W9-BNL-023

WITHDRAWN

Lost in Lumby

Center Point
Large Print

**This Large Print Book carries the
Seal of Approval of N.A.V.H.**

Lost in Lumby

Gail Fraser

CENTER POINT LARGE PRINT
THORNDIKE, MAINE

The text of this Large Print edition is unabridged.
In other aspects, this book may vary
from the original edition.
Printed in the United States of America
on permanent paper.
Set in 16-point Times New Roman type.

ISBN: 978-1-68324-515-5

Library of Congress Cataloging-in-Publication Data

Names: Fraser, Gail R. (Gail Robin), author.
Title: Lost in Lumby / Gail Fraser.
Description: Center Point Large Print edition. | Thorndike, Maine : Center Point Large Print, 2017.
Identifiers: LCCN 2017024368 | ISBN 9781683245155 (hardcover : alk. paper)
Subjects: LCSH: Large type books. | GSAFD: Humorous fiction.
Classification: LCC PS3606.R4229 L67 2017 | DDC 813/.6—dc23
LC record available at https://lccn.loc.gov/2017024368

To Karen VanCleve
and
Bill and Janet Wing
With steadfast admiration and gratitude.

ACKNOWLEDGMENTS

Heartfelt gratitude to all those Lumby fans who have waited so patiently for me to return to Main Street. Had it not been for your continued belief in the series, I might not have returned to our favorite town as soon as I did. And, as always, love and thanks to my husband, Art Poulin, who lives and breathes our world as beautifully as he replicates it on his canvases.

Deepest appreciation to John Paine. His feedback, recommendations and edits were invaluable to telling my story. And many thanks to Hope Ellis for offering her own edits and contribution to the manuscript. And again, thanks to Ron Toelke and Barbara Kempler-Toelke for their contributions and layout support of this edition.

Lost in Lumby

ONE

Running

"There never is a bad time for a margarita, is there?" Pam Walker asked Brooke as she mindlessly swirled her glass. They were watching the comings and goings along Main Street from their sidewalk table in front of The Green Chile.

Brooke Turner adjusted the dazzling yellow and green umbrella that billowed overhead. "If the margaritas are so good, why haven't you even taken a sip?"

Pam grinned. "Because I'm one drink away from becoming a blabbering idiot on the podium. I don't think anyone wants to see that."

"So you're worried that Biscuit is going to win the debate?" Brooke teased.

"Oh, he's such a good dog, isn't he? I'd even vote for him. But seriously, some name was added to the ballot yesterday, and I don't think it's another golden retriever." Pam leaned back in her chair, closed her eyes and tilted her face to the sun. "Do you ever have those dreams where you're naked standing in front of your locker in high school?"

"Yeah, I love those," Brooke said.

Pam rolled her eyes. "Of course you would.

13

And if I didn't know you so well, I'd be very worried about that comment," Pam said. "But I had one last night."

"You're just nervous about speaking in front of a crowd."

"Yeah, and look at them all!" Pam said, pointing toward the park. The crowd that had gathered for Lumby's first mayoral debate had grown larger than the park could contain, and had flowed out into the street, all but stopping traffic in both directions. "Hovering like vultures."

"Pam! They're all your friends. You and Mark are the two most popular people in town."

She ran her hand through her hair. "I just don't think this is a good idea."

"There's no one who would be a better mayor for our town than you," Brooke said.

"Gabrielle?"

"Great chef, but no," Brooke quickly replied.

Pam took a small swig of her drink. "Well, if nothing else, the amount of tequila in this margarita proves how much she loves us and wants us all to be happy."

Brooke was intently staring at something across the street. "Well, she certainly looks like she is."

Pam looked over at Brooke. "What do you mean?"

Brooke discreetly pointed toward the library, where Gabrielle Beezer was walking with an incredibly handsome man who definitely was not

14

her husband. She was waving one arm about as she laughed. Her other hand rested comfortably on his arm.

"Stunning," Pam said.

"Shocking," Brooke added.

Brooke tilted the umbrella back to improve their line of sight. It was a rare occasion when such an eye-catching stranger walked down Main Street, they didn't want to miss any details. The man was at least six feet four, and had a long, loose stride that Gabrielle struggled to keep up with. His starch-pressed, black T-shirt was tight enough to show washboard abs and sculpted shoulders and biceps, but not so tight to be offensive or appear narcissistic. His jacket hung loosely over his shoulder, hooked on one finger.

Mark stepped out of the restaurant. "Okay, the flyers are up. What's next, honey?"

Pam didn't hear him.

"What are you guys looking at?" Mark focused on where both women were looking.

"Why does he look so familiar?" Pam asked.

"Because he's gorgeous and you're just wishing he was one of your college dates," Brooke teased.

"Wow," Mark said. "That's the last person I would expect to see in Lumby."

Pam finally realized Mark was standing behind her. "Who is he?"

Mark scratched his head. "I can't remember his name, but I think he won the decathlon gold medal in the late nineties . . . maybe at the Atlanta Olympics. He was on the Wheaties box forever."

Pam slapped Brooke's arm with the back of her hand. "That's where we've seen him! In bed on Sunday mornings."

"Don't you wish," Brooke chided.

Pam immediately blushed. "No, you know what I mean—when Mark brings me breakfast."

Joshua called out from the bookstore next door. "Mark! I could use your help over here."

Mark waved back to Joshua before leaning over and kissing his wife. "I'll see you in the park in twenty minutes," he whispered. "Don't be nervous, and don't get plastered beforehand. This may be a shoo-in, but lots of folks are counting on you."

Pam took another sip of her margarita. "Please don't remind me."

Just then a commotion from down the street caught everyone's attention. Loud voices could be heard coming from the crowd in front of the park. Suddenly, the mass of people began to divide, scrambling in two opposite directions.

Pam gawked at the sight. "It's like the parting of the Red Sea."

A Clydesdale the size of a small school bus trotted into the clearing, heading straight down Main Street. Stranger still was what was riding the mare: a true knight in shining armor. Fully

16

geared in medieval regalia, the only things it was missing were a lance and a fair maiden.

But the armor wasn't holding together particularly well. The horse was of such enormous proportions that with each thunderous step it took, a piece of armor fell off and immediately became sixteenth-century street litter. First the knee coverings and elbow joints broke off, and then metal arms and headgear went flying everywhere. When a piece of armor would hit the mare's flanks, she'd shy left or right, losing the gear all the more.

The crowd collectively gasped in preparation for the unsightly accident that would surely follow.

But the Clydesdale did what the breed was known for: she put her head down and shouldered forward. Likewise, the brave knight continued in the face of adversity.

When the Clydesdale cleared the crowd, its pace quickened, and that's when odd turned to bizarre, even for Lumby. At a small canter, the vibration shook off both the helmet and the chest guard. Underneath was not some poor lad looking for attention, but instead, a full-sized human skeleton.

Only then did Pam notice that the legs were duct-taped to the cinch of the saddle that wrapped under the horse's underbelly, and its hands taped to the reins. To her surprise, the mannequin knight actually had very good riding posture.

A teenage boy was running behind the horse as fast as he could, but was clearly losing ground.

Within seconds the horse was almost to the bookstore, where Mark and Joshua were taping up posters.

"Mark! Stop the horse!" Pam yelled.

Mark spun around, his foot catching the leg of the ladder Joshua was on, forcing Joshua to grab hold of the awning and hang on for dear life. Mark bolted toward the horse and heroically dove into the air, grabbing the dummy around the waist as if he was making a football tackle. Both Mark and the dummy slid partway down the mare's side, so the dummy was perpendicular to the ground. Mark lost his grip, and in a last-ditch effort to hold on, grabbed the dummy's head, which separated from the body.

"Ew," Pam exhaled.

Now used to the commotion on its back, the Clydesdale paid little attention and never missed a beat, continuing to canter down Main Street, leaving Mark in the dust waving the skull in the air.

"He looks a little like Hamlet," Brooke commented.

Suddenly, the stranger who had been with Gabrielle ran out into the street and waved his jacket in front of the horse. "Whoa!" he said in a deep, commanding voice.

The horse came to an abrupt stop.

A few seconds later, the boy caught up and grabbed the reins.

"Thanks, mister," the kid said. "She would have run all the way to Franklin."

"She looks like a good horse," the man said, slapping the thick neck of the mare. "Perhaps she shouldn't be the butt of your pranks next time."

"Yeah, but I won the bet," the boy said, turning around to see if his cohorts were nearby.

Mark walked up to them and handed the youngster the skull. "I'm assuming this is yours as well?"

"Nice tackle, Mr. Walker," the boy said before leading the horse away.

Mark shook the stranger's hand and they spoke briefly before Gabrielle led them over to The Green Chile.

Mark was more excited than usual. "Pam, you'll never believe who this is!"

Joshua called out, waving from on top of the awning. "Mark! The ladder!"

"Oh, got to go," Mark said, dashing to Joshua's rescue.

Pam stood. "Hi, I'm Pam Walker."

"An honor to finally meet you," the man said.

His voice was so smooth and deep one could get lost in it forever, Pam thought.

"I understand the privilege is mine," Pam said. "And thanks for taking care of the horse."

"It was nothing at all," the man said, shaking out his jacket.

"You underrate yourself, Duke," Gabrielle said.

Pam wrinkled her brow, confused. "Duke?"

"Yes, Pam. This is Duke Blackstone," Gabrielle chirped in an unnaturally high voice.

Pam narrowed her eyes, taking a better look at the stranger. "So you're the one who's added his name to the ballot?" she said, forcing a smile. "I didn't know you were a resident of Lumby."

"I own a small place west of town on Cherry Creek."

Pam thought for a minute. "*You* bought the old Kremmer place last month?"

The man smiled and nodded.

Brooke sensed that Pam had been caught off guard, and immediately introduced herself. "I'm sure you'll bring a lot to the debate. The other two candidates have pretty weak platforms."

Duke laughed. "I can understand why—a dog and the deceased incumbent." His smile was utterly engaging. "Well, I'd love to talk with all of you some more, but let me go and offer Mark some help." Before leaving, he turned to Gabrielle. "I just wanted to thank you for last night," he said graciously, kissing her on the cheek. "I could not have asked for a better hostess."

"It was my pleasure," Gabrielle gushed. "We'll see you again tomorrow night."

20

Pam's jaw dropped even farther.

Gabrielle grabbed a chair as the women watched Duke saunter away.

"How can any man be that good-looking?" Brooke asked before taking another gulp of her margarita.

"He's actually nicer than he is handsome," Gabrielle said.

Pam sat down slowly without taking her eyes off Duke Blackstone. "But . . . don't you think it's odd that Mr. Blackstone shows up out of nowhere, quietly buys a dilapidated, uninhabitable shack, becomes a Lumby resident overnight, and then throws his hat into the ring for town mayor?"

"He said he's renting a home in Rocky Mount," Gabrielle said.

Pam glanced over at Gabrielle. "How do you know him?"

"I don't really," she replied. "He brought his campaign staff to my restaurant for dinner last night."

"He has a *staff?*"

"Only four or five men," Gabrielle said.

"To run for town mayor?" Pam asked in disbelief. Either she had radically underestimated the responsibilities of the position or she'd drastically misjudged the likelihood of her winning the position. Or both.

Mark called over to Pam. "Honey, you're up."

Gabrielle grabbed Pam's arm. "Be gentle with Duke," she asked.

Pam shuffled back a step. *"Gentle?"*

"He said he's new to small-town politics," Gabrielle explained. "And he really doesn't know anything about Lumby."

Pam laughed. "Don't worry. He's so charming, I'm sure he'll be just fine."

TWO

Departed

Pam and Mark Walker walked hand in hand down Main Street, as they did through life—a united front, protecting each other's back, supporting one another in times of adversity, and celebrating the other's accomplishments.

"What are all these people doing here?" she whispered to her husband.

Mark beamed with pride. "To see you, honey."

As positive as he sounded, Pam thought the turnout was almost disturbingly odd. Never had she seen the park so teeming with bystanders. Residents had filled every available space on the lawn, the Episcopal church steps, and the front porch of the Lumby Sporting Goods store. Some clever lads had strung several hammocks between the pines and were swaying gently in the wind. A few tractors were parked in front of the post office, with raised front-load buckets that were packed with blankets and being used for extra seating.

In the center of the park stood a pristine white gazebo, newly constructed after it had been obliterated from the misfiring of the town's cannon in the spring. Scurrying around close to the gazebo were a dozen free-range chickens that had taken up residence shortly after construction. A stray sheep pastured quietly in the far corner of the park, unconcerned by the commotion of the crowd. In front of the gazebo, two makeshift platforms that had been quickly fabricated out of wood pallets were set ten feet apart. Duke had already claimed the taller of the two.

Mark lent Pam a hand as she stepped up to her podium. She looked over at Duke and felt slighted—between his height and the height of his platform, he stood at least three feet above her.

"We can't see you, Pam!" a voice yelled from the middle of the crowd.

"Stand up, Pam!" another called out.

Pam turned to Duke. "Excuse me," she said, catching his attention. "Do you mind if we switch places? I don't think half the folks can see me."

Duke nonchalantly turned his back and waved to the crowd.

A thunderous applause erupted.

Pam's smile instantly froze. "What is going on?" she asked Mark through pressed lips.

"I guess word must have spread about Duke being here," he whispered back.

"So much for the home-field advantage," Pam said sarcastically.

Mark's cell phone rang. He looked at the

number and answered. "You're supposed to be here! Where are you?" A moment later, he said, "I will," and hung up. "That was Jimmy. He can't moderate the debate."

"But he's acting mayor!" Pam snapped.

"He's on Fiddlers Elbow just north of Morty Alberts's farm. Seems old Morty and his grandsons are planning a protest by herding their Belted Galloways up here. Jimmy said they would have already stampeded Main Street if it wasn't for his intervention."

"A *protest?*" Pam asked in near disbelief. "Against what?"

"Seems the town council turned down his request for free grazing rights at the fairgrounds."

Pam rolled her eyes. "So, fifty cows are headed our way."

Mark shook his head. "Oh no, Morty's got to have at least a hundred at his place." He looked out at the crowd. "Everyone's getting really restless. You need to say something, Pam. They all know you."

"You're right." Pam swallowed hard and took a deep breath. "Thank you all for coming," she began, but her voice was drowned out by the hundreds who were still talking.

"We can't hear you!" someone yelled.

Mark grabbed a megaphone that was lying on the grass and passed it to Pam. It crackled as she pushed the button.

"Thank you all for coming," she repeated, and immediately the crowd hushed. "Jimmy is tied up, so we're going to begin without a moderator. Since most of you know me, it's probably best that I introduce our guest—actually, our other candidate." She lifted a hand toward Duke. "Mr. Duke Blackstone."

As soon as Pam uttered his name, cheers broke out, and then rolling chants of "USA, USA."

"As many of you might know, Duke was a gold-medal winner at the . . ." she looked over at him.

"Nineteen ninety-six," he said with a gleaming smile.

"At the 1996 Olympics," she echoed.

"USA, USA," rippled through the drove.

Duke waved his arms and the crowd fell quiet. Pam offered him the megaphone.

"They'll be able to hear *me* just fine," he said patronizingly before turning to his audience. "It's an honor and privilege to be among you today," he began, flashing a grin. "And let's give a round of applause to Pam Walker for stepping into shoes a little too big for comfort for such a licentious candidate in Lumby, which I know a lot about because I've prepared for this moment, for serving you, the public, since I was a child."

Licentious? Pam wondered. She had never heard the word before, and assumed it was a

26

compliment. Pam nodded in thanks just as she caught sight of Brooke, who was shaking her head in despair.

"What a delight to be welcomed to such a very, very nice town, a town I know better than anyone. A town I can fix," Duke said.

More applause broke out, with some cheering, "Lum-by! Lum-by!"

"Did you bring your medal?" someone hollered.

"We'll have time for that later. Maybe I'll get you all Olympic medals. How would you like that?"

The crowd went wild, and Duke basked in their admiration.

"But friends," he continued, "We can call each other that, right? We have real problems that are here, right here and right now, that need smart people—the smartest people—to fix them because we're not going to win without a strong leader—and my gold medal proves I'm the strongest in the world—who will solve the problems that have become endemic to small towns. And Lumby's one of them, isn't it? You know that's true, don't you? Like taxes and crime, because the Olympics taught me lessons that none of you'll never know—and crime, the ugly kind with guns and rapists and murderers—that's our number one problem here."

Crime? In Lumby? Pam's jaw was open so wide she looked like a guppy gulping for air. She

27

couldn't stay silent any longer. "Wait a minute." Her hand went up as if she could stop the train barreling at her at a hundred miles an hour. "I'm sorry for interrupting, Duke, but that's not at all true. Lumby has the lowest crime rate per capita than any town in our entire state."

"That's what I'm talking about, friends. Pam and people like them—all of them—you need to watch out for because they play with the numbers, and you know numbers can be made to add up any way you want because they're numbers and only accountants, and accountants are really, really smart people, they tell you what they want you to believe. That's just Pam being petty. Petty Pam."

Pam turned bright red. *Petty Pam?*

"Petty Pam. And I have proof. So let's go ahead and ask her: Pam, did you or did you not ask me to switch podiums with you?"

"I did, but—"

"Really, friends, how petty is that? She's more concerned about her podium than about the crime rate of *our* town."

And so began the first mayoral debate in Lumby. To everyone's surprise, Duke Blackstone continued to hurl bombastic hyperbole. His ability to land a verbal punch was only equaled by his ability to throw a discus, both with perfect aim.

The medieval knight's bones weren't the only

28

remains left on the street that day, but it wasn't until the following week that the paper assessed Pam's political standing.

The Lumby Lines

WHAT'S NEWS AROUND TOWN

By Scott Stevens

It's been a busy week in our sleepy town of Lumby.

On Hunts Mill Road, Simon Dixon had no other recourse but to respond to another complaint from an Airbnb customer who had rented Sarah Bartlett's converted chicken coop for a "romantic weekend getaway in the country." While the visitors were dining in town, the coop was overtaken at sunset by two dozen determined hens, which immediately pecked their way through the guests' luggage before laying several brown, jumbo-sized eggs on their personal attire. Wanting to preserve the spotless reputation of our small town, Simon has asked the town council to reconsider their rather obscure guidelines for Airbnb rentals.

After three weeks of miserable sales,

Bob Fitzgerald and Timmy Beezer renamed and repainted their Slap Yo Mama Soul Food food truck that they purchased through craigslist last month. Now called Cluck It Up Fried Chicken, the young entrepreneurs are testing various recipes as well as lining up reliable poultry providers. Perhaps just by coincidence, many of our readers have commented that the free-range Rhode Island Red population in the park seems to have declined since the culinary wizards changed menus.

The navy-blue dog-poo box that was discreetly positioned next to the park has been removed in response to a Change.org petition signed by over 488 residents of our good town. Apparently, it had been frequently mistaken for a USPS mailbox since its installation three weeks ago. The postmaster has retrieved all salvageable envelopes and advises all poo-box patrons to retrieve their mail at the US post office, thus giving new meaning to the phrase "posting hazardous materials."

At what was expected to be a boring debate last week, Pam Walker received an unexpected shellacking when ambushed by Duke Blackstone. A stranger to our town but not our state, Blackstone stole the stage and proceeded to assault his fellow contender on every imaginable front. Blackstone's brazen and unapologetic name-calling, vulgarities and sweeping slurs have reset the tenor (as well as the G-rating) of this election. Editorial Comment: Walker is clearly out of her league and although many think she should shelter in place, she is the only viable alternative at this point, unless, of course, Biscuit has a strong surge in popularity after next week's dog show down in Wheatley.

They say when it rains, it pours, and so it was for Pam. Throughout the night, she tossed in bed. When the phone rang at three-thirty, she was wide-awake, staring at the ceiling. Cutter, their yellow Labrador, jumped on the bed and buried himself between them.

"Let it ring," Mark murmured into his pillow.

"That's your cell," Pam said, leaning over her husband and Cutter to reach his nightstand.

"Hello?"

It was Robert Day, her stepfather. His voice jolted Pam awake.

"Robert? What's wrong?" Pam's heart started to race a mile a minute. As she listened, all color drained from her cheeks, and her hands started to tremble. "When?"

Mark sat up in bed and turned on the lamp.

Pam hung up and dropped the phone. "My mother had a stroke in the middle of the night."

"How is she?"

Pam looked at Mark but didn't answer.

"Pam? How is Kay?"

Pam shook her head.

Pam wasn't crying, and that scared Mark the most. She just sat there, staring at him.

Mark wrapped both his arms around his wife. "I'm so, so sorry, honey."

She gently pulled away, shaking her head. "Is this really happening?"

After dressing and packing, Pam and Mark took off for Rocky Mount Airport, arriving less than an hour later. Standing at gate four, Mark held Pam tightly.

"Are you all right?" he asked again.

"No," she said into his shoulder.

"Is Robert meeting you at the airport?"

"We decided that it would be easier if I just get a car to drive me out to Greenwich," Pam said. "But he'll be home when I get there."

"You'll get through this."

Pam stepped away from Mark. "I've never seen Robert in my mother's house. I've never been in my mother's house without her there."

"Robert's a good man," Mark said. "I'm sure he's grieving as much as you are."

32

"I wouldn't know," Pam said abruptly, but then corrected herself. "Of course you're right. Mom and Robert were married for six years and she never sounded happier. I just feel so . . ."

Mark waited for her to sort through the raging emotions that she kept so tightly under control.

"Lost," she finally said.

"Then you can comfort each other."

Pam was confused and disoriented. "But I don't even know him. Not really," she said. "When Kay brought him to Montis, it was the shock of my life. And a week later they were married and gone. Other than a few words exchanged when I called, there's nothing between us. We are virtual strangers."

"But you're family."

"We're not family," Pam asserted. "You care deeply about family, and you talk more than once a year."

Mark rubbed her arms. "Some people would disagree."

"Robert is an acquaintance at best. Not family."

"But you both loved the same woman," Mark said.

Pam considered that for a moment. "I suppose so."

The second boarding announcement for Pam's plane blasted through the concourse. It filled her with sudden panic.

"Everything will be fine," Mark said. "Don't

worry about Montis and forget about the campaign."

"Maybe it would be better if I pulled out now," Pam said, retrieving her plane ticket from her purse.

"You just can't do that," Mark said. "There's a lot of people counting on you, and everyone knows that Blackstone would ruin our town."

"But that's my point. Duke Blackstone is the last person I want to be thinking of right now."

"I promise you, it will be fine," Mark said. "Who knows, maybe Duke will be the one to pull out."

Pam listened to the loudspeaker. "That's the final call," she said, kissing her husband again.

"Take care of everything in Connecticut. I'll be there in a few days."

Pam's eyes filled with tears.

Mark wrapped his arms around her. "Hang in there," he whispered in her ear. "If you need me, all you have to do is call and I'll come."

With one final kiss goodbye, Pam boarded the 7:50 a.m. flight that would take her through Denver and on to New York, where a chance discovery would enrich Pam's life more than she could ever dream.

THREE

Letters

Caroline Ross fingered the greeting cards as she slowly turned the carousel. She so loved the watercolor images on the front that she never bothered reading the inside sentiments of many of them.

"Caroline?" Nancy, the store manager, said softly. "How nice to see you back!"

Nancy had worked at the Lumby Bookstore for longer than Caroline could remember. They had become casual friends when she and Kai were regular customers, coming into her store several times a week, if for no other reason than to buy a book or the local paper. After Kai's departure, though, Caroline hadn't returned to the store, opting instead to order anything she needed through Amazon.

Caroline looked up with a start. "Oh, Nancy." She scrambled for an apology for the many times she had not returned Nancy's calls. "I'm so sorry—"

"Oh, that's all right, dear. I know how busy you've been," Nancy said with a sympathetic nod. "Can I help you find something?"

"A condolence card for someone I hardly know.

And Brooke's birthday is in a few weeks."

"Well, you've come to the right place." She looked at the card Caroline was holding. "Beautiful, isn't it?"

Caroline looked at the reproduced painting on the greeting card. It was beautiful—a uniquely stunning combination of hand-drawn watercolor, pen and ink, and computer graphics. "It certainly is," she said. "Such talent."

"We have several of his books in back. Did you know that the artist—" Nancy began, but was interrupted when another customer approached with a question. "Excuse me," she said to Caroline, and was off.

After choosing two cards, Caroline headed to the cash register. Nancy was already waiting for her. She grabbed a book from under the counter and placed it in front of Caroline. "It just came in a few weeks ago. Tom Candor gave it a great review in *The Lumby Lines*."

Caroline looked at the book's solid-brown glossy cover with the word "DOWN!" written in bold white letters. She thumbed through the pages. "Are you trying to tell me something, Nancy?"

"Absolutely not!" A hand of denial waved in the air. "Finn is a great dog," she said, referring to Caroline's rambunctious Irish setter. "He's . . . delightfully spirited, isn't he? Why don't I just put this on your account and if it's no help at all, just bring it back."

Caroline narrowed her eyes suspiciously. "Did the others put you up to this?"

"Not at all. In fact, Sam was in good humor when he told us about Finn's latest . . . hmmm, what word did he use? Unpredictable romp in his store," Nancy replied cheerfully. "But we all love Finn! Truly!"

"So it says on every bill for damages I receive after one of Finn's . . . romps."

"He's simply beyond description, isn't he?" Nancy said with just enough kindness, and slipped the book into a paper bag before handing it back to Caroline. "Good luck and do let me know how it goes. But you needn't bring Finn in to show us."

"I'll remember that," Caroline said as she left the store, knowing full well that the battle to preserve Finn's good reputation in town was lost after his guacamole misadventure at The Green Chile.

Caroline checked her watch and dashed down Main Street to S&T's, where Brooke Turner was already waiting.

"Over here!" Brooke called out.

She looked more disheveled than Caroline as the latter fell into the booth.

"Sorry I'm late," Caroline said.

"Not a problem. I just got here myself."

"Bad flight from Seattle?"

Brooke rolled her luggage under the table. "Frustrating, but nothing that Melanie's blue-

37

berry pancakes can't fix," she said. "Thanks for meeting me so early."

"It was hard to fit into my social schedule."

"Which both of us know would be totally empty if you didn't include feeding your dog," Brooke said tentatively.

Caroline blushed. "Oh, but Finn loves his scrambled eggs."

Brooke placed her hand over Caroline's. "I'm worried about you," she said softly. Then suddenly, she started laughing.

Caroline jolted back in her seat. "That's an odd way of showing it."

"No, look," Brooke said, pointing toward the diner's front window.

Caroline turned around just as four seniors went jogging by in the buff.

Melanie, who was standing behind the counter, waved at the octogenarian athletes.

"Are they really naked?" Caroline asked.

"As jaybirds," Brooke said.

"It's the Fossils for Fitness Club," Melanie explained. "Their motto is to keep the bones moving." Both Caroline and Brooke laughed.

"Charlotte would have liked that," Brooke said, referring to Caroline's grandmother.

"She definitely would have," Caroline said. "There's something reassuring that for all the hell we go through in our lives, Lumby never changes," Caroline said.

"But don't you think it's a little unsettling that in twenty years you and I might be streaking down Main Street?"

Caroline tried to smile. "No more unsettling than how my life is going right now."

Brooke looked at Caroline sympathetically. "Have you heard from Kai?"

Caroline leaned back. "Let me see," she began in a sarcastic tone, "I heard from Kai's brother, Jamar, explaining that the embezzlement of our foundation money was a simple misunderstanding. I heard from Jamar's attorney that the funds—*if* there were, in fact, any taken—could not be returned due to international treaties between the US and Indonesia. An elder on the island of Coraba wrote to tell me that Kai had completed his vows and had assumed his permanent role as the village minister. And, in a curt letter, Kai's sister advised me that her brother's destiny was with God and with Utari, and I should not intervene in his life any further." She paused. "So, to answer your question, I would have to say no, I have not heard from my husband since the day he snuck out of the house five months ago."

Brooke was speechless, trying to process what Caroline had said. "Who the hell is Utari?"

Caroline lifted both hands and gave her a befuddled look. "As if I knew." She ran her fingers through her hair.

"I'm sorry," Brooke said.

"I am too." Caroline closed her eyes, exhausted from scrutinizing the years of her marriage to Kai, exhausted from agonizing over what had gone so wrong between them that Kai would reach the point of leaving without a word. "Foolish me. I thought I had done everything I could to make him happy."

"I almost forgot." Brooke jumped up from her seat and pawed through her luggage. "For you," she said, handing Caroline a vinyl record.

Caroline was grateful to change the subject. Then her eyes lit up. "Bobby Hackett? This is amazing."

"I found it in a used bookstore. For the life of me, I still don't know where you picked up such a love for big bands, but if that's what makes you happy, go for it, girl. Say, I need to freshen up. If Melanie comes by, just ask her for my usual."

Caroline scanned the flip side of the record before carefully laying it down. She looked over her shoulder in the direction of the ladies' room. She was delighted to see Brooke again, but sitting alone in S&T's, the same question that kept Caroline awake every night continued to haunt her during the day. When a relationship ends, does just the marriage disintegrate, or does part of the person, the part that had been openly given to the other, die as well?

Throughout Caroline's carefully planned life, there were very few bumps in her road until her grandmother's death ten years ago. And then Kai Talin arrived, swept her off her feet, caused her to rebuild her life around him, and then left with no warning, tearing her life apart and driving her inward, both emotionally and physically.

Sipping her coffee while waiting for Brooke to return, she thought back on the caution Lumby residents showed toward Kai during their first year of carefree abandon, which was followed by a deceptively slow, almost imperceptible shift that brought him closer to God while pushing her to the periphery of his world. Frequent returns to his island of Coraba became, over time, months of separation, until his final disappearance.

In retrospect, the ending was so clearly written on the wall. *Isn't that how it always is?* she thought. Tears were pooling in her eyes as Brooke sat down.

Caroline dropped her head. "I'm sorry," she whispered.

"You're not okay, are you?"

Caroline shook her head, her straight blond hair swishing from side to side. "I've been better."

"Then do something," Brooke suggested. "Other than talking to that crazy dog of yours."

Caroline dabbed her eyes with a napkin. "Such as?"

Brooke leaned forward. "Clean out his closet,"

she said slowly and succinctly. "It would be a good place to start."

Caroline clenched her jaw.

"He won't be coming back, Caroline. The sooner you move on, the more you will live your life." Tough love was always so hard to give to a close friend.

"There they go again!" Melanie called out.

Caroline didn't even look up.

That afternoon Caroline finally took Brooke's advice, at least as far as standing in front of Kai's closet door, and perhaps, if courage allowed, looking in. Before opening the door, she pressed her palms against her temples and narrowed her eyes to avoid seeing familiar patterns of color— the blue-and-white striped shirt he had worn the first day at the fair, the yellow sweater she had bought at Wools.

Peeking into her ex-husband's closet, her first thought was one of irony: how she had so quickly surrendered the larger closet to him although he had few clothes. It was just one of a million tiny compromises she unthinkingly made during their years together.

As she stepped into the closet, her husband's scent washed over her like the tide. She breathed in the still air that drowned her in memories of the happiness they shared when they first met. Engulfed and feeling broken, Caroline dropped to her knees, grabbing a sleeve of a shirt that fell loosely from the hanger. Floating downward, it softly landed on her shoulders, each sleeve resting on either side, embracing her. She sat numbly on the ground and pulled her knees into her aching chest.

Suddenly, something struck her on the cheek: a wet, slobber-covered, stuffed purple dinosaur flown through the air. The ragged animal's stuffed yellow innards were bulging out from the ripped seam along its back. Finn, her two-year-old Irish setter, was standing just outside the closet doorway, his tail wagging violently.

"Not now," she said tenderly, reaching out to stroke his chest. He dropped down on his front paws, as if preparing to leap on top of her.

She cautioned him again. "Not now."

Hearing her hauntingly empty voice and sensing a reprimand was at hand, Finn dropped his head and squeezed into the closet, nudging himself between Caroline and the back wall. When he lay down, his paw pushed away a large box, revealing one of Kai's felt slippers. His attention immediately captured, Finn put his snout into the foot hole, claiming it as a new favorite toy. In order to bury his nose even deeper, he pushed forward with his hind legs, stretching out his young, long body, unaware that he was moving aside everything in close proximity.

Suddenly, an odd sight caught Caroline's eye.

Tucked into the far corner of the closet and well hidden from sight was a medium-sized box wrapped in glossy white gift paper. On top was tied a blue ribbon. She vaguely recalled the box, which she'd last seen a decade before when she placed it in the closet within days of her grandmother's funeral. It was the last birthday gift Charlotte Ross had bought for Caroline, one too painful for Caroline to open, and one forgotten so long ago.

Under the bow was a small envelope. On it Charlotte had written in her faint shaky script, "To My Favorite Granddaughter."

Caroline smiled weakly, and replied to the joke they had shared between them since before Caroline could remember: "I am your *only* granddaughter."

Caroline wiped her eyes and leaned forward, pulling the box toward her. At first it hardly budged from the weight inside. But Caroline slid it close enough to reach the envelope. Inside, Charlotte had written: "Happy Birthday. Love, CC."

She pressed her lips together in a tormented smile. She had always called her grandmother "CC."

"I miss you so much," Caroline said, kissing the card. Sliding the box between her legs, Caroline slowly removed the short strips of aged and curled adhesive tape. Under the wrapping was a thick cardboard box. Caroline peeled off the masking tape that sealed the box and lifted its flaps. She gasped softly.

Partially obscured by a yellowing, thick plastic cover that followed the contours of the machine, she could barely make out the gold lettering on the black, hundred-year-old typewriter: "UNDERWOOD." Caroline reached in and, with significant effort, lifted the thirty-two-pound typewriter from its container and placed it on the floor. As soon as she removed the plastic cover, she noticed a white index card held tightly against the black roller. On it her grandmother had typed:

`W ite something.`

"Wow," Caroline whispered as her fingertips gently ran over the keys of the amazing relic.

She picked up the typewriter and headed downstairs, carefully placing the Underwood squarely on the kitchen table, directly in front of the chair she always used. Tearing out a piece of paper from a pad kept next to the phone, Caroline slid the sheet behind the platen and turned the roll until it caught and the paper appeared in front.

When she tapped on one key, a metal arm lifted halfway up to the page. Hitting it much harder on the second attempt, the key struck the paper and its noise echoed through the silent room. Again and again, keys were tapped and the hammers hit the page. Each strike was surprisingly loud.

Aa Bb Cc Dd Ee Ff Ggone Hh Ii Jj Kk Ll Mm Nn Oo Pp Qq Ss Tt Uu Vv Ww Xx Yy Zz 1234567890

The "R" and "r" keys were definitely broken, but with a pair of tweezers, Caroline got them functioning in minutes. And of course, the first letter typed would be to Charlotte.

Dear CC, You are in my every thought. I'm not sure where to begin, but I'll assume you've been watching from afar and already know how badly I've screwed up.

I'm so scared that I might always need you the way I need you right now. In the hardware store the other day, a woman walked past me who wore the same perfume that you did a wonderful combination of lilacs and spring rain. It followed her between the aisles and drew me in like a magnet. I stayed close, shutting my eyes and inhaling

deeply, pretending it was you.

I discovered your gift. You couldn't have found a more perfect present. To have the old typewriter sitting on the kitchen table is oddly reassuring it waits with patience and without expectation or judgment . . . just like you used to. It anchors me and allows me to hold onto a part of our past that disappeared too quickly and without warning. I just pray that deep within me there is still something worth writing or a tale to be told other than the train wreck that has become my story.

I'm hoping you can't see from that side of paradise what has happened, what I have done, to your Foundation. It's failing, which makes total sense because it was abandoned. After Kai's brother stole the money, and after Kai left me, I had no strength to continue. I'm sorry.

Even our mill looks as

abandoned as when Kai and I bought it six years ago. I can't bring myself to keep it up. I can't even bring myself to go downstairs to his shop. I have too many mixed emotions to open those doors right now.

Perhaps writing to you will help. There is nothing more I want than to heal and open my heart to another, to give back what is offered, to find the person I lost along the way. There are days I believe that will happen. And perhaps you will see my words and send help. So, I will leave this letter by your grave, close to you so you can easily find it. I love you and miss you more than you will ever know.

Your favorite granddaughter, Caroline

FOUR

Storms

Driving along Main Street on his way back from Rocky Mount, Mark caught sight of Hank, the town's lanky flamingo that had called Lumby its home since Johnnie D (Jimmy D's son) took ownership when a misaddressed box from Amazon arrived at his doorstep. Instead of several summer-reading books his mother had directed him to order the week before, he was delighted to find a three-foot-high, vibrant pink plastic flamingo, which he soon named Hank after a puppy he had lost three years prior. With an unusually large black beak and bulbous body, Hank had a certain presence about him that was hard to miss. Shortly after being delivered to Jimmy D's Bar, the avian ventured farther down Main Street and then Farm to Market Road. So, over time, no one was ever sure where Hank would make an appearance.

A year after roaming around in the buff, as it

were, one day Hank nested in front of the Lumby Feed Store wearing a pair of custom-tailored overalls. He was thrilled that the town took note, with residents going so far as to offer suggestions for other outfits in witty op-ed articles published in *The Lumby Lines*. Within months, Hank was the best-dressed fowl in the country, although no one knew who was secretly stitching and darning for the bird.

On that morning Hank was fulfilling his patriotic duties by holding a large VOTE sign under his wing. Dressed in blue slacks and a red-and-white loosely knit sweater, he was the avian equivalent of Uncle Sam.

Running up the stairs to the second floor of the Chatham Press building, Mark came to an abrupt halt when he heard yelling down the hall. If his business with Dennis Beezer wasn't so pressing, he would have hightailed it out of there. Instead, he inched his way toward Dennis's office. The door was partly open, so he could clearly see Scott Stevens, the mediocre senior reporter for *The Lumby Lines*, squirming in his chair as Dennis hovered over him. As the head of Chatham Press, which included *The Lumby Lines*, The Bindery and the Lumby Bookstore located directly across the street, Dennis had a fairly large staff, with Scott falling toward the bottom of the ranks regarding both talent and honesty.

Thunder rolled as a squall moved over the mountains, slowly approaching Lumby.

Mark overheard Dennis read the front page of *The Lumby Lines*: "Bovine Apocalypse Coming." He slammed the newspaper down on his desk. "How the hell could you have printed this?"

Scott Stevens shrank lower in the seat.

"This is the most irresponsible crap I've ever seen you pull out of your—"

Mark's jaw dropped. He had seldom heard Dennis that angry.

Scott nervously looked at his watch. "I've got to go."

"I accept your resignation."

Scott stammered, "Th-that's not what I meant."

"I assure you, it was. It's time that you flourish elsewhere, Scott."

Mark saw Scott jerk back in his seat, stunned by what had taken place.

But the young reporter quickly recovered. "Fine," he said defiantly. "I'll swing by for my letter of recommendation after I pack up."

Dennis glared at him. "Do you want me to put my opinion down in ink?"

Mark chuckled.

"Is there someone out there?" Dennis asked.

Mark froze, as if he was caught in a wrongdoing. "It's me, Mark Walker," he announced as he strolled into Dennis's office, looking as casual as he could. "Am I interrupting?"

"Not at all," Dennis replied. "We're so done here."

"Agreed." Scott jumped up, turned on his heel and stomped out.

Dennis yelled in his wake, "The computer stays here!"

"Boy, he looked pissed," Mark said, watching Scott storm down the corridor.

"Let's just say he's leaving by mutual agreement," Dennis said, straightening the many newspapers on his desk: *The New York Times*, *The Washington Post*, and *Daily Tribune*. On top of the pile, he added a copy of *The Wheatley Sentinel*, which had a yellow sticky note by the banner with the words "CALL BACK."

"Do you really read all of these papers or just kind of have them out for show?" Mark asked, turning *The Seattle Times* around so he could read the cover story.

"Yes, Mark, I read them. I'm in the business," Dennis answered flatly.

A headline had caught Mark's eye: "Blackstone Disappears in Mountains."

"You know, I heard this Alan Blackstone fellow is Duke's twin brother. Do you think he's dead?"

Dennis, who had begun studying a spreadsheet, didn't look up when he answered. "I have no idea."

"But I hear they're total opposites," Mark said, still perusing the article. "Kind of like that Cain and Abel book we read last winter."

Dennis looked up. "*We* read?"

"Okay, well, Pam read it but she told me all about it."

Dennis strummed his fingers on the desk impatiently.

Mark continued, "I think Duke drove him nuts like he's doing to my wife. Or maybe he just went for a hike and he got lost. There's like thousands of acres of rugged terrain up there."

"More like several million," Dennis corrected him.

"Yeah. Maybe he's lost somewhere around here," Mark said, picking up some darts from the bookshelf.

"Lost in Lumby?"

"Well, not on Main Street, but up in the mountains. Or maybe he just wanted to walk— like Forrest Gump."

"Forrest Gump ran, Mark."

"Same thing. And this Alan guy has been gone for maybe like weeks. Do you think he's heading this way?"

"I wouldn't know." Dennis replied. "Is that why you're here?"

Mark aimed a dart at the board. "Twenty bucks that I hit the bull's-eye."

"I'm not in the mood," Dennis said in exasperation.

Mark tossed the dart, hitting the outside rim of the board. "Just a warm-up," he said. "You know,

I just saw your son Brian coming out of the bank. When did he get back?"

"Must have been someone else. Brian's still down in Peru working on a project for the monks," Dennis replied. "So, Mark, how exactly can I help you?"

Mark threw another dart, less successfully. "You know, Pam's running for town mayor."

"So I heard," Dennis said. "I'm sure she was madder than hell after the debate."

"Believe me, she was. She's had a rough couple of days. The debate and then her mom died. I just dropped her off at the airport."

Dennis's tenor changed. "I'm sorry to hear that. Please give her our condolences."

"I will," Mark said, tossing another dart. "So, seeing what shape she was in when she boarded her flight, driving back from Rocky Mount, I decided she needs a real campaign manager— you know, someone who has her back." He paused to take aim. "And no one would be better than me."

Dennis lifted his eyebrows. "Pam agreed to that?" he asked skeptically.

"Oh no, she doesn't know yet. But she'll love the idea. I mean, how difficult can it be?"

"To run a campaign? Very." Dennis slid his glasses down his nose. "Do you want to actually be in the debates?"

"Sure, why not?"

"Well, for one, you need to register as a candidate to participate in the debates and town hall discussions, and that would put you on the ballot against your wife."

"Yeah, but everyone would know that I'd just be filling in for Pam. I'll just swing by town hall after I leave here." Mark twirled a dart between his fingers. "I mean, seriously, what can happen?"

The newsman laughed. "Running against Biscuit, nothing. Running against the incumbent, nothing, because he's dead. But against Duke Blackstone? He'll tear you apart or eat you alive. I'm just not sure which," Dennis said. "Probably both."

"He's just all talk," Mark said with a brush of his hand and a toss of the dart.

Dennis looked at Mark in disbelief. "You have no idea, do you?"

Mark prepared to take a shot at the dartboard, this time over his shoulder with his back turned. "How bad can it be? We're talking about running for town mayor, not for like a real job."

"Well, to start, rumor has it that Duke was in prison."

"Yeah, but I hear he's also a lawyer."

"Not true. When he ran for a county office in Colorado, one opponent mysteriously disappeared and the other went bankrupt within a month of the election. Let's see, what else?"

he said, closing his eyes to concentrate. "Ah, he has more money than all of us combined and no one knows how he got it. Oh, and I hear he has connections to some of the largest crime organizations on the East Coast."

Mark didn't blink once. "Yeah, but we can handle him," he said, flipping his hand in the air. The dart slipped out of his fingers and shot upward, sticking into the ceiling. "Well, look at that," he said.

Dennis shook his head. "So, you're here because . . . ?"

"I thought we'd run some ads, maybe using some photos of Clipper and Cutter running around Montis."

"You're in fantasyland," Dennis warned him.

"No, I'm in Lumby," Mark said proudly.

Dennis sighed. "You're a good friend, Mark. I don't want to take your money. First, putting two Labs up against a corrupt politician isn't going to win you an election, and second, *The Lumby Lines* probably isn't your best bet for an ad spend right now."

"How can you say that? It's your paper," Mark asked, paying more attention to the dartboard than to what Dennis was saying.

"Haven't you noticed the paper has been a little thin these days?"

"Yeah, Pam mentioned it," he said, tossing another dart that hit the chair in the corner of the office. "Ooh." Mark grimaced at his shot.

"It was only eight pages last week," Dennis said caustically. "And we only have 184 subscribers."

"Well, that's 184 people who would see our ads and vote for Pam," Mark said, looking up at the dart still hanging from the ceiling. Suddenly, a clap of thunder shook the windows and the dart dropped down, the feathers grazing Mark's cheek. "Oh my God, did you see that?" he asked. "It could have killed me!"

"Mark, pay attention!" Dennis snapped in frustration. "I don't know how much longer *The Lumby Lines* will stay in print."

"No, everyone knows your paper will go on forever."

"And who will cover the expenses? It's been in the red for six months." Dennis cocked his head and listened to the footsteps outside his office. His wife was walking down the hall. "Not a word of this to anyone," he warned.

Gabrielle was a breath of fresh air floating into her husband's office. "Good morning, gentlemen," she said. She held a tray of coffee and pastries from her restaurant, The Green Chile. "So, what brings you around, Mark?"

Dennis jumped in before Mark could answer. "Just a social call. In fact, he's leaving, aren't you Mark?" Dennis shook Mark's hand as he led him out of the office. "Not a word to *anyone*," Dennis repeated under his breath, squeezing Mark's hand a little tighter.

"Ow," Mark said softly. "Okay, okay." Turning, he waved to Gabrielle.

"Thanks for stopping by," Dennis said loudly, before rejoining his wife.

"No need to rush him out because of me."

"I'm glad you're here." He leaned over and kissed his wife. "Mark just came at a bad time."

"It seems these last few months have always been a bad time," Gabrielle commented.

"We've just been incredibly busy."

"Well, I might not know anything about the newspaper business," Gabrielle said, "but busy isn't how I would describe this place. In fact, it looks deserted." She paused, assessing her husband. "Is everything all right?"

Dennis offered a closed-lip smile. He had done everything possible to hide from Gabrielle the unfortunate turn of events all of his businesses had taken during the last year. Although Gabrielle could have noticed the reduced traffic in the Lumby Bookstore, since it was right next door to her restaurant, he was hoping that she never gave it a second thought. He was equally hoping that she hadn't given the paper's downsizing any serious consideration.

"Everything is fine," he replied. "We're just going through some changes."

58

Just then Scott Stevens walked past his office, carrying a box of personal possessions.

"And there goes one of them now," Dennis said under his breath.

From down the hall they overheard Scott asking, "When did you get back?"

"I just flew in," a familiar voice answered.

Gabrielle's eyes opened to the size of saucers. "Brian!" she yelled as she bolted out the door. Her screeches of joy could be heard throughout the empty building.

Brian walked into Dennis's office with his mother's arm wrapped tightly around his.

"Hey, Dad," Brian said.

His son had grown an inch taller, and was now the same height as his father. At twenty-six years old, he had become a good-looking young man. Dennis and Gabrielle had seen so little of Brian during the past four years, Dennis almost felt like he was looking at a stranger.

Dennis went to shake his son's hand, but abruptly stopped. That's exactly what his own father would have done, and that's what he hated about William Beezer. Instead Dennis opened his arms and gave his son a bear hug. "How great it is to see you again, son."

"We thought you were down in Peru until September," Gabrielle said, brushing Brian's long bangs away from his eyes.

Brian resisted the urge to push away her hand.

"Brother Matthew wanted me to look at one of their new projects."

"So, how long are you here for?" Dennis asked.

"Don't know."

"Well, you're home now, so why don't you stay for a while?" Gabrielle said.

"If you two would excuse me," Dennis said, "I have a lot of work to do."

"Yeah," Brian said, looking skeptically around his father's office. Other than a few spreadsheets and a pile of newspapers, his father's desk, which would have normally been covered with piles of loose papers and galley sheets, was bare. "Seems a little quiet out there," Brian said, tilting his head toward the corridor.

Dennis offered them both a blank mask. "Just a quiet day."

Gabrielle, still in overjoyed shock, heard nothing of their exchange. "Let's go home and I can cook you your favorite meal. You look too thin."

"We'll get caught up later," Dennis assured his son as the two walked out.

When Gabrielle and Brian were gone from sight, Dennis fell into his chair. He picked up a spreadsheet and threw it across the room.

Brian, who had returned to ask his father a question, stood outside the doorway watching.

Thunder clapped outside. A squall of significant proportion was approaching.

• • •

Forty miles to the west, the storm engulfed the small town of Franklin just as the residents of the sleepy village were heading to bed and the monks at Saint Cross Abbey were beginning their nightly prayers. Deep thunder rolled in and echoed against the mountain ridges as lightning sparked for miles around.

A disheveled man, drenched and physically at the end of his rope, stood at the beginning of the monastery's driveway. Only by mere chance and good fortune had he come across the abbey that night. The few lights on in the buildings were soft and distant. He pulled the hood of his sweatshirt down over his eyes and trudged forward through the downpour.

Standing at the front door, the stranger hesitated. It had been a long, grueling journey—over sixty miles of terrain rugged enough to kill any man—one that had begun at his brother's house several weeks earlier. He knew he no longer resembled himself, but would never have guessed to what degree. The unrelenting lack of sleep and food, and his longer hair and beard, had aged him ten years. The filth that accumulated on his clothes and skin added another five years.

With the last of his strength, he knocked on the door so weakly he doubted anyone would hear.

61

He leaned forward and placed his palm on the small center window. Dried blood was between his fingers.

"Please," he whispered.

The lights came on in the abbey's entrance.

As the door was opened, the light blinded the man and he quickly covered his eyes.

Brother Michael jumped back, startled by this erratic gesture. Because the man's hood was pulled down over his eyes, the monk couldn't see his face. But he did notice his sodden clothes. One sleeve was shredded and blood stained, and it failed to cover a deep cut in the man's arm.

"May I help you?" Brother Michael asked.

With a shaking hand, the man reached out to the monk. "Please hide me."

A manila envelope, waterlogged and wrinkled, fell from under his coat. Brother Michael quickly rescued it from a large puddle. He put his arm around the man just as his body fell limp.

"Please . . ." the man mumbled.

Michael dragged the man to a bench in the vestibule. He collapsed into the seat. After walking for weeks, he had no more strength left in him.

Ten minutes later, Michael returned with a young nun.

"This is Sister Megan," he said, but the man

didn't hear a word. He was slumped in the chair, unconscious.

Megan took the man's wrist to feel for a pulse. "Wake Brother Matthew," she said. "And then call Dr. Messitt. Ask him to come immediately."

FIVE

Family

Being driven through the familiar streets of her childhood, Pam tried to recall the last time she was in Greenwich, Connecticut. It was while she and Mark still lived in Virginia, before they rebuilt their lives in Lumby, before Montis.

As the car turned into the circular driveway and approached the house, Pam's heart raced. If this had been then, Kay would have opened the door and stepped out onto the veranda to greet her. But her mother was gone.

After paying the driver, Pam stood at the base of the steps staring upward. She slowly approached the door, unsure of what to do. Should she ring the bell or just walk in as she had her entire life? It was, after all, her house now, or so she assumed.

Just as her finger was about to touch the doorbell, the door opened and Robert Day stepped out and gave her a big hug.

"I'm so sorry," he said.

"I am too," Pam said, and kissed him on the cheek.

"Let me take that." He picked up her small suitcase.

Pam walked inside and a flood of memories swept over her, carrying her back to her youth. Every detail of the house pricked her heart: the large foyer with an opulent chandelier, the curved oak banister leading upstairs, the open living room, the baby grand piano that she played. So many things were the same. But the fragrance of the house had changed. The scent was no longer of Kay's perfume and her father's cologne, but of Robert, or more specifically, Kay and Robert together.

"I thought you would like your old room, so I asked Maria to put on fresh sheets," Robert said.

"That's fine," Pam absently replied. "If you don't mind, I'll go upstairs to freshen up. It's been a long trip."

Pam ran her fingers along the railing as she walked upstairs. "The house looks beautiful."

Robert was a few steps behind her. "You know Kay—fastidious in every way. We always knew this house was too big for us, but she couldn't bear to leave it." At the top of the staircase, Robert put down the suitcase. "We're just planning a light dinner tonight, so come down when you're ready."

"Thank you," she said.

Within minutes, Pam was sound asleep on her old bed, the pillows of her childhood pulled close to her. Although she was exhausted, her sleep was restless and filled with broken dreams that stayed with her after she woke an hour later.

Walking down the hall, Pam noticed that all of the rooms had been redecorated since her last visit. She was stunned to see that one of the guest bedrooms was a nursery with a crib, a rocking chair and a changing table. *A nursery?* Pam thought.

She joined Robert in the kitchen, who was uncovering casseroles brought by friends and neighbors.

"So much food," he said.

Pam paused at the threshold before joining Robert. The kitchen had been significantly renovated and expanded. A row of windows ran from the countertop to the ceiling, and a large granite island now occupied the center of the room. Around the island were eight or ten stools. A high chair was over in the corner. The kitchen that Pam had frequented for so many years was now foreign.

"This is stunning," Pam said. "When did you remodel it?"

"About four years ago. After our culinary trip to Italy, Kay wanted a kitchen as fine as the meals we were preparing in it."

Pam noticed that Robert was arranging enough food to feed an army. "I hope you're not going to any special effort on my account."

"Not at all. In fact, I feel badly that we're just

having leftovers on your first night here, but our friends have been so generous with their casseroles," he said, tossing a large salad.

A man's voice called out from the foyer. "Dad, we're here!"

"We're in the kitchen," Robert called back.

Before Pam could prepare herself, a large group swarmed into the kitchen, her mother's kitchen, the kitchen that Kay used to shoo everyone out of.

Robert hugged all who came in, and gave the youngest, a child no more than three years old, a kiss on the cheeks.

"Pam, this is my family," Robert said. "Dylan, my oldest, and his wonderful wife, Melissa." Pam was unsure if she should shake their hands or hug them. She did neither, opting to smile and nod. "Nick and his partner, Scott. And this is Eric and his wife, Jessica, who's from England. And saving the most precious for last, this is our first and, as of right now, only granddaughter, beautiful Olivia."

Our granddaughter, Pam thought. Was he also referring to Kay?

The group gave mixed greetings.

Pam was overwhelmed, but tried to collect herself. "It's nice to finally meet all of you. I'm sorry it's under these circumstances." Her cheeks burned.

Nick was the only one who gave Pam a hug.

"We are as well," he said. "But this is long overdue."

"Many, many years overdue," another voice echoed.

"So, what have you brought?" he asked, taking a casserole dish from Jessica.

"In honor of Kay, her favorite: Irish shepherd's pie."

"Well, I would say the first order of business is some strong Guinness. We have a case in the car," Nick said.

Suddenly, everyone went in separate directions—one to the stove, another to the pantry. Olivia was placed in the high chair and brought closer to the island. Melissa began to set the table. Every person in the room, other than Pam, knew what their role was, what needed to be done, and where everything was in the kitchen. Pam also noticed that there was a rhythm and a pattern to them eating together, that had been repeated so often that everything flowed naturally.

Pam stood back and watched, feeling isolated and worthless. Worse, she felt like a complete stranger in the house, and found herself in the awkward role of an anonymous visitor.

While preparing dinner, no one made a concerted effort to bring her into the fold, although she was occasionally asked a question. Robert, though, did his best to involve Pam, including a thoughtful and touching toast he gave. But it was clear that she was an outsider, *the* outsider, who didn't belong. Had she not come for her mother's funeral, she would have slipped away as quickly as possible.

After dessert, Pam sat demurely listening to everyone else talk. It only occurred to her then that these strangers at the table, her mother's table that she had purchased with Pam during an antiquing weekend in upstate New York, were in fact her stepbrothers and sisters-in-law. Without her consent, a relationship now existed between each of them. More stunning to her, though, was the thought that all of these people were also her mother's stepchildren.

With no other relatives, no aunts or uncles or nieces or nephews in her life, Pam looked around the table at the unfamiliar people who were now her family. Other than Mark, she felt totally alone in the world and the fact that she was surrounded by those closest to her mother just made her feel less connected.

After dinner, everyone adjourned to the living room. Pam sat in her father's favorite chair, reupholstered many times over. *Did anyone even know her father's name?* she wondered.

Olivia was sound asleep in her mother's arms, so everyone spoke softly.

"Who's spending the night?" Robert asked.

"We are," Scott said, looking at Nick for concurrence. "It's too long a ride back and we're beat."

"We are as well," Jessica chimed in, with a distinct English accent. "If it's all right, I'll put Olivia down right now."

Olivia woke up just as Jessica rose from the sofa. "Mima book?" the young child asked with sleepy eyes.

Jessica lifted her higher on her chest. "No, Mima can't read you a book tonight, sweetheart. Mima is in heaven."

"How Kay loved being a grandmother," Robert said softly.

Pam blinked. Of all of the words that Pam would have used to describe her mother, "grandmother" was never one of them.

"And how Olivia loved Kay," Jessica added.

Reluctantly, Pam imagined her mother picking up Olivia from the crib, or feeding Olivia in her high chair.

Jessica looked at her daughter, who had fallen back asleep. "I think she misses Kay singing to her the most, especially in the morning."

Pam felt a pang of envy or sadness or regret, unable to recollect a single time when her mother ever sang to her.

"Do you remember the songs she brought back from Kyoto?" Jessica reminisced.

Pam looked at Robert "I didn't know you two went to Japan."

"For three weeks in March," Robert said sadly. "I never thought it would be our last trip together."

"You two lived amazingly full lives," Eric said.

Tears returned to Robert's eyes. "We certainly made each other happy." His voice cracked. "I still can't believe it. Every day she was so full of life, and now she's gone. And this house is so incredibly empty without her."

Eric, who was sitting next to his father, put his arm around the older man's shoulder. "Do you want to come and stay with us for a while? You know Olivia would love to have her Gipa wake her up each morning."

Robert offered a weak smile. "We all know Mima was Olivia's favorite."

"Well, give it some thought," Eric said as he stood up. "We should all get a good night's sleep. Tomorrow is going to be a very busy day."

"Do we need to make funeral arrangements?" Pam asked.

"I don't think so. Everything is pretty much taken care of," Eric answered. "You're invited to join us when the Episcopalian minister comes by tomorrow to discuss the details of the service."

Pam was confused. "But my mother was Presbyterian."

Robert cleared his throat. "Actually, we changed a year or two before we got married."

"Oh, I didn't know," Pam said softly.

71

Eric continued, "And we'll be meeting with Kay's attorney on Tuesday. Since you are coexecutor of her will, that's one meeting that you should attend."

I didn't know that either, Pam thought.

After everyone retired for the night, Pam sat alone in the living room listening to the soft voices that came down from upstairs. Glancing around the dimly lit room, Pam spied the only photograph of herself and Mark that Kay had put out, although it was tucked well behind a dozen other framed images of Robert and his family. Her eyes stung as she fought back tears.

Did I play such an insignificant role in my mother's life? she wondered. A tear ran down her cheek. *She was my mother and I didn't hang on to that relationship. I didn't protect and nurture it.* She wiped her tears away. *Why was I so careless?*

SIX

Interest

Caroline sat in her car, parked directly in front of the town's post office, rereading Kai's small postal card from Indonesia. There were only four words scrawled on the back side: "This is God's plan."

God's plan, my ass, Caroline thought as she tore the postcard in half.

Thumbing through the remaining mail, one letter caught her eye—one that got inadvertently put in her box. The small, handwritten envelope had her neighbors' address, but the top line read "c/o Tom Candor." In the upper left corner, where a return address would normally be found, it said only "Seal Cove." The stamp mark was dated two days before from Edmonds, Washington. Caroline set it aside, planning to leave it in their mailbox on her way home.

Instead of turning on the ignition right away, she looked out at the picturesque town she loved. Main Street was lined with Bradford pear trees from beginning to end, and they were just beginning to leaf out. Soon, the fragrance of blooms would fill the small village, and the seasons in Caroline's unyielding world would once again change around her.

She leaned her head against the steering wheel, feeling drained.

A tap on the window startled her.

"Caroline, are you all right?" the woman said.

Caroline's head shot up. Disoriented, she gave a weak nod as she rolled down the window. "I must have fallen asleep."

Gabrielle Beezer, owner of The Green Chile, knelt next to the car. "I've been trying to reach you. Did you get any of my messages?"

Caroline winced. "I'm sorry. My answering machine is acting up. Technology—what can you do?" she asked, raising her shoulders in feigned ignorance. "Is there something you wanted?"

"Just to give you an idea," Gabrielle said. "Some of us are getting together for a group cooking talk at the library. Pam, Brooke, Joan Stokes when she gets back from Cabo, Hannah—you know, the regular crowd. You might want to join us."

And cook for whom? Caroline asked herself. "Maybe," she said to appease her friend.

Glancing across the street, Caroline's eyes locked on the library—a building that only existed because of her grandmother's charity. It had always been a welcoming sanctuary that offered magical moments for her and Charlotte. The wide stone staircase leading up to the front door was once the gateway to a private world that she had shared with those closest to her. So many wonderful memories of Charlotte were behind those doors. At that moment, Caroline had never missed CC more.

Gabrielle placed her hand on the car door's windowsill, as if to stop her friend from disappearing again. "Everyone would love to see you again. I wish you'd come."

"I'll give it some thought," Caroline said politely as she started the car.

"You can stop by anytime," Gabrielle offered.

"I'll think about it. But I need to go now."

Before Gabrielle took her hands off the door, Caroline put the car in drive and slowly pulled away.

"Caroline—" Gabrielle began.

But Caroline simply waved as she drove off. Tears welled in her eyes.

Following Main Street to the only intersection in town that deserved a traffic light, Caroline turned right onto Farm to Market Road. Five miles farther, she passed Montis Inn on the left. In another mile, just before crossing the Fork River Bridge, she turned left onto a narrow, unmarked dirt road named Chicory Lane. It paralleled the Fork River for a half mile before coming to a dead end at the stone mill, which was her home since marrying Kai.

There were now only three residents on Chicory Lane, and together they owned the only two properties grandfathered in when the state acquired much of the surrounding land. The first home, immediately on the left and anchoring the corner of Chicory and Farm to Market Road, was owned by Dr. Tom Candor and his wife, Mac. They had bought the old Laningham farm shortly after the two married six years ago. Their small and beautifully kept red farmhouse set off from the road had two similarly colored barns farther back, which served as a second office and a boarding facility of sorts for Tom's growing veterinarian practice in town. Regularly, animals would come to heal under Tom's watchful care, grazing in one of the many pastures that made up their hundred-acre homestead. After being given a clean bill of health, the animals were sent home just as other patients arrived.

A half mile past the Candor's, where the lane ended, perched Caroline's home on the banks of Fork River. For over two hundred years, it had been the old Lumby Mill, which served residents from thirty miles around. Easily seen from the Fork River Bridge, the large, pale-yellow mill was a beacon next to the wide expanse of the river, whose dark waters ultimately passed under the bridge and into Woodrow Lake.

Kai and Caroline bought the mill two weeks after they were married. With the help of Caroline's friends—Brooke Turner, who provided the architectural blueprints, and Mac, being one of the finest carpenters in the area—

Caroline turned the mill into a warm home. At his request, they added an attached shop where Kai delved into the business of repairing antique furniture with a specific focus on old clocks and, of course, religious artifacts.

Driving down Chicory Lane, Caroline slowed her car before the Candor mailbox in order to deliver their letter. After clamping the mailbox door closed, she saw Mac carrying a pail into the smaller barn. Mac looked up, smiled and waved, her vibrant red hair flashing in the sun. Caroline smiled back and nodded. Mac was someone Caroline could have grown close to if the circumstances of her life were different: if she and Kai hadn't been sequestered for years as he had preferred, if Jamar hadn't filched Ross Foundation money before taking flight to Coraba, and if Kai hadn't left her with such appalling abruptness. But each of those events had occurred, and she was doing her best, albeit with varying success, to brave it alone by keeping herself separated from the world.

Continuing down Chicory Lane, at the bend of the road before the Candor farm disappeared from view, a flash of color caught Caroline's eye in the rearview mirror. Just then someone called out. Thinking someone was calling her, she stepped hard on the brake and turned in her seat to look out the window.

A man was jogging toward the barn. His flame-red sweater stood out like a flare against the muted hues of a season in transition from late winter to early spring. He waved and called out again to Mac.

Squinting, Caroline tried to recognize the stranger but couldn't.

Caroline sat still, listening to their indistinct voices—first Mac's and then the man's. Seconds later they both broke into laughter, one deep and rolling and the other higher pitched. The man took the large milk pail from Mac, freeing her to put her arm through his. Together they walked up the center steps, two at a time.

Picket rails outlined the deep front porch that spanned the length of the house and continued along their home's east side, where the last of the season's firewood was stacked. Scattered about were many chairs and wooden rockers that formed loose groupings of furniture. Several side tables were in arm's reach.

The man offered a chair to Mac and then disappeared inside with the pail. A minute later another man came outside. Caroline immediately recognized Tom Candor. The stranger was a few steps behind him, carrying a tray of glasses and a pitcher that he placed on a side table.

Tom leaned against the railing and, to Caroline's amazement, lifted a clarinet and began to play. Mac laughed and started to clap. Caroline leaned a little farther out the window but was still unable to hear the music, so she turned off the car. As soon as the engine died, the faint sound of Tom's clarinet carried down the lane.

"*Moonlight Serenade*," she thought.

The man in the red sweater bowed and offered his hand to Mac. When she got up, he began dancing with her, lifting her hand above their heads and turning her around. His body moved with supple grace and he tangoed. Mac laughed each time he dipped her one way and then another. When she tired, he gave her a kiss on the cheek before continuing his own version of a one-step shuffle.

Caroline continued to watch until a dog began to bark in the distance, probably one of their Dalmatians. The three looked toward a field just above where Caroline was parked. Although she was certain they couldn't see her car, she still blushed with embarrassment for having spied on them.

When she turned on her car, for a moment she felt unanchored. For a moment, she had let Kai and all of her life's problems slip from her attention.

Before driving away, Caroline took one last look in the rearview mirror and sighed heavily. The fondness between the three was obvious even from afar, and it deepened her unrelenting sense of loneliness. Although she had always wished for a life filled with such laughter and song, that dream was drifting further away.

She slowly continued on to her house, the old Lumby Mill, as it was referred to by the last four generations of local residents. The unique structure had sat vacant for years until Kai came across it while walking along the river's bank one day. Although water had not run through its flume, the sluice gates or the spillway for many decades, the pale-yellow, four-story post and lintel building had captured Kai's imagination. And the swish of the river that ran along the mill's long southern wall reminded him of home, which, he believed, brought him closer to God. That feeling was only compounded once they got the mill's wheel repaired and splashing water could be heard throughout the property.

Although Caroline never told Kai as much, her favorite aspect of the mill was its architectural character and its role in Lumby's history. Other than that, she thought very little of the old building. But when Kai shared his irrepressible vision of the mill becoming a home filled with the laughter of children and, of course, the ticking of beautiful vintage clocks placed among other heirloom antiques, her excitement grew and she acquiesced against her better judgment.

When they purchased the mill two weeks after their marriage, it was in a state of abandoned disrepair—the roof outside had as many holes as the floorboards inside. Laboring long hours while Caroline worked at the Ross Enterprises branch office in Rocky Mount, Kai whiled away many months converting the upper levels of the mill into a livable home. He then renovated the cavernous "gear and mill" bottom level into his antique shop with an area specifically set aside for clock repair. They repainted it the same pale-yellow, while keeping the original signage on the exterior walls.

The weeks turned into months, and without warning their one-year anniversary of buying the mill was upon them. Caroline gave Kai an engraved sign that read "Lost in Time Antique Shoppe," which he hung over the restored entrance door. Within weeks of opening, Kai's shop welcomed a fledgling customer base that quickly grew once word spread of his integrity, fairness and demand for quality in the pieces that he repaired or sold.

The sound of the mill's sloshing water was drowned out by Caroline's favorite albums of Glenn Miller and Duke Ellington, if only occasionally because of Kai's strong preference for liturgical chant. But the roots for the fulfilling, albeit predictable, pattern of their lives were drawn, and both were content.

But over the few years they were together, God and family tugged at Kai's soul so much that staying in Lumby ceased to be an option for him, although it was never discussed between them. Only after the fact, after he and his brother absconded with her heart and her money, did she face the brutal truth that she was not enough. And now all that was left was his shop.

Other than one trip downstairs to retrieve the unrepaired clocks that needed to be returned to Kai's customers, the doors to the shop had remained permanently closed. By remaining at arm's length, it couldn't resurrect more regret. Only after Brooke's suggestion and a lot of thought did Caroline come to the conclusion that the store and all of its properties within needed to be dealt with. Its proximity made it a convenient first project to be cleaned up in her life.

"Finn," she said, petting the dog between the ears, "today is the day we conquer the sad memories. Let's go down and see what he left us."

With Finn at her heels, Caroline descended to the ground level of her mill. She pulled aside overgrown vines that covered one of the windows and wiped the dirty pane with the sleeve of her sweatshirt. Standing on her toes, she cupped her hands around her eyes to peer inside. She felt like a criminal, casing a property before an illegal entry.

When she opened the shop's door, a gust of wind blew into the room, lifting spirals of fine dust from the floor in circular plumes that followed the door's swing. Caroline breathed in through her nose. The air was heavy and stagnant, but the smell was as she remembered it: a sweet blend of Kai's cologne, wood shavings and linseed oil.

Caroline took a step inside, her hand tightly gripping the doorknob as if that connection was her escape if she needed one. She glanced around the room, prepared to see ghosts, prepared for an onslaught of remorse. But the wave didn't hit, and she let go.

As she walked into the room, dust balls wafted away from her shoes like snow blowing about in a storm. Each step left a clear footprint on the dusty floorboards. Her sigh filled the room's silence. It was unnerving to see so many clocks that were all soundless and without motion. What was more unsettling, though, was the change of hue around her. Whereas the store was once colored with dark oaks, rich mahoganies and stained maples, she was now surrounded by a world of monochromatic gray. It reminded her of Finn's black-and-white photograph on the kitchen corkboard.

The glass casements that ran along the front and side walls were opaque, and the larger pieces of furniture that Kai had purchased over the last three years were encased in the same dusty film.

"This so sucks. What a waste of money," she said under her breath. "So much furniture. . . ."

She struggled to deal with her pain, trying to objectively attack the problem as she used to do so easily before Kai. She had to accept the fact that there was only one reasonable path forward: reopen the store to sell off everything, every last clock and cross. If that didn't lessen her agony, at least her bank account would be healthier.

It was getting dark by the time Caroline walked back to the house. When she heard Finn barking at a distance, she called him several times but he was nowhere in sight. So she grabbed his leash and headed down a path that ran along the river, and then through an area of heavy forest and rocky cliffs that belonged to Tom and Mac. Halfway to the Candor's, she called to Finn again, but even his barking had ceased.

Now deep in the woods, as the setting sun went behind a cloud, the surroundings darkened immediately. It was too quiet, she thought. An unsettling eeriness came over Caroline, and the hairs on her neck stood on end. Then she heard a stirring through the trees.

"Finn?" she called softly, slowly walking toward the rustling.

Suddenly, she screamed. Not far away, a man was on his knees holding a bloodied calf. In his hand was a knife that he had just used to cut the calf's throat. He dropped the dead animal and stood up. His silhouette was outlined against the rocky cliff directly behind him. His clothes were drenched in blood.

She held his stare for one moment before she turned and bolted down the path. Tripping over limbs and stumbling on rocks, she fell twice, once gashing her knee on a sharp shelf of granite. She scrambled to her feet and continued running, not once looking back. She heard steps behind her, the branches cracking from twenty feet away . . . ten feet away, gaining on her with every stride.

Suddenly Finn darted past.

"Run, Finn! Run!" she screamed in a panic.

Dashing inside the house, Caroline locked all the doors and windows before running upstairs and huddling under the sheets of her bed. She held a flashlight between her chin and her chest as she texted on her phone.

Omg Mac . . . I just witnessed a murder here. He just killed a calf. I spotted him in the woods—he had a huge knife and was covered in blood, and when he looked up at me, his eyes were bright red. I couldn't stop him, it was too late. before he could kill me, I ran back to the mill faster than ever. Finn and I are ok. I've called the police. Who would ever do such a monstrous thing to a defenseless animal? What is this world coming to? Make sure you lock all of your doors tonight. He's probably still in the area.

SEVEN

Trust

At Saint Cross Abbey, the stranger lay in a bed in one of the monastic cells for two days and three nights. He was in such a deep sleep that those watching over him were unsure whether he was alive or not. The doctor saw him each morning as best he could. The cut and infection in his arm were beginning to heal, but few other changes were noticeable.

On the third day when he woke, Sister Megan, who had seldom left his side, was sitting next to his bed in a straight-backed chair. The man's eyes opened slowly. Without moving his head, he tried to make sense of his surroundings; it was the most modest of rooms with a single bed, a chair and a nightstand, which had on it a clock and a Bible. A small three-drawer bureau was on the far wall, and immediately to the right, a narrow closet. Although the door to his room was open, it was profoundly quiet.

The sister next to him wore a crisp white cotton shirt tucked into a pair of black pleated slacks, belted at the waist. She had a lean frame and straight blond hair cut just above the shoulders with bangs cut above her brow. Had he been less groggy, he would have considered her beautiful.

"*Où suis-je?*" he asked weakly.

"*Parlez-vous Anglais?*" the sister asked, but the man faded off to sleep and dreamed of the woman sitting next to him.

Several hours later, he woke again. Without a word, the sister stood and left. A minute later Brother Michael came in.

"Do you speak English?" the monk asked.

"Yes. Why?"

"You spoke French when you first woke up, but earlier Brother Matthew thought you were speaking Arabic in your sleep."

"I do," the man said slowly. "Where am I?"

"Saint Cross Abbey," the monk replied. "If you're strong enough, I can help you clean up."

Thirty minutes later, with Michael's aid every moment of the time, the stranger returned to his room, washed and wearing a clean pair of simple cotton gray pajamas. His hair was substantially shorter and his beard had been shaved off.

"Thank you," he said once again to the monk.

"You have fresh bedding, and Brother John brought in a light meal," Michael said, nodding toward the tray on the bureau.

"Thank you."

"I'm worried those are the only two words you know," Brother Michael teased. "Is there anything else you need?"

The man shook his head just as there was a light rap on his door.

"We're done," Michael said to Sister Megan as she entered. "I'll be on morning chores if you need me."

Megan quickly dialed a number on her cell phone. "In about five minutes," she said before hanging up. "I'm sure our abbot would appreciate speaking to you if you're strong enough," she said to the stranger. "You've been a mystery to everyone in the community, and he would like to understand the circumstances of your visit."

"Does he not know who I am?"

Megan shook her head. "You're a traveler who came to our doorstep on the edge of death and asked for our help. Do you feel well enough to go downstairs?"

"Do you know who I am?" he asked.

"Yes, but I only recognized you now, after you shaved. I'm assuming you're Alan, and not your brother, Duke."

He slowly nodded. "I am definitely not my brother, Duke."

"Your clothes were beyond saving. You'll find what garments you need in the closet, and your wallet and envelope are in the drawer," she said.

Alan's eyes opened wider. "The envelope . . ."

"Your belongings are untouched. I'll wait for you outside." Upon leaving, she shut the door.

Unsteady on his feet, it took much longer than

usual to dress. He apologized for the delay when he finally joined Megan in the hall. During their walk to the monks' private living room, the man kept looking over his shoulder.

Sensing the man's anxiety, Megan said, "Don't worry. Only the brothers are allowed on this floor."

"So why are you here?"

"I'm the exception this week because I've had some experience with caring for the ill," Megan replied. "I assure you, the community will give you privacy if that's what you want."

"That's what I need right now," he said.

Megan led him through two closed doors along the main corridor, and into the monks' private living room where he sat in one of the smaller sofas. A brother came in and placed a tray of coffee and pastries on the table in front of them. He was as tall as the stranger, and dressed in a long black robe with a loose belt hanging above his hips.

Megan said, "This is Brother Matthew, the abbot of Saint Cross."

The man tried to stand.

"No, please stay seated," the brother said, placing his hand gently on the man's shoulder.

The man extended his arm to shake the monk's hand. "I'm Alan Blackstone," he said.

"It's nice to finally meet you after all these days," Matthew said as he sat down directly across from the man. "Please help yourself. You must be hungry."

"Thank you. Perhaps later."

Sister Megan said to the man, "I'll leave you to Matthew's good care." She turned to the monk. "I'll be in the back field if you need me."

Quiet filled the room as soon as the door closed behind her.

Finally Alan spoke. "I'm embarrassed to admit that I'm not sure where I am."

"A monastery in Franklin."

"Franklin?"

"By your reaction, I'll assume this wasn't your intended destination."

He shook his head. "No. I had no destination, other than . . . away." He paused. "I was lost for several weeks and then I came across your driveway in the dead of night."

Matthew smiled. "So I remember."

"I'm sorry, that's all I do remember." Alan slowly sat back. "The rest is a blur."

"We wanted to take you to the hospital, but you fought us quite adamantly—in fact, in many different languages—so we assumed you had good reason."

"I do," he said, but didn't elaborate. "I apologize for whatever I said."

Brother Matthew crossed his hands on his lap and remained silent, allowing the man to collect his thoughts.

The newspaper lying on the coffee table caught Alan's eye. A small photograph of his brother and him was on the front page. He tilted his head to read the headlines. "Blackstone Presumed Dead."

"All the papers have covered your disappearance." Matthew lowered his glasses to carefully study the man's face. "You look amazingly alike," he said.

"Do you know Duke?"

"Only from seeing him in Lumby."

Alan frowned, but was too exhausted to explain. All he yearned for was sleep. "I can't express my gratitude," he said, wanting to bring the conversation to closure as politely as possible.

"God has led many wayward souls to our doorsteps," the monk said.

Alan corrected him. "Not wayward, I assure you. But I must ask you for your sworn confidence for another day or two, until I'm strong enough to leave." Alan rubbed his temple.

"Rest assured we will give you asylum and guarantee your anonymity," he said. "But I sense your story is waiting to be shared."

Brother Matthew leaned back in his chair.

Alan dropped his head forward as he recalled the events that had brought him to Saint Cross. "I was visiting my brother, Duke, in Rocky Mount, where he is staying while he campaigns in Lumby. FedEx delivered an envelope. I was expecting some paperwork from my office, so I opened it without looking at the address. When I scanned the papers, I realized that they were for Duke. But a few words caught my eye and I began to read the pages more carefully. The first section contained undisclosed plans for a pipeline Duke intends to lay across the state. But more incriminating were papers that followed. Three dozen pages pointed to different conspiracies, embezzlements and bribes that my brother is using in order to get his project approved." Alan rubbed his hands on his knees nervously.

"When Duke returned home that afternoon, I confronted him about the pipeline and his payoffs. He said he wasn't going to let me interfere with the billion-dollar project. We argued more violently than we ever had, because I didn't let up. He suddenly lunged at me with a knife." Alan winced and then closed his eyes. "I had never seen him so angry and so determined. We fought. He slashed my arm, but I broke free and ran.

"For three weeks I've been walking through the woods, disoriented and eating little. I'm embarrassed to admit, my survival skills are less than what I would have thought."

"The mountains are treacherous," Matthew said. "Only experienced and well-equipped hikers would take on this area and this elevation."

"Well, had I not come across your monastery, I don't think I would have lasted another two days."

"That's what the doctor told us as well." Matthew thought for a moment. "Getting back to the papers you read—"

Alan interrupted. "They're in my room if you want to see them."

Mathew nodded. "That is your prerogative. But one question: Is the pipeline itself illegal?"

"I think that in politics, with our government, enough money legitimizes a lot of wrongdoings," Alan said. "From what I saw, his pipeline would tear up hundreds of miles of protected land. Duke would never have been able to get his plans passed through the legislature, or through the EPA, or a dozen other organizations that steward federal and state land, without buying or blackmailing the people he needs to approve it."

Matthew frowned. "So, why is Duke wasting his time running for mayor of Lumby?"

"Because that's the one town he needs to control in order complete his plan. The town has repeatedly voted against development, so Duke knew his only chance to successfully claim eminent domain was to ensure his own signature as the town official endorsing the project."

Matthew raised his brows. "So being elected mayor is only a means to an end for him?"

Alan nodded. "I assure you he cares nothing about the town. In fact, Lumby will be decimated just like a handful of other small towns that happen to be inconvenient obstacles to his plans."

"And you couldn't persuade him otherwise?"

Alan felt nauseous. "You don't know my brother. We always had our differences. But I kept my distance and he left me alone."

"The paper said you were . . . I'm sorry, you *are* a linguist."

Alan smiled weakly. "A theoretical linguist."

"Theoretical?"

"I study the commonalities between languages."

"So you don't speak them?"

"Oh, I do—seven fluently and another five less so. But my work is mostly academic. I do pro bono translation for an organization that helps refugees from South America and the Mideast. In fact, the day of our fight I had gone to see Duke to ask for a contribution, which I do every few years. I grovel and he writes me a check just to get rid of me. The money is really important to the families we assist."

There was a long silence between the men.

"So, now what?" Matthew finally asked.

Alan made a gesture to shrug his shoulders, but every inch of his body still ached. "I don't know."

"Would you to like to pray?" he offered.

"I'm sure your God is busy helping more deserving souls."

"I seriously doubt that," the monk said.

"If I survive my brother's wrath, perhaps we will have a long discussion about theology. I fear my beliefs, or the lack of them, will disappoint."

"I seriously doubt that as well. But I look forward to it."

Alan looked at the wall clock, and tried to focus on the challenge that lay ahead. "I need to go through the papers in detail," he said slowly. "Then I'll contact the police or the FBI, but I don't know who to trust. Duke has paid cronies at every level of the government, and I'm sure word will reach him within a week, if not days, that his papers have been disclosed. When that happens, my life will be at risk." He paused, looking up at Brother Matthew. "That probably sounds very self-centered to a man like you."

Matthew raised his brows. "Like me?"

"A monk—a person with a higher cause than living a mortal life," he answered. "But I like my life, as inconsequential as it is, as Duke has reminded me many times."

"There is no such thing as an inconsequential life."

"So I believe as well," Alan said. "If I could just impose for a short time more." He sat back as exhaustion rushed over him. With the exhaustion came utter despair. "I also don't want to put any of you in harm's way."

"I think you would be impressed just how resourceful we can be."

Alan gave Matthew a hard look. "Not against Duke."

EIGHT

Acceptance

The mantel clock in Dennis Beezer's living room chimed once, several minutes ahead of time. That's how it had always been since moving into his father's home after William's death. The fact that the clock ran fast had always gnawed at Dennis, he being an exacting type, but he intentionally never reset it out of a long-festering contempt he felt toward his father. It was just one of the many ways he still revolted against the man who tried to control his life, although William was long since buried.

Crouched over his desk, Dennis put his hands on his temples and studied the spreadsheet. The numbers, whether they were represented in digits or in graphs, told the same story: his companies were in dire condition. He was the first to admit that the failing of *The Lumby Lines* and The Bindery was due to his management skills. The downturns in his businesses were on his shoulders alone.

He took a break from the reality of his business to look at what surely would be one of the last papers he would print.

The Lumby Lines

LUMBY FORUM
An open bulletin board
for our town residents.

Let's meet for a drink. Me: Not tall, slightly rotund, graying on what's left, honest to a fault. You: attractive, witty, appreciates the challenges and foibles in others. I'll be at Jimmy D's, Wed. all day.

QUIZZIFY GHERKINS—not the pickle but the word. 429 Pts and 180 Pts respectively. Lumby Scrabblers Club looking for new members who own their own boards. No dogs with chewing issues allowed.

SWM This ad cost me $12. Needless to say, our first date is going to be Dutch. Needs to be LOL funny. Bring cell phone to share, mine's lost. See Phil in town.

Alan, I miss you. Sorry about last week— should never have given away your chair, or your clothes, or your dog. I want you back. And my birthday is day after tomorrow in case you forgot.

Lumby Real Estate

Location! Location! Remodeled 3/2 on Logger Road. Early morning traffic noise expected to end by October. Great starter home at $74,500. Any offer considered. Call Joan Stokes at Main Street Realty 925-9292. Make offer. Portable.

Office for rent above bookstore (Notes music store before they went bust). 800sq. Carpet just cleaned. Some renovating allowed. $180/mo 3 month deposit. Owners of pet stores and hair salons need not apply. See Dennis Beezer at Chatham Press.

For Rent: RV in our backyard. No wheels—no removing from property. Owners won't need it until next summer. Quaint inside, but doesn't have a hookup. Call for price. Offered by Lumby Realty. Call 925-5555.

Chicken coop built 2 years ago. Holds two dozen hens. Yearly lease only. $6/mo. 925-2985.

Certified piano teacher available to tutor your child, any age from 4–64. Very experienced. 925-0174.

One half of double-car garage. Long. Must share with bus up on blocks. Some oil on floor. $12/mo 925-5253.

The front door opened slowly and his son quietly stepped inside.

Dennis looked at his watch and was about to make a comment about his son's unnecessary cavorting until such early hours in the morning. But instead he bit his tongue. Brian was now a young man who needed to learn through the outcomes of his actions.

Dennis coughed to get his son's attention. "Odd time for a visit. Is your refrigerator empty?"

"Not quite," he laughed. "But Mom left us something in the kitchen."

"She's thrilled you're home, you know."

"I do." Brian walked into his father's office. "So, why are you working so late?"

Looking up at his son, Dennis was amazed by how much he had grown. "Do you know I barely recognize you now?"

"Hope that's a good thing," Brian said.

"It is. I might not have said it before, but you should know your mother and I are very proud of you. What you've done for the monks is impressive."

"Okay," Brian said awkwardly, not exactly knowing how to respond to his father's compliment. "So, what's up?"

"Just working on some unfinished business," Dennis said.

Brian sat down in the seat facing his father's desk. "No offense, Dad, but it didn't look like there was a lot of business going on in your building—finished or otherwise."

Dennis leaned back, wondering if Brian had the maturity to handle the hard realities of life.

"Can I see?" Brian asked, pulling a spreadsheet from under his father's arm without his permission.

"It's—"

"Dad, I know what a spreadsheet is," Brian said.

It only took Brian a minute to correctly assess the status of the three businesses that his father owned. Brian's thoughts were racing a mile a minute, as they did down in South America when he first evaluated an enterprise. Numbers churned in his head almost faster than Dennis could calculate them on his computer.

"The—"

Brian lifted a finger. "Hold on," he said as he continued to study the data on the page. Silently he ran through a SWOT analysis, considering the strengths, weaknesses, opportunities, and threats of each enterprise. *The Lumby Lines* had been running in the red for at least six months, and was in the most precarious position—it was, as the expression goes, hemorrhaging money. The

Lumby Bookstore showed flat sales against a decreasing inventory, and The Bindery was only surviving on a few staple accounts that were still using Beezer's services. However, without any one of those accounts, The Bindery also would run in the red.

After a few minutes, Brian finally returned the pages to his father. "It's a train wreck," Brian said.

Dennis tried not to show his intense disappointment in Brian's summation. "That's all you can say. It's a train wreck?"

"Oh, absolutely not," Brian said, jumping out of the chair. "But it's always good to be in agreement with where we stand, and right now we're both standing by the track, witnessing a collision of not one but three trains." Brian began pacing around the room, glancing at the books on the bookshelf that lined one wall of the office. "Hey, I didn't know you liked Paulo Coelho," he said, pulling *The Pilgrimage* from the shelf. "A friend lent me a copy of *The Alchemist* in Argentina. Epic."

"I didn't know you read," Dennis quipped.

"Huh?" Brian said, surprised at his father's assumption. He put the small paperback into his shirt pocket. "I'll return it in a few days."

"Keep it as long as you want."

Brian didn't meet his father's eyes when he asked the next question. "Does Mom know?"

Dennis blinked, not expecting that question. "No! Nor will she," he said. "Or anyone else, for that matter."

Brian shook his head. "That's not how I look at it." He returned to his seat on the other side of his father's desk. "We each create our own circle of influence," he said, using both hands to create a globe. "In there are all of your assets, and the most important consists of the relationships you have. When things are going well, they may be of less value, but as the globe gets squeezed, they sometimes become critical to your survival. You fight together and you celebrate together."

"Is that what the monks taught you?"

"They did more for me than offer a great job. They introduced me to the world. And if their philanthropic work has taught me anything, it's that life is bad when you're standing alone."

"You think that's what I'm doing?"

"You and Grandfather. The Beezer men have a strong tendency to go it alone."

"That's what you're supposed to do when you have a problem—deal with it so others don't have to," Dennis said. He then added, "Especially when the problem is of your own making."

"It's never that black-and-white," Brian argued.

"The monks have softened you."

Brian shook his head. "No, they haven't. South America has hardened me. Look at your businesses. Anyone can see they're all in trouble.

And you may be blaming yourself, but I would say that your circle is being squeezed by outside forces you have no control over," he explained. "If anything, technology is to blame. People just don't read newspapers anymore. Look how many print operations have closed in the last decade: the *Seattle P-I, The Tampa Tribune*. No offense, Dad, but if the *Rocky Mountain News* didn't have a chance, I wouldn't expect *The Lumby Lines* to either. It has nothing to do with you." He paused. "And books are now downloaded and read on tablets." He pulled the novel from his pocket. "This," he said, holding it in the air, "is obsolete. Even if you had the best management skills in the world, your businesses would still have a fate that is out of your hands. One man can't fight the trends of society, especially when it comes to technical innovation."

Although Dennis listened to every word Brian said, he refused to accept the reality.

Brian glanced at the spreadsheets. "So, who's helping you?"

"No one," Dennis said firmly. "And that's how it will be."

"But Dad, *The Lines* is down to eight pages, and there are only a handful of ads. How do you expect to cover your costs?"

"Let's just thank God you didn't go to college. That fund we had set aside has kept the paper alive. But I don't want to do that to Timmy."

Brian pressed the heels of his palms into his eyes in frustration. "God, I wish you weren't so pigheaded."

Dennis was flabbergasted. He sat back as if Brian had physically assaulted him. "How dare you say that to me?"

"I say it because I see you making bad business decisions out of some idiotic feelings you have toward your father." Brian stopped to consider what he had just said. "Or maybe it's the responsibility you feel toward the town."

"Well, you damn well need to feel responsible for all of this because someday it's going to be yours."

"Dad, you know I don't want it. I know that's not what you want to hear, but I have no interest in staying in Lumby, trying to keep some antiquated company alive."

Dennis slapped the desk. "Damn it, Brian, why do you always fight me? And since when did you get such a sharp tongue?"

Brian jumped to his feet. "When the facts are behind me and I know I'm right," he said confidently. "And I've learned how to be honest."

"And you're so sure you're right about this?" Dennis asked bitterly.

" 'This' is a big word. Am I sure *The Lumby Lines* will never be solvent? Yes. Am I sure you'll need to change The Bindery to keep that solvent? Yes. Am I sure a different type of customer benefit needs to be added to the bookstore for it to stay in business? Yes."

Dennis was almost more dumbfounded by his son's tenor than by his son's dead-on summation of the problems he faced. But he was exhausted and didn't want to fight any longer. "Sit down, son," he said. "I know you're just trying to help." Dennis stared at Brian, partly out of disbelief that his gangly, ill-behaved son was now more insightful than he, but mostly out of pride. "Is this what you do all day when you're down in Peru?"

"And Argentina and Ecuador. Some of the startups I help with are on a hundred-dollar loan. But when towns pull their resources together to form co-ops, others may have budgets of a hundred thousand."

Brian picked up the financial sheets and reviewed the numbers again. "I don't think you can turn this around," the young man said in a softer voice. "But you already know that. You've known that for the last year."

Dennis tried to explain. "It's important to the residents of Lumby. This is a small community that depends on the news the paper gives them."

Brian shook his head in disagreement. "If that was truly the case, your subscription rate would be in the thousands, not the low hundreds."

"Times are tough," Dennis said. "People have less discretionary income."

"That's crap," Brian said. "Your paper costs less than a gallon of milk. They can afford it if it gives them something of value in a way that they wanted. Your paper is obsolete, and Lumby residents are finding their news elsewhere . . . even local news."

"Where?"

Brian shuddered. *Could he be that oblivious?* He wondered. "Online. On Facebook, on Twitter, on The Huffington Post."

"But that's not news," Dennis countered.

"Some are legitimate news outlets. But all of them offer something unique to the subscriber."

"I'm talking real news," Dennis said.

"Do you actually consider the results of the pumpkin festival to be *real news?*"

"It's what readers have always wanted. It's what they expect," Dennis argued.

"They're getting the same and more online," Brian countered.

"Filled with gossip and hearsay and rumor."

"That's one of the negatives about the Internet. Unless you get the facts from a reputable source, you never know." Brian leaned back and thought about the implications of what they were discussing. "As much as you hate it, that's where your news needs to be."

Dennis eyes opened wide. *"Online?"*

Brian chuckled. "You make it sound like it's Armageddon. Do you even go online?"

"Only Amazon and Google, but as seldom as necessary."

"Well, if you want to change these numbers," Brian said, tapping on the spreadsheets, "maybe that should change right now. Spend some time and look at The Huffington Post—that started from scratch in 2005—and now they have eighty million unique visitors a month. *Eighty million!* You might not agree with what they say, but you should look at how they say it."

Dennis cocked his head, trying to imagine a world he didn't understand. "So we put our articles up on a webpage?"

Brian nodded. "It's a little more complicated than that, but yes, that's the basic idea. It's understanding your readers, knowing what news they want when they want it, and knowing the value they place in your advertisements." He picked up a copy of *The Lumby Lines* from Dennis's in-box. "It's also knowing what to keep and what to discard."

"But that could take a year," Dennis said.

"You'll be out of business by then, so we need to figure out how to transform your paper in a couple of weeks."

"It can't be done," Dennis said.

Brian created a circle with his hands again. "Remember the globe, Dad. Relationships can make it happen."

The clock chimed twice.

Dennis might not have agreed with everything his son had said, but he was smart enough to know when a battle was lost. Everything was falling apart.

"So are you planning to stick around and help your old man figure this out?" Dennis asked sheepishly.

"Sure. I'm here for a few months," Brian said. "I don't have a lot to do until my next trip, so if you're okay with me running with this, I'll bring *The Lumby Lines* into the twenty-first century."

NINE

Waking

Hank hated how the mayoral campaign was being run. Duke's aggressive tenor and rhetoric had triggered nightmares of being bullied and pushed out of the nest when he was a young fledgling. And although he would have strongly preferred to migrate south for the month so he could skip all campaign debates, he felt his town needed him more than ever. What carried him through were thoughts of leaner politics and his vacation days lounging around Hyannis Port. "If our times are difficult and perplexing, so are they challenging and filled with opportunity," his friend Bobby used to say.

But these were more than difficult times—they were ugly, filled with lies and false accusations, name-calling and personal attacks. Such gross behavior had not been seen since that crayon incident at Lumby elementary school a dozen years earlier. So Hank did something he hadn't done since arriving in Lumby: he dropped his political neutrality and officially backed Pam Walker. *Extremis malis extrema remeia*, Hank would explain when asked.

On that morning, he grabbed a VOTE WALKER sign and positioned himself in front of the Lumby Feed Store. A mannequin, well attired in the latest Caterpillar-logo garb, was with him. Not far away, Duke Blackstone stood on a pile of feed bags that were stacked on the front porch.

He yelled into the microphone. "Snarky Marky!"

Hank blinked in anger.

"He was here a minute ago. Where'd he go?" Duke yelled as he scanned the crowd of twenty congregated on the lawn in front of him. "He must be hiding inside. A real scaredy-cat! That's what we can't afford. A bunch of yellow-bellied scaredy-cats running our town. Let's get him out here." He then started to chant, "Snarky Marky, Snarky Marky." He waved his arms, encouraging others to chant with him.

Suddenly Mark walked through the swinging doors of the store carrying a new pitchfork on his shoulder.

"Hey, everyone," Mark said with a wide wave and a broad smile.

112

Duke swung around and, eyeing the pitchfork, raised the microphone closer to his mouth. "Well, you have some nerve showing up at my rally with a weapon. Look at that, folks, he's against guns but would kill a man with a pitchfork. Welcome to the thirteenth century, folks. That's where his wife will take you. What will we have next, jousting?"

Mark shrugged his shoulders. "Sam's got some nice pitchforks on sale in there," he said as he walked down the steps.

Duke pulled out his cell phone and snapped a photo of Mark walking through the crowd carrying the pitchfork. "He's crazy! The man's crazy. And people have told me that he's threatened them. Not a few, but I mean a lot of people." Duke snapped another photo. "And that pitchfork is for his Pathetic Pam," he said, continuing his tirade. "Snarky Marky needs to poke her in the ass."

Mark, who was walking away, suddenly stopped and turned. "Pick on me all you want. That's what bullies do, because you are small inside and insecure," he spat. "But lay off my wife because she is so out of your league, you have no idea."

"If she's so tough why isn't she here?" Duke yelled back. "Where's she hiding? She must be hiding somewhere."

Mark bit his lip and forced himself to take

the high road. He waved to the crowd. "Hope everyone has a great day." It took all of Mark's restraint to walk away.

That evening, after a long flight to LaGuardia Airport, Mark was almost as relieved to see Pam standing at the baggage carousel as she was to see him.

"I am so glad you're finally here," Pam said, hugging her husband. She gave him a long, overdue kiss.

"I am too," he said. "You have no idea. Was traffic bad coming in?"

"It doesn't matter," she said, holding him tightly. "It's just been so bad. I've never felt so alone in my life. And I've acted like such an idiot."

"I seriously doubt that," Mark said.

"I have. I felt like I was dropped from an airplane into a family who didn't even know I existed," Pam said, finally letting go of Mark. "But that would only make sense because I didn't know they existed either."

Mark picked up his baggage. "Come on, let's go. I'll buy you a drink and dinner once we get out of the city. Remember that place in Rye that we used to like so much? We can stop there."

The thought of not returning to her mom's home in Greenwich pleased Pam, and she was finally able to put the previous days behind her.

"So, how is it going?"

"Disastrous," Pam said. "Robert and his family have pulled together and are supporting each other, and I'm just a spectator standing on the fringe. It's really not their fault; Kay had asked that they handle the funeral arrangements."

"She could have done that to make it less painful for you."

"Maybe," Pam said. "But people keep on coming over to the house who are close to Robert and the kids, and I've never heard their names. I know I've lost my mother, but the person who was living in that house and the person who is being buried tomorrow seems like a stranger to me. When people talk about Kay, there's such a disconnect; I don't even think they're talking about my mother. It's so surreal, and I'm not sure if that's making it less painful or more painful." She stared out the window.

"That doesn't mean she loved you less," Mark reminded her.

Pam sighed. "In truth, I don't think she thought about me or us too often. I met one of her friends that didn't even know Kay had a daughter. It was so embarrassing to have to explain who I was." Pam's lip quivered as she fought back tears.

Mark glanced over at his wife and saw her pain. "After we moved away from Virginia, we just lived separate lives," he said, trying to ease her grief.

"But why am I realizing that just now? How could I have assumed we were so close when in fact we weren't?" she asked. "You know, it's times like this that I've always dreaded—the moment when you find out that you've perceived the world as something very different than what it was . . . that you've been living under some kind of delusional premise."

"I'm sorry," Mark said.

"So here I was, going under the assumption that the only family I had, that one remaining person, loved me as much as I loved her."

"Sometimes a person's love is different than we might expect," Mark said.

"But if I was wrong on something so blatantly obvious, what else have I missed?"

Pam and Mark were unprepared for the gathering at the Greenwich Episcopal Church. Because there was so much traffic, two of Robert's friends took on the task of directing traffic to adjacent parking lots after the primary areas were filled.

Inside the church, the pews were packed, and at least fifty more stood in the antechamber. Eric escorted Pam and Mark to their seats in the front of the church. Walking down the center aisle, Pam smelled the sweetness of the flowers around her. She had to give credit to Eric and Scott, who had coordinated the finer details of Kay's funeral. Although she had never read Kay's final letter of request, which had been mentioned often enough, she knew it was exactly what her mother would have liked—the setting was casually elegant with simple bouquets of baby's breath and white roses at the ends of each pew.

Once seated, Mark leaned over to Pam. "Where did all of these people come from?" he whispered.

Robert, seated next to Pam, overheard. "Kay was enormously popular," he explained. "A lot of her friends came today—from Canada and from Europe. One of her closest friends arrived yesterday from Sydney."

"Australia?" Pam asked. "I didn't know she had traveled there."

"We talked about moving there a few years ago, but we didn't want to be far away from Olivia and the kids. And of course there's Jessica's parents and a few of her relatives from Cotswold. We stayed with them regularly—it was one of your mother's favorite places to visit in Europe."

The organ started to play and the minster took his position at the podium.

"Are you speaking?" Mark asked

Pam shook her head. "No one asked me, and I didn't want to impose."

That night, after Robert had gone to bed and Mark had settled into the family room watching his favorite shows, Pam ventured into the vast attic that ran the length and depth of the house. She had not been up on the top floor since she was a child and asked to put away the Christmas ornaments. Given the dust she found, she assumed no one had ventured up there for years.

Countless boxes, furniture of every kind, china cases and old luggage formed irregular lines that she walked alongside. Most were impersonal objects, but one item piqued her interest enough for her to dig a little deeper: her father's old trunk. Removing the top blankets and his carefully folded military uniform, she found several shoeboxes of papers, all of which she removed and placed on the floor. Among the shoeboxes, she found a combination-locked safe that she had never seen before. Placing it on her lap, she tried various numbers that would have had significant meaning to her father, but nothing worked. On her twentieth try, she entered her birth date and it clicked open.

Pam removed the papers within, laid them on top of several shoeboxes, and took the entire stack downstairs to her bedroom. Carefully reading through the papers, she found several documents she'd expect in a family safe: the deed to the Greenwich house, her parents' marriage license, different insurance policies and papers for cars long since sold or given away. But she came across other items that she could not explain: a title for some property in New

118

Hampshire she didn't know they owned, purchase and sale agreements for various businesses, and a death certificate of a man named Edward Eastman. Although he shared the same surname as her father, she had never heard of him. But the address shown was where Pam remembered her father had once lived as a young man. The date of birth given for Edward Eastman was very close to her father's, but her father had told her many times that he had no relatives. Pam put it aside and continued looking through the papers.

In a sealed envelope, Pam found a birth certificate, but it wasn't hers. It was for an unnamed female born four years before Pam. The mother was Kay Holt and her father Charles Eastman. She rubbed her eyes as she read and reread the handwritten entries.

Mother had another child? Her thoughts spiraled out of control. Of course she didn't, Pam thought, refusing to accept the proof that she was holding. *My mother had another child . . . and never told me?*

"A child?" Pam asked aloud. Hearing her own voice, she quickly looked up to make sure the door to the hall was closed.

"What child?"

Pam yelped at the new voice.

Mark stood in the bathroom doorway with a clean toothbrush hanging from his mouth.

"You scared the life out of me!" she said.

"What child?" he asked again.

"My mother's," Pam said as she passed the papers to Mark. "I can't believe it. Why didn't she ever tell me?"

Mark sat down on the bed, carefully reading the document. "Wow," he said. "What a surprise."

"You think?" Pam asked, her jaw still on the ground. "I don't know if I'm more angry or hurt that she kept this secret from me." Pam thumbed through the remaining papers on her bed. "What other little bombshells am I going to find in here?"

"You know, honey, maybe you should wait until we're back home before you go through the rest of your parents' papers."

"That's just putting off the inevitable. I think they had a ton of secrets they kept to themselves." Pam's anger was surpassing her grief.

"They were private people," he said. "I don't think there's such a thing as a totally open life. All of us have forgotten things, or maybe decided not to share some messy details."

Pam looked up sharply. "Does that include you?"

"Of course not!" Mark said. "You know I would never hold anything back from you. We tell each other everything. But sometimes, I'm sure it happens in a marriage, or between a mother and her daughter."

"But a *child?*" Pam asked.

"Pam, I'm sure she died at childbirth. What else could have happened?"

Pam doubted that. "There was no death certificate for her in the safe."

"I would guess that the memories were just too painful for both of them. I mean, can you imagine losing a child like that? So they put it behind them. You can understand that, can't you?"

"I suppose," Pam lied. "Do you think I should ask Robert if he knew?"

"I think we should get some sleep, return to Montis and try to put it behind us," Mark said. "But that's not in your character, is it?"

As Pam proved when they returned home the following day, letting things go was not one of her strengths. Returning to Montis was just the beginning of a chapter in her life she was far from ready to write.

TEN
Fleeting

Caroline stood in the kitchen sipping the last of her morning tea, still shaken from the horrendous incident. She had seen Simon's police car several times the night before and once again that morning at sunrise, but she shuddered, remembering the scene.

She held back the blue-and-tan gingham curtain, keeping a sharp eye on Finn as he played in the backyard. Every few minutes she peered into the woods at distant shadows. *That's what violence does to you,* she thought, but then shook her head to push the image away.

A faint smile finally came over her as she watched Finn explore the riverbank. Being an intimate bystander in Finn's world was one of the few joys of her life. Watching him was just one notch below watching a child lick an ice cream cone on a hot summer day.

A flat rock had caught his attention. He dropped it, licked it, picked it up again and dashed ahead, with the rock clamped tightly between his jaws. Once close to the house, Finn tossed the brownish-black stone in the air, sending it flying several yards away. As soon as it landed, Finn galloped toward it, pounced on it as if it was live prey, and picked it up again to repeat the game. But just as it hit the ground, Finn froze as a cabbage white butterfly flew right over his nose.

Attention deficit disorder, Caroline thought, shaking her head.

Suddenly, the rock that Finn was playing with moved an inch, and then four inches. *What in the world is that?* Caroline thought in alarm.

Its movement pulled Finn's focus back to the game. He ran over and was about to pick it up when the stone started to scurry away. Finn dropped on his front paws, barked twice, and then nudged it with his nose. The stone changed direction and darted off to the left. Only then did Caroline see a small head sticking out of the turtle's shell.

Just as Finn grabbed it in his mouth again, Caroline ran through the door and screamed, "Finn! Drop it!"

The reptile landed on its back, its legs frantically kicking out from its shell. Caroline ran over and picked up the eight-inch wood turtle, which was covered with slime and gnawed almost beyond recognition. A part of its shell was cracked above the right shoulder and dangled from its body. It looked awful, but the turtle was still very much alive.

Caroline dashed inside, wrapped the turtle in a towel, and put Finn on the leash. Within a minute, they were sprinting down Chicory Lane. No doubt her car would have brought them to the Candor home faster, but Caroline had not yet figured out where Finn had stashed the keys.

She ran all the way to the Candor household—fearing both the killer and the turtle's imminent death. By the time she turned into their driveway, Caroline's lungs burned. She quickly glanced around the fields and barn, but not seeing anyone, she headed for the farmhouse. Smoke curled slowly from both chimneys that were at opposite ends of the long two-story home.

With Finn's leash wound tightly around one hand, and the turtle towel in the other, Caroline knocked on the door. She was about to rap even harder when the door opened.

"Caroline! You're a little early," Tom said, looking at his watch.

"What do you mean?"

"Mac invited you to dinner tonight at six."

Caroline shook her head. "I haven't talked with her."

"Ah, she took off first thing but said she was going to call you. She's probably ringing your home right now."

"I'd love to, but that's not why I'm here. This needs your help." She pushed the towel into Tom's chest.

"What's this?" he asked as he unwrapped the cloth.

"One of Finn's victims," Caroline said apologetically.

Tom nodded. "Puppies do silly things. That's one of their splendors, isn't it?"

"But he's two years old," she said uneasily.

Tom raised his brows. "That old?" He leaned over and patted Finn on the head. "Maybe it is time for you to grow up a bit." Tom gently picked up the turtle and inspected it from every angle. "Well, this doesn't look too bad. And we can't have the death of such a fine-looking turtle on Finn's conscience, can we?" He winked at Caroline. "Come in and we'll see what we can do."

Caroline looked askance at the idea of Finn going inside.

"Oh, he doesn't need to be on a leash," Tom said. "Just let him play outside. He knows his way around here better than I do."

Caroline was confused. "What do you mean?"

Tom regarded the Irish setter fondly. "He's a regular visitor to our barns. He loves the sheep. And last week he insisted on helping Mac hang the laundry on the line."

The image of Finn playing tug-of-war with Mac at the other end of a freshly washed pillowcase made Caroline cringe.

"But there's a killer out there," she said.

"Oh, that," Tom brushed it off with the wave of his hand. "Mac can explain everything. But come in," Tom said. "I'll need you to assist with the turtle."

Wondering why he was so nonchalant, she removed the leash from Finn's collar. As soon as Finn sensed his freedom, he bolted toward the chickens.

"Finn!" she yelled.

Tom laughed. "He'll be just fine. He just wants to herd them together."

"Am I interrupting?"

"Not at all," he said, leading her into his study, where shelves were overstuffed with veterinary books and tall stacks of old medical journals. Tom began rummaging through his desk drawers. On his wall was an amazing collection of cards from—and photographs of—those whom he had helped over the years.

"I think everyone in Lumby is still thankful for the day you arrived," Caroline commented, not exaggerating in the least bit.

"Not as thankful as I am," Tom replied with ease. "And there was Mac . . . waiting. Who could have asked for more?"

Caroline bit her lip. Tom and Mac formed a love story—like the one she wanted to write for her life, like the one she thought she would have with Kai.

Tom continued chatting as he examined the turtle. "Mac has a heart as big as heaven, and more resolve than a hungry bull." He frowned,

126

recalling a private memory. "When we almost lost Aaron, she stayed in Seattle for weeks, sitting by his bedside in the hospital room twenty-four hours a day, refusing to leave his side. She read volumes of books to him, although he was unconscious. After he woke up and she returned to Lumby, it took *her* months to recover, but I know that somehow her energy helped him heal. Sometimes you aren't allowed to prepare for what life throws at you, but she took it head on."

Caroline was at a loss for words, sensing the generosity but not knowing the occasion.

Tom saw Caroline's discomfort. "I'm sorry," he said, and then returned his attention to his patient. "Perhaps we could use her magic touch on this injury right about now?"

Caroline was unsure if Tom was referring to the turtle's or her own wounds.

"The killer I saw last night—" she began.

"Shh. Not another thought of that," Tom said, placing the turtle on his desk. "Why don't you hold it still while I take a closer look?"

Caroline tentatively clamped down on the turtle's frame, but the reptile struggled under her clasp.

"Gently," Tom advised. "The more you try to control it, the stronger it will react against you."

As soon as Caroline released her grip—so much so that her fingers were just barely touching the edge of the shell—the animal calmed down, allowing Tom to clean and glue the cracked shell.

"That's fine," he said, lifting it up for a closer look. "Sometimes the worst wounds are the deepest—the ones that you can't see. Those I leave in the hands of someone greater than me to heal over time." He gave the turtle a shot of antibiotics in its front leg, made one final inspection, and handed the turtle back to Caroline. "All yours."

Caroline's eyes opened wide. "What do you mean, *all mine?*"

"You shouldn't let him outside until his shell heals."

"That will take what, a few days?" she guessed.

He shook his head. "Six months at the most. Just make sure Finn understands that this turtle is his charge, his responsibility. But he's a smart dog and he'll learn quickly enough."

Late that afternoon, while baking a pie to bring to Mac's dinner, Caroline decided to spruce herself up, putting on a charming blue-and-yellow cotton dress, a few select pieces of simple jewelry and a bit of makeup. As always, Caroline looked striking. Staring into the mirror, she thought about how she had fiercely avoided this very occasion for the last five months: her first intimate family dinner as the "scorned woman." But things had to change, and reconnecting with close friends was one way to turn her life around.

Instead of taking the shortcut through the woods—*not that way,* she thought—Caroline walked down the center of the dirt lane, carefully balancing a banana cream pie in one hand and clenching Finn's leash with the other. Her eyes and ears stayed alert to any dangers as she kept Finn against her leg. She breathed a sigh of relief and slowed her pace when the Candor's farmhouse came into view.

After knocking on the front door and getting no reply, Caroline let Finn off the leash and walked over to the main barn, thinking that one or both of her hosts were tending the animals. Sliding the door open enough to peer down the darkened aisle, she saw the back of the man who she first thought to be Tom. But then she realized that the man was taller than Tom. The man stopped mid-step and glanced over his shoulder, looking directly toward Caroline.

She gasped when she saw his face. Her heart skipped several beats. *It was the calf killer!* It was the deranged murderer who she had seen in the woods! And now he was here, swinging an ax in his left hand.

Thoughts raged through her head. *He killed them!* She screamed in silence. *Oh my God, he's butchered Tom and Mac!*

In a blind rage, Caroline ran full force toward

the man and jumped on his back, smashing the cream pie into his face, hoping that the bananas would blind him long enough for . . . *For what?* She asked herself as she frantically wrapped her legs around his waist and tightened her arms about his neck. The man dropped the ax and began spinning in circles, trying to get Caroline off his back.

Suddenly, someone hit the switch and fluorescent light filled the barn.

"What are you two doing?" Tom yelled out.

Hearing his familiar voice, Caroline pushed herself off the man's back and ran to Tom's side as fast as she could. "He killed Mac!" she screamed, pointing to the stranger.

Her finger was shaking so badly that Tom took her hand in his. "Caroline, what are you talking about? Mac is fine."

"But he's the one who was covered in blood! He's the killer! He's the one who slit its throat!" she said in terror.

"Aaron?" Tom said. "He wouldn't hurt a fly."

Caroline remembered that name from earlier. "Who's Aaron?"

Tom nodded at the man who was standing exactly where Caroline had attacked him, with pie dripping from his face. "My brother."

"No!" Caroline screamed, taking a step back. "He's the one who was covered in blood!" she cried. "I saw him!"

"Oh, I understand," Tom said in a long exhale. He put his hands on her shoulders to help calm her. "Caroline, Aaron's not an animal killer. That calf had fallen off the ridge and had broken its leg. It had a ten-inch gash in its belly and had already been attacked. When Aaron found it, the animal was torn to shreds and bleeding to death. He did the only thing he could; he put the animal out of its misery as quickly and as painlessly as possible. I assure you, it hurt Aaron a hundred times more than the calf."

Caroline still wasn't sure. "But the ax . . . ?" Her accusation trailed off into a question.

Tom couldn't help but to grin. "Aaron's been helping me cut firewood all afternoon. I promise you he's very safe."

Just then Finn bounded into the barn, smelling banana cream pie on the wind. He headed right for Aaron at full gallop and greeted him with his front paws at chest level, sending Aaron flying backward. As soon as Aaron hit the ground, Finn began licking the dessert from his face. Caroline yelled at Finn, but the dog loved all kinds of cream pie.

"Let's leave those two to get acquainted," Tom said, turning Caroline around and leading her out of the barn. "I'm sure Mac has uncorked the wine and is wondering where we are."

When she looked back into the barn, both Finn and the man had disappeared.

Standing at the side table in the dining room, Caroline felt her hands tremble as she tried to fill the wine glasses while waiting for Mac to return from the kitchen with appetizers. She shook her head several times in an effort to clear the dizziness that had come over her when she ran through the barn, but that only worsened her light-headedness. So she tried the next best remedy at hand and quickly chugged a glass of wine, which immediately added to both her nausea and faintness. To steady herself, she placed her hands on the table and lowered her head, trying to breathe deeply.

Suddenly, she felt a hand on her shoulder. When she whirled around, the room began to spin. "It's you," she said. For what felt like a lifetime, she gazed directly into Aaron's smoky eyes. It was the first time she noticed a long scar over his left brow. The last thing she wondered before fainting was how odd it was that such an attractive man could also be an ax murderer.

And then there was darkness.

When Caroline came to a few minutes later, she was lying on the sofa. She slowly looked around. The only other person in the room was Aaron, who was sitting on the coffee table looking at her in concern.

"Did I faint?" she asked, rubbing her forehead.

"You did," he replied. "Are you feeling better?"

"I think," she said as she slowly sat up and straightened her dress. She then ran her fingers through her hair. "I'm still a little light-headed."

Just then Mac walked into the room carrying a tray of cheese and crackers. "Is everyone hungry?"

"Your guest just—" Aaron began, but instantly stopped when Caroline touched his arm.

Caroline shook her head. "Don't," she whispered, and then replied to Mac, "We are very hungry."

Aaron stood and offered his hand to Caroline. He had showered and changed, showing no ill effects from her attack. Before taking his hand, she stared at Aaron for an uncomfortably long time. Perhaps five years older than she, he shared Tom's good looks. His thick, wavy auburn hair, parted in the middle, was longer than Tom's, but still well above his shoulders. He shared many of the same strong features that his brother had, but unlike Tom, Aaron's eyes were the color of gunmetal gray and filled with dark portents, and his lips were curled as if set in a permanent smile.

Mac, oblivious to Caroline's staring, put a plate on the table. "You two have met, haven't you?"

"Not formally," Aaron said with an ironic smirk.

"Aaron, this is our neighbor, Caroline Ross Talin."

"Caroline Ross," Caroline corrected Mac.

Mac nodded. "Sorry—old habit. Caroline, this is Tom's younger brother, Aaron."

"The one you attacked so fearlessly in the barn," Tom added as he walked into the room.

"What?" Mac asked in a start.

"A simple misunderstanding," Aaron assured Mac. "It's nice to meet you . . . as well as your dog."

Caroline flushed with embarrassment. "I'm so sorry about that. He's a little high-spirited."

"As is his delightful owner, especially when she has a pie in one hand," Tom laughed, and she finally joined in.

Dear CC, I went to the Candor's for dinner tonight and I was so thankful for their company. Tom introduced Finn to a litter of three-week-old Dalmatian puppies. Oddly, when the puppies were jumping all over him, I've never seen him calmer.

Tom's brother insisted on walking me home, which I appreciated. I discovered that he was the person who killed the calf—for humane reasons. And although he is nice, there's a darkness that lingers just

134

below the surface. Maybe it's me—maybe I can't shake the image of him covered in blood. Once we arrived home, he seemed interested in the mill, but I didn't offer to show him around. He probably thinks I'm unfriendly, which isn't that far from the truth, I suppose.

Anyway, life goes on. But I am trying to follow your advice; pick the track you want, and then run.

Love, your favorite grand-daughter.

ELEVEN

Hoodies

The following Tuesday, the lights on the second floor of the Chatham Press building flipped on at three a.m. Two black, unmarked vans with their motors running were parked directly in front of the entrance. Several men—three, maybe four—in sweatpants and hoodies ran equipment between the building and the vans. The apparent theft would have gone totally undetected until morning had it not been for the fact that Pricilla Geer's poodle had a bout of diarrhea from eating Dickenson's raw chicken and needed to be walked every other hour that same night.

Once home, she immediately called Simon Dixon's house, who in turn phoned Dennis Beezer to tell him that his business was being robbed. Simon picked up Dennis ten minutes later and they sped off to the scene of the crime.

Slowing as they turned onto Main Street, Dennis and Simon witnessed one of the thieves caring a large computer terminal down the steps and placing it in the back of the van. They stopped the car close enough to watch but not be seen.

"How old is that thing?" Simon said.

"I don't know. Maybe eight years," Dennis answered. "What difference does that make?"

A man sitting on the van's fender suddenly bolted up the stairs.

"There's another one now," Dennis said, pointing to the man.

From behind their car, a third black van passed them, and pulled up alongside the other vans.

"Aren't you going to do something? They're robbing me!" Dennis snapped in growing frustration. "At least turn on your damn sirens."

Simon tilted his head and carefully watched a man in shorts with heavily tattooed legs run down the steps. Under each arm was a fax machine.

"Simon, do something!" Dennis barked.

Simon remained calm. "Why would someone target your business?"

"Because of all the equipment we have," Dennis answered without thinking.

Simon looked like he seriously doubted that. "Really? Fax machines? No one uses fax machines anymore."

Suddenly, the driver of the third van stepped out from behind the wheel and opened the back door. Even from their distance, Simon and Dennis could make out the Dell logos stamped on all of the boxes.

"It's a crime ring," Dennis said. "They must have hit another business before us."

Two men with dollies joined the driver and

started to unload the van. Once the dollies were stacked high with boxes, they carefully proceeded up the steps and disappeared inside.

"What the hell is going on?" Dennis said, stepping out of the police car.

A man came out and sat down on the top step, lighting a cigarette. Tossing back his hoodie, Dennis realized that it was a kid no older than eighteen. He had a pierced ring through his nose and one through his lip.

"Can I help you?" Dennis asked, running up the stairs.

"No, I'm good," the kid said.

A guy in the van suddenly called out. "Tell Beez we're missing one tower. He needs to recount."

"Will do," the kid said, snuffing out his cigarette on the sole of the shoe, and sticking the butt in his jeans pocket. The kid hurried inside.

Both Dennis and Simon followed him up the staircase.

Panting, Dennis grabbed the hand railing at the mezzanine before treading the rest of the steps.

"Good thing this isn't a robbery. We're too out of shape to keep up with him."

"Speak for yourself," Simon said, sprinting several steps ahead of him, not at all winded.

Once on the second floor, Dennis couldn't believe what he saw. The long tables he used for laying out galleys had been pushed together and bolted against the wall. On them sat a string of thirty-inch flat-screen displays, eight in all. Next to the end table were two six-foot racks that shelved equipment, whose lights were brightly flickering. Lying underneath the table, one person was feeding wires from the computers to another who was sitting on the floor in front of the racks.

"This might not reach, Beez," one of them said.

"We have thirty feet of extra cable downstairs," Brian said.

The kid smoking outside a minute before said, "Trout needs you to recount. He's missing a tower."

"*Hasta el rabo, todo es toro*," Brian said. Everyone in the room started laughing.

Simon and Dennis looked at each other in bewilderment.

"Brian?" Dennis asked.

Brian spun around. "Dad! What are you doing here?"

"I think I need to ask you the same."

"Tower four is up," someone called out from another room.

"We're going online," Brian answered, checking out the control panel above the rack.

"Who are these people?"

"Just some friends I know. Trout, JJ and Axel are from Dell. They offered to deliver your equipment and lend a hand setting it up," Brian explained. "And the others are some colleagues from Mexico."

"Mexico?"

"Este es mi padre," Brian told his team.

"Es que la policía?" the one under the table asked, staring directly at Simon.

Brian looked at Simon Dixon, saw his badge, and his eyes opened wide. *"No policía. El es mi amigo, Simon Dixon,"* he said.

"I think they're talking about me," Simon whispered to Dennis.

The others continued to watch Simon with hawk eyes.

"No te preocupes. Te lo prometo," Brian said. And then in English, he said, "Refocus, everyone. It's going to be a long night."

The kid under the table relaxed. "Not as long as it was in Buenos Aires," he said with a heavy accent.

Another joined in. "Mother, that was hot. I was sure those servers were gonna melt before they crashed."

"But what an awesome recovery," Brian said, proud of his crew.

Dennis tilted his head toward the corner of the room. "Can we talk to you for a minute, son?"

When the three were out of earshot of the others, Dennis asked, "What's going on, Brian?"

His son frowned. "We're doing exactly what you and I talked about last week."

"But why did they ask about Simon?"

Brian shrugged one shoulder. "Because several

of them are here illegally. They thought Simon could cause problems."

"Illegals?" Dennis was shocked.

"Oh, come on, Dad. Who do you think does most of the backbreaking labor in our country? Illegal immigrants pick our crops and work minimum-wage sweat jobs because none of us will. These guys are brilliant—the best of the best. They just don't have the money or the time to jump through the all the hoops to get green cards that our government keeps just out of their reach. This is the best team I know, and I would do anything for them."

"And they would obviously do anything for you if they're risking imprisonment just being here," Simon said.

"It's not that serious," Brian said, looking back at his team of friends. "Just leave them alone." It was more of a gentle demand than a request. "They'll be gone by this afternoon."

Dennis heard the familiar footsteps of Gabrielle's high heels and looked at his watch. It was 4:20 a.m. "Damn it, Brian. What's your mother doing here?"

A second later she was at the top of the stairs with two young men trailing her. One carried several closed boxes, and the other a stack of casserole dishes. Sweet aromas of Spanish food wafted across the room.

"I didn't have enough cash to buy everyone

141

breakfast," Brian admitted. "Remember," he said, forming an open ball with his two hands, "it's the people and it's the relationships inside the circle that make things happen."

Without speaking to Brian, Gabrielle told the boys where to lay out the food that she had prepared at The Green Chile the night before. Seldom had Dennis seen such a well-orchestrated catering job.

Brian whistled out the window. A minute later, three others came running up from downstairs. Before Dennis could ask any other questions, Gabrielle had all but taken over the room, speaking Spanish to the boys at a mile a minute. Conversing in her native tongue with people of her own culture, she was more demonstrative than usual—her hands waving in the air, her laughter captivating all those around her. It was a delight for Dennis to watch.

One kid, the shortest of the group, pulled off his ski cap, and long black hair fell loosely down her back. Turning around, Dennis realized it was, in fact, a young woman who he guessed was around Brian's age.

"Who's that?" Dennis asked, raising a brow.

Brian glanced over his shoulder. "Fazia. Educated in the US but she's from Argentina. She's our content design guru. And she'll be setting up your digital library."

"I see," Dennis said, hoping to get more

information, which wasn't coming anytime soon.

"You're invited to stay for a while," Brian offered more out of politeness than any need he had for his father's help. Without waiting for a reply, he excused himself and joined the others.

"There must be a dozen people here," Simon said in amazement.

"Not quite the type of workforce I'm used to," Dennis admitted as he watched one young fellow with long Rastafarian braids load tortillas onto his plate. Next to him was a kid who looked no older than sixteen, wearing a torn T-shirt and cutoff sweats.

"You know, I don't think I'm needed here, so I'm going to head off," Simon whispered to Dennis.

"Maybe you can drop me at home," Dennis said as they slid away without notice.

Just as Simon and Dennis stepped outside, six naked seniors ran by. Both men couldn't help but stare.

Simon laughed and waved to the joggers. "Well, doesn't that just make your day?"

"It's a little jarring so early in the morning," Dennis said. He didn't bother adding what else had jarred him that morning: the takeover of his business.

TWELVE

Identity

Several hours later, Pam was surrounded by a group of twenty in front of the Lumby Bookstore. What had begun as one question asked by one lady as Pam walked out of the store had become a small impromptu rally, attracting folks who were out and about in town that morning.

"It is for that reason alone, for the benefit of our residents and our businesses, that I support the town council's referendum," Pam said. The exchange had been both positive and constructive for both candidate and voters.

"Have you ever heard such nonsense?" Duke Blackstone asked from the back of the crowd.

Recognizing *that* voice, Pam's smile dropped. Where did he come from?

"Really, folks, who thinks that makes any sense?" Duke Blackstone yelled. "I'm a businessman, a really successful businessman, and I can't even figure out what she's saying. And I'm very smart, smarter than anyone here. So your time is up, Petty Pam. And I'll see you at the next debate, unless you're scared. That's what I hear from many, many people: you're just too chicken to meet me head-on. Chicken-Lips Pam. And you can't count on anything that comes out of the lips of a chicken." Duke stated, flapping his arms. "Buc buc buc buc."

Mark walked out of the post office and, hearing Duke attacking Pam, bustled across Main Street. Options flashed before him: *Do I tackle him or just come out swinging?* But a few yards before he reached Duke, someone grabbed his arm. With Mark's momentum, they both jerked forward.

"Hold on, Mark," Simon Dixon said. "Don't do anything stupid."

"But—" Mark said, staring daggers at Duke.

"I know," Simon said firmly. "Just take Pam home."

Mark wrenched his arm from Simon's grasp. "He would have been roadkill," Mark muttered as he walked away. Forcing a big smile, he waved to the group as he walked up to his wife and kissed her on the cheek. "We need to get going, honey."

"Thanks for all your ideas and questions. We'll see everyone at the next debate," she said as Mark led her away.

"Buc buc buc buc."

Mark froze.

Simon, who was in his shadow, put an arm around Mark's shoulder. "Let it go," he whispered and herded the couple toward their car.

On the drive down to Montis, both Pam and Mark were silent. They were both furious. The election had taken a toll on each of them and on their relationship. Mark felt hopeless because he couldn't protect Pam, and she felt guilty for dragging Mark into public life.

Pam stepped out of the car when they arrived.

"Are you sure you don't want to come with me to see the guys?" Mark asked, referring to the monks of Saint Cross Abbey.

"I have too much to do today. But I'm sure Brother John has some new rum sauces for you to try."

He put the car in reverse and slowly pulled away. Suddenly, he slammed on the brakes and jumped out of the car. He ran over to Pam and wrapped his arms around her. "I'm so, so sorry I couldn't do anything."

She couldn't hold back the tears. "I'm sorry I got us into this mess."

"We need to remember you're doing this for Lumby. You'll be a great mayor."

"If we survive and if we win."

"I've never doubted that for a minute."

"I love you," she said, before kissing him. "Now go. And tell everyone I send my love."

Both their hearts were lighter when he drove away.

An hour later, Mark pulled into Saint Cross Abbey. Deep in thought as to how he was going to ask for the monks' endorsement, he didn't notice the monastery's new sign:

Closed until further notice
By invitation only

Mark parked in the monks' lot in back where they always parked. As he walked to the private entrance, he waved to several of the sisters who were working out in the field, but their response was more reserved than usual. Perhaps it was because Joshua, their good friend and agricultural adviser, was not accompanying him on this visit.

Once inside the main building, Mark noticed how quiet it was. He checked his watch, thinking that the monastics might be at lunch or preparing for vespers, but it was too late for one and too early for the other. With no one around, Mark did exactly what he had done a hundred times before: he proceeded directly to the kitchen to see Brother John and sample whatever Saint Cross rum sauce he was preparing.

To Mark's disappointment, Brother John wasn't at the stove. Nor was Brother Michael, who was almost always in the community room. Not wanting to waste time until one of his friends showed up, Mark grabbed a spoon and bowl and walked into the dark commercial freezer. After considering his options, he chose a five-gallon bucket of vanilla ice cream. When he swung around, he walked into someone who had the same idea for a snack.

147

"I'm sorry," Mark said, nearly dropping the ice cream.

"My fault," the man said, trying to make a quick exit.

But as soon as he opened the door, enough light shined on his face for Mark to identify him.

"Duke Blackstone!" Mark screeched, dropping the bucket of ice cream on the floor. Fury ran through every nerve of his body. Mark grabbed the man's shirt and pushed him as hard as he could. "Get out of here!" The man fell backward, knocking a chair down.

Mark was about to lunge at him.

"Wait!" the man yelled.

Mark froze, perhaps because he was not a fighter by nature, perhaps because he was in a monastery, but probably because the tone of the man's voice sounded so different than what he had just heard in the streets of Lumby.

"Wait," the man pleaded.

"What are you doing here?" Mark screamed. "They want nothing to do with you. Stay away from the monks!"

"I can explain—"

"Bullshit!" Mark yelled.

"Mark!" a voice bellowed from the other side of the room.

Mark swung around, almost falling out of the freezer. It was Brother Matthew.

"Matthew!" Mark said, pointing at the man, his

148

fingers shaking. "He shouldn't be here! This is Duke Blackstone!"

"No, he's not," Matthew said, helping Alan stand up.

"Yes, he is! I just saw him in Lumby!"

"Mark. This is Alan Blackstone, Duke's brother."

Mark looked at Alan and then at Matthew and then at Alan. It took few seconds for Mark to get his bearings. "The dead one?"

Alan chuckled softly. "Only if you kill me first."

Mark scratched his head. "But . . ."

Alan picked up the bucket of ice cream from the floor and placed it on the table.

"What are you doing here?" Matthew asked.

"*Me?* Why don't you ask *him?*" Mark said.

"We know why he's here," Matthew said. "What about you?"

"That's not a very nice greeting, Matthew," Mark said with a slight pout while keeping an eye on Alan. "I know I haven't been here for a few weeks, but that's no reason to be mean."

"I'm sorry. It's just that we didn't expect you," he said to Mark.

"Yeah, I know, but you never expect me," he countered.

"Very true. And you're here because . . . ?" Matthew began.

"Well, that might take some explanation, and

nobody was around . . . to explain," Mark said awkwardly. "So I thought I would help Brother John out by trying his latest sauce."

Alan couldn't help but to smile.

Brother Matthew looked at Alan. "It seems you're not the only one who had that idea."

Alan raised his spoon. "Guilty as charged. And we collided in the freezer."

"Do you know who he is?" Mark asked out of the corner of his mouth, pointing at Alan.

"I do," Matthew said.

"Is this someone who can be trusted?" Alan asked.

"*Me?*" Mark asked, his eyes wide and his brows furled. "*Me* be trusted? It's *your* brother who's almost killing us out there!"

"Interesting choice of words," Alan said, glancing at Matthew.

"Alan, this is Mark Walker. He and his wife are a part of our community—really a part of our family—and he can be trusted unconditionally."

Mark spoke out of the side of his mouth, as if only Matthew could hear. "Do you know he's dead?"

"Yes and no." Matthew raised his hands. "Let's slow down. You obviously deserve an explanation."

"Over ice cream," Mark suggested.

"That we can agree on," Alan added.

For the next half hour, Matthew and Alan

explained every detail of Alan's disappearance, presumed death and concealment at Saint Cross Abbey. Mark was so enthralled in the story, he had pushed his bowl aside and the ice cream had long since melted. Every few minutes, "Wow" or a long, menacing "Oohh" was uttered under his breath.

"But Lumby . . ." Mark said, his voice trailing off as he considered the consequences of Duke's plan to lay a pipeline. "And Pam. What about her? She's going head-to-head with your brother."

Alan shook his head. "It would be too obvious if something happened to her."

"Yeah, but what happens if someone leaves a horse head in our bed?"

"You've been watching too many movies," Matthew counseled.

Alan didn't smile, though. "Your wife winning the election is a good Plan B to stop the pipeline."

"What's Plan A?"

"I haven't thought of it yet," Alan said less than confidently.

Marked leaned forward. "Wow, this is a mess."

"It's more serious than that, Mark. You understand that Alan's identity and whereabouts need to be kept confidential at all costs?"

"Yep. This is like international espionage."

"Well, I wouldn't involve Russia in this, but Alan's life does depend on your silence."

"That's not a problem. I won't tell anybody," Mark said, crossing his arms on his chest.

"Including Pam," Matthew quickly added.

It was as if Mark was snapped out of the trance. "Oh, I can't do that," he said. "You know Pam, she can see right through me. And I've never lied to her before."

"Ever?" Alan asked.

"You'll understand when you see the two of them together," Matthew explained. And then to Mark, he added, "We wouldn't ask you if the stakes weren't so high."

"But if I have to lie, that means you guys have to lie too. How are you guys going to do that? You're monks," Mark said. "You guys never lie."

"We try not to, but we also know these are extreme circumstances and that God has led Alan here for a reason."

Mark blanched at that thought. "You think *God* is involved?"

Alan shrugged his shoulders. "That's what they keep telling me."

"Have you been to vespers yet?" Mark asked Alan softly so Matthew wouldn't hear.

Alan nodded.

"It's just so long, isn't it?"

"We try not to go by the clock," Matthew added with an acerbic note. "So, you need to keep this confidential."

"You know I'd do anything for you guys,"

152

Mark said. "But wives have a sixth sense about these things, you know? Well, of course you don't know, you've never been married. I mean, you're celibate and everything. But, believe me, they do. They have this invisible radar that can pick up anything."

Alan laughed.

"See, he knows!" Mark said, pointing at Alan. "Do you have a wife like that?"

Alan shook his head, still laughing. "No, but I've had enough girlfriends to know what you're talking about."

Mark turned back to Matthew. "But I promise I won't tell her, no matter what, even if she pulls nails out of my fingers. Or drops lemon juice in my eyes."

"My God, what kind of woman are you married to?" Alan asked.

"An amazingly patient one," Matthew answered.

Mark continued. "But you have to guarantee me that you'll explain everything to her when this is all done."

"I'll do that," Matthew promised.

"Thank you," Alan said, shaking Mark's hand.

Mark stared at the man. "No offense but it still gives me the creeps looking at you."

"No offense taken. I feel the same way some-times."

A new thought came to Matthew. "Alan, you

told me that you couldn't get through to anyone because they're tracing your emails and calls. And you didn't want mail going out from Saint Cross that might give away your whereabouts."

"Yes. I'm positive they would trace anything back to the abbey," Alan said.

Matthew tilted his head, considering. "Well, we might have just solved that problem."

Alan raised a brow in interest. "How?"

"Mark, would you be willing to send some messages along for Alan?"

"You mean, like a spy?" Mark asked. "Wow."

"Huh. I think that might work," Alan said. "Assuming you're okay with this, Mark?"

"Sign me up," Mark said. "And I just thought I was coming here to ask you for a favor."

"What's that?" Matthew asked.

Mark had rehearsed his pitch on the drive over, but all of that went out the window given everything he had just heard. "Pam is running for mayor of Lumby."

"We know," Matthew said dryly.

"And is getting hammered by Alan's brother."

The monk smirked. "We know that as well. So would you like us to pray for her?"

"Not really," Mark said, and then corrected himself. "Well, not that that wouldn't help, but you know, God might not want to get involved in a small-town election. I need you guys to endorse her," he blurted out. "Maybe one of you

154

can swing by during one of her rallies or for the final debate to say a few words."

Matthew was happy to comply. "Of course we would."

"Great! That would be great, because this guy, Duke, is unbelievable. Everything that Alan says about him is true. I didn't want to drag you guys in to it, but you might be the only ones he won't bully."

"I wouldn't be so sure of that," Alan said.

That made Mark doubt his fantastic plan. "He'd never have the nerve. Would he?"

THIRTEEN

Flow

The following morning, the music of Tommy Dorsey and the aroma of freshly brewed coffee filled the air. Caroline sat at the kitchen table in her pajamas, rereading an email she wrote to Kai. There had been no communication between them for over a month, and Caroline thought the time had come for that to change.

> Kai, Your closet is now empty and your clothes are boxed up and stacked in the corner of the bedroom. I can send them to you or take them to Goodwill. Or perhaps I should perform a ceremonial cremation in a bonfire by the river. Send word if you have a preference, because I don't.
>
> I am opening the shop for three days to sell all the antiques that you so lavishly accumulated. What isn't sold will be picked up at four on the final day and taken away for donation. After all is said and done, there will be nothing left downstairs.
>
> By the way, in preparation for the

sale, I looked at your ledgers. For a man of God, you were keeping a lot of secrets.

Caroline

Caroline hit SEND.

Finn, who was fast asleep by her feet, didn't hear the steps on the front walk.

"Hello?" a man's voice called out from the yard.

The only people who ever ventured down Chicory Lane to Caroline's stone mill were either tourists who were lost or customers who came to her antique store, not knowing it was closed. Caroline assumed the latter.

"We're closed," she yelled. She held her breath, hoping whoever it was would go away. But unfortunately not.

"Hello?"

"Persistent, isn't he?" Caroline said to Finn, who was now standing by the window, wagging his tail wildly. "Why don't you bark or something?"

"I'm sorry, we're closed," Caroline repeated. "Come back on the fifth."

"Chicory Lane delivery service," the man said.

Caroline glanced at the front door suspiciously. *"What?"*

"All right then, FedEx," he replied.

157

"Leave it on the front step, please," she called back.

"That's not possible, ma'am."

Caroline begrudgingly shuffled to the front door, pulling at her pajama bottoms. Swinging the door open, she saw Aaron standing on the front stoop.

"Are you always this grumpy in the morning?" he asked.

Caroline was speechless.

"And this quiet?" he continued, his smile widening.

Her checks flushed red. "Are you always so . . . ?" For the life of her, she couldn't think of a good retort.

"Resolute?" he said. "Yes." He lowered his head in an unspoken apology. "Mac insisted I drop everything I was doing and deliver this coffee cake to you." He held out a swing-handled wicker basket.

She didn't move.

He cocked his head. "Did you just wake up?"

Caroline quickly glanced at her watch and realized that it was already ten o'clock. "No. I was working in the kitchen," she said, pointing behind her.

"I'm sorry for interrupting, but Mac is rather demanding when she has her mind set on something."

"A good quality," Caroline said.

He glanced down at her attire. "Coming from a woman wearing bunny slippers, I'm not so sure."

Her embarrassment intensified the longer she stood at the door . . . in her flannel panda pajamas . . . in front of Aaron. Caroline's mind raced, trying to decide what to do next. *Just take the basket, say thank you, and shut the door,* she told herself.

"Is there anything else?" she asked.

Surprised by her abruptness, Aaron stepped back. "Obviously not," he said with an edge in his voice.

Caroline rushed to correct the impression she'd left. "I'm sorry. I just don't get many visitors." *Great,* she thought. *He probably thinks I own forty cats.* "Please tell Mac thank you," she said, finally taking the basket.

"Trust me, it's delicious."

Caroline's thoughts were spinning. Before she could pull back the words, she blurted out, "Would you like a cup of coffee?"

He backed away slightly in apprehension. "That might be a little risky. We've gotten off to a bad start today."

"You're right." She pointed down at the wicker basket. "But I've got coffee cake here, and there's no way I can finish it alone." When she opened the lid, the scent of cinnamon and brown sugar was impossible to turn down.

"Absolutely," he said, following her inside.

"I'll be right back," she said, heading upstairs. "Just give me a minute to change."

Aaron loved the music coming from the old record player. "Huh," he exclaimed in awe of Caroline's large collection of vinyl records. "So you like the big band era?" he called up to her.

"Yeah, I do," she replied as she pulled on a pair of jeans.

"Tom never mentioned it." He continued to eye the LPs. "May I look at your collection?"

"Be my guest."

Aaron started to thumb through the records . . . Duke Ellington, Glenn Miller, Benny Goodman. "I can't believe you have this Hal Kemp. It's a classic."

"*Remember Me?* It's one of his best!" she said, pulling on a shirt. "Do you like big band music?"

Aaron nodded. "It's one of the many gifts our parents gave us. We used to listen to it every night when Tom and I were kids. I still have their JVC player at home."

"Where's that?" she asked, surprising both of them.

That was the most personal question the two had exchanged so far. Caroline had deliberately kept the conversation distant and impersonal— about the weather, the town, the economy—and he abided.

"The Seattle area," he answered.

160

Caroline reemerged, looking fresh and as pretty as ever. "How about that coffee?"

"It smells great," he said, slipping the album back in its place. He saw a slight movement from the corner of his eye and looked at the floor where Caroline had just walked. "Do you know there's a turtle following you?"

Caroline laughed. "They're more loyal than one might expect."

"A pet, I presume?"

"Finn's collateral damage, which Tom saved. But now he's a member of our family."

"So it's just you and Finn?" Aaron asked

Caroline quickly turned her back, reaching for another mug from the cupboard. She became acutely aware of how "single" everything in the kitchen must look: one coffee mug on the kitchen table, one plate and one fork in the sink, one pair of rain boots by the back door, one raincoat hanging on the hook. One of everything.

When she didn't answer the question, Aaron stumbled for words. "Of course. I'm sorry. And I'm sorry for your . . . loss." He cringed. "Mac told me only a little about it. I don't know what to say."

"No one does, least of all me," she replied. "You don't have to say anything. Actually, I'd prefer if you didn't."

"Okay. Uh, may I?" Aaron asked, pulling out a chair at the kitchen table.

"Just push everything aside."

He took a look at the two greeting cards on the table before sliding them away. Caroline caught his glance.

"They're beautiful, aren't they?"

He nodded and then turned his attentions to the old Underwood. "That's quite a typewriter."

"I use it for writing letters."

Aaron was shocked. "*Really?* In the age of emails and texting. *Why?*"

Caroline shrugged. "I love the feel of the paper, and the sound of the hammer striking the platen. It's personal." She searched for the right word. "It's more intimate."

"I see, I think," Aaron said. "This is a charming home. I heard you did quite an amazing job converting the old mill. I can't imagine taking on such a big project."

"It took us years." She looked around the room. "And it's still not done."

"Is it running?"

"The water mill? It was until a few years ago when a bottom board of the flume cracked. Since then most of the water isn't even getting to the spillway, but by that time Kai had lost interest." Caroline tried to show nonchalance, but she was bad at it. "In truth, it's a love-hate relationship. Even though none of this was my idea, it's now my home and my respon-sibility. Unfortunately, the guilt of letting it go to ruin is something that keeps me up at night."

"But it's impressive that you got it working at all," he said encouragingly.

"Kai was good with gears and pinions when he wanted to be. He had a mind perfectly suited for what he enjoyed—repairing old clocks."

"It sounds like—"

"More coffee?" she interrupted him, not wanting that conversation to go any further.

"Please."

To have a man other than Kai in the kitchen was a disconnect that threw Caroline off her center of gravity. But there he sat: a man who was handsome and nice, and offering a friendship that was missing from Caroline's life.

He walked over to the window. "Do you need a hand repairing it?" he asked, looking out at the mill's wheel.

Caroline blinked. "What?"

"Would you like some help replacing the board?" he asked before returning for another sip of coffee. "It seems like such a shame to have everything in working order except for a broken plank."

Caroline hadn't expected the offer. *Do I want the wheel turning again?* she wondered. Would it make everything right again? She finally nodded slowly. "Yes, I think I would, if you have the time."

"Then I'm all yours," he said, rubbing his hands together.

. . .

A half hour later, Aaron was lying on the plume, on the downstream side of the cracked plank. With a crowbar in hand, he pried away the old board. Caroline knelt on the other end of the gap in the floorboard. The temporary dam that Aaron and Caroline had jury-rigged to divert the water was holding, and four new twelve-foot-long slats were measured and cut, and ready to be installed.

When the final splinters of the rotted board gave way, Caroline and Aaron looked through the open bottom of the trough. The river was fifteen feet below.

"Ready?" Aaron looked up at Caroline.

Caroline nodded.

"Why don't you pass me one end of the first board? We'll position it and then you can screw your end in first."

The boards that Aaron referred to were long pieces of two-by-twelve pressure-treated western pine, and they were heavier than could easily be handled. Caroline tried to lift one end and push it toward Aaron's hands, but the board hit him in the shoulder instead.

Before she could apologize, he gave a thumbs-up. "It's all right. I didn't need that shoulder anyway."

"Sorry," Caroline groaned.

"Go ahead and drill the screw holes."

Caroline had the perfect comeback, but she bit her lip. Bent down on all fours, she drilled three-inch screw holes that aligned with a metal plate, which attached the new plank to the old one. Aaron followed suit before they positioned and attached the board with screws. They then secured the second board of the same width, the third, and then the fourth. The new floor of the plume was once again solid and ready for flowing water.

"I'm going to put in a few screws from the bottom," Aaron said, leaning over the edge of the plume.

Caroline nervously looked down at the water. "Do you think that's necessary?"

"I've done this a hundred times before," he said cavalierly. "Why don't you open the dam and let the water flow?" Inching farther over the edge, Aaron bent at the waist, hanging upside down, screwing in the final shafts. "Easy as pie. Just one more—"

Suddenly Aaron's legs flew up in the air and over his head as he somersaulted off the plume and landed on his back in the river.

"Kai!" Caroline instinctively yelled.

Aaron was so far underwater that he didn't hear Caroline's scream, nor the name she called out. A few seconds later, he popped to the surface, holding the drill above his head. Caroline slid down the embankment to help him out.

"The water is freezing!" he said as he waded to the shore.

"Are you okay?"

"Wet," he replied. After he handed Caroline the drill, he shook his head and rubbed his face. He tried to make a cheerful face. "Let's open it up."

Removing their temporary blockade, the water gushed into the plume and toward the wheel. She could hear the wood creak as the wheel began to turn, slowly at first, but then with greater momentum and force as water filled each catchment. More noises came from the mill and wheel room. The drive shaft rotated for the first time in several years.

Caroline stared in awe at the water tumbling over the wheel. "I can't thank you enough." She then noticed Aaron's condition. "Oh! You need to dry off. There are a couple of towels on the back porch. Don't use the green one—that's Finn's and it's filthy."

As Aaron headed up to the house, Caroline collected the tools they had used. When she finally joined him, Aaron was drying off his hair with the green towel.

"Ewww," Caroline groaned. "I said any one *but* the green—it's disgusting."

"Green or red—what difference does it make?" Aaron replied almost angrily.

Caroline was taken back by his change of tone. He had been so nice all during their time working

166

together. "I just thought you would prefer a clean towel."

"It's just fine," he said, picking dog hairs from his lip.

She would have laughed, but that didn't seem like a good idea right then and there. "You know, this is just like the first impression I had of you—angry." She couldn't help asking, "What is your problem?"

"I don't have a problem! Just drop it," he said, flinging the towel on the chair. "You know nothing about me."

By the time Caroline said, "Obviously," Aaron had already turned his back and was heading home.

Caroline dropped her arms by her side. She was at a total loss. Had she gone so long without company that she offended people without knowing it?

Hi Brooke, What is it with men? It infuriates me when someone acts contrary to any reasonable expectation of behavior. Not understanding why a person behaves as he does sets off all of my insecurities, because I immediately assume I've done something wrong or I'm the cause of the other person's annoyance, at best, or rage, at worst.

Why can't we all just say what's going on inside? Okay, I might not be strong in that area either, but at least I'm trying to weed out the shit and express at least some of my feelings . . . if only to my closest friends.

Anyway, I'm babbling. The reason for my note: I've asked Pam and Mac over for "the big sale." I know you'll be in Seattle, but I wish you were here. I miss you. Caroline

FOURTEEN

Followers

Unable to sleep, Dennis slipped out of bed and went downstairs to his office. On his desk sat a flat-screen monitor Brian had installed a few days earlier. Just to the left of the wireless keyboard was a new Android cell phone, with a phone number written on a sticky note taped to the screen. In the far corner, but still well within reach, was a wireless high-speed printer, and underneath that, on the floor and well protected by the overhang of the desk, was a Dell processor. Dennis pressed the only button on the front of the computer. The screen lit up within five seconds, booted up, and was ready and waiting for anything Dennis could throw at it. *Wow,* he thought. Brian had amped up everything, so what had taken an interminable time on his old computer was done in the blink of an eye.

"Impressive," he said in amazement. "But where's my email?" he asked aloud as he studied each of the icons, the number of which had grown from four to thirty. No Outlook. No AOL. He used both email servers, which was incredibly inconvenient, but history had a way of complicating life, especially when it came to technology.

Dennis was about to pick up the phone to call Brian when he spotted a folder called DB PRIVATE. He clicked it open, and Dennis was flabbergasted—on his screen were two panes: MAIL and NEWS. In the MAIL pane were all of his unread emails, sorted by date. A preview of each item showed the origin of the email (AOL or Outlook). Brian had somehow integrated his two systems. Large tabs at the top of the panel listed his saved email folders, just as they were named on his old system. The NEWS pane was spilt in half, each showing the front page of his favorite news sites. Everything was at the tip of his fingers, with just one click. "Absolutely amazing," he whispered.

He scrolled down to see if there were any important emails that needed to be read. One was from *The Wheatley Sentinel*, marked private and confidential. Another was more of a surprise than, he assumed, a high priority:

Hi Dennis, Would you please include the following announcement under Community Events in your next edition?

"Lost in Time Antique Shoppe at the old Lumby Mill on Chicory Lane will reopen its doors for a final three-day going-out-of-business sale, June

170

5, 6 and 7 from 10 a.m. to 4 p.m. All inventory must be sold. No returns, no previews, but some great deals."

Just send me the bill. Thanks very much.

Caroline Ross

After plowing through his emails, Dennis turned his attention to several notes Brian had left next to his computer. On the top page was a handwritten list entitled "News Aggregators," which included what Dennis considered to be a bizarre list of names: Fark, Feedly, News 360, and Flipboard. "Really?" Dennis said.

The next page had a list of social media sites that Brian obviously wanted his father to look at. Three were circled with the note "U need to set up your pers accts. I'll take care of the bus accts."

Sitting in front of the forty-inch screen, Dennis wasn't sure where to begin. After a moment of consideration, he typed in the obvious: "www. thelumbylines.com." A page immediately jumped up showing an image of last week's paper with key articles flanking the left and right sides of the paper's logo. A well-positioned footer read, "Site Under Construction," followed by, "Please visit us in a few days." Although each of the navigation buttons linked to well-designed subpages for contact information, classifieds, editorials, and so on, it was obvious that the data was still being loaded.

One link Dennis followed was to the paper's Facebook page, which had the same banner and profile picture as he had seen on the website. There were only eighteen followers. A little air went out of Dennis's twenty-first-century balloon.

The speed of his computer, though, was staggering. Dennis used to wait ten to fifteen seconds every time he hit the ENTER key, whereas the response he now had was instantaneous. In fact, it was so fast that he couldn't keep up with the speed of screen displays.

Dennis returned to the home page and marveled at the intuitive logic that Brian had built into the website. Even the most inexperienced of Internet users could easily navigate to their desired destination. Fixed graphics were high resolution and well positioned, video streams supplemented written copy, and hyperlinks to additional sites were plentiful.

"Damn impressive," Dennis said.

After spending ten minutes on his newspaper's site, he searched for a new website for The Bindery, and found it in the first four entries under Google. Not only had Brian brought up a site for the publishing arm of his business, he had also taken care of search engine optimization. Similar in concept and sister in design to thelumbylines.com, anyone could immediately recognize that thebinderyinlumby. com was associated with the online newspaper. Likewise, thelumbybookstore.com, which had downloadable wallpaper of a charming photograph of downtown Lumby, echoed the same style. Brian had successfully created a triad of websites for Dennis's corporation.

Just out of curiosity, Dennis next typed in "thegreenchile.com" and was immediately redirected to thegreenchileinlumby.com. Clicking through the website, Dennis was able to scan Gabrielle's menus, specials being offered that week, directions to the restaurant including a Google map, hours of operation, reviews and a page dedicated to the cook and owner which showed numerous photos of Gabrielle, mostly of herself but some with her family and friends. An announcement promising a cooking blog was posted at the top of each page.

A blog? Dennis wondered. That boy doesn't miss a beat.

He was never prouder of his son.

After Dennis searched through and wrote down comments and questions about all of the news aggregator websites that Brian had listed on his note, he went to Facebook and, with some difficulty, set up a personal account. When he was prompted to answer personal questions about himself, Dennis balked. It was foreign to him to disclose so much information, especially to people he might not know well. But he had put his trust in Brian thus far, and believed his son wouldn't lead him astray. After completing his Facebook setup, Dennis went to Brian's page. Dennis immediately noticed that Brian had twenty-eight thousand followers.

Twenty-eight thousand? How does Brian know twenty-eight thousand people? Dennis wondered.

As he looked at Brian's photographs and posting—some personal, some about his work—Dennis had an uneasy feeling of voyeurism, that he was snooping into a world in which he didn't belong.

Two hours later, just as Dennis was about to sign off, he checked *The Lumby Lines* Facebook page again. A new post had been added twenty minutes earlier, and to Dennis's amazement it now had 374 followers. How or why that happened was something Dennis didn't understand. But all he needed to know was that he had three times more readers online than he had subscribers to his paper.

The following morning, *The Lumby Lines* online visitors exceeded two thousand.

Brother Michael sat at the computer in the monks' library at Saint Cross Abbey. He had just subscribed to thelumbylines.com and was getting caught up on the town's local news.

Preparations for the town's Outhouse Races have consumed the residents of Lumby during this past week, with most stores closing several hours early to allow time for the owners and employees to give rightful attention to their respective entries. Now in its seventeenth year, the revered event has surpassed the Moo Doo Iditarod in number of applications as well as award size. (Note that the winner's pot for the best decorated outhouse increased from $50 to an amazing $500, donated by Second Nature Taxidermy, located at 16 East Main Street.)

Although some shade was thrown on last year's event after it was discovered that Jimmy D's son, Johnnie D, won by using proprietary gyroscope wheels illicitly procured from NASA, the rules have since been rewritten to clarify the definition of "advanced technologies not allowed," and Jimmy D has been banned from this year's race.

If nothing else, the Outhouse Races are providing the residents a much-needed respite from the political battle that is being waged in town. Everyone feels the best distraction to the mayhem is putting their noses to the grindstone in order to transform their otherwise functional outhouses into objects of fast-moving and esthetically attractive pieces of art in hopes of capturing any one of the smaller prizes if not the grand prize. Several of the entries have already been moved to the town square with new arrivals being pushed, pulled or hauled in by the hour.

Michael was still laughing when he heard the door open behind him.

Alan Blackstone peered in. "Do you mind if I join you?"

"Not at all," Michael said, waving him in. "I was just about to leave to prepare for vespers."

Alan pushed the door open trying not to upset all the stacks of papers he cradled in his arms.

Michael jumped up. "Do you need help with that?"

Rushing to the table, Alan dropped the pile. "No, I'm good. But thanks anyway."

"Then I'll leave you."

Alan took a seat at the table and proceeded to spread the pages out before him. Most were single-page documents, but some were stapled contracts.

Alan heard the door open behind him. "Did

you forget something?" he asked without looking up.

A woman replied. "Not that I'm aware of."

Alan swung around as Sister Megan walked into the room. He was still taken aback by her natural beauty, but kept both his emotions and thoughts in check given her religious calling.

"Sorry. I thought you were—"

"Brother Michael. I get that a lot," she teased. "I just saw him in the hall." She headed over to the computer, but before sitting down she dug deep into her pant's pocket. "Geez," she said softly as she yanked out a pair of gardening gloves, and then some twine and a handful of twist ties. Not finding what she was looking for, she tried the other pocket. Alan watched, both charmed and amused.

"Ah, here it is," she murmured. Taking a magnifying glass from the shelf, she examined a rock that looked no bigger than a quarter. Then she turned her attention to the computer and started to pull up images of stones. "Hmmm," Megan whispered.

"Stumped by a rock?"

"I am indeed," she said without taking her eyes off the screen. "Ah, here we are." She read the text. "Well, what on earth is that doing here?"

"Excuse me?"

Megan swung around in her seat. "I'm sorry, I was just talking to myself." She stood up and stuffed the stone back into her pocket. "Every once in a while we come across something unique in our upper field."

"The vineyard?"

"Yep. A billion years of rock being pushed north leaves a lot of surprises in the ground."

"An unidentified stone?"

"No longer unidentified!" She smiled victoriously. "Just very rare in this area." She noticed the papers spread over the table. "And what are you up to?"

"I'm going through Duke's papers word for word, and I'm trying to make sense of some inconsistencies."

Megan's eyes lit up. "Oh, what are those? I love a good mystery."

"I could have guessed from your rock research," he teased. "I'm afraid, the less you know the better."

Megan tilted her head and then with total conviction said, "I don't think that's ever true, regardless of circumstance."

"Appropriately said for a nun," Alan replied.

Megan looked confused. "What does that mean?"

"Only that I would expect total truth and full disclosure to be a core tenet in your life."

"And you don't think it for others?" she asked.

"Unfortunately not, but I'm quite a cynic."

"That's sad," Megan said.

"Perhaps. But if it keeps me alive, I'll hold onto my distrustful nature."

"Were you always such a skeptic?"

Alan tried to search his memory. "No, I suppose not, but I was never a dreamer. You had to be tough to survive a childhood with Duke. Our father was committed to the army, and our mother wasn't, so when he was reassigned to Japan, she left to find a better life."

"She left you?"

"All of us. Dad raised us on military bases and cold showers for as long as I can remember. Everything Dad threw at us just toughened Duke up all the more. I was . . . collateral damage. I stayed away from home as much as possible, which brought me closer to the people and the languages that were just outside the army bases. Dad always had high expectations for both of us. I think he had our political careers charted out before we finished elementary school."

Megan nodded. "Been there," she said, but it was so fleeting Alan didn't hear it.

"Duke and I both went to Georgetown to major in political science. But halfway through my first year, I left." He sighed. "I had always loved languages—really anything foreign. So I packed a duffel bag, headed to Paris and for four years worked odd jobs in France, then Spain and finally Italy. The more comfortable I became, the more I wanted to explore different cultures. So I went to the Mideast for a year and then traveled through Asia to return home."

"Did you ever go back to college?"

"No. But I have no regrets." He smiled wistfully. "There's an extraordinary freedom that comes with the knowledge that you can talk with most people in the world."

"I'm sure there is," Megan said. "On my few trips to France with my father, I felt almost foolish."

"That's being hard on yourself," Alan said. "Most people, especially in our country, have this involuntary expectation that others should speak our language, and that others are at fault if they can't, or worse, if they can but with a heavy accent. Unfortunately, my brother is the perfect example of that kind of thinking, and he's now in the position of influence, if not a great deal of power."

"So it was Duke who went on to have the political career?"

"Well, I'm not sure if you can call Duke's livelihood a political career, but yes, he's held several elected positions. He's also been convicted twice for white-collar crimes." He picked up several pages from the table and held them in the air. "But this so far exceeds any wrongdoing he's done in the past. This would send him away for life. It would also be the downfall of several officials in Washington."

Megan raised her brows. "Is it that insidious?"

Alan nodded. "Scanned images of checks made out to a state senator, emails to the assistant director of the EPA, falsified environmental impact reports."

"Everything the FBI would want to see," Megan said.

"That's the problem. I'm sure Duke has several agents in his pocket. If this gets to one of them, Duke will know I'm involved. So I can't just start calling people in the FBI."

A wily look came into her eyes. "No, *you* can't. But *I* could, and some of my friends could."

Alan dropped the papers. "I don't follow."

"How about this?" she began before sharing her quickly conceived plan.

"That's so devious," Alan said. "I wouldn't think a nun could come up with that kind of scheme."

"But that's what's perfect—everyone underestimates us," she said with a sly grin.

FIFTEEN

Adopted

Pam nervously fiddled with the stacked papers. It was late at night and the house was still, besides Mark's snoring, a sound that she found more comforting than annoying. She had spent some of the evening reading through documents that would be discussed with her mother's estate attorney the following morning. But the last three hours had been Googling the scant data she had about her sister.

Sitting in front of the computer, she closed her eyes and tried to recall every detail of the meeting with the estate lawyer in Connecticut, beginning with the ridiculously oversized mahogany table in his office. For three hours they reviewed the estate and the various steps that were needed to legally bring Kay's life to closure.

Pam was staggered by all that was required. "But this could take months."

The attorney nodded. "Perhaps a year."

"I had no idea," Pam said, staring at the four-inch-high pile of papers that was the culmination of Kay's life.

"Well, I think we made great strides today. The

rest we can do with conference calls and emails." He started to collect his work.

"If you have another minute," Pam said. "You've known my mother longer than I have, and I need to ask you something," she began. "In her safe I found this birth certificate." She slid the paper to the attorney, who quickly scanned it and nodded. "Do you know anything about it?"

Mr. Coleman withdrew a page from the thick folder lying on the table in front of him. "It was something your mother never wanted you to know because she was never proud of their decision. She directed me to keep the circumstance in utmost confidence unless you specially requested otherwise."

The certificate of final adoption was dated four months after the birth certificate.

"Adopted?" she murmured.

"Several years before you were born, your parents had a child," Coleman explained. "Your mother became very ill leading up to the birth and almost passed away during the delivery. At that time the doctors gave her a grim prognosis. Facing her own imminent death, and an illegitimate child that would need caring for, Kay and Robert decided to put the girl up for adoption."

Pam was shaken. "You're telling me I have a sister?"

"You *had* a sister, yes," the attorney said. "I

believe Kay lost touch two or three years after the adoption. Around that time, you were born and she asked that all papers regarding the adoption be sealed. We never discussed it after that." He rummaged among the papers some more. "Here they are. These papers are part of her estate so they, in essence, belong to you." He gave her half a dozen pages that were paper clipped together. "These are the last communications I had in my file."

Pam quickly read through the papers. "A baptismal certificate from Des Moines, Iowa," Pam said, studying one page. "Her name is Janet Wilson." She skimmed two brief letters that gave no more information than the child being well. "So you don't even know if she's alive?"

"No."

"But wouldn't it be your responsibility to find her to settle my mother's affairs?"

Coleman shook his head. "In every document related to and including her last will and testament, she specifically disinherits any child or children that could legitimately make claim to her estate."

"But I thought that was just a boilerplate condition in any will."

"Not in Kay's case. The wording was specifically written to ensure that you were her only heir."

Pam's thoughts were reeling. "So, I may have a

full sister out there somewhere, who may or may not even know she's adopted."

"It's possible," the attorney said.

Mark coughed, pulling Pam out of her reverie. She was exhausted and knew it was time to go to bed. When she tiptoed into the bedroom, she was surprised to see Mark wide-awake with his tablet PC resting on his stomach.

"What are you doing up?"

"I couldn't fall back asleep," he said.

"Obviously not a problem for the dogs," Pam said. Clipper was fast asleep at his feet, and Cutter was snoozing on Pam's side of the bed. "You're such a good boy," Pam said, kissing the nose of her dog. "Tell me," she said, still talking to the Lab, "how difficult can it be to find one person in Des Moines?" She pushed Cutter over and climbed under the sheets. "I just spent hours trying to find my sister, and I have less information now than when I started. I must not be looking in the right place."

"Yeah," Mark muttered.

Pam stretched out under the light summer blanket. "Oh, this feels wonderful," sliding close to her husband.

Mark was unusually focused on what he was reading. "Uh-huh," he mumbled absently.

"You sound thrilled," she said.

"Uh-huh," he repeated.

185

"What has you so fixated?" Pam said, turning the screen so she could read it. "The *FBI?* Since when are you interested in that sort of stuff?"

"I'm not," Mark said, quickly putting the tablet to sleep.

"The way you've been acting, if I didn't know better I would think that you met someone while I was away," Pam said.

"You have no idea," Mark accidentally blurted out.

Her curiosity aroused, Pam pushed herself up on her elbows. "What does that mean?"

Mark scrambled for an answer. "Nothing, nothing at all. I mean, I met Duke Blackstone . . . the *real* Duke Blackstone. That's all. He's a scary fellow, you know."

"Is that why you've been so preoccupied?" Pam asked.

"I have a lot of things going on right now."

She could guess just about all of them. "For the campaign?"

"Yeah, that's it. For the campaign," Mark said hastily. "Remember, I'm your campaign manager now, and I'm also a candidate. Those are two big responsibilities. We've got a lot of planning to do."

"Well, I think you're being weirdly mysterious," Pam said. "But it's kind of sexy." She touched his chest in an unspoken suggestion that they enjoy the rest of their evening together.

Mark slid from under her hand and rolled out of bed. "Okay, hold that thought. I have one email that I need to send off. Oh! Look!" he said, looking at his wrist as if he was wearing a watch. "It's past two, honey."

Before Pam could reply, Mark bolted out of the room. A few minutes later, Pam was asleep.

In the spare bedroom that served as their office, Mark jumped on the computer and finished reading the articles he had bookmarked about Alan and Duke Blackstone.

A few hours later, Mark returned to bed and fell into a deep sleep. Pam, on the other hand, tossed and turned about concerns both in and out of her control. Her best recourse was to meet her angst head on, so she snuck out of the bedroom and back to the PC. She was more determined than ever to find her sister.

She thought she'd make a fresh start, and begin at the beginning, with Kay Eastman. Googling her mother's name gave few results. And then she thought that her mom might have formally changed her name when she returned home after their marriage. Once she Googled "Kay Day, Greenwich, CT," ten pages of hits came up, as did several pages of images. There were even YouTube videos tagged with her name.

Pam went first to her mother's public Facebook page. She had over two thousand friends. "I can't even friend you now, can I?" she said aloud, as if speaking to a ghost.

The photographs in her Facebook albums reflected images of a person Pam didn't know: Kay and Robert skiing in Banff; Kay jumping in the waves on Block Island; Kay with Nick and Scott, who were in tuxedos, holding up champagne glasses. Those and a hundred other photographs left Pam grappling with the thought that she had somehow lost her mother along the way.

How could I have let this happen? she asked herself for the hundredth time.

She touched an image of her mother and Olivia on the screen. *I should never have let us let go.* But then again, she thought, we were never really holding on to each other throughout any part of my life. It's strange how death, the permanent absence of a person, tilts the reality of what came before.

Finding no thread that would bring her closer to her biological sister, she switched her focus from her mother to the person at hand, Janet Wilson.

On their desktop computer, she explored various genealogy and missing-person websites as well as government databases. She narrowed down the infinite number of choices to a handful to which she would subscribe.

"This is getting expensive," Pam griped as

she entered her credit card number to the fifth ancestry-search site.

Suddenly, a hand gripped her shoulder, and she screamed.

"It's me!" Mark yelled. "God, you scared the daylights out of me!"

"You almost gave me a heart attack!" Pam yelled. "What are you doing up?"

"You weren't in bed, and I just wanted to make sure everything was okay."

"It will bc when my heart starts up again," Pam said. She took a deep breath and shook her arms.

"Honey, you only had a couple hours of sleep. What are you doing now?"

"Trying to find Janet Wilson."

"Why don't you just hire a private detective?"

"I considered it, but there are so many records online now, I should be able to do this myself. It's driving me crazy," she admitted. "I haven't slept well for a week. How would you feel if you suddenly found out that you had a long-lost brother out there who you've never met . . . and who doesn't know anything about you?"

"Given my family, given I have my brother-in-law who stole a quarter million dollars from me, and how many problems I've had with Carter, I don't know if I would take the chance."

Pam was stunned. *"Really?"*

"Pam, you've only cxperienced what it feels like to be an only child. I think you have a very naïve idea that every relationship between brothers and sisters is perfect."

"No, I don't," Pam said. "I suppose I just think the worst relationship is better than none at all."

"Because you haven't been there, honey. You don't know what it's like when kinships go bad and family members turn against you, or you're forced to take sides. Family dynamics are impossible sometimes, and can turn just awful."

"But at least there is a family," Pam said. "And this Janet Wilson is the only person in the world who's related to me. And she is the only link I have to my mother."

"But isn't Robert your bond with Kay?"

"I don't know," she said, lowering her head. "I almost feel the woman Robert married wasn't my mother. She was living a different life in Connecticut for the last ten years—one that she didn't invite me to be a part of." Pam fought back tears.

"You know, Pam, this whole Janet Wilson thing could turn out badly."

She did a double take. "Since when did you become a pessimist?"

"I'm not. It's just that there are a lot of people who you might not want in your life. What happens if she turns out to be someone like Duke Blackstone?"

Pam couldn't help but to laugh. "Well that's absurd. That would never happen."

"Why couldn't it?"

"Because it just couldn't, that's why," Pam answered defensively.

"What I'm saying is that you just never know. You need to be cautious."

Pam looked at Mark in disbelief. "That doesn't sound like the 'Mark Walker, full speed ahead no matter what' guy I married."

"It's just a big nasty world out there, and we might not see all the hard realities in Lumby."

"I don't think we see any of them here. That's why we chose to live in Lumby," Pam retorted.

"My point exactly. Just go slowly," Mark warned.

"You're scaring me," she said jokingly. "I think you need to go back to bed and get some sleep."

Walking out, Mark paused at the door. "You know, there's an expression Joshua uses all the time: be careful what you wish for, because it might come true. I'm worried you have such high expectations that no matter who she is, she'll probably fall short."

By noon the following day, Pam Walker had found her sister—not in Iowa, and not named Janet Wilson. She was a fifty-six-year-old married woman named Janet Wing living with her husband, William, in Great Falls, Virginia. The background-check aggregator verified, to Pam's relief, that her sister had no prior arrests or convictions. However, the one and only photograph that Pam could find of Janet was quite blurred—Janet and presumably her husband, Bill Wing, were holding their hands toward the camera, effectively blocking the shot. From the image, Pam could only confirm that Janet, like she and Kay, had blond hair. At the bottom of the photo there was a handwritten footnote: "1997— US Embassy Rabat, Morocco."

"Morocco? Who the hell goes to Morocco?"

SIXTEEN

Living

Caroline, on her hands and knees working in the garden, didn't hear the whistling from down the road. Finn did, though, and when he caught sight of Aaron, he tore off in a full gallop to greet him.

"Caroline!" Aaron called.

She looked up with a start. "What brings you down here?" She propped herself up on her knees, brushed the dirt off her hands and waved.

"I'm on a mission," he said as he strolled up the front walk. But when he heard the sound of a big band coming from the open windows of the living room, he stopped midstep and listened, tilting his head. "Bobby Hackett?"

"I'm impressed!" she replied. "I bought it at an auction last month, and this is the first time I've played it."

Aaron closed his eyes and his body began swaying with the music as if he was dancing with Mac on the porch. "It's a classic," he said, smiling.

"It really is," Caroline said, taking his hand

193

to stand up. How incredibly nice it was to share her love of old jazz music with someone who appreciated it just as much.

"Definitely one of my favorites," he said. "Maybe I could make a copy to bring home with me."

Her smiling dream was broken. "Home?" Caroline had forgotten about that. "You mentioned you live in Seattle?"

"North of there, on the water," he said.

"The Puget Sound and the Olympic Mountains? I hear it's beautiful there."

"It is," he replied. "I'd love to show you around if you ever come that way."

All Caroline had to say were two words—"I will" or "Thank you" or "Yes, perhaps"—but instead she looked down and began pulling at the fingers of her gardening gloves.

Aaron cleared his throat. "We've known each other forever—"

"For weeks," Caroline corrected him.

"Okay, weeks, but it's felt like forever. And I think it's time we get serious."

Her eyes opened in alarm. *"What do you mean?"*

Aaron reached into his pocket and pulled out a brochure. "There's a big band concert on the green at Wheatley. What do you think?"

"Wheatley?" she said, stalling for time.

He gave her an incredulous look. "Yeah, it's that town right down the road from us. Remember?"

194

Caroline didn't hear his sarcasm. "You're asking me out on a *date?*"

"You make it sound like it's a death sentence," he said, chuckling. "Truly, I'm not that bad a guy."

"But would it be a *date?*"

Aaron ran his hand through his hair in confusion. "You can call it anything you want. I just thought since we both love Glenn Miller, we might have a good time listening to some great music. No strings, no ties, no personal questions, no talk about either of our lives," he said in exasperation. "Just a little 'April in Paris'."

Caroline noticed how soiled her fingers were and began picking at the dirt from under her nails.

When she didn't reply, Aaron threw his arms up. "Okay, this was obviously too big a leap for you. Just know I had nothing but good intentions."

As she watched him walk away, with Finn jogging by his side, Brooke's words haunted Caroline more than any ghosts could have: *You haven't chosen to live a full life. You haven't chosen to live a life without him.*

Aaron was all the way to the road before Caroline yelled out. "Wait! I know. It's a great idea, and I'd like to go with you."

Aaron spun around, beaming. "Great. I'll pick you up at five."

Caroline looked at her watch: two hours to make herself presentable. Her heart skipped one small beat.

After showering, Caroline did something she hadn't done in years: she dropped her towel and stood naked in front of the full-length mirror that hung on the back of her closet door. It wasn't that she had deliberately avoided looking at or evaluating her body, even when Kai was still a part of her life, but she never saw her body as anything other than a well-designed package that served a functional purpose. Hopefully, it would support her throughout the years without too many problems. Further, she always resented how men turned their heads to stare her down, or worse, whistle. It had been her raw beauty that she disliked the most.

Ironically, her beauty didn't bring the intimacy she craved. In retrospect, if Caroline could have fixed one aspect of her marriage, it would have been the lack of physical connection between her and Kai. But Kai was never a sensuous man, either because of his own lack of interest or his calling to higher priorities with God. Uncontrolled carnal passion, like she had read about, wasn't shared between them.

Caroline tilted her head as she examined her body. She had lost some weight over the years. She also appeared more drawn and pale, but with the summer approaching, a healthy tan would return and make her blond hair and blue eyes dazzle that much more.

She slowly turned in place, first examining herself from the left side, and then studying her back with a hand mirror on the bathroom counter. *Given everything, it's not that bad,* she thought as she picked up the towel and finished drying herself off.

She rummaged through three cabinet drawers looking for cosmetics she hadn't used for years: a face mask, skin cream, nail polish, perfume, lipstick.

"We need some music," she said to Finn before running downstairs to put on an album.

With Woody Herman's clarinet filling the house, Caroline spent the next two hours on Caroline—a long-awaited, self-indulgent sprucing up, as she explained to Finn, who was ultimately kicked out of the room when he wouldn't stop licking wet nail polish from Caroline's toes.

"This has nothing to do with Aaron," she explained to Finn, who was sitting on the other side of the closed bedroom door. "I've just really let myself go. No wonder folks look at me so weird in town. I'd turn away if I saw me too . . . I'm days away from becoming a cat lady. Brooke should have let me know years ago that I look so crappy, but I'm sure she didn't want to hurt my feelings."

. . .

At ten minutes to five, Caroline opened the door to her bedroom and stepped out feeling like a new woman . . . nervous but new. She wore an enchanting red-and-white striped dress with spaghetti straps that was long-ago buried in her closet, a pair of red sandals that needed to be dusted off and a red sweater over her shoulders, thinking it would probably turn chilly as the evening progressed.

Had Caroline turned off her record player instead of humming to the song in the kitchen, she might have heard Aaron drive down the road. But not until she answered the door did she realize the vehicle he had come on.

"That's a motorcycle," she said, before greeting him.

"It is. And you look beautiful," he said, smiling.

She blushed. "Thank you. It took a while. I don't do this often."

He grinned. "I gathered."

"Let me get my car keys," she said.

"I thought we would take the bike," he suggested, handing her a helmet that he'd had behind his back. *"Pour toi,* Madame."

She blurted out the first excuse she thought of. "But I'm wearing a dress."

"Don't worry," he said, trying to lead her out of the house. "It's not against the law and we're just going on back roads. I promise, no faster than thirty miles an hour."

"But if it rains?" she stuttered.

Aaron looked up at the clear blue sky and shrugged.

"Bugs," she said.

"Bugs?"

"In my teeth."

Aaron eyed her suspiciously. "Have you ever been on a motorcycle, Caroline?"

She shook her head.

"Then tonight will be a first."

In more ways than one, she thought as he dragged her down the path.

"You may want to put on your sweater," he advised as he mounted the bike.

After donning her helmet, she lifted her dress a few inches and sat directly behind him. There was a basket strapped above a caddy over the rear wheel.

Caroline tentatively placed her hands on his upper arms.

He turned around to talk to her. "Not there— you could impact my steering. Put your arms around me."

Caroline leaned forward and wrapped her arms around his waist. This way, there were no more than a few inches between their bodies. She smelled his cologne, and for a passing moment she was lost. Then suddenly, the engine roared to life. The noise and the vibration caught her by surprise. When the bike rolled forward, she instinctively tightened her hold around him. He smiled and released the clutch.

When they drove past Mac and Tom's home, she was holding on for dear life.

"You all right?" he asked.

"I don't know," she yelled back.

"Just relax and move with the bike."

Once they turned left onto Farm to Market Road, the ride was much smoother, but she still kept her head tucked into Aaron's back. For Caroline, it was unnerving to give total control over to another person who literally held her life in his hands. One bad turn, one moment of indecision, and she would surely meet her maker. But a stronger feeling was the exhilarating freedom of total abandon. The wind blew against her body and the world passed by as if they were standing still in time.

"Take a deep breath and enjoy the ride," he called back to her.

After a few miles, she got used to the feel of the wind against her skin and the swaying of Aaron's body as he gently banked the bike on curves and leaned into turns. By the time they approached Wheatley, Caroline had loosened her grip from around his waist, and for one fleeting moment she even held out an arm to feel the rush of air against her skin.

When they came to the first light in town, Aaron put his foot down once the bike rolled to a stop. Twisting around to talk with her, he casually placed his hand on her upper thigh to keep himself balanced.

"We may have to circle the green to find a parking spot," he said loudly over the rumble of the engine.

Caroline nodded, and then tapped his shoulder and pointed forward when she saw the light change. He removed his hand from her thigh and drove off.

To their luck, Aaron found a parking space directly across the street from the makeshift stage, in between two other motorcycles.

"So, what did you think?" he asked.

"I've never felt anything like it," she said, still feeling the adrenaline from the ride. She shook her hair after he removed her helmet.

"I hope that's a good thing."

"Me too," she said under her breath.

After finding an open space on the green, Aaron unfolded the blanket and spread it out on the grass. From the basket he withdrew a bottle of wine, a loaf of rustic bread and a plastic bag that held various cheeses.

"You thought of everything," she said.

"I was worried that asking you to dinner before the concert might be too much, and I didn't want to chance it," he teased, "so this is the next best thing. What a beautiful night," he said as he sat down on the blanket and made himself comfortable. "This is a great spot to watch the band."

"It is," she agreed, glancing over her shoulder.

"I have another throw in the caddy if you get cold," he offered. "But how about some wine to start the evening?"

He opened the bottle and offered her a glass. Only then did she sit down next to him. She drank half of it before he had finished pouring a glass for himself.

Aaron laughed. "A little thirsty, are we?"

She looked at him with bright-blue, wide eyes, like a deer caught in the headlights. "Nerves."

He laughed as he topped off her glass. "Caroline, the hardest part was over when you said yes."

Thirty minutes and two more glasses of Pinot later, Caroline let her guard down and finally began to enjoy the evening. The conversation they had before the music started was delightful, and fairly impersonal. They shared a lot: both were fiscal conservatives and social liberals who supported medicinal pot, neither had strong religious leanings, both enjoyed being outdoors more than indoors, both loved problem solving and did crossword puzzles in pen, both watched the NASA channel, and both were rock hounds. And although Caroline had a higher distrust of strangers, as it turned out, she held a stronger faith in the goodness of the human spirit, while Aaron placed his values on family, but never offered to discuss his own—other than, of course, Tom and Mac.

Caroline and Aaron laughed often and freely as they told each other silly stories from their past. They both delighted in watching the children playing on the green while the music of the big band era filled the town.

Shortly after the band began its second set, the sun went down, the children tired and the atmosphere changed dramatically. The town's green, lit only by the soft lights of the lampposts that followed the sidewalk, became incredibly romantic. When slower and softer tunes played, some couples moved closer together while others began to dance.

Aaron stood and offered Caroline his hand. "May I?"

She had only danced with Kai once or twice years before, and wondered if she still remembered how.

Once in Aaron's arms, though, she realized that she didn't need to remember anything— her body instantly responded to his lead. His gentle touch on her waist or the feel of his palm on her back moved her through turns, dips and swing outs—some that she had forgotten long ago, some that were new to her. And never once did she feel his touch was too personal.

Together, their bodies fit next to each other like two contoured halves of a greater whole. When they moved close, Caroline felt her breasts pressing against his chest, and sensed the rub of his leg between hers when their footing was just inches apart. Every touch ignited a sensual spark, a burst of erotic sensitivity that she had assumed was extinguished forever. When Aaron placed his hand on the small of her back, she felt her knees buckle and her heartbeat quicken. She closed her eyes and felt the arousal in her body.

As the band began playing the closing piece of the night, a slow rendition of "Stardust," Aaron drew Caroline close and they began swaying in unison, lost somewhere between the music and the movement of their bodies. Caroline rested her head on Aaron's chest, feeling his warm breath on her neck, hearing the beat of his heart. She inhaled the sweet scent of his cologne. On impulse, she pulled him closer.

When the music ended, the two continued to sway back and forth until the laughter of nearby children broke their trance. They looked into each other's eyes, their lips inches apart.

Suddenly Caroline pushed away, putting her hands up to her flushed cheeks.

No matter what he wanted right then, Caroline's cue took precedence. "I'm guessing it's time to go?" he asked.

• • •

On the ride home, Caroline kept her arms wrapped around his waist. It was a night like no other—in the embrace of a man who shared her passion for music . . . and for dancing. As the town lights faded behind them, Caroline buried her face into the hollow between his shoulder blades. Any remorse or guilt she felt about her failed marriage lessened with each mile they traveled, so by the time they arrived at the mill, Caroline knew that it was time to put Kai behind her and move on with her life.

On that night, though, she wanted to move on alone, so she didn't ask Aaron inside. Instead, she crawled into bed with Finn, turned off the lights and slept more soundly than she had in years.

SEVENTEEN

Burned

At the far table in the otherwise empty Green Chile restaurant, an impromptu Beezer family meeting was in progress.

Brian sat next to his father, nursing a Corona with lime.

"You're not the beer drinker you used to be," Dennis remarked.

"I'm not the goof-off I used to be," Brian replied, tapping the neck of his beer bottle against his father's Corona.

"You're certainly putting in some long hours. Will I be shocked when I see your bill?" his father asked, half serious.

"The equipment is discounted sixty percent and will be invoiced to your company. You're covering mileage and four hours for three of my team to deliver the stuff. I've already paid the rest of the crew in cash—nine hours for eight people each. You can repay me later."

"I thought you were broke and couldn't afford a pizza."

"God, no. The monks are more than generous with my salary, and I have no living expenses when I travel." Brian took a sip of beer. "I just needed to get to the bank to convert my money from Peru."

"How about your own time?"

Brian shrugged. "Consider it pro bono."

"You know that's not necessary."

"I'm good," Brian said.

Timmy moved restlessly in his chair. "Are we done?"

"Not quite," Gabrielle chimed out from the kitchen.

Dennis pulled idly at the label on his bottle. "The amount you paid the kids, was it enough?" He hesitated. "The only reason I ask is because some of them were wearing really tattered clothes, and I just wanted to make sure that—"

Brian interrupted his father with a loud laugh. "Dad, three of those *kids* are worth more than you a couple times over. Another wasn't . . . until last month when he sold his startup for four million dollars. Coming to Lumby was the excuse they needed to go heli-skiing up north."

"Wow." Dennis chuckled. "I read that wrong. I imagined them all cramming into a broken-down van praying that they could make it back to Mexico."

"Maybe if the van is a Mercedes," Brian joked. "They came here on a private plane skirting customs and immigration, so the only thing they prayed for was that they wouldn't be picked up by the police." Brian smiled to himself. "We just enjoy working together. We learn something new from each other on every job we do. You know, the circle," he said, again making an open globe of his two hands.

Dennis was so impressed with his adult son. "When did you become so smart?"

"Somewhere between Lumby and Argentina, I guess."

"When are you going back?" Gabrielle asked, still in the kitchen.

"In a while," Brian said.

Dennis put his hand on his son's arm. "Don't go there," he warned Brian. "She misses you so much when you're gone."

Brian looked apologetic as he leaned forward. "What can I do?"

"Nothing more than you are, son. You have your own life to live and she knows that."

"I heard that," Gabrielle called out.

"We're both very proud of you," Dennis said loudly. "Aren't we, Gabrielle?"

"This is getting creepy. Can I go now?" Timmy asked, standing up.

He was almost as tall as Brian.

"I don't even recognize you anymore," Brian joked.

"Two more months and I have a learner's permit," Timmy said.

"And *Dad* is going to teach you how to drive?" Brian asked doubtfully.

"Yeah, the day I get my permit," his brother said. "Then maybe I'll drive down and hang out with you for a while."

"That's not going to happen," Gabrielle yelled.

The three Beezer men laughed.

Timmy pulled out his iPhone and scrolled through his gallery. "Can I put one of my videos on your site?"

"This isn't a game," Dennis said.

Timmy handed Brian his phone. "This is a good one."

Almost immediately, Brian started to laugh. "What the hell is that moose doing?"

"Crazy, isn't it?" Timmy said. "He was always hanging out by the mannequin at the sporting goods store, so we put wheels on the base, sent the mannequin rolling down Main Street. The dumb moose just ran after it."

Brian continued to watch the video, slapping his hand on the table. "Priceless," he said. "I think we can use it."

Dennis looked concerned. "You're not going to turn *The Lumby Lines* into a cheap, gimmicky site, are you?"

"Not at all," Brian assured him. "But we need hits. We need subscribers. And we're going to get them by offering lots of free content for the first couple of weeks and then they can subscribe at a nominal rate. We're also offering free advertising for the first two weeks."

Gabrielle leaned out of the kitchen. "Are you paying attention to the time? You're due at the abbey pretty soon."

Dennis turned to Brian. "I've got their manuscript in the car. If you're interested, you can take a look at it during the drive over. You mentioned you wanted to get your feet wet in the publishing business—this might be a good opportunity to take a book through the entire publishing cycle."

"Are we done?" Timmy asked.

"We're done," Dennis said, watching his younger son tear out the door.

Dennis always enjoyed returning to the quaint village of Franklin. It reminded him of what Lumby was like twenty years before, and it never changed. The monastery had stayed the same as well, except of course, when the sisters and their wine business joined the monks six years earlier.

However, approaching Saint Cross that afternoon, Dennis saw something he had never seen before: a CLOSED sign.

"How odd is that?"

"Do you think we should go in?" Brian asked. "Maybe something has happened."

Dennis shook his head. "Brother Matthew would have called us."

He turned into the driveway but drove slower than normal. At first glance, everything appeared to be normal: monks were walking between the buildings, and several of the sisters were working out in the fields. But something was off, a sense Dennis couldn't put his finger on.

When they knocked on the front door, Brother Matthew answered right away.

"Wonderful to have you here," he said, shaking Dennis's hand. "And Brian, you have been away for too long. Why don't we go directly into our community room?"

On the main table were stacks of papers that Matthew hastily turned over, stacked and put to the side. "Let's take a look at your galley," he said.

Dennis removed it from his pack. "I enjoyed it a great deal."

"We're pleased to hear that," the monk said. "This is the first collaboration of the two communities. It wasn't always easy, but it taught us so much about each other. It was almost an enlightening experience."

A man passed quietly down the hall.

"Brother Michael?" Brian said. "I had some questions to ask him about his Bolivia trip." Brian got up and was about to follow Michael down the hall.

"Brian! You and I have some matters to discuss as well, so why don't you stay here?" Matthew said with some urgency. "We need to talk about your next assignment."

Brian was jarred by his uneasy tone. Then he became aware of the unnatural quiet in the building. Usually monks were walking in and out of the community room, and most certainly Brother John would have emerged from the kitchen to say hello by now.

Brother Matthew thumbed through the galley. "Is this something you wanted me to review right now, or can we get back to you later in the week?"

"Whenever is convenient," Dennis replied. "Our run schedule doesn't have it in press for another ten days. Going forward, you can work directly with Brian on this. He'll be overseeing the publication."

Matthew was pleased with this news. "Very good, Brian. I look forward to that," he said, tapping his finger almost impatiently on the galley. "If it is anything like the results you have given us in Peru, I'm sure we will be delighted. I read your last report just the other day, and I want you to know how pleased we are with your accomplishments. And at the same time we can walk through our thoughts about a mission that is opening in Paraguay. What you started as an experiment in Mexico City is now the working model for our entire philanthropic effort throughout South America. To say that you are needed in Asunción is an understatement." Somewhat abruptly, Matthew stood up. "That is for future discussion, though. Until then, if there is anything we can do for you, please don't hesitate to call. Otherwise, I will plan a trip to Lumby and see you in your office as soon as the books are ready."

Dennis and Brian followed Matthew's lead to the front door.

"A wonderful visit," Brother Matthew said, shaking their hands. "So good to see you both."

Before they could say goodbye, the door closed behind them.

Dennis and Brian stared at each other.

"What just happened?" Brian asked.

"I was going to ask you the same."

Driving away from the monastery, both men mulled over the visit.

"That was the strangest meeting I've ever had, with or without monks." Dennis said. "Is everything all right between you and Brother Matthew?"

"Dad, of course it is!" Brian said, annoyed by his father's line of questioning. "He was just busy. Let it go."

"Well, if anything, at least now you know that the next stamp in your passport will be from Paraguay."

Brian looked out the side window. "I suppose . . . if I want it. But I guess I don't know what I'm going to be doing."

"Really?" Dennis looked at his son doubtfully.

"I thought your primary goal was to get out of Lumby."

"It was," Brian said. "But digital news and digital printing have changed everything. There are opportunities to transform the businesses for the better."

"My businesses?" Dennis asked wearily.

"Yeah, yours and others," Brian answered.

Once back in Lumby, Brian returned to the Chatham Press building to post the moose video. Within hours, it was viewed by four hundred thousand people.

Brian smiled. "Epic."

At home, Dennis also went online. Thelumby bookstore.com was now up to 14,221 visitors. He pulled a clean sheet of paper from his printer and wrote out the final front-page announcement in his newspaper.

Obituary

THE LUMBY LINES
1942–Next Week
Wake Thursday Night 6:30 p.m.
The Fairgrounds, Lumby
No donations.

EIGHTEEN

Searching

If nothing else, the residents of Lumby always knew how to throw a great town wake for anything that had fulfilled its natural purpose on this planet, whether it be human, animal or, as was often the case, neither of the above.

After the life-sized, carved moose was irreparably decapitated while standing watch in front of Lumby Sporting Goods, a nice requiem followed. But all would say that Lumby's finest waking hour came when the town gathered to bid farewell to one of the barns of Lumby, which was dismantled and stolen shortly after the internationally famous painting *The Barns of Lumby* had met the same fate. On that evening, people came from around the county to find hundreds of torch poles placed throughout Katie Banks's property, lighting several acres that surrounded the missing barn. Where the building once stood, a large bonfire was raised, and for

215

hours people sat around the stone foundation watching the flames blaze and then slowly die. As with most wakes in Lumby, Brother Matthew gave a heartfelt eulogy that would be deeply appreciated and long remembered.

And so once again the town came together to offer homage and find comfort in the strength of their community. On that afternoon, they were laying to rest an institution that had been around longer than most of them had been alive: *The Lumby Lines*.

Beginning at dusk, friends and families converged on the fairgrounds just north of town, setting up chairs and laying down blankets in front of the makeshift stage from which a local band best known for their standing appearance at Jimmy D's was already playing. The Bounty, Lumby's very own hot air balloon, had been inflated earlier that afternoon and was gently floating well above the ground.

Enterprising high school students were strolling throughout the crowd selling everything from popcorn and sodas to fireworks to old editions of the newspaper. Children ran untethered, waving sparklers and small American flags.

Hank stood in between The Bounty and the stage, wearing a casual but smart outfit of khaki shorts (which he thought drew unnecessary attention to his legs, if the truth be known) and a dark-blue polo shirt. A bag of marshmallows hung from his beak. So as not to annoy any part of the populace, Hank had left his WALKER sign behind, but his thoughts and loyalties were, by that time, well-known in town.

Dennis Beezer, leaning against the stage, watched Brian supervise the last delivery of the stockpile of unsold newspapers amassed in the basement of The Bindery. The payload included moldy, unreadable issues as far back as 1942.

Brian dusted off his hands. "Good to go."

"So, that's all of it from The Bindery?"

"Yeah, about ten tons of old newsprint," Brian answered. "The basement's empty except for some old filing cabinets."

"I'll go down there tomorrow," Dennis said absently, scanning the crowd. "There must be two thousand people here."

"*The Lines* was around a long time."

Dennis turned to slap his son on the back. "And it will continue to be, thanks to you."

"Did you see the bump in paid subscribers this week?" Brian asked.

Dennis laughed. "I would have never expected it."

"I don't want to jinx our luck, but I don't think you've seen anything yet."

Dennis looked at Brian. "Well, I don't think it has anything to do with luck, son."

Jimmy D joined them. "Are you ready to get this show on the road?"

"Let's get it over with," Dennis said.

Jimmy jumped up on the stage and grabbed the microphone off the stand.

"Glad to see all of you here. It's quite the turnout," Jimmy started. "Since we don't have a mayor, I'm just filling in."

A small group began chanting "Duke . . . Duke . . . Duke," throwing their fists up in the air.

Jimmy raised his hand. "Okay, folks, this isn't a political rally—keep it for the debate on Wednesday." He paused until they quieted down. "Let's give a shout-out to everyone who helped with the balloon—doesn't it just look great?" Jimmy said looking up at The Bounty. "I'm told that free rides will be available after the eulogy. Speaking of which, why don't we bring Brother Matthew up here to . . . do what he does best. Brother Matthew?"

The abbot of Saint Cross Abbey, dressed in a long black robe, walked up on the stage and accepted the microphone. "Thank you, Jimmy," he said, bowing slightly. As soon as he started speaking, silence fell over the fairgrounds. "I am again humbled to find words of comfort for this town in transition, a town that was once a part of my life and Montis Abbey, and one that all the monks and sisters in Franklin hold dear in our heart. I have never given a eulogy for a newspaper before, and worried that the words it so steadfastly communicated would be diminished in such an observance. But then I saw The Bounty," he said, looking up at the balloon.

"It doesn't seem like that long ago when the residents of Lumby faced the unprecedented challenge of building something that was initially so foreign to them they might not have been able to envision what we see here tonight. But I believe that call to action many years ago became one of the town's finest moments." He paused. "Those two thoughts are on my mind tonight: time and community. Because I believe it is those two principles that *The Lumby Lines* weaved into a rich tapestry. For over sixty years—and I fear to admit, I was there near the beginning—*The Lumby Lines* has reflected the best of the people of Lumby. Dennis Beezer, and before him, his father William Beezer, ensured that the one newspaper we depended on would bring our lives together in truth, humor and moral decency."

Brother Matthew spoke for another ten minutes. By the time he was done, there wasn't a dry eye to be seen. His final words warmed the heart of each Lumby resident with humor, with compassion and with sadness.

When the last words were spoken, Dennis Beezer ceremoniously lit the bonfire, and the largest blaze ever seen in Lumby lit the sky.

Pam and Mark stretched out on her large blanket, with Caroline sitting close by.

"Boy, you don't see that every day," Mark

said. "The flames must be twenty feet high."

"I'm glad we didn't bring the dogs. I think that would terrify them," Pam said.

"It's the end of an era, that's for sure," Mark said, mesmerized by the fire.

"I think it's sad," Caroline said. Her gaze drifted to the hot-air balloon. "Seeing The Bounty again just brings back too many memories of Kai. Sometimes I wonder if I should just move away so I can start a new life without so many reminders."

Tom and Mac Candor strolled up, holding hands and swinging their arms.

"Hi, guys," Mark said. "Have a seat—there's plenty of room on the blanket."

Caroline stood up and brushed off her pants. "Take my spot. I'm just leaving."

"Not on our account, I hope," Mac said.

"Not at all," Caroline said. "All of this forces a walk down memory lane that I'd prefer not to take right now."

"Aaron is just over there," Mac said, pointing toward the bonfire.

"Not tonight," Caroline replied. "I'll be over at the stage looking at the kites."

Pam watched Caroline disappear into the crowd. "It must be hard for her, seeing The Bounty again."

"I'm sure," Mac agreed.

"But Kai certainly did an amazing job," Tom

said as he continued to marvel at the balloon.

Aaron walked up to the group. "An amazing job with what?"

Tom nodded at The Bounty. "Caroline's husband built that for a town he had never heard of and for residents who were less than welcoming when he arrived. I give him lot of credit."

Aaron perked up. "Caroline is here?" he asked, looking around.

"She just headed over to the other side of the stage," Mac said, and then cautioned, "It's a hard night for her."

"Well then, she just might need a friend," Aaron replied.

A few minutes later, he found her lying on her back on the platform, staring up at the sky.

"It's not quite dark enough for stargazing," Aaron said.

Startled, Caroline bolted upright. "I didn't know you were here."

"A funeral for a newspaper? I wouldn't miss that for the world." His smile was contagious.

Caroline laughed. "Yeah, it's a bit odd, I suppose. But it's Lumby." She leaned back, resting on her elbows. "Did you notice the kites?" she asked, pointing. "In the glow of the bonfire, they really are quite spectacular."

A handful of kites danced in the sky, each ablaze with color from the flames.

"The yellow is so brilliant," she said. "And I like the light-blue one as well. Which one is your favorite?"

For a peculiarly long time, Aaron scanned the sky. "I don't know." Within seconds, both his mood and his tone had changed noticeably. A dark storm rolled in with no warning.

"Which one would you pick?" she asked.

"What difference does it make?" he barked crossly.

Caroline bit her lip, grasping for any reason for Aaron's abrupt shift of mood. *Absolutely none, so why is it such a big deal to you?* she thought. "I just asked which kite you liked."

"Just drop it, Caroline," he warned.

It was already a bad night for Caroline, and it was getting worse by the second. She had had enough of his mood swings. "What the hell is going on?" she snapped.

Aaron took several steps back, trying to extricate himself from the looming argument. "Nothing," he said. "Nothing at all."

"Then why are you so pissed?"

"I'm not!" he yelled.

"Bullshit!" Caroline said. "I just asked you which kite you liked."

Aaron glanced up at the sky. "The one on the right. Are you happy now?"

"Not really," she said.

NINETEEN
Memories

A United moving van with a Connecticut license plate arrived at Montis shortly after breakfast. Although Pam and Mark weren't expecting the movers that early, several of their friends who had offered their strong backs were on call. An empty U-Haul destined for Caroline's shop waited in the parking lot.

"Is Joshua back?" Pam asked as she looked for her work gloves.

"They got in last night. They're swinging by S&T's and will be here in a few minutes."

"Great," Pam said, heading out the door. She kissed him. "Okay, you ready?"

"And able," Mark said, tripping over his own feet. "Well, not *that* kind of Abel. Not like the brothers Cain and Abel."

Pam wondered if her husband had lost his mind. "What are you talking about?"

"Nothing," Mark said quickly before scrambling out of their house.

Pam followed in his wake. "Some of the furniture will go into the main building, the other pieces to Caroline's. I'll tag what needs to be moved into the U-Haul."

"Does Caroline know we're coming?" Mark asked.

Pam shook her head. "Not exactly. I think she's having a hard time getting ready for the sale, so I'm a little worried our idea could just make the situation worse. Once we get there, if she doesn't buy into the idea, we'll just head down to Wheatley."

Joshua and Brooke arrived as the movers were opening the rear doors.

"I am so glad you're here!" Pam said to Brooke. "I can't tell you how much I've missed you."

"It's good to be home," Brooke said, looking into the van. "Wow, it's a lot of furniture."

"It's only about a tenth of what was in my mother's house. The Realtor suggested I take the pieces of sentimental or financial value, and leave the rest in the house so it would show better."

"And what are you going to do after Kay's house sells?"

"Either the furniture will stay with the house or I'll arrange for a consignment company in Greenwich to sell it." Pam's voice broke on the last words.

"Are you okay?"

Pam had spotted an armoire from her mother's room. She remembered climbing into the bottom of it when she was a child. "I don't know. I think the last couple of weeks have been a little overwhelming."

"Step aside, girls, the men are here," Mark announced. His arm was wrapped around Joshua's neck. "Gosh, it's so great to have you guys back. I think you should blow off Seattle and stay forever."

Joshua laughed. "Not possible. But your timing couldn't be more perfect. Do you wait until we come home to schedule a major project?"

"We just don't want you to miss out on the fun," Pam said, winking at Brooke.

"Okay then, let's get at it," Joshua said. "We're flying back to Washington in three days, so no lolling around."

"Three days?" Mark whined. "Is that how long you think it's going to take us to move all this furniture around?"

"Mark, I was teasing." Joshua looked inside the van. "It will take us four hours at most."

Joshua's estimate was spot on. The empty moving van pulled out before noon.

"Why don't we grab some lunch before we go over to the mill?"

"Okay, honey," Mark said, sounding artificially gay. "Why don't you bring some sandwiches out back? I need to talk to Joshua for a minute. Just guy stuff. Just catching up on what he's missed."

Joshua grabbed his shirt and pulled him away. "Why are you acting so weird?"

Mark's good cheer collapsed in a moment.

"I'm a nervous wreck. I have a secret—a monk secret—that I have to keep. But it's driving me nuts. I'm more scared that I'll accidentally spill the beans than some mafia goon is going to shoot us down in the middle of Main Street." Mark stopped short. "I shouldn't have said that."

"I have no idea what you're talking about, but I think you're letting your imagination get to you," Joshua said.

"I'm not," Mark protested. "You have to believe me."

They sat across from each other at the picnic table farthest from the house.

"Would you just go and see Brother Matthew?" Mark asked. "And when you're there, look around. Maybe even check the ice cream freezer."

Joshua was mystified. "For what?"

"I can't tell you."

"Look, I'm going to the monastery tomorrow to pick up some papers to bring back to Seattle. Do you want to come with me?"

Pam came around the corner carrying a plate full of sandwiches. "So, what are you two talking about back here?"

Joshua shrugged his shoulders. "Believe me, I wish I knew."

"No, you don't," Mark said under his breath.

Caroline was rearranging some artifacts in the shop's glass case when she first heard the sounds of a vehicle approaching on the dirt road. Finn had already run to the door. *Was it Aaron's motorcycle?* she wondered. Her heart raced as she listened closer.

She hadn't seen him since their fight at the fairgrounds, since she'd left him standing alone by the stage. Once at home, her anger had morphed into sadness that Aaron's volatility was, in sense, a deal breaker. And by midnight, sadness had churned into regret for ever meeting Aaron and putting herself into a new relationship. It was too soon. And he was not the right person.

The sound grew louder. But could it be him?

When the engine's vibration started rattling the windowpanes, Caroline knew it was a truck. Three bellowing honks preceded a high-pitched beeping, indicating that the truck was backing up.

She opened the shop door just as a huge U-Haul jumped the curb and rolled onto her lawn.

"Wait!" she yelled, running out and waving her arms. "You're on my grass!"

But the truck kept to a straight line as it crept backward toward the shop's entrance until it was no farther than five feet away.

Caroline ripped off her gloves. "Are you crazy?" she screamed as the motor turned off.

Both doors swung open.

"Always! That's what keeps us sane!" Mark said, sliding out of the driver's seat. Pam was right behind him. From the other side, Joshua and Brooke jumped out.

"What are you guys doing here?" Caroline shrieked in joy.

"Killing your grass, for one thing," Brooke said, giving her a kiss.

"Sorry," Pam said. "But I'm hoping you'll forgive us when you see what we brought you."

Mark swung open the back of the U-Haul, and Caroline's jaw dropped. The truck was packed to the brim with furniture—very expensive furniture. The boxes were carefully marked with their contents: "Crystal," "Lamps," "Fine China."

"The best from my mother's estate," Pam explained.

"I don't understand."

"We thought we might help each other out. I need to sell some furniture, and you might benefit from having additional furniture at your final sale."

Caroline was amazed. "I would. But these look like they're high-end antiques."

"Some of them are," Pam said. "Let's move them into your shop, and I'll help you price them." She hesitated. "But I didn't want this to be any more of a burden than what you're already facing."

Caroline looked at Brooke. "Is she really playing the 'let's not hurt Caroline any more than she's been hurt' card?"

"Only because she loves you," Brooke said.

"So are we good to go?" Mark asked.

Caroline nodded. "If you are, I am."

Mark and Joshua began to carry the valuables into the shop.

"It looks great in here," Mark called out to Caroline. "Looks like you're ready to go."

An hour later, the shop was rearranged to make room for "Pam's plunder," as Mark lovingly referred to the consignment.

Caroline caught Pam running her fingers along the back of a large upholstered chair. "Are you okay?"

Pam sighed. "This was my dad's favorite chair." Her voice cracked. "It all happened so quickly. I wasn't ready to let go of Mom, to let go of all these memories."

"You never lose the memories," Caroline said. "But if you ever want something back, just call me." She suddenly remembered something. "Wait a minute, guys! I forgot to inventory!"

"What inventory?" Brooke asked.

"There's got to be over fifty thousand dollars' worth of furniture here. I need to inventory and track the sale of each piece so I know how much I owe you."

Pam didn't see it as a problem. "Just assume anything you didn't have this morning is what we brought in. Put a price on it and take out your commission. Whatever is left over will be fine with me."

"That's how Kai would have done it, and that's why his business was in such shambles," Caroline pointed out.

Pam looked up. "I would have never thought it given your business background."

"I promised Kai that this was his world and I wouldn't intrude. It worked for both of us—his hobby slowly became an occupation, and I was always busy with Ross Enterprises. I thought he was taking care of the paperwork and the money. I'm just now finding out how messy it was."

"I'm guessing that was a shock," Pam said.

Caroline nodded. "I wasn't expecting a lot of things."

"There are secrets in every relationship," Mark said, trying his best to sound casual.

"Yeah, but I thought we were rock solid. I never saw the cracks." Caroline exhaled loudly. "But I don't have anything to compare it to. Maybe I wished we could have shared the same passions, but he had God and his clocks, and twice a year, his island and his family. And I had—"

Pam picked up the sentence. "A very full and happy life before Kai came along."

"Exactly," Caroline agreed. "And look what happened to it. Look what happened to me."

"You'll find a way through," Brooke assured her.

"That's what Aaron said a few days ago."

Pam raised her brows in interest. "Aaron? As in Tom's brother?"

Caroline saw Pam's antennae rising. "Oh no, no, no, no," she said. "Don't look at me like that. He was just talking about getting through, saying that sometimes having hope for something is as good as having *it,* and that sometimes, when hope is all we have, that's what carries us forward."

"Good advice," Brooke sad.

Caroline's smile was thin and fleeting. "I thought it was at the time."

"And?" Pam asked.

"And nothing," Caroline insisted. "Sometimes I don't even know if a friendship is possible. His personality can turn on a dime."

"A little like you recently," Pam said to her husband.

"No, this is serious. Something comes over him, and suddenly he's filled with rage. His anger really scares me."

"But he's never—"

"Oh God, no," Caroline said. "But I could never live with someone so unpredictable."

"But you like him?" Brooke asked.

Caroline rolled her eyes. "Okay, you take away his moments of rage and he has some redeeming qualities; he's funny and loves big band music. The more I get to know him, the more impressed I am. But then he snaps and we're back at square one. And . . . oh, wait . . . one other thing: *I'm married!*" Caroline paused, and then continued in a more serious voice. "But it just keeps gnawing at me; as good-hearted and carefree as Aaron seems, I feel there's some dark secret that's under the surface. I don't know if it's anger or sadness, but there's a raw wound that gets scratched and he becomes a totally different person. Who knows? Maybe I just can't shake the image of when I first saw him, covered in blood." She shrugged her shoulders. "But it really doesn't matter—I have no plans to get to know him any better than I do now. Believe me, that door is permanently closed."

TWENTY
Waves

At Saint Cross Abbey, Alan stood over the table, his shoulders hunched. In front of him were stacks of copies that needed sorting—six full sets of forty pages each. FedEx envelopes were piled next to address labels to be filled out only after being hand carried by Joshua to Seattle.

"You look busy," Megan said, walking into the room. "Or bored."

Alan always thought Megan was a breath of fresh air whenever he saw her. "Probably the latter. But the packages are going out today."

Megan looked wary. "Why would you mail them from Saint Cross? Wouldn't that be telling the world exactly where you are?"

"It would, so I'm not," Alan explained. "A friend of Brother Matthew's is going to pick them up and mail them from another city."

"And who would that be?" she asked.

"A fellow by the name of Joshua."

A wave of relief visibly passed through Megan. "Perfect," she said.

"Do you think that's someone I can trust?" Alan asked, although Matthew had tried on several occasions to calm his fears.

233

"Totally. Joshua lived with the monks over at Montis, and now he works for my father. So yeah, he's as trustworthy as they come."

Alan sat down. He still hadn't recovered from his time in the woods, and was constantly frustrated by his lack of strength.

"You look tired," Megan said as she headed over to the bookshelf on the far side of the room.

"I am. Or maybe it's just that I haven't been outside since arriving here."

"I'd go stir-crazy," Megan said.

"Brother Matthew and I thought it was best that I stay inside because of the parishioners who work here," Alan explained. "Please don't misunderstand—I'm not complaining in the slightest. In fact, I don't know how I'm ever going to thank all of you. But I think I have cabin fever."

"Understandable," Megan said. She tilted her head and thought for a moment. "Do you trust me?"

"Of course I do."

"Then come on," she said, reaching out to take his hand. "Let's break out of here."

Leading Alan to the back entrance, Megan grabbed a wide-brimmed gardening hat and a smock. "Put these on, and keep your head down," she said. "We'll go directly to the truck. Just follow me."

Stepping outside, Alan was almost blinded by

the bright light of the full sun. The intense smells of pine trees and mulch washed over him.

Megan coughed to get his attention. "This way," she said softly.

Once in the truck, Megan told Alan to sit low in the front seat to avoid being seen.

Alan buried his chin in the smock and pulled the hat over his ears. "Where are you taking me?"

"Kettle Pond," she said. She was quiet for several minutes of driving before continuing. "I'll have you know that moving from Oregon to join the monks at Saint Cross was a difficult time for me. I always supported the idea because I knew our abbey and our wine business needed more space than what was available to us in Troutdale. But my emotional side didn't quite see it so clearly. I felt I had left my home in Oregon and left the one monastery I knew." They were now several miles from Franklin. "You can get up now," she said, removing his hat for him. "So," she continued, "instead of turning to the community for support, I turned inward. In my little free time during that first year, I went off on my own and explored the area."

"Did you ever tell anyone how you felt?"

"No, but I should have," she said. "And they know now."

"Was it God who kept you here?"

Megan blinked, startled by such a direct question. "Wow, you go right to the bottom line."

"I'm sorry. Was that inappropriate to ask?"

Megan shook her head, her blond hair breaking over her shoulders. "No. Just unexpected." Megan looked over at Alan. He had one arm out the window, and his face was lifted up to the sun. "So, one fall day I stumbled on this small lake. None of the monks knew about it, and it was only referenced once on a US geological survey map in 1952."

"So you named it Kettle Pond?"

She nodded.

"Why that name?"

"It's more of a geological name. Kettles are bodies of water formed by retreating glaciers." She paused. " 'I went to the woods because I wished to live deliberately.' "

"That sounds familiar."

"Thoreau. Walden Pond is another kettle hole."

"Who knew?" Alan teased.

Megan blushed. "Only a geek geoscientist."

"You know a lot about the earth."

She grimaced. "It was my college major."

"I'm so surprised."

Her brows rose. "Because I'm a woman?"

"Because you're a beautiful woman, yes. Because you're a nun, yes. Because of how you cared for me, yes. And a handful of other reasons I can't think of right now. But I just have to ask; were rocks something that weirdly fascinated you as a child?"

Megan laughed heartily. "I so wish it was, but it's a more convoluted story than that."

"I'm all ears."

Alan had turned in his seat and now had his back against the door, looking directly at her.

"My father owns one of the largest vineyards in the country—Copeland Vineyards."

"Huh. I didn't expect that either."

She nodded as she tightened her grip on the steering wheel. "It was always assumed that I would take over the family business."

"Not a bad business, all in all," Alan said, laughing.

"Better than pig farming, I suppose." But then she frowned. When she spoke her voice betrayed some bitterness. "That expectation hung over me for as long as I can remember. My father had me sampling wine when I was four years old. After my mom died when I was six, it was just him and me. He so loved his grapes that he wanted to share his knowledge and his passion with me. And without a mother at home, when I wasn't at school, I was with him in the vineyards or at one of his processing plants."

"Did you enjoy it?" Alan asked.

"I don't remember ever thinking about it. I was just like any other kid growing up in familiar circumstances that surrounded me. Comparing a Merlot and a Bordeaux at my twelfth birthday party was just normal. And when I went away to college, I followed the one curriculum that best prepared me to carry on my dad's business." She sharply braked to avoid hitting a squirrel. "After graduating, I worked next to him for several years, but then . . ."

"Then you found God," Alan suggested.

"I don't know if I found God exactly. But it was the only reason for leaving the business that my father would ever accept."

"Do you at least enjoy the wine?"

She thought for a moment. "I *appreciate* wine. I think wine is a lot like opera. Those who immediately love it will love it forever. Those who don't can learn to appreciate it."

"So you told your father you wanted to be a nun?"

"That sounds so simple, but it wasn't. It was painful. I disappointed him in ways I can't ever imagine."

"I'm sure that's not the case," Alan said.

"Yes, it is," she said unequivocally. "Family is hard sometimes."

"Agreed, more than you would ever know."

"It baffles me when people say they wished they had a larger family. I feel they don't understand all of the complications that those relationships come with. But Dad and I are good now. We support each other every way we can."

"So God was your out?"

Megan blinked. Again, she was startled not

only by what Alan said but by his unapologetic directness. "The pond is down this road," she replied, avoiding the question.

Turning onto an old logging trail with deep ruts and a high center ridge, the truck bottomed out every hundred yards. Megan slowed to a crawl.

Sensing he had gone too far, Alan leaned his head out the window. He was in awe of the surroundings; the trees were some of the tallest he had ever seen, and the peaks of the mountains looked close enough to touch. "This is incredible."

Megan smiled. "You haven't seen anything yet."

The road ended a mile farther on, where an enormous boulder twice the size of the truck blocked their way.

Megan jumped out. "It's another half mile."

"Lead the way."

They didn't talk while they walked through the dense woods. Again, Alan was overcome by the scents of the forest. Fifteen minutes later, they came to an opening, and Alan couldn't help but to be awestruck.

"My God," he whispered.

In front of him was one of the most pristine sights he had ever seen. An eagle screeched, its call echoing against the mountains. The water was deep-azure blue, and rock formations of massive cliffs jutted straight up from the water. Between the cliffs, right next to the water's edge, were large evergreens. A flock of geese paddled along the surface at the far side of the pond.

"This is indescribable," Alan said.

"Breathtaking, isn't it?" Megan asked.

"Have you gone swimming here?"

She pulled back slightly. "On occasion."

"Do you mind if I go in?" he asked as he longingly looked at the water. "It's been so long since my body has felt good."

"If you don't mind the cold." Megan laughed. "It's fcd by the snow melt."

"Do you want to join me?"

Megan was intrigued by the offer but passed. "No, thanks. I didn't bring a suit."

"Neither did I, but it's all innocent, I assure you."

She believed him, but it was beneath her decorum. "I'm sure, but thank you anyway. I'll be over by the cliff. Take as much time as you want."

A few minutes later, Megan heard a splash and looked over her shoulder. There was a frothy ring where Alan had entered the water after diving from a rock overhang not far from where they had parted. The ducks scattered and took flight.

A few seconds later, he bobbed to the surface. He screamed out. "It's freezing!"

"I know!" she called back.

He started swimming toward the far beach and then swam back. He was so enjoying himself that he appeared to forget about Megan and didn't look in her direction. Standing behind several trees, Megan watched him out of curiosity, remembering earlier days when she skinny-dipped with boyfriends.

When Alan pulled himself out of the water, she gasped. He was naked. And he had a great physique. He climbed up on the rock and, running at full speed, pushed off and stretched out his body before hitting the water. He swam back and forth again, occasionally disappearing under the surface, only to reappear with a big smile. Every so often, he would wave to her from the water before continuing to swim in random circles.

The drive home was quiet. Alan had immediately fallen asleep. Every few minutes Megan looked over at him. By the time they returned to Saint Cross, she had memorized his profile perfectly.

TWENTY-ONE

Guise

Pam sat at the kitchen table, nervously tapping her pencil on a pad of paper.

"Do you think we should offer a complimentary stay at Montis?"

"No," Mark replied without paying attention. "We're already overbooked for the next six months." He was thumbing through a copy of *Handyman*. "Hey, look at this cool chop saw."

"Mark! Are you listening? I think we should give a courtesy stay at Montis," she said.

He briefly looked up from the paper. "We have too much to do as is. Don't you think we're busy enough?"

"Yes, but it might be nice to have some kind of drawing. We can just pick a name—any name—from the phone book," she suggested.

Mark looked at his wife suspiciously. "The Lumby phone book? I think the last one was printed ten years ago, and some of those folks have died since then."

"Well, not the Lumby phone book exactly." Pam stalled. "Maybe one from, I don't know, Virginia."

"*Virginia?*"

Their two dogs looked up, hearing Mark's disbelief.

"Well, it only makes sense," Pam retorted. "We both lived there for most of our adult lives."

"It makes no sense at all, and I know you too well to suggest something that makes no sense," Mark said, putting down the newspaper on his lap. "So, do you want to tell me what's going on?"

Pam pushed away the pad of paper in frustration. "All right. I want to meet Janet Wing. There, I said it. I want her and her husband to come to Montis, and I don't know how to lure them here."

"Lure or trap?" Mark asked with a soft laugh.

"That's not funny," Pam said, throwing a pencil at him.

"No offense, sweetheart, but you've been stalking them online every day since your return from Connecticut. Your obsession might be getting a little out of control."

Pam was about to argue the point, but she knew Mark was right. Janet Wing had become an obsession—her obsession, and everything else in her life had suffered because of it.

Mark became pensive, which he rarely did. "If you need to fabricate a lottery to get her here and bring this to closure, then you have my support."

"But I don't want to bring anything to closure,"

Pam said. "Just the opposite—I want to start something that I'll have the rest of my life. I want to have an incredibly close relationship with my sister."

"Who you've never met," Mark reminded her. "Who might be a—"

"Criminal? She's not!" Pam jumped up. "I paid for a full background check."

"You didn't," Mark said. "Did you?"

"Well, I had to know something about her," Pam protested.

"And what did you find out?"

"Almost nothing. Just the bare facts. Either she's in a witness protection program or she's as pure as the driven snow."

"Like I said, honey, be careful what you wish for. She might not be someone you want in your life."

"She has a credit card at Neiman Marcus. How bad can she be?"

"How do you get *that* information?"

"Don't ask," Pam said, closing that door. "But she lives a clean life. She hasn't had a ticket in ten years. Not even a parking violation."

"Well, you said that her only photo was taken in Morocco. Maybe they haven't lived in the States that long."

"Those are the things I want to find out, and to get her here, I need—"

"A hook."

Pam chuckled. "I was going to say, a legitimate reason that doesn't make them suspicious."

"Yeah, a hook. I'm great at that sort of spy stuff. Have you Googled their house?"

"A very nice estate in Great Falls."

Mark thought about the problem she had posed. "So, assume that she subscribes to at least one of the higher-end culinary or home-decor magazines. Send her a letter saying that we drew her name from the subscribers of a select handful of publications for a complimentary midweek stay. She just might believe it."

"And what happens if she doesn't?" Pam asked.

"What happens if she does?" Mark asked ominously. He picked up the newspaper and flipped through the pages. He stopped when something caught his eye.

"Hey, honey, do you like these socks?" He lifted the page and pointed to a photo of a man sitting cross-legged wearing a pair of vibrantly colored socks.

Pam studied the image. "Why is his face all smudged?"

"Oh, it's from that espionage trial in DC. They do that to protect the identity of the spies," Mark explained with full gravitas. "But I've never seen socks like those." He studied them a bit longer. "I like them."

"Your birthday is coming up. Tear out the photo and put it by the computer."

"Thanks, honey. I'll love wearing them downtown."

"I'm sure you'll be setting new style trends along Main Street in Lumby."

"And I think they might look sharp at our next debate. It might even make Duke Blackstone a little jealous."

"I doubt that, but I love you anyway." She kissed him on the forehead. "If nothing else, you're so easy to please. Remember, Brooke and Joshua are coming over for dinner tonight. They're flying back to Seattle early tomorrow morning, so it won't be a late night for any of us."

"They're going to miss the debate?" Mark asked.

"Yeah. Aren't they the lucky ones?" Pam replied, walking out of the room.

As soon as their guests arrived, Mark grabbed Joshua by the sleeve. "We're going outside to look at the—the—roof." Mark stumbled over his words.

Pam spun around. "What's wrong with the roof?"

"Nothing at all," Joshua said. "I just wanted to ask Mark a question about your soffits," he said over his shoulder as the two men walked out. Clipper and Cutter ran after them, thinking that a game was about to begin.

Once they were out of earshot from their wives, Joshua asked, "What's wrong with you?"

"I just can't lie to Pam. I know she'll see right through me."

"Well, you need to keep up the guise for another couple weeks," Joshua said.

"Did you go to Saint Cross?"

"I had a long talk with Brother Matthew and, yes, I met Alan Blackstone. Nice fellow," Joshua said. "He certainly is in a bad way."

"So they told you everything?"

Joshua laughed. "Probably more than they explained to you. There have been a few new developments since you were there, and Alan asked that I explain them to you."

Mark cringed. "I don't want to know. The more I know, the worse I feel, and I'm sure I'm just going to spill the beans one of these nights."

"You know you can't do that, Mark. Get a grip," Joshua said. "Alan's life is definitely in danger, and he has reason to believe that he has been tracked to this area."

Mark was stunned. "How can that be? No one knows he's with the monks."

"As it turns out, one reporter tracked him into the woods, heading west. That would bring him to Lumby or Franklin."

Mark's eyes opened wide. "What is he going to do?"

"I hope you don't mind, but I told Alan that

if he had to get out of Saint Cross quickly, he should come here, to Montis."

"I guess that would work, but Pam would have to be told." Mark was thinking out loud. "But then again, she's so focused on meeting her sister and getting through this campaign that she might not notice another guest checking in."

"Alan asked me to mail several packages once I get back to Seattle. I'll use the addresses that Megan checked out, and will anonymously deliver them to the police and to the FBI. There'll be less of a chance of crossing paths with one of Duke's paid cronies. If anything needs to be sent back to Alan, I'll mail it to you and you can drive them to the monastery." Joshua paused, rethinking the conversation with Alan. "I think Alan believes this has become bigger then Duke wanting to lay a pipeline across the state, and now it's involving elected officials in DC."

"Officials?" Mark asked.

"Senators."

Mark's jaw dropped. "Wow."

Brooke walked into the front yard with two cold beers. "What are you two up to?"

"Just getting caught up," Joshua said casually.

Mark exhaled. "God, for a former monk you're so good at this," he said under his breath, but a bit too loud.

"Good at what?" Pam asked as she joined the others.

"Juggling our travel to and from Seattle," Joshua said without skipping a beat.

Pam put her arm around Brooke. "You know how much we miss you. I hope you'll be back for our July Fourth celebration."

"We'll try not to, but I'm not sure when we'll be back," Brooke said, looking at her husband.

"Well, you have to be here," Mark said. "I'll need some help with the fireworks."

"Serious help," Pam said.

"We'll do our best," Joshua said, jabbing Mark in the side.

"And perhaps you'll even get a chance to meet my sister," Pam said. "I mailed off an invitation this afternoon."

"Are you sure you know what you're doing?" Brooke asked, concerned.

"Ha! See, Pam, I'm not crazy," Mark said, before turning to Brooke. "That's exactly what I told her!"

"He might have a point," Brooke said. "I want a family as much as anyone. And I know how awful it feels to be alone in the world. But life is more complex now. People aren't who they say they are or who they appear to be. Maybe it's a sign of the times, or just the technology that's allowing all of these lies. You just hear so many stories of folks making up their own identity, or worse, assuming someone else's."

"I think all of you are a bunch of naysayers," Pam said.

"We're just trying to protect you, honey."

"As long as you can protect me from Duke Blackstone, that's all I want."

As Pam learned that Wednesday, nothing could have protected her from her opponent's onslaught. Simple lessons of behavior and common courtesy learned during adolescence fell by the wayside, as did the core principles of truth and respect. Of the two hundred town residents who attended, assuming that serious issues would be addressed in open discussion, more than half left as soon as it became obvious that it was no more than a platform for Duke's personal attacks on Pam. Even Biscuit and his owner excused themselves from the stage less than ten minutes into what Pam would later call "the carnage of politics."

That night in bed, Pam tossed and turned as she replayed snippets and sound bites in her head, over and over again. With no sleep, she finally rose several hours before dawn and started her day.

When the Inn's phone rang at 9:05 a.m., she was on her fourth cup of coffee and feeling no better.

"Montis Inn," Pam answered, feeling exhausted.

"Good morning, I hope I'm not calling too early," a woman with a chirpy voice said.

"Not at all," Pam replied, rolling her eyes. "How can I help you?"

"This is Janet Wing."

Pam almost dropped the phone. This was it.

"I received an invitation from your inn," she continued. "I'm sorry, but I was unsure if it was genuine."

Pam was unprepared for the call. "As genuine as Montis Abbey," she said, smacking herself in the forehead. *How stupid did that sound?* she thought. "Your name was drawn from a pool of subscribers."

"That's what I didn't quite understand," Janet said politely. "Although I read most of those magazines, I don't believe I've ever subscribed to any—they're mostly given to us by our friends. Although that might disqualify us from your drawing, I didn't want there to be any misunderstanding."

At least she's honest, Pam thought. "None at all," she said, trying to think of a reasonable-sounding explanation. "I'm sure the names that we received also included potential subscribers."

"Is there someone in management that you would like to check with?" Janet asked.

Pam laughed. "That's not necessary. I'm Pam Walker, owner and occasionally referred to as the management."

"Oh! Excuse me," Janet said, her voice lifting in delight. "It's so nice to talk with you!"

"Likewise." *You have no idea,* Pam thought.

"So, may I confirm our dates with you?"

"Definitely."

"We thought we might arrive on July second and stay for eight days if that's not too much of an imposition."

July Fourth weekend, one of their busiest of the year. "That sounds perfect," Pam said. "And there will be two of you?"

"Yes, my husband, Bill, and I."

"Consider your room reserved," Pam said. "And do you need a ride from the airport?"

"Oh, definitely not. We're quite self-reliant, and Bill is tremendously resourceful. But thank you, anyway."

"All right, then. If you have any questions in the meantime, please don't hesitate to call."

"Oh, we don't want to impose any more than we have already, but I do have a question about your restaurant. The reviews that I've read are so charming, and they all mention that your restaurant is unmatched in the entire area."

"We take a lot of pride in our menu," Pam said.

"Are reservations needed for dinner?"

"Not for guests staying with us."

"Then we'll plan to see you on the second," Janet said happily.

"I can't tell you how much I'm looking forward to meeting you."

"Until then," Janet said before hanging up.

TWENTY-TWO

Endings

Caroline retraced the same route she'd driven at least three times a week since laying her grandmother to rest ten years ago. From Farm to Market Road she turned onto a roughly paved road that ended at a one-room, nondenominational church not used since 1954. Next to the church was Lumby's town cemetery, which held hundreds of tombstones, most so worn and weathered that the etchings were no longer legible. One, though, was newer granite with intricately carved wording:

CHARLOTTE CAROLINE ROSS

The caretaker, a deaf man who still remembered the rainy day seventy-four years before when he stood next to the raging river and threw dirt onto his great-grandfather's coffin, tended the grounds seven days a week for lack of any other interests. For the longest time after her grandmother's death, he was the only person Caroline was comfortable being around. Perhaps it was because Old Josiah couldn't hear her sobs as she stood over the grave, but it was probably because Old

Josiah thought nothing more or less of death than he did of living—in his mind, it was two sides of the same coin, a cycle unnaturally incomplete until the soul was finally laid to rest. For that reason, he expressed no remorse or sympathy and showed no awkward self-consciousness when he and Caroline exchanged glances or a gentle nod of the head when she visited the cemetery regardless of the weather.

When she arrived that day, Old Josiah was sitting on the stone wall that ran between the graveyard and the road, where she usually parked. He lifted his hand, swerving it back and forth in the air as if it was a fish swimming upstream.

"No," she said, facing him squarely so he could read her lips. "Finn's not with me today. He's at home, sleeping."

Old Josiah pressed his hands together in prayer and looked to the heavens as if to thank a distant god.

Caroline patted him lightly on the shoulder as she walked by—her way of saying that she understood. The last time Finn had joined her, she naïvely let him off the leash while she stood by CC's grave. When Caroline finally glanced up, the cemetery looked as if a small tornado had passed through: limbs were dragged from the woods, holes dug in sacred ground, and a shoe had appeared out of nowhere, its origins disturbingly unknown.

She tucked her most recent letter into the ground next to the cold granite.

> Dear CC, Today I learned that you can never go back. I feel naked and stupid and utterly lost. If there is a reason for everything that's happening to me, I certainly don't see it. Would you please reach down from heaven to explain it to me because I can't figure it out on my own!
>
> All I know is that I'm no longer the person you used to admire, who you entrusted your companies to. I am abandoned and alone.
>
> Love, Caroline

When Aaron walked into the shop that afternoon, Caroline was focused on sorting through Kai's old notes. Each page needed to be carefully reviewed and then filed or trashed.

"You look busy."

Caroline jumped in her seat, knocking a pile of papers from her lap.

"God, you scared me!" she said.

"I'm sorry. I thought you heard me knock."

Caroline collected the scattered papers from the

floor. "Not when I'm working on something. I tune everything out."

"You're still shaking. Take a deep breath," he said as he looked around the shop. "Wow, these antiques are stunning."

"And soon they'll be out of here," Caroline said.

"I can't tell if that's something you want or you're dreading," he said, pulling a four-wheeled stool out from under the table. It was Kai's stool. A stool she had nicknamed Zippey but never sat on herself.

"Don't—!" Caroline screamed.

Aaron was startled. "What!"

"The stool . . ." she began, reaching out.

"Is it broken?" Aaron asked, rolling it back and forth a few times.

"No," she said softly, as if defeated. How could she ever explain?

Aaron sat down and spun around several times. "This is great," he said as he forcefully pushed off. The stool carried him across the room at a surprising speed.

Caroline knew her rising anger was unreasonable, so she sat there, speechless. Since she couldn't share what Zippey had once meant to Kai and to her, she shut down. She just wished Aaron would leave.

"Are you okay?" Aaron asked as he wheeled his way toward her.

"Fine."

"Fine, really? Or fine, it's time for you to go."

"The latter," she whispered.

Aaron was clearly baffled. "Not until I get an explanation."

"For what?" Her entire body went rigid.

"For what just happened between us."

"Nothing," Caroline snapped.

"I deserve more than that from you."

"You must be kidding me! I can't believe you just said that!" she screamed. "For no reason, you turn into a storm of thunderous rage, and then you say it's nothing!" Caroline looked away as she started crying. "And you would never understand."

"If you give me a chance, I might."

She whipped around and exploded. "Why do I always have to explain?" Her anger was compounded by her sadness, and those emotions were all directed at Aaron. "Maybe I don't want to have to explain everything. Maybe I don't want to tell you how important that stool was to Kai." Her voice was getting louder. "You will never understand what I'm going through! In a few days I will be getting rid of everything that mattered to my husband—to us—and that pain of utter failure hasn't diminished one bit. It's deeper now because I have had to live with it every day—seeing how people look at me, knowing how I let him change me."

257

Rather than retreating, Aaron pushed the stool next to Caroline's chair and went to put his arms around her, to ease her pain with his tenderness. But she wouldn't allow it. She pushed him away.

"Just go," she said, sounding utterly exhausted and totally defeated.

"I'm not going anywhere."

"Get out! You're not wanted here. You're not wanted in my life," she yelled.

The words had been said, but they both knew she didn't mean them.

Her demand turned into a heart-wrenching plea so soft he could barely hear her. "Please go."

And Aaron finally complied. He rolled the stool back to where he'd found it and walked out the door, as frustrated and confused as ever.

Given how miserably the last couple of days had gone for Caroline, when Brooke suggested a girls' night out with Pam and Mac in Wheatley, she quickly accepted. If nothing else, close friends and a few glasses of wine would improve her mood.

"This is fantastic," Brooke said as she gazed around the restaurant. Crystal glasses glistened on freshly starched tablecloths. Large hurricane candles burned in the middle of each table.

"They opened a few weeks ago, and the reviews have been great," Pam said. "They might attract some of our business, so I've been wanting to see firsthand."

Mac leaned in and said in a whisper, "Are you sure we can afford this?"

"Worst case, we can just get an appetizer and blame it on our diets," Caroline said.

Brooke laughed. "And what diets would those be?"

"The ones we're women enough to ignore," Pam quipped.

"At least for tonight," Caroline said.

"Look at that," Mac said, drawn toward an expansive mahogany bar just off the dining room. "That's stunning craftsmanship."

"The man or the wood?" Brooke teased.

"Actually, both," Mac replied.

Pam led the way to the bar. "I think we should begin with appletinis. Any other suggestions?" she asked.

After spending an hour at the bar, the women had a spectacular four-course dinner. Afterward, at the suggestion of the bartender, they walked a block up Maple Street for after-dinner drinks at the White Hart Inn.

It was a Friday night and the bar was bustling. Bodies bumped and meshed, drinks were poured, and boisterous laughter came from all corners. The women had two rounds of lemon drop shots on the house before they were able to grab an empty table. After one more round, paid for by interested fellows, Caroline was asked to dance but declined.

"You should go out there," Pam said, nudging Caroline.

"I'll pass. Or pass out. My head's already spinning," Caroline said.

"To my soul sisters, one and all!" Mac toasted before emptying the shot glass. "I haven't partied like this in ages."

"Me neither," Pam said, pushing her empty glass toward the center of the table.

Caroline gazed around slowly at her friends. "Am I totally drunk, or do all of you ladies look absolutely stunning tonight?"

"You're drunk," Pam shot back.

Brooke gave Caroline a hug. "I was about to say the same thing about you."

Caroline glanced down at her clothes, saw the wrinkles in her blouse and began pressing her hands down the silk, trying to smooth out the material.

"It's nice to see you out of your sweats," Pam added.

Caroline crunched her nose. "They need to be burned, don't they?"

The responses came in a chorus. "No, not at all," Pam and Mac said.

"Well, maybe returned to the closet," Brooke suggested.

"But they're so comfortable."

"I'm with Caroline," Mac said. "I vote for comfort. Thank God I'm married to a veterinarian who has such low expectations of my wardrobe."

"Well, that's because Dr. Candor is perfect in every way," Pam teased.

Brooke laughed loudly. "As if Mark isn't?"

Pam rolled her eyes. "You have no idea what I have to deflect every day. He's like a fly to a light bulb—he just can't stay away from . . ." They all waited for Pam. "Mishaps."

Mac burst out laughing. "Is that what you call them now?"

"But he has such good intentions," Caroline said. "If I could find the combination of your two husbands—"

"And what's wrong with Joshua?" Brooke asked.

Caroline blushed. "Well, he was a monk!"

"I guarantee you, he's not now," Brooke said, raising her eyebrows. "Carnal knowledge and all that religious stuff, you know what I mean?"

The women started laughing so hard that many in the bar turned and looked.

A round of drinks arrived at the table, courtesy of two men standing at the bar. One of them raised his glass and nodded at Caroline.

"Caroline can pick them up a mile away, even when she's not trying," Brooke said.

Pam watched the men watching Caroline.

261

"That's because she's the only one not wearing a wedding ring."

"Yeah, you go with that thought, Pam," Brooke said. "The reality is, we just don't have the 'it' factor."

Pam ignored her. "He's trying to get your attention," she whispered to Caroline.

Caroline didn't even give the man a second look. "I'll pass."

"I'll take care of it," Brooke said.

"Take care of *what?*" Caroline asked.

Without answering, Brooke sashayed over to the bar and introduced herself to their benefactors. After a minute of conversation, Brooke stumbled back to the table.

"Girls, the one on the left is Jason, and Doug is his friend."

When Jason nodded, his dirty-blond hair fell over his eyes.

"He wants to know if we'd like another round," Brooke said.

"He's gorgeous," Caroline mumbled.

One more round of drinks later, the two men finally got the message that it was a girls-only party, and disappeared into the crowd. While Mac was making her final toast of the evening, a noise at the front of the bar drew Caroline's attention. Although the room was spinning around her, she was able to make out a man walking in the front door.

"Aaron?" Caroline said. But the man was a blur.

Pam raised her brows. "Aaron?"

"Is that Aaron?" Caroline asked, squinting as she tried to look through the crowd.

The last thing Caroline remembered that night was getting up from her seat and staggering in a very crooked line toward the man she thought was Aaron.

When Caroline woke, before opening her eyes, she noticed the smell—it was the scent of starched bed sheets. She buried her nose in the pillow and inhaled deeply. It was definitely not her pillow. She opened her eyes just enough to look around; there were two queen-sized beds. The morning sun was already above the trees.

She pressed her hands against her temples, trying to suppress the worst hangover she'd ever had in her life. *Where am I?* She peered down at herself under the sheets. *And why am I naked?*

The bathroom door was ajar and she held her breath, dreading hearing a man's voice. *Oh God, is that Aaron?*

The front door to the room burst open and she screamed.

"Good morning," Brooke sang out as she walked in carrying three large paper coffee cups.

Mac was right behind her with a tray of pastries.

Caroline slid farther under the sheets, trying to remember what happened the night before. "Where are we?"

"At the White Hart Inn," Brooke answered. "We were all too drunk to drive home last night."

"And who's in the bathroom?"

"It's only me," Pam called out.

Caroline stayed under the covers. "You three were here all night?"

"All night," Brooke promised.

Caroline's head spun. "So Aaron wasn't here?"

Mac gave her a penetrating look. "Not that I'm aware of."

"The man who came into the bar?" Caroline asked.

"The guy you walked up to before you sort of passed out?" Pam asked. "His name was Steve and he was looking for his wife."

Caroline sighed, but it wasn't necessarily a sigh of relief. She shook her head, trying to clear her thoughts through the hangover. "What time is it?"

"It's six forty-five. Time to rise," Mac said, throwing Caroline her clothes. "We need to get back to Lumby. I'm supposed to be on a job site, and today's your big day."

"The shop! It's supposed to open in a couple of hours." Caroline yanked on her shirt. "And poor Finn!"

"Don't worry, I'll go back with you. Everything will be fine," Brooke said.

When they arrived at the mill, Caroline immediately ran inside, expecting to find the disaster that always followed when Finn was left alone for too long. Instead, she found him asleep on the sofa. Other than an empty food bowl, everything in the house was in order.

"So much for thinking he was wildly missing me all night," Caroline quipped as she leaned over and kissed the dog on the nose. "You're such a good boy, I hardly recognize you."

Going into the kitchen to feed Finn, Caroline spotted an unfamiliar basket on the table. Inside were dozens of freshly baked muffins, and on top, a handwritten note: "Sorry about yesterday. Wishing you all the success. Aaron."

Brooke looked over Caroline's shoulder to read the note. "Aaron?" Brooke asked. "They're still warm—he must have brought them over this morning. Did you give him a key to your house?"

"No! Absolutely not. But he knows my door is always unlocked," Caroline explained. "And don't give me that look. It's not what you're thinking."

Brooke feigned innocence. "All I'm thinking is that any man who offers blueberry muffins must be worth his weight in gold."

After grabbing coffee and several of Aaron's

muffins, Caroline and Brooke headed downstairs to open the shop doors.

"Pam and Mark should be pulling up any minute," Brooke said.

"It's nice that they offered, but this is a little embarrassing . . . a lot embarrassing. I feel like I'm washing the dirty laundry of our marriage in public. And just to ensure I haven't been humiliated enough, no one's going to show up."

"I like that positive thinking," Brooke joked.

Hearing a car approach, they both looked down Chicory Lane just as a DHL truck came into sight. Once parked, the driver jumped out with a clipboard and large envelope in hand.

"Caroline Talin?"

Caroline raised her hand. "That's me."

"Sign here, please."

As soon as he gave Caroline the envelope, she ripped it open. After reading the first few lines, she shook her head. "Unbelievable!" she gasped. She continued to read, quickly flipping the pages.

"What is it?" Brooke asked.

Caroline exclaimed in disbelief, "Kai is suing *me* for divorce."

Brooke found this funny. "Okay, at least you now know where he stands."

Caroline smacked Brooke's arm with the papers. "Kai has ordered me—*ordered me!*—to ship all the furniture to Indonesia. Like I'm going to do that. Ha!"

"Are you going to call Russell?" Brooke asked, referring to Russell Harris, their acquaintance and attorney in town.

Caroline fought to push her crushing disappointment aside. "Soon enough," she said. "But not today."

"So what are you going to do with the furniture?"

Caroline stuffed the papers back in the envelope and marched to the shop.

"Sell it all!" she yelled defiantly as she lifted her fist in the air. "Kai just pushed the wrong button, and there is no turning back now."

Dear CC, You always used to tell me that one of the secrets in life is to pick a lane, keep your head down and move forward. Well, last weekend I did, and I ran the first race toward fixing up my life. The ground floor of the mill is now empty other than the pinions and gears that operate the wheel. The shop is closed.

On Saturday morning, we had more dogs than people with Pam and Mark's Labs and Tom's Dalmatians. But soon a long trail of cars formed in and out of Chicory Lane. Most were acquaintances from Lumby who arrived early, just wanting to wish me well, but Sunday brought at least a hundred serious buyers. Pam's furniture from her mother's estate sold within hours, as did most of the clocks. When all was said and done, the donation truck that came at the end only had a few boxes of knickknacks to take away.

I know you're smiling. I know you're thinking that it's past time I pick a lane and fight those battles.

Love, Caroline

TWENTY-THREE
Selfies
The Lumby Lines

**WHAT'S NEWS
AROUND TOWN**

The town council has repealed all permits issued to the thirty-six cows expected to run in this year's Moo Doo Iditarod. Although the long-standing event is a favorite among residents, the cleanup of the "residual droppings" along Main Street cost the town $2,300 last year, with that line item being contentiously dropped from the budget shortly thereafter. The town council's decision to discontinue the Moo Doo Iditarod is expected to be one of the more divisive issues in the next mayoral debate.

Dr. Tom Candor reports an unusually high number of office visits for canine dermatitis, and suggests that his clients refrain from artificially bleaching their dogs' coats, contrary to what many have read in the recent BuzzFeed article. When asked if he endorses any pooch hairstyles lauded on social media, Dr. Candor replied, "Tempting, but no."

Sheriff's Complaints

SHERIFF SIMON DIXON

7:02 a.m. Moose vs MINI Cooper on State Road 541. Moose wins.

7:12 a.m. Lumby Sporting Goods reported that someone strapped a bra (size 48DD) on the wooden cow in front of the store. Said bra has since been tacked to the wall behind the bar at Jimmy D's.

7:29 a.m. Phil Conner requested any information about owner of said bra. He can be reached at 925-3928.

2:09 p.m. Postmistress reported noxious odors coming from PO Box 17. LFD called and post office evacuated. No follow-up provided.

4:17 p.m. Caller reported draft horse trotting down Farm to Market Road at MM6.

3:35 p.m. Reverend Olson reported burst pipe over crucifix at Holy Episcopal. Sunday's sermon changed to "The Mystery of Holy Water."

Brian Beezer sat at his father's desk in the Chatham Press building reading the morning's *New York Times*.

"Since when are you ever on time for a meeting?" Dennis Beezer asked as he walked into his office.

"Since when are you ever twenty minutes late for a meeting?" Brian retorted.

Dennis looked down at his watch. "You're right about that, sorry. I got tied up with a call at home."

Brian started to stand but his father waved him down. "No, stay there," he said, grabbing a seat on the other side of the desk. He looked around his office. "I don't know if I've ever sat here before. Quite a different perspective."

Brian stacked a tall pile of envelopes scattered on his desk. "You should go through your mail, Dad," his son advised.

"I've already pulled out the bills, but be my guest."

Brian thumbed through the mail. One had a return name of "Pat Petrosyan."

He raised his brows. "Petrosyan?"

"The one and only, I imagine."

"Why is she writing *you*?"

"I'll try not to take that as an insult," Dennis said.

"You have to admit, you and Petrosyan are worlds apart on so many levels."

271

"Well, you've underestimated your father. She called the other week asking about our publishing services for her daughter's book, *Turn the Paige*. After she explained the project, I told her that The Bindery was not the type of publisher she needed, but she insisted on sending us her blanket contract-and-confidentiality statement."

Brian ripped open the envelope. In addition to the document his father had mentioned, there was also a four-sentence description with sample photographs.

"Paige Petrosyan wants to publish a book of her *selfies?*"

"Evidently," Dennis answered with disdain.

"That's epic," Brian said with a smile. "They are masterminds of media. But why would Pat Petrosyan want Chatham Press when they could have their pick of any publishing house in the world?"

"I asked the same question. She said a few reasons; it seems her first husband brought her to Lumby when they married forty years ago, so she has always been fond of the town. She's also wildly paranoid about leaks, and said that a small press wouldn't present the risks of pre-release copies getting sold to the press, or of any unauthorized interviews. And, finally, she's a huge fan of the monks."

"Of Saint Cross Abbey?" Brian was shocked.

"Well, of their rum sauce. And she likes their

books that we published, which amazes me because I wouldn't have thought she knew how to read," Dennis said in a condescending tone.

"Dad," Brian warned. "No matter what you think of the Petrosyans, only one face is more recognizable than Paige Petrosyan in the world, and that's the Pope."

"I know who the Petrosyans are, and I know the rest of the world does as well, but, Brian, they have done absolutely *nothing* to justify their fame or their money." Dennis was just getting started. "Worse, they've contributed nothing to society. They are the bottom-feeders—they are the takers. They take everything they can, and they give nothing back."

"Per you."

"Yes, per me, and I own The Bindery and still decide what gets put on paper. And a selfie of Paige Petrosyan's breasts is not what I consider of any value to anyone."

"So you now have ethical requirements for publishing a book?"

"I refuse to be a pawn in their shallow, narcissistic world."

"Dad, Paige Petrosyan has eighteen million twitter followers. She has one of the world's highest Snapchat numbers."

"Whatever that is."

"You're sounding obsolete."

"And so I am." Dennis slapped his hand on his

desk in frustration. "I don't want to live in a world where Facebook followers take precedence over content. Petrosyan's book is nothing more than a self-absorbed, trashy collection of pornographic photos that you can get from any hooker in the bowels of Chicago."

"But there's a big difference: I unconditionally guarantee that her book will come out as number one on the *New York Times* Best Seller list, and it will stay there for at least six months, and it will be published in no less than six languages. Dad, what I'm saying is that that one book would bring in more income than the combined revenues for all of the books you've published since you've had the business." Brian studied his father's intransigent face. "It would be a financial game changer . . . for you . . . and for Mom."

"No, it wouldn't because it's not being published under my imprint." Dennis abruptly stood up, ending the conversation. "Let's get over to The Bindery and see what that basement looks like now that you've pulled out fifty years of old newspapers."

"I have one call to make," Brian said, picking up the phone. "I'll meet you over there in a minute."

After he heard his father's footsteps on the stairs leading outside, Brian picked up the documents and reviewed the contracts. "Sorry, Dad, but it's for your own good." He signed his name, committing Chatham Press to printing Paige Petrosyan's breasts. A minute later, Brian dropped the envelope in the mailbox directly in front of their building on Main Street.

The Bindery, a highly reputable publishing and book-binding operation located on Cherry Street, a half block away from the Chatham Press building, had been founded by William Beezer, Dennis's father, to print and distribute *The Lumby Lines*. Shortly after acquiring The Bindery's building, William brought in a massive Harris-Seybold press that served the business well for more than thirty years, when ultimately it was replaced with two other machines that used more advanced technologies. It was those machines that, if running full-out, could be heard by those walking down Cherry Street. Dennis had not yet embraced the paradigm shift to digital or print-on-demand publishing, and as such hadn't upgraded his equipment in a decade.

Although Brian had spent very little time in The Bindery during his youth, only on those rare occasions that he visited his grandfather, he had always liked the building a great deal. The two-story, brick-and-mortar building had large Palladian windows disproportionate to the front façade but designed to bring as much light as possible into the print room. On most days, a metronomic hum emanated from the presses and cutting machines, located in an adjacent room. There was an ever-present but imperceptibly thin layer of dust on everything, along with deeper pockets of sawdust in each of the corners. The smell of paper and ink was one that could never be forgotten.

"Dad?" Brian said, walking up to his father, who was staring at the silent printing presses.

"These used to run eighteen hours a day," Dennis said sadly. "And we employed so many from the town to operate the machinery and stack the publications. That's what's wrong with your technology, Brian. It doesn't connect people."

"Not like it used to, no," Brian agreed. "But if we converted this to a print-on-demand shop and added some space for self-published authors, I think you would be amazed by how quickly this business could turn around."

"You're probably right, son," Dennis said. "But I don't know if I have the energy or the desire to go through that kind of change. As much as I hate to admit it, I'm getting tired and I just want to stick to what I know."

"You sound like you're fifty and about to retire."

"I *am* fifty!"

"But, Dad, even if *you* want to stand still, your company shouldn't. If it does, you'll lose everything." Brian paused. "Just look at this month's numbers for *The Lumby Lines*; you have thirty thousand subscribers. I doubt your company has ever seen those kinds of revenues."

"It hasn't, and I appreciate everything you've done. But *The Lumby Lines* will never be the newspaper it was."

"It could be something better," Brian said. "It's reaching more people and you have a better chance to impact those lives with the content you choose to provide."

"That's exactly my point about Petrosyan's book. I don't want to impact people's lives with that trash."

Brian had to suppress a guilty look. "Unfortunately, the readers decide what is and what isn't trash. Millions of people find some kind of benefit in what Paige Petrosyan is doing."

"I don't get it," Dennis argued.

"You don't have to," Brian replied. "Determining value is no longer your job. What you do is provide content that your readers perceive as valuable."

"I always wanted to walk the high road of journalistic integrity." Dennis sounded miserable.

"You always have, Dad. But the world has changed under your feet."

"You're right. And I think *The Lumby Lines* needs a new president and editor-in-chief." He paused a moment. "So?"

"So?" Brian was unsure what his father was suggesting.

"Do you want to take over the paper?"

Brian stepped back as if he'd been pushed. During his long hours of transitioning the paper online, not once did he give any thought to the possibility that his father would turn editorial control and operations over to him. In fact, he would have never gone down that improbable path. Although he had built good momentum heading up the monks' philanthropic efforts in South America, and although Matthew had voiced his desire for Brian to continue, he was even unsure if that's what he wanted.

"I don't know what to say," Brian finally replied.

Dennis put his arm around his son's shoulder. "If nothing else, say you'll give it some thought."

"I will."

Dennis wasn't going to push too hard. "Let's see what messes are left in the basement," he said, flipping on the switch at the top of the stairs. The room below suddenly glowed under fluorescent lights.

They walked downstairs together.

Dennis was flabbergasted when he looked around. *"Look what you've done!"*

Several tons of old newspaper stored in the large basement had been hauled off and the floor swept clean. Other than several oak filing cabinets that Brian assumed were true antiques, the room was immaculate.

"It's been years since I've been down here,"

Dennis said in awe, scanning the vast room. "It's just been used for storage. Papers and out-of-print copies were stacked to the ceiling."

"Why do you think the bonfire burned so strongly?" Brian asked with a smile.

"What you've done is incredible, Brian."

"Hey, wait a minute," Brian said, pulling out his phone. He quickly put his arm around his dad and snapped a selfie of them standing in the empty basement.

"So not necessary," Dennis said.

"But now we'll have that moment forever," Brian said, assessing the image on his phone before showing his father. He put the phone away and looked around the basement. "You know, you have a great opportunity here," Brian said. "This could be the foundation for a print-on-demand imprint for The Bindery. This floor alone could hold all of the equipment for self-publishing and order fulfillment. And then you have the traditional presses upstairs for printing full runs of the books you put under contract."

Dennis shook his head. "I see what you're trying to push me into, but I just don't have the passion."

"Then find someone who can."

Dennis stared at his son and smiled. "I think I'm looking at him."

"Dad, that wasn't my intent when I offered to help you out."

"I know that. But sometimes life has other plans that you might not be aware of."

"I could say the same to you," Brian said. "I need some time to think about all this. But if it's all right with you, I'd like to set up a print-on-demand shop down here. I can guarantee a positive cash flow in six months."

"Then it's all yours," Dennis said, shaking on the deal.

"And one final thing I need you to do," Brian said. "Would you go through those filing cabinets? There are some old manuscripts, like from 1913. No title, no author. Maybe you know who they belong to."

"I'll take a look, but I'm sure I don't know a thing about them," Dennis said. "Consider them all yours. I don't even want to know what's in the drawers. But be careful what you come across—you could be unearthing ghosts that don't want to be disturbed," he teased.

TWENTY-FOUR

Decoys

After receiving word of her imminent divorce, Caroline removed the few remaining mementos from the kitchen corkboard. In place of images and keepsakes that reflected a past life with Kai, she pinned up two new photos of Finn—one of him playing with Tom's Dalmatian puppies, and the other with Finn standing next to Aaron by the riverbank. Among several other photographs she posted one of her favorites of Aaron, who was looking directly at her with bright eyes and a wide, easy grin surrounded by a two-day-old beard. Although she felt conflicted, almost certain that their relationship shouldn't be taken any further, she couldn't help but smile each time she looked at it. Tacked below was a recipe for a cake she wanted to bake for Aaron as thanks for his blueberry muffins. Additional clippings hung from the board about shows she wanted to attend and classes she might be interested in.

But it was the calendar on the corkboard that had changed the most. Instead of blank boxes of days that merged into blank rows of weeks, Caroline had filled many of the dates with specific times and appointments she didn't want to miss: Tom's obedience lessons for Finn, an invitation to Montis Inn, dinner at Mac and Tom's, and a lunch date with Gabrielle at The Green Chile. Caroline was choosing a life she wanted to live.

From the corkboard she removed an advertisement for a swing-dance class in Wheatley and slipped it into her pocket. She took a deep nervous breath.

"Let's go, Finn," she said as she headed out of the house.

When they turned the bend in the road and the Candor farm came into view, Finn darted off at full speed in search of—in order of importance— Mac's peanut butter cookies, Tom's doggie treats, and some lost calf in need of his herding skills.

Walking up the driveway, Caroline saw Aaron and Tom working on Aaron's motorcycle in front of the main barn. Aaron was lying flat on his back, his nose inches away from the engine and his hands held overhead.

"Try it again," he said.

Tom turned over the engine; it sputtered several seconds and then died.

"One more time," Aaron said.

One more time the engine started, sputtered, but this time came back to life.

"Fantastic! I think we're good," Aaron said.

Tom looked at his watch. "I'm due in Wheatley in a half hour. Are you coming along?"

Aaron put down his wrench just as Finn dashed past. He immediately looked around for Caroline. "Well, this is unexpected," he said, his smile widening.

"We're just heading off to some field trials," Tom said. "I think Finn could learn lots, and you might enjoy it as well. I'm only going to stay for a few hours. Mac and I are flying to Denver for a couple of days, and we need to be out of here by five."

Aaron jumped to his feet and brushed the dust off his pants. "Come with us. It should be fun."

Caroline felt the warmth of his invitation. "I think I will."

The local kennel club had taken over the south fields in Wheatley. There were more dogs than Caroline had ever seen in one location. Countless Irish setters were being walked in the grassy parking area, sleeping in crates, and swimming in the lake. There were also many different types of setters as well as other sporting dogs: spaniels and retrievers of varying coat colors and textures and sizes, Weimaraners and vizslas of identical size and color.

As soon as they arrived, Tom headed off to the main tent to check in as one of the veterinarians on hand for the field trials.

Caroline stood outside the car talking softly to Finn, trying to coax him out. But Finn was so dumbfounded by the commotion around him that he glued himself to the front seat and refused to move. When Caroline finally dragged him to the ground, he nervously farted and then sat down. When a dazzling female trotted past him, he got so anxious that he squatted and peed right where he was standing. She wasn't impressed. Poor Finn.

Aaron and Caroline, keeping a tight leash on Finn, passed by a canine agility area. A course of different obstacles and various-colored flags had been carefully placed within the quarter-acre boundary marks.

They stopped to watch a handler and her German shepherd.

"Aren't they amazing," Caroline said in admiration.

"How do they know where to go?"

"It looks like the course might be color-coded."

Aaron stiffened up.

"Are you all right?" Caroline asked.

Forcing a smile, he gave a lighthearted chuckle. "I'm as lost as Finn is at a dog show." He started to walk away. "Let's head over to the lake."

Caroline looked at Aaron's back, wondering

what had just happened. "If that's what you want, lead the way."

When they arrived, a golden retriever was obediently sitting by its owner's side, intensely focused on the decoy in the handler's hand. The decoy was thrown and only after it landed in the middle of the pond did the owner release his dog, who galloped down a makeshift pier, flew into the air and landed in the water. The dog then swam to the decoy, grabbed it with its mouth and swam back to the shore, returning the decoy to the owner.

The decoy, or perhaps the dog leaping through the air, caught Finn's attention. Despite his usual attention deficit, Finn suddenly became laser attentive, his eyes tracking the second decoy, his muscles twitching, ready to be released at full run. Decoy after decoy, dog after dog, Finn became more excited to the point that he started to whine.

Caroline laughed. "I've never heard him make that noise."

"He's reacting to his instincts," Aaron said. "He sees what the other dogs are doing and he's making the connection."

Caroline scratched Finn between the ears. "I always feel so guilty that I haven't been a better owner for him." She spoke softly, as if to herself. "It was Kai who wanted a dog, and I just agreed . . . like I always did. Just like it was

Kai who wanted the mill and an antique shop."

"How could someone close to God want so many things in life?" Aaron asked.

"I've wondered that myself." She gazed ahead. "But Finn and Kai were inseparable. After he left, it took months for Finn to stop looking for him and then finally turn to me. I wish I could explain to Finn that Kai dumped him as well. If he knew that we were in the same sinking boat together, he might have liked me a little sooner." Suddenly she looked up at Aaron. "Oh, I'm sorry," she said, blushing.

"For what?"

"Way too much information," Caroline said, and immediately changed the subject. "Why don't we head over there?" She pointed toward a distant field, needing to escape.

After exploring the fairgrounds and the different competitions that were taking place, Caroline and Aaron found a shaded knoll overlooking the main field, sat down and watched a hunting exhibition. They watched champions and amateurs locate pheasants, quail and partridge in the tall grasses. When the dog found a bird, they held as still as statues until the owner flushed the bird from the tall grass. Caroline was fascinated, but Finn was bored. He fell asleep at her feet and began having dreams of herding calves, with his legs moving a mile a minute and his tail helicoptering behind him. When he started alternating between snoring and farting, Caroline nudged him awake.

Caroline slid the advertisement out of her pocket. "I saw this a few days ago. Would you like to go?" she asked, passing the small slip of paper to Aaron.

"A swing-dance class? I would love to!"

"With me," Caroline added.

Aaron laughed. "I assumed as much. That only makes it better."

"I accidentally tore off the date. It's in two weeks," Caroline said.

Aaron's smile faded.

"What's wrong?" Caroline asked.

"I might not be able to make it."

"Because you have such a full social schedule?" she asked teasingly.

"I wish," Aaron said. "I just don't know when I'll be heading back home."

"Home?"

"The one in Seattle, remember?" Aaron said. "I don't want to overstay my welcome with Mac and Tom, and I have a job to get back to."

Caroline froze, keeping her eyes on the dogs in the field. She had taken a huge step that led her right off a cliff. She didn't want to look at Aaron for fear of saying something she would later regret, for fear of feeling more vulnerable than she already did. She leaned over to pet Finn in order to put more space between them.

"But I appreciate the offer," Aaron said, giving

her back the advertisement. "Maybe next time."

"Maybe," Caroline said, crushing the ad in her hand, desperately trying to hide her disappointment. "I think it's time to go," she said without looking at her watch.

"If that's what you'd like," Aaron said, jumping to his feet and offering her a hand.

On the way back to the car they passed the main retrieving pond. From the corner of her eye, Caroline could see a decoy being tossed. Just as Caroline unsnapped his leash, Finn bolted away from her, darting across the parking lot. He galloped down the pier and with all of his might launched off. He sailed twenty feet through the air before hitting the water in a huge splash. And then to everyone's amazement, Finn sank like a stone.

Caroline panicked, thinking he was going to drown. "He doesn't know how to swim!"

Aaron ran down the dock and, seeing Finn was in trouble, dove in. Finn was frantically bobbing at the surface, trying to keep his head above water by paddling just his front legs. As people would say for months to come, it was the oddest thing to watch. Finn was swimming up and down, as if he was trying to stand on his hind legs. His paddling kept his head above water but didn't provide any forward movement.

As Aaron approached Finn, his foot hit the bottom of the pond, which was only five feet deep. He stood up, wrapped one arm around Finn's waist, grabbed his collar with his other hand and steered him back to shore.

Both shook off the excess water when they got onto dry land.

"How can that dog not know how to swim?" Aaron asked, squeezing his shirt-tails, which dripped water all around him. "You live next to a river!"

"He's never gone in the water. He only walks along the bank," Caroline said. "I was going to ask Tom to teach him."

"Sooner versus later," Aaron advised, shaking a stern finger at Finn.

"And that's when you're leaving as well? Sooner versus later?" Caroline asked acerbically.

Aaron was about to reply when Tom joined them.

"Nice save, Aaron. I'm assuming you're ready to go?" Tom asked.

"Evidently some more than others," Caroline said sarcastically.

On the ride back to Lumby, Caroline sat quietly staring out the car window, pretending to listen to what Tom was explaining to Aaron about the dog show. *Going home?* she thought. Caroline hated surprises as much as she hated unwanted change. Yet she was most angry at herself for never considering the possibility— no, the inevitability—that Aaron would leave and return home. She was angry for not having time to protect herself, to pull away and prepare for life after Aaron. But of course there would be, just like there was life after CC died and life after Kai walked out. Why is it, she wondered, that she was so unsuccessful in starting up a life again after being left behind?

TWENTY-FIVE

Engaging

Four days later, by two o'clock that afternoon, Pam's nerves were on edge as she paced around her house, waiting for her sister to arrive. The inn had never been cleaner, nor the grounds more manicured.

A car passed on Farm to Market Road, prompting Pam to look out the window. Another car, another glance.

Finally, a car slowed in front of Montis Inn and pulled into their drive. Mark, who was sweeping the front porch, put aside his broom to greet the visitors.

The car looked familiar to Pam—one that she saw many times a week. Mac stepped out from the driver's side and began talking with Mark. Although Pam couldn't hear what was being said, both Tom and Mac were laughing. The trunk popped open as Mark circled around to talk with Tom, who remained seated in the car.

Suddenly the rear door opened and a woman stepped out, her face turned away from Pam. What Pam noticed, though, was the woman's blond hair, cut shoulder length. She was slightly taller than Mac but just as lean. Mac removed

291

several pieces of luggage from the trunk and placed them away from the car. She embraced the woman and then got back into the car next to Tom. From the back seat behind Tom, a man stepped out and immediately shook Mark's hand. He stood several inches taller than Mark, and looked to be in his sixties. Even from that distance, Pam could see the man's broad smile. He laughed and tapped the roof of the car just before Tom and Mac pulled away.

The woman turned around, and Pam gasped. They not only looked like sisters, but from a distance, one could almost confuse them as twins.

"Pam!" Mark called. "The Wings have arrived."

Pam dried her damp hands on the kitchen towel and opened the door. Both Clipper and Cutter barged past her and dashed toward the car.

"Grab them!" Pam yelled.

But Mark wasn't fast enough. Clipper greeted Janet with full exuberance. Never jumping up on guests, Clipper had an odd way of sideswiping strangers to get attention.

"Unh-unh," Janet said, putting her finger up. Clipper immediately sat in front of her.

Cutter went after Bill with the same level of commitment.

"Who do we have here?" Bill asked.

"Our poorly trained dogs, I'm afraid," Mark said.

"Dinner!" Pam yelled from the porch.

Hearing that word in their one-word vocabulary, the dogs froze, then turned and galloped back to the house. Once they were locked away, Pam ran outside.

"Pam, this is Janet and Bill Wing," Mark said, looking back and forth between Pam and her sister. "They met Tom and Mac on the flight up from Denver, and Tom insisted that they drive them here."

"Those two are the greatest people," Bill commented as he shook Pam's hand. "Hi, I'm Bill Wing." His smile was as contagious as his cheerful disposition.

"Pam Walker."

"And I'm Janet Wing." Her eyes sparkled and there was a song in her voice. "We've read so much about Montis Inn since we spoke. I especially enjoyed the cover story about you in *Vintner's Fare*."

Now that Pam was standing only a few feet away, she noticed more differences between them than she had originally thought. Although both had natural blond hair and blue eyes, and although both were lean, Pam was at least five inches taller and looked ten years younger. And Janet was . . . cuter, from head to toe. Pam wondered if Janet noticed the likeness between them.

"Christian Copeland is always spot-on in his

recommendations," Bill said, glancing around the property.

"You know Christian?" Pam asked in surprise.

"Oh no. We've only met him twice. But we so enjoy his magazine each month. Janet, do you remember his recommendation for that small chalet in Annecy, France? It was so perfect we stayed for three weeks."

"It was," Janet confirmed.

"This is just beautiful," Bill said, eyeing the main building. "It's quite a compound. Christian's article mentioned a library."

"Right over there," Pam said, pointing to one of the two smaller buildings next to the dining room and grand kitchen. "It used to be the monks' scribing room."

"Oh, I almost forgot—this is for you." Janet said in a chirpy voice as she handed Pam a glossy gift bag stuffed with brightly colored tissue paper. "Some cheese and crackers made in Virginia."

"This isn't necessary, but thanks so much." *Does she notice our similarities?* Pam wondered again. "I'm sure you're both tired. We have a suite prepared for you in the guest annex."

"Annex?" Bill asked.

Pam laughed lightly. "Some of our names are left over from when Montis was a monastery. The annex," she explained, pointing to the long building behind them, "was the monks' sleeping quarters and private living area, and it now contains our largest guest suites. The main building of the inn—which was their chapel and community room—just has single rooms."

"How delightful," Janet said.

"Mark will take you to your room. Will you be having dinner at the inn tonight?" Pam asked.

"We would love to," Bill said, "but Tom and Mackenzie insisted that we join them for margaritas and some tapas at a restaurant called The Green Chile."

"It's just up the road," Mark said. "You can borrow one of our cars."

"If it's not an imposition," Janet said sincerely. "Otherwise we can easily make other arrangements."

"No problem," Mark said, picking up the two pieces of luggage. "If you'll follow me."

And as quickly as they arrived, they left. Pam stood alone, not knowing what to do.

Two hours later, Pam was pacing the room, waiting for Mark to return. *What could he possibly be doing?* she wondered as she looked out the window. Each time she was about to venture over to the guest annex to see what they were up to, she restrained herself. She didn't want to appear overly friendly, or worse, overly interested.

Mark finally breezed inside. "They are the

nicest people in the entire world, honey."

"Where have you been?" Pam asked, trying not to sound annoyed.

"After we dropped off their bags, I showed them around the place—Janet walks like a bat out of hell. We ended up having a cup of coffee in the library. They're just so laid-back, really comfortable with themselves and with each other. They're amazing, and so nice."

"You said that already."

"You know, Janet looks cute and all, but she's as sharp as a tack, and has her wits about her. Oh, and they travel all the time. They go everywhere. As soon as they finish one trip, Bill's on his laptop planning their next adventure. They just pick up and go on a whim, just like that." He snapped his fingers. "They're heading off to England and Sweden next week. And then the Maldives at the end of the month."

"Where's that?"

"I don't know, but it sounds like they have tropical umbrella drinks there. And then they might go on to Singapore. Singapore! Boy, wouldn't that be a dream come true?"

"I thought we loved being at Montis," Pam said. "I thought *this* was our dream."

"Well, we do, and it still is, hun, but to have the world at your fingertips and just be able to pack up and go, just like that." He snapped his fingers again.

"They must be retired," Pam said flatly.

Mark hesitated. "Yeah, they must be, but they don't seem the type to be slowed down by jet lag or anything."

"Huh?" Pam asked, looking at Mark, but he didn't reply. "Did you talk about anything other than Singapore?"

"Oh yeah, we talked about everything. They are the nicest people."

Pam rolled her eyes. "So, you know nothing more about them?"

"Not really, other than . . ."

"They're really nice. Yeah, I got that."

"They have a couple of grown kids who also live in Virginia. Campbell and Hayden."

"Sons or daughters?" Pam asked.

"One of each, I think, but I'm not sure," Mark said, scratching his head. "They didn't say."

Pam tried to suppress her impatience. "Did they tell you anything about themselves? What he used to do for a living?"

Mark tried to recall. "Come to think of it, not really. They asked a lot about us and the Inn. And we talked about their travels."

A car started up outside, and they both looked out the window.

"That must be them," Mark said. "I gave them the keys to the Jeep. It would have been fun to go to The Green Chile with them."

Pam looked at her watch. "Well, in an hour

we'll have a dining room full of guests, and if we don't set the tables, they'll be eating with their fingers."

By six the following morning, Mark was already distributing copies of *The New York Times* to each of the guest rooms. Walking into the Inn's lobby, he saw Janet and Bill Wing sitting in the lounge. Bill was at a side table by the window, peering at his laptop, and Janet was sitting on the sofa knitting.

"Good morning," Mark said softly, not wanting to wake any guests upstairs.

Bill waved Mark over.

"You two are up early," Mark commented.

"We like to walk for an hour before breakfast," Janet said with a smile.

"Are you heading out now?"

"No," Bill replied. "We got back about ten minutes ago. You have a delightful orchard."

"It is, but growing a bunch of apples is more work than you can imagine. Did you have a nice evening?"

"It was perfect," Janet said perkily. "Tom and Mackenzie were a total joy to be with."

Bill nodded in agreement without looking up from his computer. "They'll be coming to stay with us for a week in . . . when did they say, Janet?"

"October. Then they're heading up to New England to see the fall colors."

"That's right," Bill said. "Just before we leave for Italy."

Janet continued knitting. "The food was delicious. Gabrielle and Dennis . . . hmmm."

"Beezer," Bill said.

"Yes, Gabrielle and Dennis Beezer joined us. And then Jimmy and Hannah came in for coffee. Just a delightful time." Janet smiled to herself. "And what a charming town you have, Mark. After dinner we all walked along Main Street and wc were told a little about Lumby's history."

Mark laughed. "That must have been interesting. Stories are usually embellished over the years because not a lot happens around here."

"We understand that you two are running for a political position," Bill said.

"Yes. Mayor. But I'm not. I just filled in for Pam when she went to Connecticut. But if Pam can survive her opponent, she'll be great for the town."

"We heard all about the other candidate," Bill said.

"Biscuit, the golden retriever, or the deceased incumbent?"

"No, the other fellow. What a nasty business that must be," Janet said, gently shaking her head.

Bill looked up from his PC. "So, Mark, have you ever been to Edinburgh?"

"Scotland? Oh no," Mark shook his head. "We

haven't traveled much. Too busy working and all."

"There's this little restaurant right down the street from the fort. Do you remember the name, Janet?"

"Bourbons or Whiskies. Something like that," she replied.

"They have the most delicious sticky toffee pudding. Janet makes a perfect replica. Perhaps you can make that for the Walkers, honey."

"Perhaps," she said with a smile.

"We were talking about that place last night. We should go back there next month," Bill said.

He leaned back in his chair and crossed his legs. As his cuffed khakis rode up slightly on his leg, his brilliant socks caught Mark's eye. Mark studied them, trying to remember where he'd seen them before. Suddenly his eyes opened wide.

"Okay, I need to go," Mark said abruptly. "Papers to deliver. Have a great day," he said over his shoulder.

Once outside, Mark hurried back to their home. Inside, he grabbed the newspaper article he had torn out for Pam.

"Look! It's him!" Mark said excitedly, shaking the article inches from Pam's nose. "I just saw his socks. They're identical. I think he's even wearing the same pants. And the way he crossed his legs." Mark pointed to the blur-faced secret informant testifying for the government against the Iranian spies. *Or was it the Mafia?* Mark wondered. "It's him! I bet they're in the witness protection program! Maybe coming to Lumby is part of their cover."

"Mark, that's ridiculous," Pam said. "I found those socks online."

"On Amazon?"

"No, in a specialty store."

"Well, if they're not on Amazon, no one buys 'em. Except this guy," he said, pointing to the photograph, "and Bill Wing, who are one in the same." He stared at the picture again. "Wow, maybe that's why they're so nice. You don't want to be shot by gangsters . . . or Russian spies."

"You've gone way overboard," Pam said. "Did you finish delivering the papers?"

"No. After I saw Bill's socks, I ran over here as fast as I could."

"Remember, Chuck is coming by," she called to Mark as he walked out the door.

When Mark returned to the sitting room, Bill and Janet were in their same chairs, but one other guest had joined Janet on the sofa. The three were laughing about their traveling exploits.

"We still get bills for a parking ticket in Venice from three years ago!" Bill said.

"Which we've already paid twice," Janet chirped.

"Do you go to Italy often?" the guest asked.

Bill tilted his head, thinking. "Not often. Three

to four times a year at most. Would that be about right?"

Mafia, Mark thought.

A man called out from the front porch. "Hello?"

Mark recognized the voice immediately. "In here, Chuck."

Chuck strolled in carrying some beehive equipment in both arms. "Good morning, all."

"Chuck Bryson, this is Bill and Janet Wing. They'll be staying with us for a few days."

"Wonderful. Very nice to meet you," Chuck said, bowing slightly. For a moment he stared at Janet as if she was someone he knew. He then turned to Mark. "Will you be joining me up at the apiary?"

Mark held out a stack of newspapers. "I can't. I haven't gotten to any of my morning chores."

Bill Wing stood and stretched his back. "Do you have beehives here?"

"About a dozen hives in the upper field of the orchard," Mark replied. "And Chuck ensures I don't do anything stupid with them."

"What an interesting job," Janet said.

"Actually, Chuck is a physics instructor at Berkeley," Mark explained. "In his free time, he maintains the Montis hives, which were originally established by the monks who used to live here."

"Berkeley? What a great school that is," Bill said.

"It's been an honor," Chuck said.

"I'd love to hear more about that."

Chuck raised his brows. "If you're free, you're invited to join me."

Bill looked at Janet. "Do you want to go?"

"I think I'll stay here," she said, continuing to knit. "I'm almost done with a sleeve."

"Then we're off," Chuck said.

"Is this all right to wear?" Bill asked.

"I don't mind if the bees don't mind," Chuck joked. He handed Bill a smoker and a hat, and they were off.

Mark waited for the men to leave. "I noticed Bill's socks," he said casually, straightening out a stack of magazines. "I've been looking for something similar."

Janet laughed like a bird. "Bill loves his socks. I think those are his favorite pair. I can give you the name of the store we buy them from."

"Perfect," Mark said, leaving two newspapers on the coffee table. "It must be nice to be retired. What did Bill do before that?"

"He just did some intelligence work for the government."

"Oh? Doing what?"

"Oh, I'll let Bill explain," she said. "But I warn you, it's awfully boring."

I doubt that, Mark thought.

TWENTY-SIX

Fireworks

Although arrangements for Pam and Mark's Independence Day party had been made weeks in advance, the serious work began just after dawn the morning of July Fourth. Their chef, André Levesque, was already in the kitchen preparing for the feast that he and Pam had agreed upon. Additional help arrived a short time later to set up the outdoor tables and chairs delivered the day before. In all, several hundred people were planning to come to Montis Inn to enjoy a buffet and a spectacular fireworks display.

Mark was hanging strings of white lights from the trees in the backyard. Yet, after plugging them into an outlet, only half of them came on. "I wish Joshua was here. He knows how to fix these better than anyone," he said to Pam.

Hank stood quietly by the pond, keeping one eye on the koi and one on the lights.

Pam jammed another bamboo-lantern post into the ground.

Mark noticed his wife's bad mood. "You don't seem that thrilled about tonight. Is everything okay?"

Pam stepped closer to Mark so as not to be overheard. "Do you know we haven't spent more than five minutes with Bill and Janet since they arrived?"

"They're having a great time, honey."

"With all of our friends!" she said. "They now know more people in Lumby than we do. And everyone loves them! Do you know last night they had dinner with Adam and Katie Banks? *We've* never been invited over to their house for dinner."

"They're really interesting people and seem to get along with everyone."

"I know how fascinating they are. Would you please stop saying that?"

Mark shrugged. "For what it's worth, I haven't talked to Bill very much either. He's been spending most of his time with Chuck." Mark climbed up on the ladder and began to hang another string of lights. "But they're on vacation, honey, and are just relaxing."

"No, Mark, they're not on *vacation*. They're *retired*. There's a world of difference. And there is no such thing as a vacation or taking a break from retirement."

"You sound angry," Mark said.

"I'm envious of how free they are. They have absolutely no responsibilities. And I'm totally frustrated." Pam ran her fingers through her hair. "I have a sister who would rather spend time with *our* friends than with us, and who would rather fly around the world than be here."

"Well, when you compare Montis to Bali—"

"Don't even go there," Pam warned.

"Yeah, I'm jealous too."

"I'm *not* jealous!" Pam snapped a bit too quickly. "It's just that our lives are so different. And what do we have in common? You and I run an inn and a restaurant three hundred and fifty-four days a year. We help the monks with their business, and we support our community. And they . . . they go off to Paris and Sydney and Marrakesh. Who the hell goes to Marrakesh?"

"Wow. They've been to *Marrakesh?*" Mark started singing, " 'Wouldn't you know we're riding on the Marrakesh Express.' "

Pam rolled her eyes. "Crosby, Stills and Nash? You're showing your age, dear."

"Nothing's wrong with Marrakesh," Mark said, continuing to hum the song.

"I'm using that as an example." She took a deep breath and then dropped her shoulders. "You have to admit it, we're just boring, and people like Bill and Janet Wing aren't."

"But you're running for mayor!"

"For a town of five thousand in the middle of nowhere," Pam said. "And I've been shredded by a narcissistic, misogynistic racist who has better polling numbers than I do. Fantastic," she said sarcastically.

Bill and Chuck walked around the corner.

"Help has arrived," Chuck said in his normal jovial fashion.

"We never turn down that kind of offer," Mark replied. "Maybe you guys can finish staking the lanterns for Pam."

"That sounds easy enough," Bill said. "Where would you like me to put them?"

Pam waved her hand vaguely. "We're just scattering them throughout the backyard. The tables will be set up by the pond, so maybe you can add some extras over there." Pam looked around. "Is Janet with you?"

"She went to Wheatley with Mackenzie and Gabrielle. A girl's shopping trip and then they were talking about getting their nails done, I think."

Pam hid her sweeping disappointment. "They'll have a wonderful time. A lot of nice boutiques and stores."

"And Janet loves shopping, whether it's the Christmas shops in Germany or a farmer's market in Dublin."

"Your exploits still amaze me," Chuck said.

Mark finally had an opening to ask more about

Bill's mysterious background. "Did you used to travel a lot for work?"

"In the early days. We lived in Europe for several years and then in Asia."

"And what did you do there?" Mark asked casually.

"Just some government work," Bill said. "Certainly too boring to talk about."

"No, I think it's cool," Mark said. "To have the chance to live abroad."

"It kept us busy, no question," Bill replied before changing the subject. "So, Chuck, do you have a problem getting up your road in winter?"

"You went to Chuck's house?" Mark asked.

"He drove me there yesterday afternoon. Just stunning views."

"We know," Pam said under her breath.

"When a bad storm is in the forecast, I just stay put," Chuck answered. "But that only happens once or twice a year. I'm more concerned about wildfires that can whip through the valley faster than you can imagine."

"I hadn't thought of that," Bill said.

Chuck nodded as he buried another lantern. "When we go up north, I'll show you a scorched area from four years ago. As devastating as they are, it renews the forests."

"I'm looking forward to that," Bill said.

Mark's ears perked up. "Are you guys going out tomorrow?"

"No, they have some other plans for the next few days," Chuck said. "But we're looking at Friday for Bill and I to hike up and see the eagles."

"That's incredibly rough terrain," Mark said.

"So I've been warned," Bill said. "But it should be quite an experience."

Mark stood on the ladder, waiting for an invitation to join them. But it didn't come.

Although the party was to begin at seven o'clock, friends and neighbors began to arrive at six. Chaperoned children ran through the orchard, picking low-hanging fruit, while others played with the many dogs that were invited and equally welcomed. Clipper and Cutter were among them, being sure to visit everyone not much taller than themselves, since children were the most likely to offer them treats.

Most of the guests from Montis emerged from their rooms to join the festivities when the sun set. Fireflies filled the air and the lanterns were lit. When the Christmas lights came on, Montis looked like a fantasyland.

Janet found Pam and asked if there was anything she could do to help.

"Just enjoy yourself. We don't usually put our guests to work," Pam joked as she poured ice into a large metal barrel.

The grill was filled with barbecued chicken and

burgers, while corn on the cob steamed in a large kettle. Bowls of salad and baskets of chips were placed on the tables. Pam brought out the rest of the plates and silverware.

"Are the fireworks ready?" she asked Mark, who was a few steps behind her carrying sodas and beer.

"Yeah, but I wish Joshua was here. He's always taken care of all of that."

"Just don't blow off a finger, honey," she said, half serious. "You'll need both your hands to help clean up afterward."

Laughter broke out from a table where Bill and Janet Wing were sitting with Chuck, Tom, Mac, Gabrielle and Dennis.

"They're having a great time," Mark said as he and Pam headed back to the kitchen.

"They are indeed."

Once inside, Pam grabbed an oversized tray filled with condiments and paper towels. Turning around, she bumped into Janet. The tray almost went flying.

"Please let me take that," Janet offered. "You two are working like slaves, and we're not doing anything to help."

Pam could have refused, but Janet's offer was so well-intentioned that Pam handed her the tray. "Is it too heavy?"

"Absolutely not," she said, and flew out the door.

A minute later, she was back with an empty tray. "Where do you keep your trash bags?" Janet asked.

"Over there," Pam said pointing at the far pantry. "Why?"

"I just wanted to pick up the empty cans that are lying around," she said cheerfully.

"Are you always so helpful?" Pam asked.

"I think it's nervous energy," Janet said. "I'm not very good sitting around unless I'm knitting. And I love entertaining. When Bill and I are in town, we seldom have a dinner alone—it's either with neighbors or friends."

Pam grabbed the chance to finally talk with Janet. "Have you always lived in Virginia?"

"No, I'm from Iowa and Bill's from Illinois. We met in college and as soon as we married, he signed up with the Company and we moved to DC."

"The Company?"

Janet froze for a second. "Oh, the government," she said. "There were a few assignments abroad and then we found our home in Great Falls."

"Do your parents still live in Iowa?"

Janet's smile waned. "They were both killed in an accident in 1992."

"I'm sorry," Pam said.

"It was hard to lose both of them at the same time, and we were abroad when it happened," she said. "I'm glad Bill was with me."

"Do you have any brothers and sisters?"

"Oh my word, yes. I have four brothers and three sisters—there were eight of us. Other than Woody, who passed away two years ago, most everyone is still in Iowa and doing well."

"Pam!" Mark called from outside. "We need the burger rolls, tomatoes and onions."

Janet jumped into action. "Here, let me do that," she said, stacking up the tray. "I'll be back in a minute."

To Pam's relief, Chuck managed the fireworks that night without incident. Most of their guests had moved across the street and were sitting on the hill looking down to Woodrow Lake a short distance away. Chuck, Bill and Mark set the launch bench on the sandy beach. And then the show began.

As the fireworks exploded in succession, exclamations and applause were heard all the way down the valley.

"Wow, look at that one," Mark said as a massive red chrysanthemum formed in the sky.

"You have a fine collection here," Chuck said.

"That's Joshua's doing. He bought them a couple of months ago on one of his trips to Helena."

"So, Chuck," Bill began, "have you ever studied pyrotechnics?"

"Just enough to answer the few questions I

had. I find it amazing that they've been around for two thousand years, and it took us almost the same amount of time to duplicate similar chemical reactions for different purposes." Chuck lit another string of fuses and within seconds a sequence of explosives lit the sky overhead.

For an hour, the three men scrambled on the beach, loading one Roman candle after another into six separate launchers. To everyone's delight, the fireworks kept the sky over Woodrow Lake ablaze with color.

Near the orchard high on the hill, Caroline and Aaron were watching with Tom and Mac. Caroline lay back on the blanket. She stared straight up in the sky, watching blues and reds brilliantly dance before fading out.

"Look at that one!" she said in awe.

Aaron didn't look up, seeming more interested in watching the people around them.

"Do you not like fireworks?" Caroline asked.

Mac and Tom looked over at Aaron, waiting to hear his answer.

"Perhaps I don't see them the way everyone else does," he said.

Mac patted Aaron on the knee. "Good answer," she said softly.

"Well, I love them. In fact, this is one of the dreamiest evenings I've had in a long time," Caroline said, watching another burst of color.

"Did you come here last year?" Mac asked.

"Not for the last five years," Caroline replied. "Kai wasn't one for celebrations and big gatherings. The last July Fourth party I attended was when Mark accidentally set fire to a rowboat." She turned to Aaron to explain. "That's because he had the crazy idea of launching some fireworks from the middle of the lake."

Tom and Mac joined in Caroline's laughter.

"Oh, I remember that like it was yesterday," Mac said. "A classic Mark Walker move. That boy's kept us amused over the years."

"But the man has a good heart, you've got to give him that," Caroline said.

"It sounds like you two like him a lot," Aaron said.

Mac looked down at Mark on the shore, barely making out his silhouette. "I respect him. He's crazy and out of control at times, but he's someone you can depend upon no matter what."

"He certainly is," Caroline said thoughtfully. "And isn't that what really matters when all is said and done? Knowing the other person will be there come hell or high water?" She forced herself not to look over at Aaron, but instead kept her gaze on the stars. *But why am I angry?* she wondered. After all, what they shared was never more than friendship. She had nothing more to give. But could there have been a different ending, one in which Aaron stayed in Lumby, if she had not pushed him away so many times in so many subtle ways? Were her own actions undoing the very happiness she craved?

A firework exploded overhead and transformed into an immense yellow chrysanthemum that covered the night sky. Would she ever find a love that big?

TWENTY-SEVEN

Pines

Whatever fleeting thoughts of romance the fireworks might have conjured up the night before, the light of day had brought her back to reality. Caroline's feet were once again planted firmly on the ground as she sat on the front porch steps waiting for Aaron, although her heart sped up when she heard his motorcycle approach.

"Mac said lunch wasn't until noon."

"It isn't," Aaron said.

"But it's only eleven o'clock. Why did you want to pick me up early?"

"It's a surprise," Aaron said.

"Any hints?"

"You'll see soon enough," he said, not giving her a clue. "Are you ready?"

She took the helmet he offered. He held her hand to help her get onto the motorcycle.

"For balance, not for romance," he assured her.

She wrapped her arms tightly around his waist as they slowly drove up Chicory Lane—for contact, not for balance, she knew deep down.

He stopped before turning onto the main road.

"Are we going far?" she called out.

He pointed to the mountain on the other side of the river.

After turning onto Farm to Market Road and crossing over Fork River, Aaron made a left onto a dirt trail that was no wider than five feet at best. It was a path that Caroline had never noticed before. Looking across the river, she recognized Mac and Tom's property, where she regularly walked Finn.

Then her yellow mill came into sight, with its large wheel revolving slowly.

She tapped Aaron on the shoulder. "Can we stop?"

Aaron braked but kept the engine running. They both removed their helmets.

"I've never seen it from this angle," she said loudly, looking at her property.

"Seriously?" Aaron asked in amazement. "Of all the times you looked across the river from your home, didn't you ever wonder what was over on this side?"

Good question, Caroline thought. "I suppose I did every once in a while. But Kai was always there, and I never . . ." Her voice faded against the sound of the engine. She glanced down at the rushing water. "Maybe I thought the river was the back boundary of my life."

After staring at the mill for a bit longer, she donned her helmet. "Ready," she said, tapping him on the shoulder.

Following the water's edge for another mile, Aaron veered right, away from the river and onto an even tighter trail that began to gradually climb the mountainside she had frequently viewed from her kitchen window. Once deep in the woods, Aaron stopped and turned off the bike. It was totally silent.

"It's through here," he said, taking her hand.

Walking into the woods, Caroline noticed a distinct change to the air—it became heavy and more pungent with pine and decaying wood. Fifty yards farther, they came upon the most spectacular pine grove Caroline had ever seen. Huge trees hundreds of years old reached for the sky, the boughs breaking the sunlight into fragmented patterns that shone through the heavy mist just above the ground.

"This is awesome," she whispered as if she was in a cathedral. Walking through the grove, she touched the massive trees with her outstretched fingers.

Underfoot was a soft, thick layer of pine needles built up over decades. Their footprints showed as if they were walking on a dense carpet.

"I'm certain it's a virgin forest." Although Aaron spoke softly, his voice hauntingly carried between the trees.

Caroline turned in a full circle, dazed by the natural beauty that surrounded her.

"I can't believe this was always here and we

never knew it . . . I never knew it," she said, walking up to Aaron.

"I discovered it a few years ago when I was hiking. I think I'm drawn to it because it's so monochromatic."

She looked up at the sun's rays filtering through the forest. "It's surreal."

When she turned around, Aaron was only inches away.

He kissed her in a way no one ever had. It was intensely passionate but yet so tender she barely felt his lips. Caroline's knees weakened as he wrapped his arms around her and pulled her body close to his. She closed her eyes as the primal smell of the land enveloped her.

"I've wanted to do that since the first day I met you. You have consumed every moment and every thought." He pulled her closer so there was no space between their bodies. "I can't be this close and not want to make love to you," Aaron whispered in her ear. When Caroline didn't respond, Aaron released her. "I know this isn't what you want right now, but sometimes life gets in the way and we don't have control over our futures."

"What do you mean?" Caroline asked.

"Just that I'm with you now, and it means more to me than anything."

He pulled her close and kissed her again, more urgently but with the same tenderness.

Suddenly, she stepped away. "But I'm married. I'm wearing a wedding ring." She held up her hand as if to prove her point.

"Why?" Aaron asked harshly. "Explain to me why you're wearing a wedding ring for someone who is halfway around the world, who you will probably never see again. It makes no sense!" His voice boomed and ricocheted against the trees.

Disturbed by his outburst, Caroline turned to walk away, but he held onto her arm.

"Just tell me," he pleaded. "I'll understand."

Caroline began crying. "I can't because I don't understand. All I know is that the vow I took was supposed to be forever. I can't give up simply because Kai did."

"But a relationship needs two people, Caroline. You can't be in it alone."

"I've been alone my entire life, so this is no different."

"I love you and there's nothing I can do to help you," Aaron said, finally letting go.

Caroline turned away from him and quickly headed down the path, leaving Aaron standing among the trees.

Tom and Mac were on the porch holding champagne flutes. An opened bottle and two more glasses were on the side table.

"I see the party has already begun," Aaron said, stepping off the motorcycle.

He took Caroline's hand and gave it a gentle squeeze as they walked to the house. "Are you okay?" he asked softly.

She gently nodded. "A party, huh?" Caroline said, raising her brow suspiciously. "What's all of this about?"

"It's a tradition," was all Mac said as Aaron and Tom followed the women in to the dining room.

"Not long-standing, but deeply appreciated," Aaron added.

Mac placed an arm around Aaron, giving him a kiss on the cheek. "A very sad one, I would say."

"A rolling stone gathers no moss," Aaron countered as Tom filled each glass with champagne.

"This is delicious," Caroline said after taking a sip. "It's been years since I last had champagne."

When they sat at the table, Caroline immediately noticed three differences from the other meals she had had there: the finest china and silverware were set, a prayer was said and, after that, Tom lifted his glass to make a toast.

"To my brother—it was wonderful having you here, but another visit is over," Tom said sadly. "We'll miss you, Aaron."

Caroline froze in disbelief. "You're leaving?"

Her heart raced and she felt flushed, as she had just before she'd fainted that day in Aaron's arms. And now his arms wouldn't be there to catch her.

Aaron took a sip of champagne. "In a few hours. It's time for me to go home."

How can you be leaving? Caroline thought, feeling dangerously unmoored. As she sat motionless at the table, she was flooded with emotions—both anger for not being warned that Aaron was leaving and regret for keeping Aaron at arm's length.

Caroline was being left . . . again.

Walking back to the mill with Aaron was almost unbearable, knowing that each step was that much closer to having to say goodbye. What Caroline couldn't process was why she felt so much pain. After all, Aaron was nothing more than a casual friend, as Caroline had repeated over and over to anyone who would listen.

Aaron put his hand lightly on Caroline's lower back as they approached the mill. "You were awfully quiet at lunch. Is everything all right?"

She remained silent until they reached her front walk. "You could have told me."

Aaron took hold of Caroline's shoulders and turned her so they were facing each other, just inches apart. She tried to pull back, but he pulled her closer and then kissed her. It was a long, soft, sensuous kiss that wrapped around Caroline like a warm wave, pushing her body next to his. He kissed her once more before stepping back.

"I tried, but I couldn't." He kept his hands on

322

her shoulders. "Caroline, I was hoping we could have gotten to know each other better, but you keep saying that you're not ready."

"So you're just going to move on?"

He smiled at the suggested insult. "No, I don't cut and run that easily. I need to get back to my job." Aaron looked at her with empathy. "I feel so sorry for you. Even now you just can't bring yourself to say or ask anything too personal or too intimate." Then he shook his head in frustration. "Trying to build a relationship with someone like you, someone who has built up so many walls they can't even see out, is almost maddening." He paused. "But I've enjoyed trying, and I'll remember every minute we've spent together." He kissed her on the forehead. "I don't know what you need, Caroline, but if it's time and distance, here's your opportunity."

"But . . ." She couldn't find anything else to say, and that one word just hung in the air between them.

"Exactly," Aaron said with sincere regret. "Don't worry. I'm certain our paths will cross again, sooner or later. Perhaps then you'll be ready. Perhaps then there won't be any 'buts.' "

He kissed her on the cheek, turned around, and walked out of her life.

TWENTY-EIGHT
Winged

Pam, already drenched from making several trips between the buildings at Montis, once again stepped out into the rain, carrying a large hamper of dirty bed linens. Sometimes owning an historic inn was far from either romantic or pleasurable, and this was one of those mornings. Strong winds during the night had loosened a shutter on the main building, about which one guest complained incessantly during breakfast, which Pam had had to prepare because their chef, André Levesque, was delayed while waiting for a shipment of lobster at the Rocky Mount Airport. Adding to that, Anna, the inn's housekeeper, had called the night before in excruciating pain from a cracked tooth that needed immediate attention that morning.

Pam heaved the basket a little higher as she dashed between the guest annex and the library. All in all, it was a miserable morning. Under the sheets, well protected from the rain, were a dozen books and magazines that needed to be returned to the library. Although guests were always bringing reading materials back to their rooms, the books were seldom returned to the library and needed to be collected after the guests checked out.

Yet one more of a hundred tasks she and Mark did every day.

The old library was a classic sanctuary within the larger refuge of Montis. Bookshelves surrounded large, curtained windows and antique library tables sat at the far end of the room. A flat-screen TV flanked the stone fireplace for those who wanted to watch the news that Pam turned on for her guests each morning. Throughout the room were comfortable chairs and worn leather couches that fit like a glove for those who sat in them.

Rushing through the door, Pam dropped the hamper on the floor. She was as wet as if she had stepped out of the shower, and her sneakers were covered with mud.

"How delightful," Pam said, rummaging through the stained pillowcases and dirty towels in the hamper for the books. One aromatic sock fell out from between sheets. "Ugh," Pam said, picking it up with the tips of two fingers. It would need to be washed and mailed to its rightful owner. *Add it to the list,* she thought.

Pulling together the magazines, she noticed someone had torn the cover off their *Saveur* magazine. "Perfect," she snapped. "Why the hell can't people—"

"Good morning, Pam!"

Pam bolted upright, letting out a quick shriek. She thought she was alone in the room.

"I'm sorry. Did I startle you?" Janet asked.

With the chairs so large and Janet so small, it was easy to understand why Pam didn't notice her.

"No, not at all," Pam said. "I just didn't see you." She caught her breath. "Good morning," she said in an artificially cheery tone.

"Is there anything I can help you with?" Janet asked as she put her knitting needles to the side.

"No, thank you," Pam said, returning the books to the shelves. "Just straightening up a little."

"This is a delightful room," Janet said, marveling in the rich colors and warm comfort around her.

"It is one of my favorites," Pam replied.

Even though this was one of the few times that Pam had been alone with Janet since her arrival, she had no desire to talk to anyone that morning. Pam rearranged the magazines throughout the room and moved on to untangling the Internet cables at the table. She then restarted the printer and made a fresh pot of coffee.

"Coffee will be ready in a few minutes. Will Bill be joining you?" Pam grabbed a clean washcloth from the hamper to remove some dust she saw on the windowsill.

"Not this morning. He and Chuck headed off to

a nature preserve. So we had an early breakfast with Chuck, Jimmy and Hannah at S and T's."

"Oh, did you?" Pam replied, biting her tongue.

"You and Mark are so fortunate to live in such a charming town. We've never met so many warm people."

"They are."

Janet laughed lightly, as if sharing a private joke. "By the time we finished coffee, there were ten people sitting around the table. It was great fun."

"That's nice," Pam said.

"And Duke and his wife are so funny."

Pam balked and spun around. *"Duke Blackstone?"*

Janet nodded, a smile never leaving her face. "Yes, I think so. Yes, Duke and Helen. They invited us for dinner tomorrow night."

Pam tried to control her rage but couldn't. She threw down her rag. *"That's it!"* she shouted. Right there and then she emotionally unraveled. All of the angst and frustration that had built up inside during the week erupted to the surface. Her face turned bright red. "You can come here as our guests and ignore us during your entire trip. You can even make best of friends with everyone in town. But you cannot—*cannot*—have dinner with Duke Blackstone! He has made our lives miserable." Tears began to fill her eyes.

Pam's verbal assault pushed Janet against the

back of her chair. She looked like a fawn caught in a trap, scared and not knowing what to do.

"I've had it," Pam said, storming to the door.

"Wait!" Janet called out.

Pam had one hand on the doorknob.

"What in the world have we done?" Janet asked sincerely.

Pam spun around. She pushed the tears from her face as she stared at an older version of herself. And then something snapped within her. *"Are you that unaware?"* Pam yelled.

Unfortunately, Janet was the only person in Pam's firing range when everything finally came to a head. Pam's anguish ran deep: from losing a mother she had lost touch with so many years earlier, from feeling betrayed by both of her parents for not telling her about Janet and from the profound disappointment that some kind of natural, unspoken connection had not sparked with her biological sister when they finally met. *"I'm your sister!"* she yelled.

The questions came like a flood that couldn't be held back. "Did you not wonder why you were invited here? The questions I asked about your family? Did you ever notice the likeness between us?" Pam collapsed into the chair closest to her, more emotionally spent than frustrated. "Did you not once wonder about any of this?" she pleaded.

Janet blinked several times. *"Sisters?"* The chirp in her voice was gone.

Pam's pained stare never shifted away from Janet. "And to hear that you're befriending Duke Blackstone—the one person who's making my life a living hell—is just too much." Her fingers trembled as she ran them through her hair. "Mark was right. I regret ever meeting you. Having you as a sister, trying to have a relationship with you, is just too heartbreaking." More tears rolled down her face.

"There's nothing heartbreaking, Pam," Janet said steadfastly. "You have obviously made a mistake. It's as simple as that." Janet picked up her knitting needles and fiddled with her yarn. "Mistakes are made all the time."

"But this isn't one of them," Pam shot back. "I have your birth certificate and your adoption papers, and you are the only person they lead to." Pam paused before making her final admission. "I asked you here under false pretenses. There was no contest. It was all a ruse. But I wanted to meet you. I have no other blood relatives except for you."

Pam wiped her eyes with the back of her hands. Although her heart ached, she felt a tremendous weight lifted from her shoulders. She no longer felt smothered by the unspoken secrets and bottled-up emotions that had all started with Robert Day's early-morning phone call weeks earlier. "Our mother was Kay Holt and our father was Charles Eastman. Dad died years ago, but

Mother just passed away last month. When I was going through her personal belongings, I found your—"

"Not mine!" Janet emphatically said.

"Yes, *your* birth certificate and adoption papers," Pam insisted.

Janet sat up in the chair, stiff backed and impenetrable. "Pam, I'm sorry you feel so alone in the world that you need to contrive relationships that aren't there."

"Contrive?" Pam asked in bewilderment. "Do you think I'm making this up?"

"Certainly not maliciously. But you're . . . mistaken. I'm no more adopted than you are," Janet said unequivocally.

Their discord was quickly spiraling into rancor.

"Wait here," Pam said, holding up a finger. Within seconds she was out the door, running to her home. When she returned a few minutes later, more drenched than ever, she pulled two papers from under her jacket.

"Here," she said, almost throwing the documents onto Janet's lap.

Janet set them aside without a glance.

Pam was furious in disbelief. "You won't even look at them?"

"That's someone else's private business. I don't like prying," Janet said.

Pam dropped down next to Janet on the sofa, all but blocking her escape route, and read the birth certificate aloud, her trembling fingers following each word she spoke. "Born May first . . . Charles Eastman . . . Kay Holt . . ." Pam held up an engraved disc that hung from a gold necklace around her neck. " 'KH'—Kay Holt," Pam said. "I found this in the same box as the birth certificate."

"Your parents weren't even married," Janet commented.

"Foolish mistakes are made."

"And I'm not one of them," Janet snapped back.

"No, you were a consequence of their love and young passion. But our mother did the right thing under the circumstances. They said she was deathly ill, and wasn't expected to live past childbirth. Knowing the orphanage was the most probable solution, she wanted to give her daughter, give *you,* a chance at a good life."

Janet struggled to stand, but Pam kept one firm hand on her leg, while holding the adoption papers and baptismal certificate with the other. Pam read, "Janet Wilson . . . Des Moines, Iowa." She glanced at Janet. "Are you really going to tell me that this isn't you?"

"This could be anyone," Janet insisted. "I don't know where you got those papers, or why they were fabricated, but I have a birth certificate at home." She removed Pam's hand and jumped from her seat. No longer pushed into a corner, she quickly regained her composure and returned to her familiar persona. "You're right about one thing, though, I need to cancel our invitation with Duke Blackstone. We would never want to do anything to offend you." She walked toward the door and then turned around. "And given the unfortunate misunderstanding and all that you have been through, we'll be sure to pay our bill in full."

TWENTY-NINE

Harbored

Every time Joshua visited Saint Cross Abbey, his spirit was renewed. This trip was quite a different matter, but as usual, Brother Matthew smiled as soon as he saw him.

"You're spending too much time in Seattle with Christian and not enough time here, my friend," the monk said. "Did you come for vespers?"

"I'm afraid not," Joshua said. "We have a problem. And I need to talk with Alan."

When Alan joined them, Joshua continued.

"Last night, Brooke and I were having dinner in Rocky Mount. Your brother and several of his associates were at the table next to ours," Joshua told him. "Since we've been gone most of the summer, no one recognized us. They spoke freely over the noise in the restaurant, and we overheard much of the conversation. From what was said, I'm certain Duke is going to launch a full search to find you. He's bringing in the FBI."

"On what grounds?"

"Duke has told the FBI that you embezzled millions of dollars from his company, and that's why you disappeared."

"That's insane!" Alan spat.

"No one who knows you would believe that," Matthew concurred.

"That doesn't matter," Joshua said. "Duke needs to get the FBI behind him so they will allocate the manpower to find you dead or alive."

"He's right," Alan said. "The FBI doesn't have to believe it—they just need a request or complaint. And I'm sure Duke has already paid off the right people to make it happen."

Joshua leaned forward. "There's something else. Duke has reason to believe that Alan is somewhere in this general area."

"General area?" Brother Matthew asked. "Would that be the northwest or Franklin specifically?"

"I don't know, but one of Duke's buddies at the table was talking about a two-hundred-mile grid from where Duke and Alan first fought in Rocky Mount. The same fellow said that the FBI is issuing plenty of search warrants."

"Since embezzlement is a federal crime," Alan thought aloud, "that gives them the right to search wherever they want."

Brother Matthew was stunned. "Including Saint Cross?"

"I know nothing about the law, but we have to assume yes," Joshua replied.

"Why would they come here, though?" Matthew asked. "I am positive that no one from here has said a word."

"And I can say the same for Mark," Joshua

said. "The poor guy is a nervous wreck for fear of accidentally saying something. But with Saint Cross falling within their grid, you're a target." Joshua paused. "And if you think about it, they'll assume the monastery is perfect cover. These government guys are good. If they can find one terrorist in all of the Middle East, finding one person in the foothills of the Rockies isn't rocket science."

"I agree," Alan said.

"I think we need to get you out of here," Joshua said. "That's why I came."

Matthew frowned. "But don't you think that the abbey is large enough to hide Alan for a few hours while the police are here? Between the Sisters' compound and ours, we should be able to come up with a plan."

"If they bring one or two men yes, but not if they bring a full team with dogs."

"So, where do I go?"

Joshua smiled, looking like a fox about to outwit its prey. "I know one place where they won't find you: Montis."

"That's too obvious," Matthew said.

"Isn't that the monastery owned by Mark and his wife?"

"Yes, but it's now an inn," Matthew explained.

"Duke might ask the FBI to harass your friends all the more just as retribution for going head-to-head with him in the election," Alan said.

"To put me in the mix is just asking for more trouble."

"Not if they had no idea you were there," Joshua replied.

Matthew looked at Joshua, wondering why he would recommend Montis. Suddenly, his eyes lit up. "Of course, the cottage," he said. "Very good, Joshua," he said, putting his hand on his friend's shoulder.

Joshua explained to Alan. "It's a small stone outbuilding at the back of their property that Brooke and I stayed in when we first got married. Less than a handful of people know about it, and it's so deeply buried in the woods that no one would ever see it, even from an aerial shot."

"Even though it might be only a couple of miles from where your brother is campaigning, the cottage might be the best place in the world for you to hide," Matthew agreed.

"I'll explain further on the way over," Joshua said. "Be packed and ready to go before sunrise."

Early the following morning, a Volvo drove through the town of Franklin unnoticed, heading toward Lumby. An hour later, just as the sun was rising, Joshua and Alan, who sat low in the back seat, skirted the village, weaving their way on back roads just outside of town. From Perimeter Road they turned right onto Deer Trail Lane. Alan nervously fidgeted behind him.

Joshua looked at him out of the corner of his eye. "Just a few miles farther."

Several minutes later, he slowed the car. They had reached the end of the dirt road. "There," he said, pointing to a broken-down mailbox that barely read 18 DEER TRAIL LANE. The driveway was unrecognizable, covered with years of overgrowth. A single-bar gate set ten feet off the road was lowered. It appeared that wild vines had been torn away from the padlock, which hung from a heavy chain on the post.

Joshua got out and opened the gate, drove through, and then closed it behind them. The driveway, if one could still call it that, had not been accessed for several years. The overgrowth was so thick and tall that it came halfway up the side of the car.

Alan looked out the window suspiciously. "Not that I'm doubting you, but . . ."

"I don't believe there's a safer place for you right now," Joshua said, looking over his shoulder at Alan. "It's just ahead."

Beyond the tall grasses and overgrown shrubs stood a stone cabin with ivy encasing its southern and eastern sides. The hand-hewn-oak front door hung on wrought-iron hinges forged during the century before.

Stepping out of the car, the two men trampled through the underbrush to get to the front stoop. Inside, Alan found a comfortably sized living room with a wood-burning stove and ample furniture to make any visitor welcome. The windows were small but well-placed to maximize the sun during the summer and defend against the cold of the winter. Immediately to the right of the front door was a staircase leading to a loft. The far side of the living room had a dining table with six chairs, in close proximity to the kitchen. To the right of that was the master bedroom, and to the left a full bathroom. Overall, it was a charming cabin, although a little rustic for any urbanite.

"I spoke to Mark last night. He must have come over and personally cleaned it up for your arrival."

"Please tell him how much I appreciate his efforts. Does anyone else know about this?"

"No. Since the monks owned it for so long, it's not even on any of the area maps," Joshua explained. "There's no possible way anyone could find you here, unless they were specifically told where to look."

Alan breathed a sigh of relief. He was finally able to relax.

"Okay, I need to go," Joshua said. "If there's an emergency, Montis Inn is a short walk through the woods heading west. A phone in the kitchen rings directly through to the Inn's lobby. Dial nine for an outside line. Mark knows you're here and will keep an eye out as well as bring some food over for you. He's probably already stocked the refrigerator to tide you over."

Alan shook Joshua's hand. "I don't know how to thank you."

"I know you would do the same," Joshua said. "Without hesitation."

After Joshua left, Alan unpacked his few belongings and settled in. Well after sunset, Mark arrived with a bounty of breads, cheeses, a casserole, and a selection of desserts, enough to feed a small army. He also brought several bottles of the Inn's house wine.

The following day was one for the books in Lumby. Duke Blackstone was driving himself to a rally, and had it not been for a moose that was crossing the road at Priest's Pass, all would have gone according to Duke's plan. However, he was a bad driver, and misjudged either the car's maneuverability or the moose's movements. To avoid damaging his car by hitting the animal, he veered and hit a guardrail, throwing one tire off its rim. The moose was both unhurt and undisturbed, and continued along its path in the woods.

The next car that came along pulled up behind the accident. Duke was just stepping out of the car.

"Looks bad," Brian Beezer said.

"I wouldn't know," Duke said.

"Can I give you a lift?"

"Where you going?"

Brian laughed. "This road only leads to Lumby, so that's your choice."

"Then I accept," he said, instinctively opening the back door.

"The front seat is available," Brian said.

But Duke sat in the back anyway.

There was little discussion between the two men during the ride, which Duke appreciated. He was poring over an FBI report on activities related to Alan's search.

"Where would you like to be dropped off?"

"Chatham Press."

"Do you have business there?"

"I need to give the idiot owner of the newspaper a piece of my mind."

"Oh?" Brian asked.

"You know, small towns are shit holes that burn through state funds. And independent newspapers and their scumbag editors are worse than that. And this little shit of a paper is no different." So began Duke's rant on *The Lumby Lines*, which continued until Brian pulled up in front of his father's building.

Duke pulled out his wallet to pay the driver.

"That's not necessary," Brian said.

"It's always necessary," Duke hissed, throwing a hundred-dollar bill on the front seat as he stepped out of the car.

Brian picked up his iPhone and began snapping photos as Duke climbed the stairs. Brian stayed in his car long enough to see Duke go inside. *Dad is going to be so pissed,* he thought.

As Brian was about to turn off his car, Brother Matthew drove past. What struck Brian as extremely peculiar is that Matthew didn't drive . . . ever. Brian slowly pulled onto Main Street and followed the monk, who turned right onto Perimeter, hitting the curb on the way.

Where is he going? Brian wondered.

Staying a good distance back, Brian watched Brother Matthew turn onto Deer Trail Lane. At the dead end, Matthew stopped the car, got out, looked around and quickly disappeared into the woods.

At Montis Inn, Mark hammered several nails into a loose shutter on the second floor. He looked down from the ladder when a car pulled into the parking area.

"Well, if it isn't young Mr. Beezer. This is an unexpected visit," Mark said as he climbed down. "I've been meaning to tell you that *The Lumby Lines* website looks great. We subscribed weeks ago."

"Glad you like it," Brian said.

"I hear your dad's mighty proud of you," Mark added.

"It's been a great experience. I appreciate all of the trust that he's put in me."

"Trust is a funny thing," Mark said. "It takes so long to be earned but can be broken as easily as a twig. So, what can I do for you? Run a few ads?"

"Answer a fairly straightforward question."

"Fire," Mark said.

"Why is Brother Matthew hanging out at your cottage on Deer Trail?"

Mark blinked, and then his eyes opened wide. If that wasn't evidence enough that he was surprised by the question, his jaw dropped open. "What do you mean?"

"Matthew—Deer Trail. You guys own the property at the dead end. It's pretty straight-forward."

Mark tightened his lips in a pout. "Maybe it wasn't Matthew."

Brian rolled his eyes. "Mark, I work for him."

"Okay, then I don't know," Mark said, trying to bluff.

Brian came a little closer. "My father says you blink a lot when you're bluffing in poker."

"Wow, that's exactly what Pam says."

"They're both right. And you're blinking a lot right now."

Mark froze, fearing that a carefully constructed plan was about to spiral out of control because of his blinking. "I can't say anything, Brian. I promised."

Brian shrugged as if to plead innocence. "You know, for *The Lumby Lines* I've got to be a reporter, just like my father and his father before him."

"But they both knew when to back off," Mark said sternly.

"Dad did," Brian admitted. "But I'm sure Grandfather went to the grave regretting a lot of bad decisions in life."

Mark looked for a way out of this mess. "I can promise you, Brian, if you press this, you'll be doing the same and you have no idea how much you'll regret it."

"But I know there's a story there, and it's got to be big."

You have no idea, Mark thought.

"Okay, if I stay out of it, you need to offer me something in return," Brian said firmly.

"Where did you learn how to negotiate? Your dad's not even that good." Mark was stalling as he considered alternatives. "All right, then," he said. "How about a compromise: you don't print or say one word *to anyone* and I'll guarantee you an exclusive interview that will explain everything when the time is right."

Brian thought long and hard about his proposal. "I already have photographs," he bluffed.

"Delete them all, Brian," Mark said. "You have a reputation and you have morals—both

343

are more important than some photos that could do a lot of damage now and will be forgotten in a month. I know you don't want to go back to being the jerk that you were. No offense."

"None taken," Brian said.

Mark continued in a softer voice. "I can tell you that if you push this, the way you say your grandfather pushed too often, you would do— not could do, but *would* do—irreparable harm to some people's lives, and you would lose the trust of more people than you can imagine." He paused, hoping his words would sink in. "Forget the entire incident, and get on with your business until I call you."

Brian conceded. "And we have a deal?"

Mark shook his hand. "On my word. But you tell absolutely no one."

As Brian Beezer drove away, Pam came out of their home. Although she hadn't been eavesdropping, she sensed something was up. She had heard Deer Trail mentioned and tried to figure out why. She did know their thirtieth anniversary was approaching, and she thought that perhaps Mark was planning a romantic getaway at the cottage.

"What did Brian want?" Pam asked.

"Not much. He was just . . ." Mark tried to come up with a reasonable excuse.

"Yes?" Pam asked.

"Wanting advertisements. That's it—for his new

website. I told him he needed to talk with you."

Pam doubted that. "So why didn't you send him over to the house?"

"Oh . . . he had to go. And so do I. Need to get to my chores. See you later." Mark dashed off.

"Remember the shutter on the second floor," Pam called out.

"Already done, honey!"

Pam headed for the restaurant and kitchen to discuss the menu with André. After planning the meals together, Pam was going to return to their house, but her curiosity got the better of her. Instead, she followed the trail that first traversed the small Montis cemetery and then went on to their cottage.

As the cottage had been vacant for several years, Pam was shocked to see two cars parked in the driveway.

She threw open the door, assuming it was trespassers.

There, she came face-to-face with Duke Blackstone, Mark and Joshua. If that wasn't surreal enough, Brother Matthew sat close by with his hands crossed on his lap.

Before Pam could scream, Mark cried, *"It's not him!"*

By midnight, Mark had explained every last detail to Pam, and had answered most of her questions.

Pam was neither upset nor disappointed. "You did a good thing, honey," she said as they climbed into bed. "I'm sure the monks and Alan appreciate it."

Mark was dumbstruck. "But aren't you angry I lied to you?"

"Not at all," Pam said nonchalantly.

"Well, wait a minute. I thought we agreed to never lie to each other, no matter what. And at one point, I'm sure you would have done bodily harm if you knew I wasn't honest with you."

Pam knew that was probably true. "Maybe I've changed."

"No, no, no," Mark said, wagging his finger. "A person doesn't *change*. They're not honest one minute and dishonest the next. Either a person is or they're not. I thought that was important to you."

"It was."

"It *was?* But now it's not?" Mark asked.

"It's different now."

Mark's concern was growing. "How?"

Pam shrugged her shoulders. "Maybe I don't see everything in black-and-white anymore. Maybe I believe that if you can't tell me the truth, there's a good reason. I trust you, honey." She kissed him on the lips. "Now go to sleep."

Two hours later, Mark turned on the bedroom lights. "Pam, wake up," he said, shaking her. "Is there something you want to tell me?"

Pam was half asleep. "No, I'm sleeping. Turn off the light."

"I'm serious, we need to talk." Mark said, sitting up in bed. "Maybe you don't have a problem with me being honest because *you* might not want to be honest."

Pam opened one eye and tried to figure out what Mark was saying. "What?"

"Well, maybe you think it's okay that I didn't tell you about the monks and Alan Blackstone because you have something that you don't want to tell me, so it's like equal." Mark paused. "Is there something you want to tell me?"

"Yeah, there is," Pam said. "And I haven't told you because I knew you'd be upset."

"I knew it," Mark said. "Go ahead, say it."

"The shutter fell off the inn again. Now go to sleep."

Mark gave a weak laugh. "That's not funny at all."

"Not if it hit one of our guests. Would you please use longer screws next time?" Pam rolled over and put a pillow over her head.

THIRTY

KH

Janet's dreams always reflected the grace and good fortune of her life. They gently carried her through each night with loving images of those people she kept close to her heart, and held soft reflections of a cherished home in Virginia that, throughout the ever-changing seasons, kept her, Bill and her two grown kids safe and warm. Occasionally, her sleep would take her back to her childhood, in Iowa, where she was always playing with one of her many siblings, always picked up and coddled by a devoted mother and father.

That night, Janet tossed in bed as she was carried through a dream of her young childhood. It was around her third birthday, and she was sitting alone in a playpen close to the kitchen. Snow covered the trees and a strong wind rattled the siding, but inside, a fire burned in the hearth. Although she couldn't see her mother, she could hear her singing just feet away. In the pen was a new stuffed rabbit that she had swaddled in her favorite old quilt, which also covered her own shoulders. The worn comforter was pink and yellow—her favorite colors—and offered

348

comforting warmth. Pretending that the rabbit had started to cry, little Janet picked up the corner of the quilt to dry its eyes. Only then did she notice the initials beautifully embroidered in dark-blue thread: KH.

Upon waking, Janet remembered the dream in vivid detail. She hadn't thought about that quilt for almost fifty years. And she was quite certain about the initials, if for no other reason than for the punishment she received when, at the age of five and not knowing any better, she traced the letters with a black marker.

" 'KH,' " Janet whispered as she showered that morning. Who was KH? No doubt a friend of her mother's who had used the quilt as barter, as was common in their tight-knit community. The fact that they were the same initials as Kay Holt—Pam's mother—was purely coincidence, Janet assured herself. But to dispel any lingering doubt, Janet would call her oldest brother in Iowa later that day to ask if he remembered the quilt and who KH might have been.

After dressing, she and Bill had their morning walk before joining Pam and Mark for breakfast. André, the Montis chef, had gone out of his way to prepare one of his more memorable meals.

"André must have come up with a new recipe for the croissants," Pam said. "These are delicious."

Janet beamed. "Actually, I bought them yesterday from a small bakery in Wheatley. They're Alsatian croissants with walnut, almond and hazelnut cream," she said sweetly.

"Mrs. Loundons?" Pam asked.

"That's the one!" Janet said, going out of her way to reconnect with Pam. "I thought you might enjoy them."

"That was very thoughtful," Pam said politely.

Mark wiped crumbs from his shirt. "So, do you two have any plans today?"

"We've already had our walk down to Woodrow Lake," Janet said. "You're both so lucky to live in such beautiful surroundings."

Pam smiled at Mark. "We are, but it comes at a high price."

Bill nodded. "But who wouldn't want to work here?"

"Spoken like a true retiree," Pam laughed, thinking about her endless list of chores. "So, more sightseeing?"

"No. Chuck Bryson asked if I wanted to join him to check out the golden eagle's nest at . . . hmm . . . I think he called it Dead Man's Bluff. Want to come?"

Before Mark could respond, Pam smacked him on the arm.

"Oww," Mark winced. "I think that's Pam's way of saying, 'No, I wouldn't because my to-do list is a mile long.' But thanks anyway."

"True enough, but that's not the exact reason,"

Pam said. "Do you want to show them your scars?"

Mark flinched. "We had a small incident the last time Chuck and I went up to see the eagles."

"*Incident?*" Pam said sarcastically.

"It was a one-in-a-million thing," Mark said. "I dropped my corned-beef-and-cabbage sub, and one of the eagles took it for roadkill. Before you knew it, this bird and I were waging a full-out war for the hoagie."

"With talons three inches long," Pam added.

"Yeah, but who knew that eagles had such great eyesight?"

Pam rolled her eyes. "I think everyone does."

"But he saw that corned beef from five hundred feet up," Mark said, still in amazement several years later.

Everyone laughed, except Pam.

"It's intense there. Really rugged," Pam said more seriously. "Just be careful."

"But you couldn't have a better rappelling partner than Chuck," Mark said.

Janet's ears perked up. "Rappelling? You didn't tell me that part," she said to Bill.

Mark explained. "You need to get to their nest, which is on the ledge halfway up—"

"Or down," Pam added.

"Yeah, the rock face is perfectly sheer."

"Sounds exciting," Bill said, rubbing his hands together. "I'm ready for the challenge."

Pam looked toward the door as someone arrived. "Speaking of the devil himself."

Chuck Bryson waved.

"No crampons allowed in here!" she called out.

"You'll never let me forget that, will you?" he laughed as he walked up to the table. "A few small holes in the hardwood floor, and Pam didn't speak to me for a week."

"I thought it gave our floors a vintage look," Mark said, coming to his defense.

"Because you were one of the offenders," Pam reminded him.

"May I?" Chuck leaned over and helped himself to a croissant. "Absolutely delicious," he said after taking a big bite. "So, who's joining me today?"

Bill jumped up. "Ready to go. But I think I'm the only one."

Chuck looked around the table. "No other takers?" Everyone shook their heads. "All right then, we're off."

"Do I need to bring anything?" Bill asked.

"Lots of medical supplies," Pam quipped.

After the men left, Pam and Janet sat at the table. Janet looked around the room and Pam stared into her cup of coffee.

"You're angry?" Janet asked hesitantly.

Pam wouldn't go there. "Disappointed, maybe. If you don't want to believe something—"

"It's not that I don't *want* to believe it," Janet began. "But you just can't decide to believe something you know isn't true."

Pam almost dropped her mug on the table. "But how can you be so certain?" she asked, her voice filling the empty room. "Stranger things in life have happened."

"I'm sure they have, but not in this case." Janet saw Pam's brows rise. "And I'm not being stubborn. I even called my brother earlier this morning to ask if he knew of something I didn't, and he assured me he didn't."

"But, Janet, that doesn't prove anything," Pam countered.

"Your suggestion is almost preposterous. And this isn't just about you and me. If what you said is true, it would be about my parents, who would have lied to me, and about my brothers and sisters, who wouldn't be my siblings . . . and about my own children." Her lips tightened. "I know who their grandparents are. My son looks just like his grandfather."

"But that could be a coincidence," Pam argued.

Janet took a deep breath, trying to calm herself down. "Pam, I can't imagine being in your position, not having a family of your own. But I'm not it, no matter how badly you wish it was otherwise."

"Or how badly you're afraid of the possibility?" Pam countered.

Janet slapped her hands on her thighs, startling Pam.

"All right, then," Janet said, trying for reconciliation. "If you must be certain that I'm not your sister, I . . ." She paused for a moment. "I would agree to a DNA test."

Pam's eyes lit up. "I don't want you to do it for just for me," she said. "I want you to want to know the truth as well."

"But I do," Janet said. "The only thing I ask is that you don't tell Bill."

Pam's jaw dropped. "I thought you two shared everything."

"Almost everything."

THIRTY-ONE

Talons

A half hour later, seemingly in the middle of nowhere, somewhere north of Lumby, Chuck pulled the car off the road.

"Are we in Canada yet?" Bill joked.

"Follow that road and you'd be there for dinner time."

Unloading the trunk, the two men continued their discussion about travel, which began shortly after leaving Montis Inn.

"So you liked India?" Bill asked.

"I'm not sure if 'like' would best describe it. Jaipur was . . . fascinating—total chaos and an assault to every one of our senses. Nothing can prepare you. But I'm glad I went."

"Most beautiful place you've been?" Bill asked.

Chuck thought for a moment. "I really haven't traveled the world like you have, but I would have to say the South Island of New Zealand. How about you?"

"Wherever I am," Bill answered. "You could put me in the middle of Morocco during the worst damn sandstorm the planet has ever seen, and I would love it."

Chuck laughed. "You don't let moss grow under your feet."

Bill lifted his shoulders apologetically. "I just find the world and the people in it fascinating, and the farthest corners of the globe are the most interesting of all."

"So, Lumby must be pretty tepid for your adventurous nature."

"Meeting new friends is never boring," Bill said, gently slapping Chuck on the back. "Most of the time, for me it's not where we are but who we get to know. I find people so interesting. It's always fun to hear what they think—see the world through their eyes."

"That's certainly refreshing to hear. I'm afraid most people have no interest," Chuck said, picking up a handful of carabiners. "You grab the ropes, and I'll take everything else."

Chuck swung a large backpack over his shoulders, and they headed off into the woods in a single file.

"So where are we?" Bill asked.

"This is Bryson's Bird Sanctuary."

"Yours?"

Chuck laughed. "I suppose it once was, but I donated the land to the town and they made it into a wildlife preserve."

Bill looked back toward the road. "We haven't seen a soul for twenty miles, and there's no sign. How would anyone know there's a bird sanctuary here?"

"Well, there's no need for a sign." Chuck slowed as the path narrowed and increased in slope. "Anyone who has any business being here knows it's here. It's pretty much by personal invitation and word of mouth in the town."

Two hours later, they had hiked a mile in the deep forest and climbed two thousand vertical feet.

Standing at the summit, Chuck looked over the ledge as he pulled on his gloves. "The nest is a hundred feet below us."

Bill was still appreciating the panorama. "This is beautiful. You think you're the only person in the world."

"And that's how we want to keep it," Chuck said, stepping into his harness. He ran the rope through several anchors, a grappling hook that was deeply embedded into the closest tree, and his carabiners.

"What do you want me to do?" Bill asked.

"Nothing right now. I'll go down, take my measurements of the eaglets and then we'll get you strapped in so you can take a look firsthand."

Bill was awed by the complexity and volume of ropes and connectors. "Looks like you've done this before."

"Hundreds, maybe thousands of times." He grabbed one rope in front of him, and another behind, and walked backward until he was at the ledge. Suddenly, Chuck leaned out and pushed off.

Before Bill knew it, his friend had vanished. He ran toward the edge but not so far as to be able to look straight down. "You okay?"

"Just fine," Chuck called, hovering about fifteen feet below the ledge. He began to let out rope to lower himself to the nest.

A high-pitched screech shattered the quiet.

"The female is watching us," Chuck said.

Suddenly, an eagle swooped down with talons facing Bill's head. He ducked just in time.

"The bird!" Bill screamed, waving his arm in the air, although the eagle was long gone. "That's the fastest thing I've ever seen."

Chuck didn't hear. "Be careful. She can be a little ornery."

Ornery? Bill thought. "She almost took my head off."

Another screech followed by another attack. This time the eagle flew parallel to the ledge, clearly heading for Chuck. Bill watched as if it was a *National Geographic* film in slow motion. Her talons extended in front of her body.

She screeched again, right before Chuck screamed. Both were bloodcurdling shrieks.

The rope suddenly went loose and dropped slackly to the ground.

"Chuck!" Bill yelled.

There was no response.

Bill's heart raced. He lay down on his stomach and wormed his way to the precipice, pushing over the edge as far as he dared. Seventy feet below him, Chuck was sprawled out on a ledge no larger than a double bed. Beyond that was a drop of another five hundred feet.

"Don't move!" Bill yelled in a panic. "Chuck, can you hear me?"

Bill couldn't hear Chuck groan, but saw his mouth move.

"Her—" Chuck tried to say something.

"Don't move!" he yelled again. "You're on a small ledge." The eagle screeched somewhere above Bill. "Can you hear me?"

Chuck moved his head very slowly. "Her talon," he said almost inaudibly.

Bill pulled up the rope Chuck had been hanging from. The end looked if someone had cut it with a razor blade. "Are you all right?"

Chuck shook his head once. "Something's in my back," he said weakly. Chuck winced as he moved his hand under his back.

Both of them saw the blood when he brought his arm up.

"I landed on a branch." He coughed and spit out some blood.

Bill tried not to panic. "I have to go for help. But don't move. You're right next to a huge drop-off." He looked at his watch. It was 2:14 p.m. "I'll be back."

Bill scooched away from the edge and stood up. He grabbed the car keys from Chuck's jacket, looked around and took the path that he thought they had used on the hike up. Unfortunately, it wasn't.

Bill tried to run on the deer trail, but he tripped often. His hands were cut up and throbbing from breaking his falls. Not until the path began to ascend an hour later did he realize he was on the wrong trail. Another path veering to his left continued downward, so that's the one he took.

Two hours later, he was very lost. Had he known that he had increased, and not decreased, the distance from the road by several miles, he would have panicked. Had he known that he was surrounded by tens of thousands of acres of wilderness, he would have panicked that much more.

In the kitchen at Montis, Pam smelled the dill she had collected from their garden that morning. "Perfect," she said aloud as she began to dice the new potatoes that she would serve at dinner. She glanced over at the clock above the stove: 5:35 p.m.

Mark opened the swinging doors enough to stick his head in. "Have you heard from Chuck?"

Pam shot him a quizzical look. "I assumed they got back a while ago. Is he in the library?"

Mark shook his head. "No, they haven't returned, and they're about two hours overdue. And Chuck is always on schedule, especially when he's hiking."

"They might have stopped off at Gabrielle's for a margarita."

Mark immediately shook his head. "No way—not without letting us know. He's too responsible."

Pam dried her hands on a towel and picked up the phone to call Chuck's cell number. It immediately went to voice mail. "Chuck, it's Pam. Call us right away."

"What do you think?" Mark asked as soon as she hung up.

She stared at the phone, expecting Chuck to call right back. When it didn't ring, she frowned. "I don't know. Are you worried?" she asked, trying to temper her nerves.

"A little," Mark said, although his concern was a lot more than a little. "I'm going to drive up to the preserve. I'll probably pass them on the way."

"Take your phone and call me," Pam said.

Mark spun around and ran straight into Janet, who was standing directly behind him.

"Have you heard anything?" she asked.

"No, but you know Chuck," Mark said, casually waving his hand.

"Actually, I don't."

"He can get lost up there . . . well, not lost in the 'I'm lost' sort of way. Chuck would never get really lost like that." He told himself to stop talking, but nervous words just kept coming. "But lost as in being distracted because of the mountains and the eagles and stuff."

"They should have been back hours ago. Bill doesn't know how to hike," Janet said, wringing her hands.

"Yeah, but Chuck is the best of the best. He knows what he's doing."

"Are you going up there?" Janet asked impatiently.

Mark tried to force a calm tone. "I thought I'd just take a drive to the preserve."

"Please. They might need your help."

"That's right, they have a lot of equipment." Mark stumbled over his words as he fibbed. "Why don't you go in and talk to Pam?"

"All right, but let me know if you hear anything," Janet said.

"Will do." As soon as she was gone, he dashed out of the room.

Pam had overheard the conversation, and she was prepared when Janet came into the kitchen. "Don't worry. Everything will be fine."

"You don't know Bill," Janet said.

"No, but I know Chuck. And I know Mark, and he will dig his way to China to find them if they're in trouble," Pam reassured her as she continued chopping the carrots. "I haven't seen you all day. Is everything all right?" she asked, deliberately changing the subject.

"I've been in my room," Janet replied.

"I hope you're not avoiding me."

"No, just with a good book." She paused, not liking to lie. "But it is a little awkward, isn't it? I don't quite know what to say to you."

"Well, FedEx delivered the DNA test kits this morning, so whenever you're ready, we can spit and see what happens," Pam said, forcing some levity into their conversation.

"Spit?" Janet asked.

"Into a small flask. The packing is pretty clever—it looks very simple." Pam glanced over at the clock again. "We might have a bit of a wait until Mark calls us, so why don't we go over to our house and I'll show you."

Twenty minutes later, Pam held up the two vials of saliva that would prove whether or not she was sitting next to her sister. Not only would the test tell them what they now both wanted to know, but it had also been a good distraction while they waited for Mark to call.

But still no word from anyone.

THIRTY-TWO

Found

Fifteen minutes later, after driving eighty miles an hour once he reached the outskirts of town, Mark reached Chuck's parked car. Pulling up behind it, Mark jumped out and looked inside. All the hiking gear was gone, so he knew that they were still up on the mountain. Mark cupped his hands around his mouth. "Chuck!" he yelled as loud as he could. But there was no reply. He honked his horn several times. Still no response.

He quickly dialed Pam, but the connection was poor. "His car is here," he cried into the phone. "I'm going up the trail. If you don't hear from me, call Simon."

Mark had hiked the preserve many times with Chuck over the years, and knew the way well enough to find the eagle's nest. He bolted up the path at a full run. Within minutes his heart was pounding in his chest and his leg muscles burned.

I so need to start exercising, he thought.

As soon as he reached the summit, he saw Chuck's backpack and gear scattered around. He picked up the cut rappelling rope, and panicked.

"Chuck!" he screamed.

He heard a faint reply: "Help me."

Mark knelt down and crawled to the edge. He saw Chuck spread out on a ledge directly below him. Within feet of where Chuck lay was a sheer drop-off down into the ravine.

"Chuck, it's Mark. Are you okay?"

Chuck remained still. "No," he said weakly. "Her talons cut the rope."

"Where's Bill?"

"Went for help."

"How long ago?"

Chuck's eyes were closed. He didn't answer.

Mark assumed Chuck was drifting in and out of consciousness. He quickly grabbed a spare rope and tied a large loop at the end. He lowered it down to Chuck.

"Chuck, listen to me!" Mark yelled. "Put the rope under your arms." When the rope reached Chuck, he said again, "Under your arms."

"You can't pull me up," Chuck said weakly.

"I know, but you're right next to the ledge. If you roll off, you'll die."

Chuck did as he was told, although he cried out in pain when he tried to lift his upper body. Mark tied his end around the base of the tree.

"Should I come down?" Mark asked.

Chuck coughed and a small amount of blood landed on his shirt. "You'll kill yourself."

Mark couldn't argue that point. He looked at his cell phone, although he already knew there was no coverage. He checked the time. "Pam should have already called Simon," he said. "I'm going to stay with you."

"You need to find . . ." Chuck's voice faded.

"Bill. I know," Mark yelled back.

But Mark wouldn't leave Chuck. If no one showed up, he would go down to help Chuck himself.

The next hour was one of the longest in Mark's life. Dusk wasn't far off. Mark began to look through the gear to figure out the best way of rappelling down. Just as he was untying a rope, Simon Dixon and Dennis Beezer came running up the trail.

"Thank God," Mark said.

"Where are they?" Simon asked.

"Chuck's below on a ledge. He's hurt."

"A chopper is on the way," Dennis said.

Simon looked over the cliff edge to assess the situation. He pulled out his walkie-talkie and started talking.

"Where is Bill?" Dennis asked.

"Chuck said he went for help, but I haven't seen him."

Dennis noticed that there were several paths leading away from where they stood. "Bill probably took the wrong trail."

"I'm afraid so," Mark said.

Within a minute, the men spotted a helicopter in the distance.

Simon continued to talk to the rescue team in the chopper. "No, there's nowhere to land," he said loudly into the walkie-talkie. There was a pause while a question was being asked. "Enough room for one person to stand, but that's it. It's a narrow ledge."

Another minute later, the helicopter was hovering overhead. The side door opened, and a cage was swung out. A rescuer stepped in and motioned his arm. The cage dropped and disappeared from view.

Several minutes later, the cage was winched up. Simon continued talking with one of the rescuers as Chuck was lifted to safety.

The helicopter hovered for several minutes more, and then they spoke to Simon.

"Roger," Simon said, and turned to Mark and Dennis. "They need to air evac Chuck to Rocky Mount Hospital. They think a limb punctured his right lung, and his vitals are weak."

The helicopter pulled away from the mountain, rotated and headed southeast.

"If it's still light enough, they'll be back to help with our search," Simon said, looking through Chuck's backpack. He pulled out a map, two flashlights, one flare gun and a handful of smoke flares. "If nothing else, he certainly was equipped."

"I'll head back to the car and call in for more help," Dennis said.

"Okay," Simon said, opening the map. "Mark and I will split up. I'll head north and Mark can take the trail to the west. When the others get here, tell them that we think Bill headed in the wrong direction, away from the road."

Simon split up the gear between him and Mark. "Here," he said, handing Mark the backpack. "Take this. If you find him, use the flare gun and then stay put. Don't move a foot."

Mark grabbed everything handed to him and took off down the trail that headed west. In the fading light, he noticed the ground had recently been scuffed up, but that was no guarantee Bill had taken that route—a deer could have easily caused it.

Every few minutes, he stopped and hollered Bill's name. But there was no reply. He thought he heard Simon doing the same, but one thing Chuck had taught him is that sounds do funny things when echoing against the cliffs.

When Mark reached an intersection where one path headed back up the mountain, and the other down, he took the path of least resistance.

Back at Montis, Pam held out the phone so both she and Janet could listen. The connection was bad, which made it all the more frustrating as Simon gave them an update: Chuck had been found and was being medevaced from the cliff. He was alive but in serious condition. Bill was not in the recovery area, so two search teams had been—

The call disconnected.

"Deployed," Pam said. "That's what Simon was going to say. And those mountain rescue teams are unbelievable."

Janet's eyes were wide with fear.

"He was wearing Reeboks," Janet said helplessly.

"Reeboks?"

"He didn't even have boots. He was wearing the sneakers that he wears when he's walking around the neighborhood in Great Falls. Why would he think he could use them to go mountain climbing?"

Pam shrugged. "It's a guy thing."

Then Pam did what she always did when she got nervous—she cleaned. Only this time, Janet was just a few steps behind, following her from one building to another, from one room to the next. After they made their way to the library with an armful of books and magazines that had been collected throughout the inn, Janet began dusting the leather upholstery.

"He worries me a lot sometimes," Janet finally said. "He wants to take on all of these adventures, charging full speed ahead. He says he doesn't want to miss anything before he dies."

Pam continued straightening the room. "Well, there's nothing wrong with that, is there?"

"No, but I don't think he is careful enough. He doesn't always calculate what can go wrong."

"But all men are like that, Janet. A half-million years ago, the first time they saw a woolly mammoth, they ran after it without thinking it through." Both women laughed. "It's just who they are. In fact, I think that's one of the roles of a husband." Pam paused, thinking back on her spouse's misadventures. "I can't tell you all the predicaments Mark has gotten into over the years. Sometimes I'm amazed he hasn't broken every bone in his body."

"But none of us are twenty-year-olds anymore. Our bodies break easier."

"You're right, but if we ask our husbands to act their age and be more cautious, they'll just grow older that much sooner. And look at Bill, he's in great shape."

"For a suburban life in Virginia. But he even complains when he has to mow the lawn."

"Because he doesn't want to do it," Pam said. "No husband likes to do anything on a honey-do list."

"But I think mountain climbing and rappelling fall outside of limits of responsible behavior."

"I suppose that's just what we have to do sometimes—put up with their craziness," Pam said.

Janet was the first to sit down at the card table. Pam quickly joined her.

"You shouldn't worry. Mark and Simon and the others will find him."

Janet looked outside. It was pitch black. "You said there are thousands of acres out there."

"And the guys know the area incredibly well. Also Bill seems to have a good head on his shoulders."

"Most of the time but he gets carried away— that's what I'm worried about. And if he knew Chuck was hurt, he would have gone for help."

"Did I tell you the time that I walked into the lower barn and found Mark hanging from the ceiling of the crossbeam with one end of the rope tied around his waist, and the other end tied to a bumper of our Jeep? He was throwing his shoe at the car, hoping to hit the gas pedal."

Janet couldn't help but to laugh. "Why?"

"To this day, I don't know. I asked him if he needed any help, and he said no. And that was the last time we ever talked about it."

"But he must be incredibly handy. The two of you rebuilt the inn."

Pam burst out laughing. "Oh my gosh. During the restoration, there was an 'incident' almost every day, and an ambulance here almost every week. We became such good friends with the Lumby EMS team that we invited them over for Thanksgiving. But Mark came out of it in one

371

piece, no worse for wear. It will be no different for Bill."

Janet took Pam's hand and held it in hers. "Thank you for being so sure."

The search went on through much of the night. It wasn't until midnight, when Mark's hoarse voice yelled out Bill's name for the hundredth time, that Bill was found.

He froze when he heard a faint reply. "Over here."

"Again," Mark yelled out as he ran toward the sound.

"Here! Here!"

Mark burst through an opening and fell into a stream. He scrambled to his feet.

"Bill?" he yelled, waving the flashlight.

"I'm here," he said, running up to Mark. "Is Chuck okay?"

"Yeah, they airlifted him to the hospital."

"I heard the helicopter but couldn't see it. And then with all the echoes, I got turned around again."

"Are you okay?" Mark said, placing his hands on Bill's shoulders.

"Exhausted," Bill admitted. "Do you know how to get out of here?"

"I have no idea. I'm as lost as you are," Mark said. "But . . ." He swung the backpack to the ground and pulled out Chuck's flare gun. He counted out five bullets. "We'll send up the first three flares fifteen minutes apart, and then another two ten minutes apart. They'll find us in no time."

Mark had underestimated the search team's size and capabilities. He only had to shoot two flares to be rescued.

The hike back to the car was slow going; it was dark and both Mark and Bill were physically spent.

"You know Chuck thinks the world of you," Bill said as they walked single file through the woods, each carrying a flashlight and following several men in the search party. "We talked all the way up to the bluff. He said he wished he was more like you."

Mark was stunned. "He's a physics professor from Berkeley. Why would he want to be more like me?"

"He loves your attitude toward life," Bill said. "And he said you're the most loyal friend a man could ever have."

"I would have to say the same about him."

"We also talked about the town election. Chuck said there's a lot of dirty politics going on. I might know some people who could help."

Mark stopped dead in his tracks, shining a flashlight in Bill's face. Mark's thoughts were racing a mile a minute. "Like hired spies?

Like the Mafia knocking off Duke Blackstone? I knew it! I knew you did something under-cover!"

Bill lurched back, startled by Mark's reaction. "What in the world are you talking about?"

Mark's eyes were open wide. "I knew you were a spy or something. Were you in the CIA? Or maybe that secret organization that no one talks about."

Bill laughed. "I was in intelligence, yes. But the people I know are a couple of well-respected senators."

"What a contradiction," Mark joked.

Bill tried to laugh but his whole body hurt. "Washington is in shambles isn't it? That part of the business drives me crazy."

"What business? Like the spy business?" When Bill didn't answer, Mark pressed further. "Do you know the president?"

Bill chuckled as he shook his head. "Not really. I've only met them a few times. If you want, I can see if there's some way we can lend Pam a hand."

"I'm not sure what she would say, but if there is any way to help her, I'm all for it."

"No promises, but I'll see what I can do."

Bill was never so glad to be lying on a bed in his life. Exhausted, bruised, and badly scratched up, he felt ten years older.

"Have you heard anything about Chuck?" he asked Janet, who was in the bathroom rinsing out a washcloth.

"Simon called from the hospital. Chuck had surgery for a punctured lung but is expected to make a full recovery. He'll be there for two or three days."

"Nicest guy in the world. We really need to go and visit him."

Janet walked back into the room and sat on the edge of the bed. "You're not going anywhere for the next few days."

"But we're scheduled to leave tomorrow," Bill said.

"We need to talk about that," Janet said cautiously. "You're hurt and I'm exhausted."

Bill sat up. "From what?"

"Mostly worrying about you," she began. "But I'm also tired of the pace we're keeping. During every trip we're going from place to place, not even staying long enough to unpack our bags. And then after we return home, it's only long enough to do the laundry and catch up on our mail, and then we're off again. We don't even have time to spend with our own kids or all of our friends."

"But this is what we said we wanted all along— that once I retired, we would travel the world," Bill said.

"But not every week of every month. And

375

definitely not when it jeopardizes our health and peace of mind."

Bill looked crushed. "So what are you saying?"

"I would like to stay here for a while longer. I really have no interest in going to England. We've been there so many times and we don't even enjoy the folks we stay with." Janet considered telling Bill the more pressing reason she wanted to stay in Lumby: to learn what the DNA results were. But it had been a long day, and she wanted time to sort through her feelings before sharing them with her husband.

Bill groaned as he lay back down. "Maybe that's a good idea. I haven't been this sore in years." He thought for a moment. "You know, if we're going to stay here, I'd like to give Bones a call and see if he can join us."

Janet's brows shot up. "That's a surprise."

Bill closed his eyes and spoke very slowly. "It will make sense after I tell you what Chuck said."

Before Janet could reply, Bill was sound asleep.

Janet grabbed the ice bucket and snuck out of the room.

The night-lights in the dining room allowed Janet to make her way to the kitchen. She swung open the door and found Mark standing by the island, holding a sandwich. His head was tilted and his eyes closed.

"Mark?"

He opened one lid and then took another bite of the sandwich.

"Are you all right?"

"I was lying in bed starving."

"Can I get you something else?"

"No, I'm almost done here," he answered before taking the last bite. "Is Bill doing okay?"

"Very sore, but he's sound asleep." She filled the ice bucket. "I can't tell you how much I appreciate everything you did . . . how grateful I am that you found Bill."

"I wasn't alone—everyone was looking for him," Mark said casually.

"Yes, but you went out to find him. You could've stayed where you were until the rescue team came, but you didn't. You risked your own safety for his."

"He would have done the same, I'm sure."

"I am too," Janet said confidently. "But I wanted you to know how indebted we are to you."

Mark chuckled lightly. "You're not. In fact, Pam and I were going to apologize for being around so little. We've been so preoccupied with the election and so beat up by the campaign that we just haven't given our guests the attention we usually do."

"Pam hasn't really talked about it," Janet said, slightly uneasy.

"No, she wouldn't," Mark said. "She doesn't like sharing her troubles with anyone. She thinks she needs to solve every problem herself. I love her, but that woman drives me crazy sometimes."

Janet saw a possibile opening. "Well, maybe we can help. Bill and I thought it would be nice to stay in town for a few more weeks—that is, assuming our room is available."

Mark was surprised by her suggestion. "I'm sure it is. But I thought you two were off on another whirlwind adventure."

"We were," Janet said, "but I think today took a lot out of Bill. Maybe it's time we unpack our luggage and slow down a little."

"I'm sure Pam would love for you to stay," Mark said eagerly. "The election is taking a toll on her and you guys are about the only distraction she has in her life right now. If it wasn't for our guests, she would be campaigning from morning to night. She really wants to do what's right for Lumby."

"Doesn't Pam have any volunteers?" Janet asked.

"Certainly our close friends. But people are busy and she would be the last to ask for help. She feels it's an imposition."

"What does she need help with?"

"She really needs people to go door to door and introduce themselves, explain the town issues and how Pam would deal with them. And if they don't agree, that's okay. What's most important is for everyone to vote so their voices will be counted."

After saying good night, Janet headed back to their room with an ice bucket under her arm. She was more confident than ever that there was a higher reason why she and Bill had to stay in Lumby.

THIRTY-THREE

Color

Several days later, before joining Pam for coffee at the Lumby Bookstore, Caroline stood in front of the post office. Her fingers trembled as she opened an envelope that she had just received, with the return address:

seas the day
seal cove marina, pier #2, slip #9
edmonds, washington

hello Caroline, trust me when i say i'm not an author. in fact, i'm as drawn to pen and paper as a fish to a bicycle. but you seemed quite enamored with your old typewriter and the letters written on it, so i'm game—i'll gladly humiliate myself if that makes me more honorable in your eyes.

  i fear we ended on a bad note, more so because of my impatience and frustration than anything. so please accept this as an apology.

  for lack of anything else to discuss, i'll start by answering questions that you never asked: i live on a boat. my home is a 42' irwin ketch sailboat named "seas the day" that is docked at a small marina in edmonds. in tow is a dinghy on which i spend most of the day, painting buoys and boats for a handful of very loyal customers. i spend the two coldest winter months hibernating in her warm cabin, reading the books i have collected throughout the year. after several turns in the road, this is where my journey has brought me so far, and i'm happy for it. although my life is not well anchored, literally and figuratively, it's one that's deeply lived and appreciated by me every day.

i hope to receive word from you soon.

aaron

"Caroline!" Pam called from across the street. "Are you coming?"

"Yeah." She waved back. Her broad grin couldn't be missed.

"You look stunning," Pam said when Caroline joined her. "It's nice to see you smiling again."

Caroline blushed. "It's nice to feel happy again."

Walking into the store, the women split up.

"I'll be back in the genealogy section," Pam said.

Caroline stayed by the front corner of the store.

"Here for a card?" Nancy, the store manager, asked as she walked by.

"Hi, Nancy. It looks like you have twice as many as you did last time I was in," Caroline said, turning the carousel.

"No one buys books anymore," she said in dismay. "So I'm hoping I can sell more cards and magazines to make up the difference." She looked at the cards that Caroline was studying. "The wood duck—that's one of my favorites."

Caroline picked up the card and held it close, studying the fine details of the image, which she guessed was pen and ink on dry watercolor with complimentary computer graphics in the background. "It's stunning," she said. "I've never seen a style like this."

She returned the card to the carousel and looked at the others—probably two dozen—by the same artist: all of wildlife, all with exacting details, all in brilliant colors. "I also love this one," Caroline said, pointing to a card that showed a pair of mountain bluebirds surrounded by Heavenly Blue morning glories. "And the Black-capped Chickadee is precious."

"I think they're all exquisite. And that the artist is one of our own means that much more, doesn't it?" Nancy added.

Caroline pulled back in disbelief. "He's local?"

"Well, not exactly local, but close enough,"

Nancy replied as she began to stack some books. "He's Tom Candor's brother."

Caroline felt like a bomb went off in her head. *"Aaron?"*

Nancy nodded, "Didn't you know?"

"Clueless, as usual."

"Clueless about what?" Pam asked as she joined the women.

"That Tom's brother, Aaron, is an artist," Caroline replied.

Pam looked at the card Caroline was holding. "I'm surprised you didn't see Aaron's prints hanging in Tom's clinic."

Caroline thought back to the many times she had taken Finn in for his shots. "I did, but most veterinarian clinics have prints on the wall. I never knew there was a connection."

"He's a famous wildlife illustrator," Nancy said. "Mac told me that the BBC did a documentary on him years ago."

Pam chimed in with her own knowledge. "And the post office just released a new set of stamps that uses four of his images. We've even used his wallpaper at Montis."

"Ah," was all Caroline could say as one question rolled in and stayed like heavy fog enveloping a bay: *Why didn't he tell me?*

"I think we have two prints left from when Aaron was here a couple of weeks ago," Nancy said. "He offered to sign a dozen illustrations—I only wish I had more in stock. We sold out within a few days."

Caroline frowned. "Why do you call them illustrations and not paintings?"

"I'm not quite sure, but he calls himself an illustrator," Nancy said. "I wish there were newer images, but Mac says he hasn't picked up a paintbrush in years. I heard that five or six years ago, he just pulled out of the art scene—stopped painting, stopped giving interviews, and he stopped licensing his artwork. There was a wild rumor floating around that he destroyed hundreds of illustrations that he was preparing for an Audubon book."

That reminded her of his unexplained outbursts. *Maybe he is crazy,* Caroline thought. But why didn't he tell me? Although Aaron had never lied to her, assuming omission isn't a lie, Caroline nonetheless felt misled, even deceived.

When Caroline saw Tom working outside as she drove home, she couldn't help but stop. She jumped out of the car and marched up to him. "Why didn't you tell me about Aaron?"

He was startled by her onslaught. "Tell you what?"

"That your brother is a famous illustrator. That his designs are shown all over the world." Caroline was exasperated. "That he was on BBC, of all damn things!"

Tom laughed. "Oh, the Brits wouldn't like to hear that," he teased.

"This isn't a joke!" Caroline snapped.

Tom shrugged his shoulders. "I assumed you knew. Everyone in town does."

"Well, I didn't," Caroline said belligerently. "Why didn't Aaron tell me?"

"That you need to ask him."

"But . . ." she began before realizing that Tom was right—she was talking to the wrong person. She turned on her heel and headed back to the car. "I'll do just that."

Dear Aaron, I just tried calling you, but no answer. When you wrote that you painted boats and buoys, I assumed you meant you worked as a harbor hand, not that they were subjects in one of your illustrations! You never once suggested anything about your career. I feel like an idiot. And I was told that you destroyed most of your illustrations. Is that true?
Caroline
PS—Your artwork is stunning.

Caroline carried the phone with her throughout the day, hoping that Aaron would call. Four hours later, she received his response via email.

dear Caroline, i never thought about it. i wasn't hiding some dark secret—it was a past life which i needed to leave behind. i suppose i also wanted us to have more time together before answering the questions that you were bound to ask. so, i'll explain now.

shortly after i found my artistic style, my hand as they call it, an improbable mix of luck and persistency hit and my illustrations caught on.

five years ago, on august 5, when mac and tom were visiting, one day tom dragged me away from my work to go kayaking. the sky was clear blue, but the winds were blowing unusually strong from the northwest.

as we paddled along the rocky coast, a storm blew in faster than we ever thought possible, and before we could make landfall, i lost control of my kayak and flipped over. a relentless series of waves threw me against the rocks.

five days later, i woke in the hospital with a traumatic brain injury or a 'tbi,' which sounds less daunting. there were no long-term effects from my skull being as shattered as a light bulb dropped on cement, except one: cerebral bilateral achromatopsia. the optical tissues in the cerebral cortex of both hemispheres in my brain were torn up. so, now i'm completely color-blind, and the world is nothing more than shades of gray. everything i see is a black-and-white photograph.

when i first woke, i assumed i had died because everyone was an ashen gray. most startling was when i looked in the mirror and saw a man with no pigment, a man with gray skin and gray eyes and gray hair. for a long time, food was so revolting i had to close my eyes while I ate—pasta, which had always been my favorite, had become gray noodles with black sauce . . . lettuce, strawberry ice cream . . . it didn't matter, everything was gray. for a long time, i couldn't remember or even name any colors. and my career as an artist was over.

tom was as devastated and tormented by the guilt. but he and mac saw me through, emotionally and physically. after several weeks, tom had to return to his practice in lumby, but mac stayed on, encouraging me day after day. with therapy and practice, i was taught to compensate, and everyday tasks, such as driving, were relearned.

when i was finally released from the

hospital, I went back to a black-and-white studio. i tried working in just pen and ink but it was impossible. i knew that chapter in my life was over. one night i burned the stack of illustrations i had tried painting after the accident so no one could ever see them. i then packed up the odds and ends of my studio and put everything into storage, where it remains to this day.

my spirit was pretty much broken.

it took months for the headaches to go away, but when they finally did, i bought a boat—being color-blind out on the water is quite easy—actually, i often forget what was taken from me. for eight months, i sailed along the west coast, finally ending up in edmonds, where i found a small marina in a secluded cove.

it was here where i finally became comfortable with the distance between my life and my art. i'm still not totally at peace with what happened, and sometimes, especially when called upon to tell one color from another, i snap and become so angry that it's as if another person takes over. i know that happened a few times when we were together . . . i'm sorry if my anger scared you.

so, that's my private story, as black-and-white as it is. oh, and yes, i really do paint boats and buoys to pass the hours—the cans are numbered before i head out on my dingy and only once has that system failed me, with more humorous than serious results.

i appreciated your last comment about liking my art—i wish some of my critics were as generous in opinion, but to each their own.

always, aaron

Caroline slowly closed her laptop. She thought back on the incident with the towel, about his disinterest in the fireworks, about a dozen small things that triggered his anger, and she finally understood. Aaron's darkness existed because he couldn't see any color.

Caroline printed out Aaron's email and slipped it into her pocket, gave Finn some toys and went out alone. By the time she walked to the Candor farm, the urgency to have someone close, to share her sadness, had welled up to the brim of overflowing. Quickly knocking on the front door, she prayed that someone was home.

When Mac opened the door, tears had formed in Caroline's eyes. "Caroline?"

She held out the letter. "He told me." Her voice cracked. "I didn't know where else to go."

Mac led her inside.

"You knew . . . you were there," Caroline said. "But you didn't say anything to me."

"It wasn't our story to tell. Aaron needed to share it in his own way, at his own time."

"But we were all together at Montis, sitting on the hill, when I asked him if he liked the fireworks."

Mac nodded. "And if I remember correctly, he said that he saw them differently than everyone else. He didn't lie to you."

"No, but that's worlds away from the truth of his accident," Caroline said.

"Caroline, the accident was devastating in so many ways. We didn't think Aaron was going to make it, and then when he did, we didn't think he wanted to live. But he's accepted the breaks that fate has handed him, and he's trying to move on."

"God, I'm so tired of life being this hard—for me and for the people I love," she whispered as she dropped down onto the sofa. "To lose such a talent."

"He's a brilliant artist," Mac commented.

"He *was* a brilliant artist," Caroline said. "Isn't that the tragedy? That he no longer is?"

"We see it differently," Mac said, demurring. "The tragedy is that Aaron hasn't found another way of expressing the passion that drove him to spend hours painting one wing of a cardinal. He'll always be a brilliant artist, with or without color. He just sees his world differently . . . like a photograph. Ah, wait a minute." Mac leaned over and pulled out a large manila envelope from the coffee-table drawer. She handed it to Caroline. "A psychiatrist that worked with Aaron gave this to us so that we could better understand what Aaron was going through."

From the envelope, Caroline pulled out a twelve-inch-square piece of dark plastic filament.

"It's a filter," Mac explained. "It removes all color."

Caroline held it up to her face and looked out into a world of black-and-white. It was so disorienting, Caroline almost became light-headed. She looked at Mac and gasped.

"Oh God," she whispered.

As she eyed the world through Mac's filter on the way home, nothing seemed familiar; common objects were only vaguely recognizable as shades of gray bled into other shades of gray. Chicory Lane was an unwelcoming dirt road of black-and-gray blotches, the trees were almost impossible to demarcate, and her yellow mill was a dreary light ash. The only thing she saw that registered as normal was the overcast sky.

Once inside, she viewed Finn through the filter. No wonder Aaron had asked what breed of dog he was, she thought. Instead of a rich, vibrant burgundy-chestnut, his coat was dark charcoal, the color of soot.

Only then did Caroline realize how differently Aaron must have perceived his own image that first time she saw him in the woods. Instead of being covered in red blood, he was covered in gray.

Dear Aaron, I've reread your letter, and I'm without words. One afternoon, one wave—I really can't understand the improbable chain of events that leaves a life so radically changed. I cringe thinking that, for the longest time, I felt I was the only one who was dealt an unfair hand in life, that I was the only one who had to go through the kind of pain that rocks your faith and shuts you out from the world. You have shown me otherwise.

I don't know how to offer you comfort. What can I do or say?

Always,
Caroline

PS—Can I ask two questions: Is there a chance that, over time, you may see colors again, and, do you dream in color?

dear caroline, just being there, at the other end of my letters and at the other end of my calls, means everything. to answer the easier question first; to the best of my recollection, i didn't dream at all for six months after the accident, but when the dreams slowly returned, they were in black-and-white. i think i do dream in color every now and then, but it's so vague that when i try to remember, the feeling slips away. it's almost impossible to describe which is one of my regular frustrations.

as far as the future, the doctors don't know. in fact, they know very little about the human brain, either how it works or how it heals itself. recently i think i have seen hues of green—perhaps not green, but i know for a fact it wasn't gray. the color would stay for a few hours before fading. but that hasn't happened for a while and it might not ever happen again. if it does, it does. if not, my life will continue on. all is good.

except, right now i miss you with alarming intensity.

love,
aaron

Love? Caroline's slightly jilted world blurred just a bit more.

THIRTY-FOUR

Ansel

The Lumby Lines

**WHAT'S NEWS
AROUND TOWN**

A busy week in our sleepy town of Lumby.

Uber, the international online transportation network, finally came to Lumby last week. The service, which allows customers to request transportation for themselves or their personal items via a mobile app while allowing drivers to earn income by providing said transportation in their own vehicles, hit some unexpected road bumps on Main Street. Uber corporate officials were reluctantly dragged into a quagmire of legal definitions when Mr. Reynolds hired an Uber diver from Wheatley to transport twenty-seven chickens to the processing plant two hours away. The driver, having recently purchased a Lexus RX, refused the fare. Another unfortunate turn of events occurred when

Bob Fitzgerald and Timmy Beezer used their Cluck It Up food truck to shuttle a wedding party of seven from Hunts Mill to the Presbyterian church. Uncapped barbecue sauce was to blame for the ruined attire of bride, groom and guests.

LUMBY FORUM
**An open bulletin board
for our town residents.**

Unemployed minister seeks mature parishioner who is a whimsical beauty with infectious laugh. Must love all sports, except lacrosse. Agnostics acceptable.

The top half of a naked female mannequin was found in Porta Potty #3 at the fairgrounds. The owner can claim it at Brad's Hardware—she's waiting behind the plumbing counter.

Last seen in front of Jimmy D's where I parked it on Sat.—a green, 2014 zero-turn John Deere lawn mower. The wife is on my case, so call if you see it. Jerry 925-9173.

Exceptionally gifted writer with over-weight cat, a healthy ego and OCD seeks well-educated reader of any sex to share immaculately clean apartment. Adoration and encouraging feedback preferred. Editing skills a must. Let's meet at library Fri. 6 p.m. Bring own dictionary.

Free to a great home. One-year-old bicolored Great Dane. Needs own mattress. Neutered like one of the family.

You can benefit from an unexpected upswing in my fortune-telling business! Prices slashed by 50% and mood rings same price as last year. Joy at 14 Cherry Street behind the barber.

Hookers wanted. Wed. afternoons. Second floor Lumby Feed Store. Bring own blades and yarn.

Within a day of receiving Brian Beezer's call for help, Trout, JJ, and Axel had arrived from Dell headquarters to set up Brian's print-on-demand business. A day later, Fazia joined the rogue group, which had camped out in the basement of The Bindery so that they could work around the clock. Hardware was connected, software installed and custom programs written that linked the modules needed to edit, lay out and transfer digital manuscripts to and from any point around the world.

Dennis stayed clear of the area, whereas Gabrielle came by every few hours to ensure all were well fed.

"Epic," Brian said as he paged through a mobile app that JJ had pulled together.

Then the FedEx Ground trucks arrived and delivered the most advanced printing presses and binding technologies, which offered pages-per-minute capacity that was ten times faster than what was available upstairs.

With his team knee-deep in cables and code, Brian turned his attention to the filing cabinets, more out of a necessity to get them off the floor versus any curiosity about the contents. On one side of the table were a dozen stacked boxes filled to the brim with old papers. On the other side were loose documents: old town and county maps, rejected manuscripts, even scrolled sheets of original calligraphy done by the monks when they lived at Montis Abbey. One pile that caught Brian's eye contained dozens of thick cardboard monochromatic photographs of leaves and bugs. Leafing through them, he found a handful of dramatic black-and-white landscape photographs. They were of the American west, the Grand Tetons possibly.

Brian rubbed a layer of dust from the bottom border of the first image, and read the faded handwriting: "Ansel Adams—1916." The next photograph, in fact all the photographs, had the same name and date.

Now handling the photographs much more gingerly, Brian laid them out on another table. There were eighteen in all, and most appeared to be in good condition.

"Fazia, look at this," he said, waving her over.

As she examined each photograph, Brian was Googling information on his tablet.

"What do you think?" he asked.

"I don't know. They could be by Ansel Adams."

"The year is right," Brian said. "Wiki says his first trip to Yosemite was in 1916. Do you know anybody who could authenticate these?"

"I think Scott Crowley could be who you want."

"I also have this," he said, handing Fazia a single page.

She began reading the contract. "William Beezer?"

"My grandfather," Brian replied.

Her mouth opened to form a gentle "o." Her eyes grew wider as she kept reading. "So, Ansel Adams gave your grandfather perpetual rights to these images?"

Brian nodded. "That's what it looks like to me."

Fazia was dumbfounded. "Do you know what just dropped in your lap?"

"Our first book."

"It's so much more than that." Fazia shook her hand, trying to slow down their racing thoughts. "But we're not set up for a full-bleed ten-by-fourteen."

Brian picked up the phone and dialed. "Dad, I'm at The Bindery. Would you get over here? . . . Yeah, it's important, it's very important."

Brian then made a second call.

A few minutes later Dennis walked down the steps into the basement. He wasn't sure what amazed him more: the equipment installed over the last several days, or seeing a woman standing next to Brian with her hand resting intimately on his shoulder.

"You're making impressive headway," Dennis said, crossing the room.

"Dad, this is Fazia Torres. Fazia, my father."

Fazia's smile was dazzling. The first time he had seen her was on the second floor of the Chatham Press building when Brian's crew was installing the servers for the newspaper's website. At that time, it was at a distance and only for a few seconds. Now that she was standing a few feet away, Dennis realized how beautiful she was. With black hair almost down to her waist, the woman had raw beauty and sensuality about her. She reminded him of Gabrielle.

"Nice to finally meet you, Dennis," Fazia said,

shaking his hand. "Brian's told me quite a few stories."

Dennis was taken aback by her casual informality, although clearly no disrespect was intended.

"Nice to meet you. I think we crossed paths last time you were here."

"Possibly," she said with a smile.

"Dad, I came across these old photographs and a contract. Do you know anything about them?"

Dennis leaned over the table. "Wow," he said quite loudly.

"My thoughts exactly," Brian said.

Dennis continued to study the prints. "Eighteen? Is this all of them?"

"Not sure. I haven't gone through the other boxes yet."

Fazia handed Dennis the contract. "This was with the photographs."

Dennis brought it closer to the table lamp to read it. "Interesting."

"So, do you think they're ours?" Brian asked.

"Possibly." Dennis checked the photos again. "Your grandfather was a stickler for copyright protection. He might have bent a lot of rules, but that was one he never wavered on. You might want to pass the contract by—"

"Russell Harris," Brian interrupted. "Yeah, I called him after I called you. He's expecting me in an hour."

"Extraordinary," Dennis said, still astonished by the discovery. "Do you know much the originals are worth?"

"No, but this one Ansel Adams book could sustain this press until you and I are both long gone."

Fazia put her hand on Brian's arm. "But we can't run it down here," she reminded him.

"You're right. Dad, we don't have the capability of running a full-bleed ten-by-fourteen layout on these 'POD' presses. If Russell gives his okay, I'd like to bring the job upstairs and get it scheduled on your machines."

"I don't see why not," Dennis said. It wasn't the time or the place to talk about the future with Brian, but Dennis had some plans in the works that needed his undivided attention. "I was hoping you'd be interested in assuming the responsibility for press operations, at least for a while."

"Are you retiring, Dennis?" Fazia asked.

He smiled. "No. Just moving on to new challenges." He turned back to Brian. "The only priority you have is the monks' book, which needs to be run next week. Other than that, they're not too many books on the line."

"And that's what we're going to turn around," Fazia said confidently.

"I like your attitude," Dennis said.

The crew headed for the door. "Beez, we're

breaking for lunch. Do you guys want to come with us?"

"I will," Fazia said, jumping at the chance. "I just love this town."

"I need to pass, but would you bring me back something?"

"Your regular?" Fazia asked.

"Fine. Thanks, babe."

"Babe?" Dennis asked as soon as the others were gone.

"Drop it, Dad."

The rapid-fire questions began.

"I thought she lived in Argentina."

"She does."

"And she works there?"

Brian chuckles. "She's good for a while."

"She's *good?* What does that mean?"

"She really doesn't need to work, Dad," Brian said.

"Then why is she here?"

"Because she wants to be, and I asked her to come up."

"When did she get here?" Dennis asked.

"A while ago."

"Where is she staying?"

"Why the fourth degree?" Brian asked.

"Just curious. Where is she staying?"

"With me, at my place," Brian said. "We're friends with benefits."

"Oh," Dennis said, letting out a breath. "I see."

"No, you don't. If anything serious happens, I'll let you know."

"Actually, it's your mother who's worried."

"Bullshit," Brian said. "Mom loves Fazia. They talked for hours last night." He knew that there were better opportunities to break the news, but he continued nonetheless. "I'd like Fazia to stay on long-term, to handle the front end of our print-on-demand business. She's great with customers, and she'll do a great job helping out other authors."

Dennis looked at his son and suddenly saw a man whose life was coming together, just as his had. "Are you going to marry her?"

Brian laughed. "She is so out of my league, you have no idea."

"No one is out of your league, Brian."

"Believe me, she is in every possible way." He immediately changed the subject. "The print-on-demands will be run down here, but sent upstairs for binding and distribution. We'll need a one-ton incline belt conveyor."

"Agreed," Dennis said. "With all you have going on, don't let the monks' book slip."

"I won't," Brian assured him. "But you do know it will lose money, don't you?"

Dennis looked at his son. "Sometimes it's not about money, it's about people."

"I agree. But sometimes it's only about the money. The Paige Petrosyan selfie book would easily cover all of your losses."

Dennis threw his arms in the air, his face turning beet red. He exploded. "Don't *ever* bring that name up again!" he yelled. "I'd torch this building before printing her book."

"But, Dad—"

"This meeting is over," he snapped before storming out.

THIRTY-FIVE

Proof

Pam tapped the envelope lightly against the kitchen table, anxiously fidgeting with the certified letter that had arrived that morning.

"You seem a little stressed. You okay, honey?" Mark asked as he passed through on his way outside.

"It just came," she said, holding up the envelope.

Mark stopped at the door. "What's that?"

"The DNA test results."

Mark's eyes came alive with interest. "How cool is that! I so want to do that. Maybe I'm Chinese-Afro-American-Scottish."

"You think?" Pam asked mildly.

"Well, you never know, do you? That's what so cool about it. Maybe I'm the great-great-great-grandson of a famous Russian czar. Or Peruvian—I've always been drawn to the Andes, like the Incas. Maybe my people built Machu Picchu."

"*Your* people?" she asked.

"Sure. We're all members of a larger tribe. That's what the whole DNA ancestry is—finding out which tribe you're in."

"But Mark, your family name is Walker. I would bet the ranch that you are no more Incan than I am," she said. "Anyway, this isn't that type of test. All it does is show the probability of a familial relation."

Mark plopped down next to his wife. "So, go ahead, open it," he said, nudging her arm.

Pam shook her head. "I'm waiting for Janet. She should be here any minute. And I'd really appreciate you distracting Bill for a while. This is something that she wants to do alone."

Mark blinked several times. "You mean, they have secrets from each other? Wow, I'm like shocked."

"I wouldn't call them secrets."

"Exactly!" Mark said. "That's exactly it. It's like when I couldn't tell you about Alan. It drove me nuts, but there was a good reason."

"And I'm sure Janet has hers, so I'd like to respect that."

There was a tap on the door.

"There they are. Remember, keep Bill away for a while," Pam said softly.

Mark jumped out of his seat. "Got it." Swinging open the door, he hooked his arm around Bill's. "You're coming with me. We've got some work to do down at the barn."

"I'm your man." Bill was all-in for a new adventure, although he had not recovered fully from the preserve hike.

"Come sit," Pam said brightly to Janet.

"You're making me nervous," she said. "Is there something wrong?"

Pam picked up the envelope from the table. "It arrived this morning."

For a moment, the women stared at what could change both of their lives forever.

"Are you ready?" Pam asked.

Janet nodded. "Yes, but I'm worried you'll be disappointed."

That made Pam hesitate. *Could I have been wrong?* she wondered. Would this end in a colossal disappointment? But then she looked at Janet, looked at her eyes, her smile, her blond hair, and Pam only saw a vision of herself in five years.

Pam's fingers trembled as she opened the envelope and unfolded the page. Without reading all of the text, her eyes immediately scanned down to the center of the page.

MATCH PROBABILITY: 99.999%

Janet gasped. Pam continued to take in the percentage. Dead certain. They remained silent for the longest time.

When Pam finally dared to glance at Janet, she saw tears in her sister's eyes, and the elation she felt drained away.

"I'm sorry," Pam faltered. "I know this isn't what you wanted."

Janet blinked and the pool of tears broke over

the rim and trickled down her cheek.

Without saying a word, she stood and walked out the door.

Pam could have said something; she could've called out her name, or gotten up and followed her. But she didn't. She was not alone in the world. She was now a sister, and, in turn, a sister-in-law and an aunt. Her tribe had grown disproportionately within a few minutes.

Pam had been sitting at the table lost in her thoughts for over an hour when she heard Mark yell and the bell ring from the barn. It was their signal that help was immediately needed down below. "Now what?" Pam asked as she raced out the door. Regardless of Janet's state of mind, she might be needed as well so Pam pounded on her door, and the two women took off in the Jeep toward the barn.

Upon arriving, they saw Mark standing near the center of the barn with a rope tangled around his body. "Don't move!" he yelled. "He looks like he's about to blow."

All the women could see were two horns and Bill, perched higher than the sides of the stalls. One end of a heavy rope was tied around his waist, and from there the rope went straight up, around a pulley hanging from the beam above, and then down to Mark.

As they approached the stall, Mark put out

his arm. "Not too fast," he cautioned them.

Peering into the stall, they saw Bill sitting on Old Jesse's back.

"What the hell is he doing?" Pam screeched.

Jesse snorted and threw his head into the air.

"Everyone, stay calm!" Mark said in a low voice. "Every time Bill moves, Jesse goes a little berserk."

"An animal weighing over a ton doesn't go *a little* berserk," Pam said, annoyed.

"Well, I can't distract Jesse long enough to lift Bill off his back." Mark paused. "In fact, I can't lift Bill—he's too heavy."

"How did he get in there?" Janet asked.

"Well, Jesse was sleeping." Although he spoke softly, Mark stumbled over his words. "Bill said he had always dreamed of riding a bull, so I just lowered him onto Jesse's back to give him that real living-in-the-country experience."

Pam glared at Mark. "Are you nuts?"

"Well, Jesse has calmed down over the years. He hasn't hurt anyone in forever," Mark said defensively.

"That's because we give him full access to his own private pasture."

"So, maybe Janet can hold out a bucket of oats while Pam and I try to lift Bill off him."

Twenty minutes later, Jesse was standing in his stall, calm and without a rider. Bill and Janet were sitting on a pile of hay watching Mark put away the rope and bucket.

"Another successful adventure at Montis," Mark said, slapping his gloved hands together. "You have to admit, this place is great."

"It is indeed," Bill said. "Assuming one survives to tell about it."

"This is extraordinary!" Mark said with child-like enthusiasm. "I think you're the first to ever sit on Jesse's back!"

"I'm not quite sure what that says about the judgment of either of you," Pam added with a smirk. She tugged on Mark's sleeve. "We'll see you two up at the inn."

When Bill started to stand, Janet put her arm on his leg. "Can we stay here for a minute?"

"Sure. I could certainly use a break."

Janet waited until their two hosts were well out of earshot.

"I need to tell you something," Janet began, but before she got the words out, she started crying.

Startled, Bill put his arm around her shoulders. "What's wrong? You're not upset because of Old Jesse, are you?"

"No, although I agree with Pam—probably not your smartest move."

"So, what it is?"

Janet tried to gather herself. "I need to start at the beginning . . ."

Bill was delighted by the revelation. "Sisters? You and Pam? Well, I'll be gobsmacked. The moment we arrived at Montis, I noticed you two looked incredibly alike, but I thought it was purely coincidence. You hear stories how each of us have a twin somewhere in the world—I just assumed she was yours."

Janet's head was hanging so low, her hair covered her face.

"So, I only have two questions: Why are you so sad, and . . ." he paused. "Why didn't you tell me from the start?"

"I'm not who I was," Janet whispered through her tears.

"That's ridiculous. Of course you are," Bill said, taking hold of his wife's hands.

"I'm not from Iowa. I'm not the daughter of Barbara and Bailey Wilson." She wiped her face with the sleeve of her blouse. "And Pam is my only sister. My upbringing was a pretense . . . a lie."

"Wasn't it more of an omission?" Bill suggested.

"That's why I didn't want to tell you," she said, sitting up a bit straighter. "Nothing ever fazes you. You never think there's any hard consequences in life," Janet said. "But this is something that your rose-colored glasses can't change. I have been deceived, and I don't want you to say it's nothing and sweep it under the rug."

• • •

Later that afternoon, Mark gave Pam another bear hug. "I think it's wonderful, honey! You have a sister. This is exactly what you wanted."

"Well, maybe not exactly—or maybe not like this. I was so excited for myself that I didn't think of how this might affect her. I watched Bill and Janet come up from the barn. She was really upset, so I'm probably the last person in the world she wants to talk to." Pam thought this was ironic. "But I'm one of the few people who knows exactly what she's feeling, who knows how painful it is to realize that your parents weren't honest with you, and to regret not knowing that secret for all these years." She looked out the kitchen window to see if the Wings had come out of the room.

"Maybe you should go talk to her."

"But I'm the one who brought all of this on. I can understand why she would hate me."

Mark led her to the door. "Go. You two need to talk about it."

Walking into the guest annex, Pam ran into Bill, who was carrying a full trash can under his arm.

"Let me take that," Pam said. "Was your room not cleaned this morning?"

"It was, but Janet asked me to throw this out."

Pam looked into the wastebasket. To her surprise, it was stuffed with all of Janet's

412

knitting materials: various skeins of colored yarns, straight and circular needles, patterns and hooks.

Pam rummaged through the supplies in disbelief. At the bottom was the half-finished sweater Janet was working on the day before. "What is she doing?"

Bill shrugged. "Janet's mother taught her how to knit . . . actually taught all her daughters how to knit. It was a big thing in her family. That's how they spent the long cold nights in Iowa," he explained. "And now she wants to throw it all away and break that tie because she says it was a sham. She doesn't know who to trust. She doesn't know if anyone else in the family knows about her adoption. She's even wondering if her brothers and sisters were also adopted."

Pam felt horrible. "I'm so sorry."

Bill shook his head. "Don't be. She deserved to know the truth."

"Let me keep this," Pam said, clinging onto the trash can. "And give us a few minutes."

Pam's knock on the door produced no answer. "Janet?" she said, peering inside.

Janet was sitting on the edge of the bed, her hands folded on her lap.

"Can I come in?" But Pam didn't wait for an answer. "I think we need to talk."

"There isn't anything more to be said," Janet said softly. "You have your answer."

"Well, *we* have our answer," Pam corrected her. "And we're in the same boat."

Janet finally looked up. "In what way?"

"We both feel betrayed. We both had our lives redefined, without any warning or permission."

"I just keep on going over everything in my head. The million opportunities—"

"Mom had to tell me the truth," Pam quickly finished her sentence.

Janet's eyes opened wider. "Yes, that's exactly it."

"And you wonder why they took that secret to their grave."

Janet nodded. "Did they intentionally want to hide it from me? And who else knew?"

Pam placed the wastebasket on the bed next to Janet. "I think you're making a big mistake by throwing this part of your life away," Pam said. "You love knitting, and you're great at it. That's a part of who you are regardless of who your parents are."

Janet glared at the yarn on top of the heap.

"Regardless of who you're angry at, you're only going to hurt yourself by giving up something that means so much to you," Pam said.

Janet pursed her lips, and her chin quivered.

Pam continued. "After my mother died, after I found your birth certificate and adoption papers, I felt the ground shift underneath my feet, and everything I knew about myself had changed.

414

But when I came back here, I had a lot of time to think things through." She sighed. "I'll never know why my parents didn't tell me, but I hope it was out of their love for me. We were never close, but I always knew they would do anything to protect me. And I truly believe that's how your parents felt about you. I know the circumstances of your adoption, and there's no question that our parents loved you enough to give you to another family than risk the chance of you being brought up in an orphanage." Pam sat down next to her sister. "It would help if there was someone you could talk to about everything you're going through. What does Bill say?"

"Nothing," she said. "Nothing ever fazes him."

"Well, who else can you talk to?"

"I don't know who I can trust. I don't know who has been honest with me."

"But there must be someone," Pam said. "You have a thousand friends all over the world."

"We do but they're just acquaintances—no one I would ever . . ." her voice trailed off.

So much for having a long Christmas card list, Pam thought. "Maybe that's the difference between us. We only have a handful of very good friends who are closer than family because they are in our lives by choice, not by happenstance. And I could talk to any of them about anything."

"But I don't even know who I am," Janet said.

"I don't think being adopted diminishes who

you are, I think it adds to who you are. You're already the by-product of your upbringing in Iowa. And now you can add to that whatever genetics our parents have given you."

"I'm one half my mother and one half my father, neither of whom I have ever known."

"Well, we can certainly do something about that."

"Exhume them?" Janet said darkly.

"Very good—dark humor always comes in handy." Pam laughed. "But I have something better than that. I have a thousand hours of videos that our parents took over the years. A cabinet full of tapes starting with black-and-whites in the forties going through my mother and Robert's last trip abroad. I'm sure once we binge-watch the videos together, you'll know your place in the universe."

Janet gave a weak smile. "Could you promise me one thing?"

"Anything."

"Please don't tell anyone," Janet pleaded.

Pam lifted her eyebrows. "Being adopted is nothing to be ashamed of."

"I just don't know what people would think." Janet nervously wrung her hands together.

"Janet, everyone already thinks you're perfect. This would just add a layer of intrigue."

"Please," she implored.

"If that's what you want, your secret is safe

with me," Pam said. "Now, Mark is a different story, but I'll talk to him."

Janet let out a small sigh of relief.

Although she stayed in her room for the next two days, Bill told Pam that Janet was consumed by the photo albums Pam had dropped off. Perhaps that was her way to relearn who she was.

THIRTY-SIX

Boxes

The winds blew viciously as Caroline headed out the door, planning to stop by the cemetery before meeting with Russell Harris. Her mood perfectly matched the ominous weather. The events of the prior week had dragged Caroline through an emotional chasm that began with self-doubt and ended in self-criticism. As much as she tried to change the course of her life, she couldn't take the next step.

Standing by her grandmother's tombstone, she began to cry. "I wish you could help me," Caroline whispered as she tucked a letter next to the cold granite. She kissed her fingers and then touched the headstone.

> **Dear CC, Today I will either be free of Kai and reclaim our family name or be told that I will be dragged through muck for the next two years in an ugly legal battle that would stretch from Lumby to the island of Coraba. As much as I want to be done with Kai, I**

now realize that he was a good excuse for all of my wrong turns. Shame on me.

I miss you terribly.

Your granddaughter, Caroline

Just as Caroline turned to walk away, a heavy gust blew through the graveyard. A small piece of old, wet newspaper hit her chest and stuck to her shirt.

Pulling it off, her eyes caught part of the caption of the torn article: PICK A LANE.

From the few words that followed on the shredded piece of paper, Caroline speculated that it was about one of the more eccentric challenges hosted by the town—the Outhouse Races. But her eyes blurred as she gaped at the bold words: PICK A LANE.

She spun around. *"Is this from you?"* Caroline shouted at the headstone. She was so startled, she shook.

As suddenly as the winds kicked up, they died again and it was calm around her.

"Of course it is," she said. She kneeled down and leaned against the headstone. Bursting into tears, she clutched the piece of paper close to her heart. After several minutes, her tears finally subsided.

She regarded the words again. "I will," she promised.

She carefully placed the torn page in her pocket. "I will pick a lane," she told her grandmother. "And that lane will be my life—a life that we're both proud of."

Although earlier that morning Caroline had dreaded the thought of returning to Russell's office, she now drove into town with a clear head and focused vision. She was possessed by a clear-minded determination that she hadn't felt in years.

Driving over Goose Creek at the far end of town, Caroline slowed the car and rolled down her window. Slipping her wedding ring off her finger, she unceremoniously tossed the ring into the water. "It's so over, no matter what you say," she said, as if Kai was in the seat next to her.

When she arrived at her attorney's office, Russell immediately noticed the change in her demeanor—how she sat at the table, how she was present and engaged in their conversation.

"You must have had a good night's rest," Russell said.

"Far more than that," Caroline replied, but didn't explain any further.

"As you requested, I submitted your letter of resignation to the board of directors at Ross Enterprises, and they have voted."

"Their decision?"

"I recused myself and abstained from the vote

because of my conflict of interest, so I wasn't present and they haven't told me. But they would like to talk with you."

"A sweet parting of the ways, no doubt," she said. "That's nice of them."

"Have you received an email about the board meeting later this week?"

Caroline nodded.

"Your resignation is first on the agenda."

Caroline raised her head. "It's hard to have one's fate in someone else's hands, but I trust that each one of them voted in the interest of the company."

"I'm sure they did as well."

"And I'll accept their decision and work with them on a smooth transition."

"That's good to hear." Russell pulled out a set of papers from one of the many folders on the table. "Moving on with better news, I have your final divorce decree and release papers. Kai and Jamar are legally out of your life. I'll retain the originals if you want, but here is your copy."

Caroline's heart skipped a beat when he handed her the papers.

"The deed to the mill has been reissued in your name alone," he said, giving her the stamped deed. "The home is now yours to do with as you want."

Caroline put the documents in her purse, thanked Russell and walked out of the office. She crossed the road and hurried down Main Street.

Her pace was quick and her steps were light. This was how she used to walk, before slowing her gait to match Kai's shorter and more shuffling stride.

She walked up the path to the unassuming office of Main Street Realty.

"Look who's here! Come and visit," Joan Stokes said when she saw Caroline at the door.

"I wish I could stay, but I just wanted to put a bug in your ear," Caroline said. "I'd like you to list the mill for sale."

Joan was shocked. "Today?" she asked half jokingly.

"Yes. If possible, today."

"I'm so surprised, dear. Are you sure?"

"I've never been surer of anything in my life. Here's the deed," she said, handing Joan the envelope. "Could you possibly come by today or tomorrow so we can go through the listing?"

Joan checked her schedule. "This afternoon, if that works for you."

"Excellent."

"Can I bring my photographer?"

"I'll be ready," Caroline said, already heading for the door.

"Then a quick sale is what we'll go after," Joan said. "I'll see you soon."

Joan arrived just as the living room clock was striking two. Caroline stepped outside to greet her.

"Your reputation for punctuality precedes you," Caroline said.

"Time is money . . . and respect," the Realtor replied. She took several steps back and scanned the front of the home while her photographer fetched his equipment out of the trunk. "This is Nick," she said, introducing him before getting to work.

For the next hour, while they took pictures of the place, Caroline hibernated in her bedroom, rummaging through old boxes that she hadn't opened since moving to the mill. She came across a box from her childhood and reveled in her findings. Carefully laid out on her bed were four cameras that Charlotte had given to her when she was young: an 1860s wet-plate Bellows camera, a vintage Kodak folding camera, and two other cameras both from the early 1900s. She immediately thought of Aaron. Since the cameras could only take black-and-white, Aaron might value them differently than anyone else. What he saw through the lens finder would match exactly what it would be in print. She somehow thought of it as a simpler process, since his brain wouldn't have to mentally convert something in color.

Just as Caroline finished wrapping up the last of the cameras for mailing, there was a slight rap on the door.

"Can I shoot this room?" Nick asked.

"Sure, just give me a second."

"Wow, what a great antique," he said, picking up the Bellows camera. "Do you know this is over a hundred fifty years old?"

"No, I didn't know that."

He turned it over in his hand several times, looking at it from all angles. "Does it still work?"

"They all did when I was a child, but they haven't been used since," Caroline said as he handed it back to her. She carefully wrapped it up and added it to the shipping box.

Within no time, her house was officially for sale. A large FOR SALE sign was hanging by a post close to the road.

As Joan and Nick drove away, Caroline raised her head to the sky. "I've picked my lane, CC."

She went into the kitchen and began removing everything from her corkboard, including the pictures of Aaron and Finn. Once empty, she took the corkboard down and brought it out to the car. Caroline left Finn sleeping in the living room and headed into town to mail Aaron's box and drop off several items at Goodwill.

Approaching Lumby, still some distance from Main Street, Caroline noticed that several cars were parked along the side of Farm to Market Road, with people walking into town. The traffic was unlike any she had ever seen before—it took her ten minutes just to drive a few blocks, where she was lucky to find a parking space behind the library. Grabbing Aaron's box, she was headed for the post office when she saw Pam Walker walking a few yards ahead of her.

"Hey, Pam!" she called.

Pam turned around. As soon as she saw Caroline, she stopped and let her catch up. Pam looked around nervously at the crowd.

"What's going on?" Caroline asked.

Pam was rattled. "Are you here for the debate?"

"No, I'm sorry. I didn't know. I just needed to mail a package," Caroline said. "Is that why everybody's in town?"

"Yeah, it's over in the park and starts in . . ." Pam looked at her watch. "Twenty-two minutes."

"You seem a little edgy," Caroline said. "Are you all right?"

"No." Pam said in exasperation, running her fingers through her hair as she did when she got nervous. "I'm not all right. I feel like I am about to be slaughtered. For the last two hours Duke Blackstone has been serving free beer and pumping up the crowd." Yells came from the park. "What a fiasco. I so regret my decision to run for office."

Caroline looked around. "I wouldn't say that too loudly. People might get the wrong idea."

"I don't care what idea they have right now!" She suppressed a scream. "I've been called every name in the book, our lives have been dragged through mud, and now he's threatening to sue us."

"So fight fire with fire." Caroline said promptly. "Get as nasty as he is."

"I can't," Pam said, but then quickly corrected herself. "I could, but I won't. I don't want this election to turn me into the type of person I'm running against. Mark and I couldn't live with ourselves or each other."

THIRTY-SEVEN

Support

The following week, Caroline stopped by Tom and Mac's to deliver Finn for a private lesson. Since the dog-show fiasco, Tom had been patiently teaching the Irish setter basic hunting and swimming skills.

Finn bolted toward the barn as soon as he was let out of the car, and Caroline headed for the house. Mac was just hanging up the phone.

"Where are you off to looking so nice?" Mac asked, admiring Caroline's crisp blue-and-white collared shirt and pressed blue skirt.

"A board of directors meeting," she said. "I submitted my resignation and now it's a formality."

Mac pursed her lips in surprise. "Do you want to leave?"

"I think that's best for Charlotte's company."

"Do you?" Mac asked. "But you're her granddaughter."

"Yes, but when I met Kai, I allowed myself to be sidetracked, and I barely pulled my own weight. And after he left, I neglected the company altogether," Caroline said. "I would have voted no differently."

"Well, I'm sorry," Mac said. "I know Ross

Enterprises was part of who you were for a long time."

"And it always will be, as will Charlotte. I can only manage what's in my control."

"Like selling your house?" Mac asked sadly.

"That's certainly one of them."

"We saw the FOR SALE sign. I can't tell you how much we'll miss you . . . and Finn," Mac said. "I hope you don't mind, I told Aaron. I was hoping he might be interested because every time he comes for a visit, he talks about moving here—especially since the accident."

Caroline asked sharply, "What did he say?"

"That it's a beautiful old structure."

"I suppose it is," Caroline said.

"I'm sure Aaron will find his own path to his own home."

"Pick a lane," Caroline said to herself.

"What?"

"It's just something Charlotte used to say to me. It means make your own destiny. Decide what's important, what you want to do, and just put your head down and run."

Mac was distressed by this sort of talk. "So, where will you go?"

"I don't know," Caroline replied. "Soon enough I'll have no job and no home, so I suppose the possibilities are endless."

"I would think you would sound more excited," Mac said honestly.

"I am in a way, but maybe having endless possibilities isn't what's important. I just want one or two that fit perfectly into my life."

"And is Aaron one of those?"

Caroline scrunched her nose. "Maybe, if the timing was different."

"I was just talking to him when you came in," Mac said. "He loves the cameras you sent him. He says he uses them every day. He has even begun to digitally change some photographs he's taken."

"But they're not digital cameras—they're a hundred years old."

"He said that after the film is developed, he has the black-and-white negatives digitized so he can load them into his computer."

Caroline smiled. "So he's using technology from both centuries. That's pretty cool."

Mac imparted another piece of news. "He sounds totally different now—a little like you. He's back to being how he was before the accident. A beautiful spirit who sees nothing but beauty in the world."

"That he is," Caroline said. Instead of feeling regret, though, she was pleased that he'd touched her life when he did.

"And he quit his buoy job, which he had just to fill the hours. I think he's serious about photography or some variation of it."

"Please tell him I'm happy he found his lane in life."

Going up Farm to Market Road, Caroline noticed more election signs, reminding her that she had two VOTE WALKER campaign yard banners in her car that needed to be dropped off at Montis. Although the election was just days away, the town was much less busy than the last time she was there.

On the second floor of the library, in a conference room that was occasionally used for private meetings, the board was waiting for her. After politely greeting everyone, Caroline took her seat at the head of the table. Russell Harris, the attorney, sat opposite her at the other end.

"As you know, I abstained from the vote of your resignation due to my conflict of interest. As such, I'll turn this over to Ethan."

Ethan Townes leaned forward and crossed his arms on the table. "Caroline, we had quite a long discussion about the future of Ross Enterprises. As you're aware, the sales have shown a downturn during the last five years, and the philanthropic efforts have all but ceased."

Caroline concurred. "I'm sorry to interrupt, but I must say that I believe both of those are a result of my own doing and not reflective of the products we sell or the mission my grandmother wanted for her company."

Ethan looked around the table at the other board members. "We're actually in agreement with you. We believe that with proper management, the financial future of Ross Enterprises is very promising. Likewise, the board feels that with a dedicated focus, Charlotte's grants for the arts program would once again thrive."

Caroline sat motionless, waiting for the sentence to be pronounced.

"You successfully led both endeavors for over ten years. Each one of us believes that you could do it again if you decided that this was a priority in your life."

Caroline looked puzzled. "I'm sorry, I don't understand."

"The board voted unanimously *not* to accept your resignation. Although we have some concerns, we want you to continue in your position as president. We believe all that you have lived through these last few years will enable you to bring a greater wisdom and maturity to the position."

Caroline couldn't help but to smirk. "Wisdom?"

Finally Russell spoke up. "One doesn't go through the turmoil that you have without coming out the other end a little smarter and a lot stronger. We have all had our own challenges, to some degree and in some fashion, and we have each benefited from the experiences."

Caroline was stunned. She had never considered the possibility of continuing in her position. Her thoughts were swirling. She didn't want to simply accept their offer because it was made. What was right for Ross Enterprises? Could she do what they were asking? Could she recommit her life to the company? And if she continued as president, would she be able to give her responsibilities the focus that was needed if other circumstances in her life changed? The mill was now for sale. She had even thought about moving away where she could have a fresh start.

She stood up shakily. "Do you mind if I take a minute?"

When Caroline left the room, she walked past a long line of bookshelves on each side of her. Reaching her arms out, she ran her fingertips along the spines of a hundred books. They were all there because of her grandmother's generosity and perseverance. In fact, the town library itself existed because of Charlotte, and it would remain a cornerstone of the community because of the grants it received from the Ross Foundation.

Caroline sat on the top step of the enormous staircase that connected the two floors. She slowly looked around, and her mind filled with memories from the past. She and CC used to come each Sunday morning to read, from children's books when she was young to sharing *The New York Times* when she was grown.

Caroline inhaled deeply. She had always loved the smell of the library, the combined fragrance of leather and paper and ink. If there was one place that she felt connected to CC, it was her library. The library was CC's legacy.

Caroline put her hands on her knees and stood up. *Now was not the time for weakness,* she heard her grandmother's voice say. If this was the lane she wanted, she had to run down it.

When she returned to the conference room, all conversation stopped.

Caroline reached the head of the table and spoke. "Thank you for your endless commitment to Ross Enterprises. If nothing else, I'm positive we all have the company's best interest in mind. And thank you for your display of grace under pressure. I have put all of you in a difficult position, especially Russell. Charlotte would be proud of her board, as am I." She paused for further reflection. "I always listen for Charlotte's voice, and if I could hear it now, I'm positive she would advise me to continue leading the company. But now I also hear my own voice, and perhaps that's the difference—perhaps that's part of the wisdom you mentioned. And that wisdom has me believing that I will be a stronger leader moving forward than I was in the past. So, I humbly accept your offer for me to continue as president and commit to you everything I have."

After the meeting, Caroline cast an early vote for town mayor and drove down to see Pam and Mark. Several workers were already staking lanterns in the ground and putting up tents for the consolation party.

"What are you doing here?" Pam asked as she walked out of the inn's main building.

Caroline grabbed the signs in the back seat and handed them to Pam. "Sorry, but Joan suggested I take these down before there are any showings," she explained. "It doesn't matter. I don't think too many people saw them in front of my mill anyway."

"Except for Finn," Pam teased, "and he's not voting."

Caroline laughed. "If he did, I'm afraid he'd go with Biscuit."

"Believe me, he's not alone. At this point, I'd vote for Biscuit." Pam gave Caroline the once-over. "You look awfully smart."

Caroline blushed. "Mac said the same thing. Did I look that crappy before?"

"You might have . . ."

"Let myself go?" Caroline offered. "Yeah, I know. But that chapter is over."

"Good for you!" Pam said. "And I'll be able to say the same as soon as the results come in. Are you coming to our consolation party?"

Caroline frowned. "Yeah, but why are you so convinced you need consolation? If anything, today has proven to me that you never know what's going to happen."

Pam broke the Walker signs in half over her

knee. "There's no question. *The Lumby Lines* polls have Duke winning by a landslide, and the paper hasn't been wrong in fifty-eight years."

"That's unbelievable," Caroline said. "How do you explain it?"

"I can't," Pam said. "But polls don't lie."

"But Duke embodies everything this town is against."

Pam shrugged. "I always thought so. But there's so much anger and fear in the world right now. I think that our economy has been bad for so long and it's all crept up on us. And now we're turning around and realizing that we're no better off than we were twenty years ago. Duke touched a nerve."

"Of bigotry," Caroline retorted.

"Of resentment. I'm just hoping that he'll straighten up, drop the ugly rhetoric and use his connections to do some good for the town. I overheard him talking about some major construction project he wanted, so we'll see." Pam looked down at the broken signs. "The whole thing is pretty disheartening."

435

THIRTY-EIGHT

Grant

"Wiilllsson!" Mark called out. "Geez, I just love this movie," he said as he clicked off the DVD player.

Pam, Janet and Bill were comfortably huddled on the sofa with popcorn bowls balanced on their laps.

"I love Tom Hanks no matter what movie he's in," Pam said.

"Me too!" Janet exclaimed. "He's average sexy and just a really nice guy."

"Well, we're not exactly chopped liver," Mark said, fiddling with the DVD case.

"Of course you're not, dear. I would never think you're pâtè," Pam said.

"Thank goodness for that," Bill quipped, at which everyone laughed.

Flashing red-and-blue lights streamed through the windows of the library, illuminating the

436

opposite walls. Cars could be heard pulling into the drive.

"Are we expecting anyone?" Pam asked, looking at her watch. It was eight-thirty.

Mark shrugged. "Not that I know of." He looked out the window. "It looks like Simon's police car. No, wait. It's a black SUV with flashers on top. Oh, there's another."

Pam jumped from the sofa. "What's going on?"

They all went outside as a caravan of three security cars, followed by a limousine, pulled into Montis. Even from that distance, everyone saw a state flag waving from the antenna.

"Bones!" Bill cried out.

"Bones?" Pam asked.

Bill was bursting with excitement. "Remember when I asked if you had any rooms available this week? Well, I hope you don't mind, but when you said you did, I invited a friend."

"And your friends travel in limos?"

"Well, this one does, but he really prefers driving his own tr . . ." Bill's voice trailed off as he dashed across the courtyard with Janet following right behind.

By the time the Wings reached the limousine, a man just as tall as Bill was stepping out of the back seat. They all gave one another a demonstrative embrace. When Bill pointed over toward the library, the man turned. Only then did Pam and Mark recognize who it was.

"Is that Senator Grant?" Pam mumbled.

"Come over," Bill called out, waving to Pam and Mark.

Pam and Mark couldn't walk fast enough.

"Bones, this is my sister-in-law, Pam Walker, and her husband, Mark," he said. "This is John Grant."

"It's a privilege to meet you, Senator," Pam said nervously.

"It's John," he said, shaking her hand. "Nice to finally meet you, Pam. I hear you're running for office."

Pam was stunned that he knew. "Trying to."

"Sometimes it's a nasty business, I'm afraid," the Senator said in dismay.

"No exception here," Bill added. "It's as low-down as you'll find in the capitol building."

John nodded in understanding. "Well, Pam, let's see what we can do about that. I've been known to give a good speech or two in my day." He then shook Mark's hand. "And Mark, you need to fill me in on some of the stories I've heard these last couple of weeks."

Mark's eyes opened wide. "Stories?"

"We're in the middle of a critical vote on immigration and I get a tweet about some eagles that are trying to knock off Bill. Oh, and then during our day-long filibuster, another tweet about a bull named Jesse?" the Senator laughed.

Mark was uncharacteristically flustered. "Oh, those were nothing," he said, waving his hand.

"Just as long as you keep old Bill alive. I need him home in one piece," John said, slapping Mark's shoulder.

Bill laughed. "That's because I'm the only one who lets Bones win."

"Can I ask why he calls you 'Bones?' " Pam said.

The Senator rolled his eyes. "Bill has called me that ever since our first racquetball game thirty years ago." Then he leaned closer to Pam. "That's when I was twenty pounds lighter but don't tell anyone."

Pam laughed, still dizzy with disbelief that the senior senator of their state was at Montis.

An aide approached with his luggage.

"Let me show you the way," Mark said. "We'll give you a suite in the Annex."

"The Annex?" John asked apprehensively.

"Sounds ominous, doesn't it?" Bill said, putting his arm around his friend's shoulder. "I'll explain. It's a total delight—you'll see."

"Does your staff need a place to stay?" Pam asked before the men walked away.

John stopped in midstride. "No, they're all set," he said. "But you and I need to strategize. I've never met a crooked politician who got the better of me."

"I'm afraid I have," Pam confessed.

"But that's going to change." John raised a finger in the air. "Tomorrow morning you and I are going to take on the world. I'll see you at breakfast." He waved to his driver as Bill led him off to the guest quarters.

The following morning after a cup of coffee, Janet was out the door without being noticed. Carrying a Lumby map in one hand and a dozen VOTE WALKER platform sheets in the other, she jumped into the Jeep. Before heading north on Farm to Market Road, she checked her references one last time. "Blueberry Lane," Janet said to herself. "That sounds delightful."

She was right. "B'berry," as the townsfolk called it, was a softly meandering street lined with maples and modest but well-maintained Craftsman bungalows, each with a small front yard separated by low evergreen hedges.

"Very Norman Rockwell," she said. "This should be easy."

Parking at the northern start of the road, she grabbed her papers and set off. Her stride was quick and determined.

"Good morning!" Janet said in a singsong voice as she walked up the steps of the first home she came to.

A woman twenty years Janet's senior sat on the front porch, rocking slowly in a worn bentwood chair.

The woman squinted. "Are you a Jehovah's Witness sort?"

Janet laughed softly. "No, I'm not."

"Then come up here so I can see you better."

Janet kneeled down directly in front of her chair. "I'm Janet Wing."

The woman stopped rocking and took a closer look. "You're not from around here, are you?"

"No, I'm from Virginia . . . well, originally from Iowa."

"What's your name again?"

"Janet Wing. I . . ." Janet balked—she was at a total loss for words. After so carefully thinking through how she would help Pam with her campaign, Janet forgot about the details. She hadn't prepared her "pitch," as Bill would have called it.

"Yes? What is it?" the woman said impatiently.

A flush covered Janet's face.

"Speak up and speak quickly. I'm ninety-eight if not a day closer to a hundred."

Janet shook her head. "I'm sorry. I don't mean to waste your time." Seldom was Janet in such an awkward situation, especially of her own making.

"Get on with it, then."

Janet was so flustered, she froze. "Here," she said, shoving a flier at the woman. She then forced a smile.

The woman glanced at the page. "I can't read

this." She handed it back to Janet. "The writing is too small. What does it say?"

Janet wasn't exactly sure. "Let me read it for you," she offered.

For the first time Janet actually read Pam's platform. It was smart, well organized, to the point and perfectly phrased. All the words that Janet was missing a few minutes before fit into place like pieces of a puzzle.

Janet stood up when she was finished.

"How long have you known Pam Walker?"

Janet wasn't prepared for the question. "A few weeks," she confessed.

The women frowned. "You're not from these parts, and you don't know her. So what are you doing here?"

Janet shrugged. "Just trying to help, I suppose." She quickly added, "Regardless of who you support, your vote is important." As she looked down at the woman, who had probably lived in Lumby her entire life, an unexpected sense of empathy came over Janet, forcing her to deviate from her agenda. "Do you need a ride to the voting booths?"

"Seth is driving us," she said, feebly pointing at the house next door.

There, on a similar porch in a similar rocking chair, an older gentleman waved back.

"I heard every word," he called out. "Pam has my vote."

"Thank you!" Janet replied loudly.

The next one will be better, she thought as she walked down the sidewalk. And she was nearly right. But it took another dozen houses on the upper half of B'berry to refine her pitch.

When she knocked on the next door, a boy no older than eight answered. Janet heard an infant crying inside.

"Are your parents home?" she asked.

"Mom, a lady is here. I'm going on my bike," the boy said, brushing past Janet.

A woman in her late twenties came to the door, a baby resting on her right hip. Then a girl, a little younger than the boy, bolted out the door.

"Be careful!" her mother yelled before turning her attention to Janet. "How can I help you?"

"I'm Janet Wing. I'm here to answer any questions you might have about the mayoral race and about Pam Walker's platform. I believe she best represents the long-term interests of your town, and is the strongest candidate on the ballot."

"Are you one of those paid campaigners?" the woman asked cautiously.

"No, I'm just a very close friend who knows that Pam has the best interests of Lumby at heart. She has realistic goals for strengthening the economy of the community and the quality of everyone's lives. But it seems your hands are quite full and this might not be the best time to talk. If you have any free time, this might help." Janet gave her a flyer. "I wrote down my cell number on the bottom if I can be of any help."

"You know, that Duke Blackstone makes a lot of sense," the young mother said.

"He might," Janet replied.

"And he won the Olympics," she added.

"He did. But does he know how to best spend hard-earned taxpayer dollars? Pam wants to increase school funding, whereas Duke wants to cut all areas except for intramural sports. Pam believes in protecting the town's cemeteries and parks, and wants to set up an endowment to double the size of the Bryson's sanctuary."

"That doesn't do me much good," the mother quipped.

"But it will do your children good, and their children," Janet said with conviction. "She wants to ensure that personal property and small businesses in town are taxed fairly. Pam has offered a balanced budget to show how the town can better maintain its streets and utilities, bringing cable to every home regardless of population density. She has supported the community and its residents for over a decade, and knows the town better than most. She has only the best intentions for Lumby."

At that moment the baby started wailing. "I need to go, but I'll read this."

"That's all I ask," Janet said.

444

Two hours later, Janet arrived at her last house. Before she knocked on the door, a middle-aged man walked out on the porch. Janet thrust her arm out, shaking the man's hand.

"I'm Janet Wing, Pam Walker's sister. She's running for mayor and we would like your vote."

Not only had André prepared one of his finest meals for the senator, but everyone also pitched in to help. Although it had always bothered Pam to have others in the kitchen, for some reason that evening was different. That evening was with family.

Janet was extraordinary in seeing what needed to be done and doing it without having to be asked: setting the table, decanting the Bordeaux, lighting the candles, warming the plates. With Janet's support, Pam had very little to do.

"Are you sure you don't want to stay here forever?" Pam joked. "You could come out of retirement and put me out of a job within a week."

Janet didn't stop for a second. "But don't you think," she began as she peeked into the pantry to find a new box of crackers, "that all kitchens are basically the same?" She pulled out a box of Carr's.

Pam had never really thought about it because she had not been in many other kitchens. "I suppose they are," she said as she watched Janet open one drawer and then another in search of a cheese knife.

Janet found one. "Perfect for sharp cheddar."

An outburst of laughter came from the corner table in the dining room, where Senator Grant, Bill and Mark exchanged stories as they nursed their glasses of wine.

"It's wonderful that Bill has a chance to spend some time with John," Janet said.

"They seem to be good friends."

"They are, but they don't see each other too often because of John's schedule." Janet looked around before folding a towel and placing it on the island. "I think we're ready, André," she said to the Montis chef as if she had known him for years.

Pam had put Senator Grant at the head of the table and Bill at the other end.

As the appetizers were placed, Senator Grant moved forward in his chair, sitting a bit taller. He lifted his glass. "To old friends who I don't see often enough, to new friends who I hope to see more of."

"To friends and family," Janet added, smiling at Pam.

There was a knock on the door and it opened slowly.

"Now, *this* is what I was waiting for!" Mark said excitedly.

Pam shot Mark a look of concern.

Robert Day poked his head in.

"Robert?" Pam said, jumping from her seat.

"Am I interrupting?"

"Absolutely not!" she said, rushing over to give him a kiss on the cheek. Everyone, this is my . . ." She hesitated for a second.

"Stepfather," he filled in.

Pam blushed. "And dear friend." She took his hand and started to walk toward the table.

"Mark called and told me about your campaign," Robert explained.

"Which I'm going to lose miserably," Pam retorted.

"Either way, I wouldn't miss your party for anything," Robert said.

"Have you had dinner?" Pam asked.

"No, and I'm famished. But I don't want to impose—I can make do with a sandwich."

"It's never an imposition," Pam said, laughing. "And a simple sandwich is out of the question."

"I think we can do a little better," Janet said, already heading into the kitchen. "Just give us a minute."

"Let me introduce everyone. That beautiful whirlwind who just went into the kitchen is my sister, Janet," Pam began, before continuing on to the rest of the crowd.

On that evening, the three families—the Wings, Robert Day and the Walkers—became one seamless clan. Pam quietly sat back and relished the laughter and genuine warmth between them.

Mark leaned over and kissed his wife. "For someone who thought she was alone in the world, you have a quite a family."

Pam smiled, looking around the table. "I do, don't I?" she said. "And you're at the very center of it. I can't thank you enough for what you've done. I'll always love you."

THIRTY-NINE

Détente

Dennis Beezer sat at his desk in the Chatham Press building, deeply engrossed in spreadsheets with the header, "*WHEATLEY SENTINEL* WKLY CASH FLOW."

Impressive, he thought. He knew that the city had the population and the demographics to sustain its own local paper for at least another eight to ten years, until he would be ready to retire on his terms, but it was a big change and any change comes with its share of risk. He had always liked that paper from the first day he began working there as a young college graduate who had returned to his hometown with his new wife, Gabrielle, and son. Although his stay at the *Sentinel* was only for a few years until he took ownership of *The Lumby Lines* after his father passed away, he looked back at that time and those people he'd worked alongside with great fondness.

Had Dennis not been distracted by the reverie or the dreams of "Chapter Two," as he secretly referred to his planned second career that he had not yet shared with anyone, he might have looked out the window and noticed a UPS freight truck driving through town. It turned off Main Street and parked directly in front of The Bindery.

As he had done every morning for the last three weeks, after reexamining the financials, Dennis picked up the *Sentinel* to analyze the stories they were covering, the position of the articles, the quality of the writing and of course the advertisements that played an unfortunate but necessary role in any newspaper business.

On page four, a small two-inch-long article caught his eye:

Niche Publisher Strikes Gold

The niche printer, The Bindery, owned by Chatham Press out of Lumby, has broken all publishing records for the size of its first-edition printing of its *New York Times* bestseller *Turn the Paige*. Coming in at #2 three weeks prior to its official release date, the book, an erotic collection of selfies taken by the media mogul Paige Petrosyan, is guaranteed to be an enormous windfall for the publisher. Their first run is set for one million copies with projected unit sales expected to surpass ten million within the year.

"Damn it, Brian!" Dennis yelled, slamming his fist on the desk.

He couldn't run down the stairs fast enough.

As soon as he turned the corner, he saw his son standing by the truck, examining a pallet of books that had just been loaded.

"Brian!" Dennis hollered from halfway across the street.

Brian kept on counting the boxes.

"Brian!" Dennis screamed. "Look at me." He grabbed his son on the shoulder and spun him around. "What the hell are you doing printing that book?"

"Keeping this company alive," Brian said as calmly as he could.

Dennis was flushed with rage. "I told you never to print it."

Brian's temper began to boil. "You gave me total control! You said, 'Take it, it's yours.'"

"I said you could print anything but this," Dennis screamed. He looked around and realized that a crowd was growing around them. "Get in here," he hissed under his breath as he grabbed his son's shirt and pulled him into The Bindery.

Fazia, who was working in the basement, took three steps at a time as she bolted upstairs.

"What's going on?" she asked Brian.

"Stay out of it," Dennis barked. "This has nothing to do with you."

"It has everything to do with her," Brian said. "We're a team."

"Well, you and your team have made some lousy decisions," Dennis said sarcastically.

Without another word, Fazia disappeared out the front door.

"How the hell could you do this to me?" Dennis shouted. "You're going to ruin us."

"I'm doing just the opposite," Brian said, standing his ground.

The argument went on for several minutes, making no progress, with neither side giving in.

"I've had it up to here!" Dennis smacked himself in the forehead.

"Stop it! Both of you!" Gabrielle shouted.

Both men froze, stunned to hear her voice. It was one of the few times in their lives that they'd ever heard Gabrielle yell in anger.

"You both sound like a couple of children!" Gabrielle hollered.

"He has ruined my company!" Dennis snapped back.

"I've saved your precious company!"

With that, their fight started all over again, this time louder and more furious.

"Shut up!" Gabrielle yelled. "Just shut up!"

Both men instantly recoiled. It was an expression that neither had ever heard Gabrielle use.

Gabrielle's face was bright red. She was angrier than anyone in the room.

Fazia stood behind her, a hand on Gabrielle's right shoulder.

"You are both acting like brats, and I will not

have my husband and my son show such blatant disrespect for each other."

"But—" Brian started.

"Shush! No buts. The first thing you will do is apologize to each other and shake each other's hand."

Father and son stared at each other.

"Do it, Brian," Fazia said.

"You too, Dennis," Gabrielle said.

They both mumbled something under their breath, shook hands and quickly stepped away.

Gabrielle continued. "Brian, did your father tell you not to publish that book?"

"Yes, but—"

"Uh-uh," Gabrielle said putting her hand up to stop him. "Not another word. And Dennis, did you not turn the business over to Brian and give him total control?

"Yes, but—"

"They certainly are cut from the same cloth, aren't they?" Fazia asked Gabrielle.

Gabrielle leaned back to answer her. "Both are as stubborn as mules." Then she spoke to her husband and son, in a calmer voice but with the same intensity as before. "If I remember correctly, I'm one of the three officers of this company—silent but I still have a vote. Brian how many copies of the *Paige* book have you printed?"

"Two hundred color galleys."

"We're scheduled to run the presses on Thursday," Fazia added.

"Destroy them all," Gabrielle said.

"Good!" Dennis said.

"But, Mom—"

"I'm not done. Create a new imprint and print the book under that imprint, making no reference to The Bindery or Chatham."

"What?" Dennis asked.

"Dennis, you're concerned about the reputation of your company," Gabrielle explained. "I can understand that. I can't imagine that the monks of Saint Cross Abbey would be too happy if their books were packaged between Paige Petrosyan's breasts. And Brian, you're most concerned about the financial strength of the press."

"I am," Brian replied.

"Then destroy the galleys you've produced, create your own imprint, your own publishing name, and print the book separate from Chatham Press."

Both men had to think through the solution Gabrielle had presented.

Brian looked at Fazia. "I think we could do it. What do you think?"

"An easy enough change," Fazia said. "It shouldn't affect our release date."

Dennis spoke up. "No reference to The Bindery in any of your press releases."

"I guarantee it," Brian said.

"All right, then," Dennis acquiesced. "Go ahead and build your empire."

"It's *our* empire. And this imprint will be the cash cow that will fund everything you'll want to do until you are too old to care."

"That day will never come, I assure you."

That night, well past ten o'clock, Brian walked quietly into his father's office.

"I'm glad you're still up. I wanted to apologize," Brian said, sitting down across from Dennis. "I guess I stretched the boundaries a little. I knew you were against that book, but I knew it would save your business."

Dennis looked at his son, who seemed to have matured a year since that afternoon. "I'm sorry for losing my temper. When you own a business, it becomes one of your children, and you want to protect it as best you can."

"I know," he said. "That's another reason why am here. I could use your advice."

Dennis leaned back in his chair. "What's that?"

"These *Lumby Lines* election polls—they just don't make sense to me. I've been away for a while and probably don't know what's going on in town, but these numbers are crazy nuts. I think it's some kind of bug with the old algorithm we're using. I wanted to get your take on it. Maybe we could look at it when you have a minute."

FORTY

Stars

The following morning, Caroline had a clear goal in mind: tackling the attic. Her awakened optimism and self-confidence permeated her every thought, and she was filled with energy and intent. Each minute spent cleaning out her house was one minute closer to putting Kai, and that part of her past, behind her.

After a long shower followed by reading *The New York Times* over coffee, she tuned to her old Underwood typewriter. One final letter needed to be written.

> Dear CC, It's been a long, bumpy road, but I have walked it and it's now past me. I am resuming the leadership of Ross Enterprises. I am positive I will not disappoint them, nor you, again. More important, though, is that I will ensure I don't disappoint myself.
>
> I have needed you by my side, and I'm so grateful your spirit was there with me. But now I

know I need to go forward on my own. I can no longer blame or rely on others for the core of who I am and what happens in my life.

But I want you to know that I'm fine—stronger and happier than I've been in such a long time. If it happens that some-one enters my world, I will accept his love with an open heart. But I will stay true to myself. It's no longer needed for me to be happy. Maybe that's the difference.

I will write you every now and then, but if you don't hear from me, know I'm well.

I love you, Caroline

As she was slipping the letter into her pocket, Mac called, asking her and, of course, Finn, to come over that afternoon to lend a much-needed hand in a three-person project.

"No loafing around for us today," she told Finn after hanging up the phone. "First to the cemetery and then it sounds like we've got some work to do."

Arriving at her neighbors' just after lunch, Caroline found Tom and Mac standing by the sliding doors of the big barn. They appeared to be waiting for her.

"Thanks for lending us a hand," Tom said as he bent over and petted Finn on the head. "You too, Finn. You'll learn a lot today."

"How can I help?" Caroline asked.

"We have a project," Tom began as he led the women into the barn and closed the door tightly behind him. "We need to mark the calves."

Caroline stopped in her tracks. "With a branding iron?"

Tom laughed. "Absolutely not. We paint them."

Caroline looked at him skeptically. "Paint?"

"Well, spray paint to be exact," Tom said, kicking a box filled with cans of spray paint. "Animal safe and environmentally friendly."

As they walked past the stalls to the far end of the barn, Caroline heard what sounded like a car starting up outside. "I think someone's here."

"Just the wind," Mac assured her.

"Are you sure?"

"That's right, the wind," Tom agreed. "Now let's get to work," he said, leading them as far away from the door they had just entered as possible.

Caroline was mystified. "I don't mean to question your methods, but wouldn't this be easier if we were at the other end, closer to the calves? If we're way down here, we need to walk each one of them the length of the barn . . . twice."

Tom quickly looked at his wife.

"We don't want to spook them," she blurted out.

Suddenly, they heard a commotion outside.

"I really do think someone might be here," Caroline said.

"It's just the dogs playing around," Mac said calmly. "They make such a racket. Why don't we turn on the radio?" she suggested to Tom.

A moment later, the barn filled with a tune from the forties. Tom twirled Mac on his way to get a stool. Caroline watched the couple with delight.

"One afternoon I saw you and Aaron dancing on the porch," Caroline admitted.

"Oh, Aaron's a wonderful dancer," Mac said, swaying back and forth.

He certainly is, Caroline thought. "Have you heard from him lately?" She did her best to sound detached.

Caroline assumed Mac didn't hear her question because it went unanswered.

"All right, ladies, we're ready," Tom said as he organized the stools. "Caroline, if you don't object, perhaps you could bring each calf from the stall to us, and then you and I will hold it while Mac marks its rump."

Caroline looked perplexed. "Do you think all

three of us are needed? I can just take the paint and mark each one standing in the stall."

"They're dangerous animals," Tom said, shaking his head.

"The calves?"

"Unpredictable," he added.

Mac slapped her hands together. "Enough talk," she said. "Let's get started."

So began the most bizarre afternoon that Caroline had ever spent at the Candor farm. If the task of marking the animals wasn't weird enough, the frequent fifteen-minute breaks when one or both of her friends would disappear made it even stranger. But she continued working without question or comment.

By the time they finished and left the barn, it was well after sunset. Although Caroline was expecting the Candors to invite her in for dinner, they simply thanked her and said good night.

Walking back to her house, Caroline shook her head in near disbelief. "Finn," she said, "that was the oddest experience I've ever had." Caroline replayed the afternoon in her head. "If you ask me, they're either on drugs or they're losing their minds."

As she turned the bend on the road, she slowed her pace. She spotted lights in her front yard, which was odd for two reasons: she hadn't turned on any lights earlier in the day, and she had no lamp-posts where those lights shone.

She shortened Finn's leash to keep him closer to her side. When her house came into full view, she gasped. The lights she had seen from the road formed a path. Every few feet, on both sides of the path, was a softly glowing paper bag that flickered gently from the candle placed within. The line of candles began at the road, crossed the front yard, and disappeared around the right side of the house. With the house disappearing in the darkness, the path looked dreamlike, beckoning her to follow it.

Passing the side of the house, when the back-yard came into full view, her breath was taken away. Glowing bags continued every few feet along the back of the house, and a thousand white lights hung in the trees that surrounded the back lawn. In the middle, two quilts were spread out with candles surrounding them. On one quilt was a wine cooler and plates of food ready for serving.

Caroline put her hand up to her mouth, gasping. It was without question one of the most beautiful sights she had ever seen. It was as if she was in a dream.

Aaron, who was standing in the shadows of the mill, stepped into the light. In his hand was a bouquet of roses.

"Aaron?" she whispered.

"You look gorgeous," he said, approaching her. He handed her the roses. "For you." He took her in his arms and kissed her gently.

She gazed into his eyes in disbelief, thinking he looked more handsome than ever. His smile carried her away and when she smelled his cologne, her knees weakened. "When did you get back?"

"Today."

He was bathed in the warm light of the candles. Caroline was never happier to see anyone in her life. Tears filled her eyes and quickly rolled down her cheeks.

"That's not quite the reaction I was hoping for," Aaron said.

"Everything fell apart," Caroline said, crying softly.

"I know. That's why I am here. You never said as much, but—"

Caroline wrapped her arms around his neck and kissed him. *It was a dream,* she thought. Nothing so perfect could ever happen in her life. But here he was, when she needed him most.

She looked at the candles surrounding them. "How did you—" she began, still stunned by the beauty he had created in the backyard.

"Shh," he said as he drew her near, kissing her on the lips, more urgently this time.

It's a beautiful dream, Caroline thought, melting in his arms. She had longed to be kissed like that—passionately, with total abandon. They explored each other's lips with an intensity that made her body shudder.

When they finally separated, he looked into her eyes. "I have missed you more than you can imagine."

Aaron took Caroline by the hand and led her to the quilts where she sat down, encircled by soft, iridescent light.

"I'm speechless," she said. Her heart beat so loudly, she was sure Aaron could hear it.

He stared at her. "I've been thinking of this moment since the day we said goodbye."

"It's unbelievable."

He wiped the remaining tears from her cheek. "Better?"

She nodded.

"We can talk about everything later. But first, some wine."

Pouring her a glass, he toasted, "To seeing you again . . . and again."

Caroline wanted time to stop, to freeze and never move forward or back. If that moment could just stand still, they would be together, like this, forever. "How did you do all of this?" she said, looking at the Christmas lights strung through the tree limbs.

"With plenty of help from Mac and Tom," he admitted. The lights glistened; the water wheel of the mill turned slowly, the sound of water gently lapping at the bottom. "It wasn't hard turning this into paradise—you have a beautiful home."

"It's for sale," she said softly.

"I know."

"So you're trying to soften me up so I'll sell you the mill at a low price?"

"I won't deny it—the thought crossed my mind when Mac told me. But no," he said. "This was your life, your past. I know you don't belong here and I want to be wherever you are. If we are to have a chance, it won't be in a home you don't want. And I would never want to force you to go against your feelings."

"Thank you for that," she said, thinking back on Kai's insistence that they buy the mill because it made *him* feel comfortable.

"And if that's not reason enough, I almost killed myself on that wheel," he joked. "I'd probably drown in the first week if I lived here."

Caroline laughed for the first time since seeing Aaron.

Her eyes traced the line of lights hung between the trees. What had seemed so bizarre all afternoon—the odd project, the stalling for time, the sounds she had heard outside—made total sense now. "So, the whole marking-the-calves thing?"

Aaron laughed. "A decoy. We're not very good liars, and we're not that creative in making up excuses either."

"Maybe that's a good thing," Caroline said. "But I'm gullible—I bought into it."

Aaron removed the lid of the glass container.

"How would you like steamed crabs from Washington?"

She took another sip of wine. "This seems so implausible," she whispered. "But you are here next to me." *I can feel the warmth of your body,* she thought.

"Well, you probably deserve more than this, and definitely more than me, but it's the best I can do."

Caroline and Aaron were soon talking as if they had just seen each other the day before. Aaron laughed over Finn's capers and Caroline listened intently when Aaron talked about his boat, Seattle and his photographs. And Aaron asked intelligent, caring questions when Caroline told him everything about Ross Enterprises. There were no secrets between them, no areas off-limits.

After dinner, they lay on their backs and looked up at the star-filled universe.

"I used to love looking at the stars," Caroline said, thinking of the many nights during the beginning of her marriage when she and Kai watched for shooting stars. "But it's different now."

"They're up there, Caroline," Aaron said, taking her hand in his. "It's just beautiful, infinite space. Wait one minute," he said, getting to his feet.

"Where are you going?" she asked with a touch

of panic. For a second, she feared he would leave her and the dream would come to a heartbreaking end.

"You'll see," he said as he unplugged the lights and snuffed out each candle.

"Wow," Caroline whispered.

"What?"

"As you blew out each flame, it was like a dimmer was turned up in the stars. Come look," she invited him. She held out her hand and prayed that he would take it. He did.

When he lay down, he moved his body close to hers.

The stars were as brilliant as she had ever seen.

"Thank you for such a wonderful night," she said, turning to look at him. "I don't want it to end."

He slipped his arm under her head and pulled her closer. "It doesn't have to."

Caroline allowed her emotions to take over. She moved her body on top of his, kissing him on the lips and then on his neck. She sat up, her knees straddling his waist.

"I haven't done this since—"

"Me neither," he whispered. "But before we go down that path, I need to ask you a question."

Caroline frowned. "What is it?"

"Will you share your life with me?"

Caroline leaned over and kissed him. "I will."

She unbuttoned his shirt before removing her

blouse. Her naked body radiated warmth in the starlight. Aaron lifted the quilt over her shoulder and gently pulled her on top of him.

And there, under the open sky, Caroline and Aaron made love and began their life as a couple, together.

FORTY-ONE

Surge

Lying in the bed in his cottage, Alan Blackstone looked at the alarm clock. It was 5:45 a.m. He took out a piece of paper from his wallet and dialed a number he had never dialed before. The phone rang twice before it was answered.

"Hello?"

"Megan, it's Alan. Did I wake you?"

"No, I was just preparing for matins," she said. "Are you all right?"

"Yes, but I wanted to talk to you."

"What is it?"

"I just wanted to thank you for everything you have done since the night I arrived at the abbey." He paused. "Your friendship has meant more to me than you'll ever know."

"Alan, it's not even six," she laughed. "Why are you telling me this now?"

There was a much longer pause. "I'm going to see Duke this morning."

"You can't!" she yelped. "Not alone."

"I have no choice," he said firmly. "I refuse to live in hiding for the next two years while the FBI tries to sort through all the criminal activities my brother is in. I'm not willing to give my life up that easily."

Megan's head was spinning as she considered the consequences of Alan confronting Duke. "But you could just leave. You speak a dozen languages. You could live anywhere in the world and he would never know . . . he would never find you."

"I would know, Megan," he said. "Every day I would feel resentment toward my brother and disappointment in myself. I would know that I let what's fundamentally bad have the upper hand, and I just can't do that."

"He'll kill you this time," she pleaded. "I just sense it."

"I'm willing to face that possibility. At this point I don't care."

Megan held back tears, more of fear than sadness. "But I do. I don't understand it and I can't explain it, but I can't lose you."

Alan replied slowly. "I have no choice, Megan." He hung up and turned off his phone.

All too soon, Alan was standing in front of Duke's rented home in Rocky Mount. A couple of months ago, he was looking at the front door over his shoulder as he ran toward his car, his face beat up, his arm slashed. More painful than his physical wounds was the knowledge that his brother was a criminal who tried to kill him to cover up the truth.

Alan knocked on the door. When there was

no answer, he pounded it with his fist.

When Duke finally answered, it was obvious he had just woken up. He was in his robe and slippers, and his eyes were half closed.

Duke had a great poker face and he showed no signs of surprise. "Well," he said in an aggrieved tone, "if it isn't my born-again brother. I thought you died in the woods."

"Good to see you, too," Alan said.

A neighbor walking her dog looked up at the brothers. When she turned away, Duke grabbed Alan's shirt and pulled him inside, slamming the door behind him.

"What the hell are you doing here?" he yelled.

Alan remained calm. "We need to talk."

"Like hell we do," Duke spat. "I should have finished the job I started last time you were here."

"Duke, that would have been insane. Lots of people knew I was here," Alan lied. "And if I disappear again, they know exactly who's to blame."

"I'm above the law," Duke bragged. "Haven't you figured that out yet?"

"You're delusional."

"Sit down!" he yelled, pushing Alan into a chair. Duke started pacing the room back and forth, like a caged animal.

"I—"

"Shut the hell up," Duke snapped.

Alan withdrew a manila envelope from inside his jacket and threw it on the floor. "This is what you wanted," Alan said. "Was it really worth my life?"

Duke scrambled to pick it up. He looked inside and saw that it contained the originals. "You have no idea."

"It's just money," Alan said.

"No," Duke countered. "It's better than money. It's power."

"Over who?"

"*Everyone*. Every spineless politician who laughed behind my back, who didn't return my calls, who didn't support me. All of them are going to rot in hell, but I'm going to make sure they kiss my rear first."

"Not everything is about you."

"It's *all* about me," Duke hissed. "You didn't understand that when you were ten years old, and you don't understand that now. How stupid can you be?"

"And you think Dad would be proud of you?"

Duke burst out in a sinister laugh. "My God, how gullible are you? He was the first damn person who taught me how to blackmail. And I was only nineteen."

Alan was stunned. "No, he didn't."

"He wanted that sniveling, kindhearted judge to give me a hard punishment for that misdemeanor at school. So he hired a prostitute to put our dear

471

judge in a compromising position. Four photos later and his threat to publish them, and I was behind bars for a month before the case was dropped. Just like Dad wanted."

"Dad wasn't a bad man," Alan argued.

"You think? When you were beat up in school, Dad told me to stay out of it. He said you needed to learn to hit back ten times harder than you were hit." Duke walked behind his desk, throwing the envelope on the stack of papers. "You were a disappointment to both of us."

Before Alan knew what happened, Duke was holding a small pistol, pointed directly at him.

"Are you mad?" Alan yelled.

"Get up!" Duke shouted. "You and I are going for a little drive."

"You know you'll never get away with this."

"I get away with everything."

Suddenly the front door flew open, and a dozen men barged into the room, all of them wearing FBI jackets, all of them holding guns in their hands. Duke was so startled that he dropped his arms.

"Hands up!" one of them screamed.

Duke pointed at Alan. "Arrest him!" he yelled. "He's the one you've been looking for."

Several guns were pointed at both Blackstones. Duke let the pistol slip from his hand.

One of the FBI agents turned to Alan. "Alan Blackstone?"

Alan nodded.

The man looked at the other twin. No one was able to tell them apart at first glance.

"Duke Blackstone?" the lead agent asked.

"Yeah, that's me," he said in impatient disgust. "Just take him away and get out of my house."

"Duke Blackstone. We have a warrant for your arrest on thirty-nine felony counts of"—he checked the paper he was holding—"obstruction of justice, tax evasion, aggravated assault, grand larceny, bribery, murder, and attempted murder."

Before Duke could explode, two men pulled his arms behind his back and handcuffed him.

"Take those cuffs off me!" he yelled. "None of you will have a job by the end of the day."

"Take him away," one of the men said.

As he was led outside, the team of agents dispersed throughout the house and started a search that would last until sunset.

Alan's whole body shook. "How did you know?"

"We received a call from a woman at Saint Cross Abbey in Franklin. She told us you were here and in danger."

Alan tried to clear his thoughts. "But your letter said that it would take years for the investigation—"

"There was no letter from us, sir. We were within days of arresting your brother based on the evidence you provided. If you received contradictory information, it was probably written by someone your brother hired."

Alan walked over to the desk and grabbed the manila envelope. "Here are all the original documents." He was greatly relieved. The original papers were finally in safe hands.

"Thank you," the agent said. "Where will we be able to reach you if we have any questions?"

Alan considered that and then smiled. "Saint Cross Abbey," he said, walking out of the house.

Standing on the porch, he took a deep breath. It was over.

By four o'clock, Alan was back at the cottage, fully packed and closing up his duffel bag.

There was a knock.

"You here?" Mark Walker called out.

Alan opened the door with his belongings in hand.

Seeing that Alan was about to leave, Mark grabbed the satchel and threw it back into the room. "Where do you think you're going?"

"Didn't you hear what happened?" Alan asked.

"We heard there was an FBI bust, and that you were involved and that Duke was dragged away." Mark's eyes were bigger than normal. "Wow, it must have been something."

"And thanks to Megan, I have a full life ahead of me," Alan said. "This chapter is done with. I think I've overextended my welcome."

"Actually, you haven't," Mark said, putting his arm around Alan. "I've been sent here with explicit instructions to bring you back to Montis. An election party is just getting under way, and there are a lot of people there who are very worried about you and would like to see you."

"Thanks, but I don't think so."

"You have no choice in the matter," he said, leading Alan down the stairs and away from the cottage.

Following Mark's dogs, they took a path that Alan had been told about but had never used. It led them directly to Montis Inn. When they strolled into the backyard, Clipper and Cutter took off to join the party. Alan immediately saw Megan standing under the lights of the nearest oak tree.

Mark went up to her. "See, I told you he was there," Mark said. "Keep an eye on him—I hear he's had a rough day."

"What are you doing here?" Alan asked Megan. He unconsciously reached for her hand.

"We've all been waiting for you." She nodded toward Matthew and Michael, who were standing with Joshua. "Maybe some more impatiently than others." She grinned.

FORTY-TWO

Champagne

The party at Montis Inn was well under way.
Hank, being the loved flamingo that he was, stood
by the road attempting to direct traffic. A bottle
of champagne was tucked between his legs, since
this might be the night that more libation was
needed to drown the sorrows of Pam's stinging
loss. Hank had worked tirelessly, campaigning
door to door, caucusing with whomever would
listen. And clearly he was Pam's staunchest
supporter. Had his financial reserves not been
depleted by a bad investment in Belize, he would
have contributed significant funds to the Walker
campaign.

Pam was watching Hank when Dennis and
Brian Beezer arrived at Montis. From a distance
she could tell that father and son were having a
serious conversation when they got out of the car.
Brian pointed to a stack of papers that he was

carrying. Dennis nodded and placed his hand on his son's shoulder. He then surveyed the crowd. When he spotted Pam, they headed directly over to her.

"So, where are your better halves?" Pam said.

"Gabrielle and Fazia will be here in about an hour," Dennis explained. "But we . . . Brian . . . needs to talk with you as soon as possible."

"If it's work related, let's wait until tomorrow," Pam said.

"It's about the election," Dennis said. "He has some news."

"Dennis, you sound way too serious," Pam said. "How about a glass of champagne?"

"Not right now," Dennis said. He turned to his son.

"Pam, our paper's poll results—" Brian began.

"Hold on. If this is about the election, Mark should be here," Pam said, waving her husband over.

Mark swaggered over and put his arm around his wife's waist. "Thanks for coming, gentlemen. Nice weather for a shellacking," he joked. "Why do you guys look so serious?"

"I'm not quite sure," Pam said. "But I think there's a problem with the polls."

"Oh God," Mark moaned. "Is Biscuit going to beat us as well?"

"No," Brian said. "The poll results are wrong,"

he said. "And I take full responsibility. When we brought up *The Lumby Lines* website, we were so close to the election that I decided to use the old algorithms layered on a new app, which we embedded into our platform instead of building our own." The young man looked down at the stack of papers and shook his head. "I should have realized that something was wrong with the numbers sooner. But strange things happen in politics, and that's why I never really thought about it until a couple of days ago."

"What are you saying, Brian?" Pam asked.

"When word got out that Duke was arrested this morning, I saw a significant bump in his numbers. It was crazy nuts, regardless of the populace behind him."

"Well, I've always thought that his numbers were too high," Mark said lightheartedly. "So, honey, this is good. Instead of losing by an embarrassing amount—"

"We'll lose by a smaller amount to a felon," Pam said, rolling her eyes.

"Actually, you won't lose at all," Brian corrected them.

"What do you mean?" Pam asked.

"The poll numbers were flipped," Brian said, holding out the papers and pointing to one line to help explain the anomaly. "This line of code is wrong. There's an ascending sort to the names.

Blackstone 'B' and Walker 'W.' And then there's a descending sort to the numbers."

Both Pam and Mark were confused.

"So . . . ?" Pam said.

"It means you've always had a huge lead over Duke Blackstone," Brian said. "He never polled at more than eight percent."

Pam was stunned. "So, I won?"

"Well, not until the election results are in," Dennis interjected.

"We've corrected the program and updated our poll results online. What it shows now is a strong victory in your favor," Brian said.

Mark shook his head. "But I just checked your website ten minutes ago," he said. "The polls still have Duke winning with eighty-seven percent."

"Refresh the page. It will show the right numbers," Brian said.

"You're going to win, that's what counts," Dennis said.

Pam was still a little shocked, but she quickly came to her senses. "I think what counts is that very few residents bought into the hatred and divisiveness that Duke Blackstone represented." She gave Brian a hug. "Thanks for telling us."

"We're sorry," Dennis said.

"I'm the one who needs to apologize," Brian said. "It's not your responsibility, Dad. Especially now."

Pam raised her brows. "Especially now?"

Dennis looked at his son. "Chatham Press is in Brian's hands."

"We're still in negotiations," Brian said jokingly.

"I'd like him to take it over if he wants to," Dennis said.

"And what will you do?" Mark asked.

Dennis tried to hold back his grin. "I bought *The Wheatley Sentinel* last week, and I'll be its publisher."

"Congratulations!" Mark said, slapping Dennis on the back. "That's like ten times bigger than *The Lumby Lines*."

"Not quite, but close," Dennis said, smiling proudly.

"That's huge news for both of you!" Pam said, giving Dennis a kiss on the cheek. "Why don't you two go and get a drink?"

"I think we will," Dennis said, grabbing Brian's arm.

After they left, Mark whispered in Pam's ear, "You did it."

Pam looked around the party. Already fifty people had come to support her and Mark. "I guess so," she said more soberly.

"Then why don't you sound happier?"

"I guess I've realized that *this* is what really matters—being with family and friends. Not being mayor of Lumby. Regardless of who holds what job, we'll always carry on the fight for everything we believe in for this town. And I guess it's just been such a long fight, I'm not going to hold my breath until the election results come in."

By seven o'clock, more than a hundred people were celebrating friendship, their commitment to the town and their shared belief in a future. Joshua and Brooke, who had returned from Seattle the day before, were talking with Bill and Janet Wing. The monks were sitting with Chuck and Robert Day, discussing philosophy. Mac and Tom were already on their third glass of champagne by the time Caroline and Aaron arrived on his motorcycle.

At nine o'clock, Mark's cell phone rang. He looked at the caller ID. "It's Simon Dixon."

He answered and then listened. "The election results are in," Mark said loudly.

Everyone hushed to hear the news.

"Total votes cast was 4,382." Mark yelled out over the crowd, repeating word for word what Simon was telling him. "One percent for Biscuit . . . three percent for Duke Blackstone . . . four percent for Mark Walker . . . eight percent for Pam Walker."

Pam looked confused. "How can that be? That's only sixteen percent."

Mark held the phone tightly and covered his other ear in order to better hear. "And eighty-four percent write-in for 'Walker.' "

Everyone broke into robust cheers.

"We won, honey!" he said, ending the call.

"But which one of us?" Pam asked.

THELUMBYLINES.COM
Town Events

The steadfast residents of our small town have seen more than their fair share of political pandemonium during this year's mayoral election. Although the voting stations at both the Lumby Feed Store and Lumby's Sporting Goods were officially closed at 8:00 p.m., and all votes tallied within an hour, subsequent confusion rolled down Main Street when the town council revoked the certificate of nomination for Duke Blackstone due to his apparent incarceration. Unrelated to any felonies, but further complicating the election results, candidate Mark Walker withdrew his name from consideration due to a "conflict of interest."

The final popular vote has been recorded as follows: Pam Walker (designated winner) 92%, Biscuit (runner-up) 3%, Mark Walker 0% (withdrawn), Duke Blackstone 0% (rescinded). The seventeen absentee ballots have not yet been counted, but town officials are certain they won't affect the final results as published on this website.

Mayor-elect Walker will begin her term in an inauguration ceremony at the fairgrounds next Tuesday from 7:00–7:15 p.m. Simon Dixon reminds everyone that Porta Potties will not be provided due to the length of the swearing-in ceremony.

FAIRGROUND ROAD

NORTH DEER RUN LOOP

NORTH GRANT AVE

MAIN STREET

CHERRY STREET

FARM TO MARKET ROAD

SOUTH DEER RUN LOOP

To Wheatley

Town of Lumby

Est. 1862

Gail Fraser is the author of the acclaimed Lumby series, which thus far includes *The Lumby Lines*, *Stealing Lumby*, *Lumby's Bounty*, *The Promise of Lumby*, *Lumby on the Air*, and *Lost in Lumby*. She also co-authored *Finding Happiness in Simplicity* with her husband, folk artist Art Poulin. Together they live and work at Lazygoose Farm in rural upstate New York, which has been featured on PBS and in numerous national magazines.

When not writing, Gail tends to her vegetable garden, orchard and beehives. She is also an avid long-distance swimmer and flute player.

Prior to becoming a novelist, Gail Fraser had a successful corporate career holding senior executive positions in several Fortune 500 and start-up corporations, and traveling extensively throughout the world. She has a BA from Skidmore College with undergraduate work completed at the University of London, and an MBA from the University of Connecticut with graduate work done at Harvard University.

www.lumbybooks.com

Books are produced in the United States using U.S.-based materials

Books are printed using a revolutionary new process called THINKtech™ that lowers energy usage by 70% and increases overall quality

Books are durable and flexible because of smythe-sewing

Paper is sourced using environmentally responsible foresting methods and the paper is acid-free

Center Point Large Print
600 Brooks Road / PO Box 1
Thorndike, ME 04986-0001 USA

(207) 568-3717

US & Canada:
1 800 929-9108
www.centerpointlargeprint.com